continued . . .

A Lady Betrayed

Nicole Byrd

BERKLEY SENSATION, NEW YORK

THE BERKLEY PUBLISHING GROUP
Published by the Penguin Group
Penguin Group (USA) Inc.
375 Hudson Street, New York, New York 10014, USA
Penguin Group (Canada), 90 Eglinton Avenue East, Suite 700, Toronto, Ontario M4P 2Y3, Canada
(a division of Pearson Penguin Canada Inc.)
Penguin Books Ltd., 80 Strand, London WC2R 0RL, England
Penguin Group Ireland, 25 St. Stephen's Green, Dublin 2, Ireland (a division of Penguin Books Ltd.)
Penguin Group (Australia), 250 Camberwell Road, Camberwell, Victoria 3124, Australia
(a division of Pearson Australia Group Pty. Ltd.)
Penguin Books India Pvt. Ltd., 11 Community Centre, Panchsheel Park, New Delhi—110 017, India
Penguin Group (NZ), 67 Apollo Drive, Rosedale, North Shore 0632, New Zealand
(a division of Pearson New Zealand Ltd.)
Penguin Books (South Africa) (Pty.) Ltd., 24 Sturdee Avenue, Rosebank, Johannesburg 2196,
South Africa

Penguin Books Ltd., Registered Offices: 80 Strand, London WC2R 0RL, England

This is a work of fiction. Names, characters, places, and incidents either are the product of the author's imagination or are used fictitiously, and any resemblance to actual persons, living or dead, business establishments, events, or locales is entirely coincidental. The publisher does not have any control over and does not assume any responsibility for author or third-party websites or their content.

A LADY BETRAYED

A Berkley Sensation Book / published by arrangement with the author

PRINTING HISTORY
Berkley Sensation mass-market edition / November 2007

Copyright © 2007 by Cheryl Zach.
Excerpt of TK Copyright © 2007 by Cheryl Zach.
Cover art by Leslie Peck.
Cover design by George Long.
Hand lettering by Ron Zinn.

ISBN: 978-0-425-21843-3

BERKLEY® SENSATION
Berkley Sensation Books are published by The Berkley Publishing Group,
a division of Penguin Group (USA) Inc.,
375 Hudson Street, New York, New York 10014.
BERKLEY SENSATION and the "B" design are trademarks belonging to Penguin Group (USA) Inc.

PRINTED IN THE UNITED STATES OF AMERICA

10   9   8   7   6   5   4   3   2   1

For Marcia,
and a cherished friendship that dates back
to the times when we shared study hall
but didn't study—
sotto voce conversations were
so much more interesting!—
and made mud pies.

One

A dagger pierced her temple. . . .

Pain washed over her in waves so intense that her body shook with the force of them. Pushing back the nausea that came close to overwhelming her, Maddie fought for every breath.

She had hoped to make it home before she lost control of her limbs, but the weakness had increased too quickly. Staggering along the overgrown path among the trees, she paused to thrust aside a low-growing branch. As she did, she glimpsed the abandoned structure, its bare wooden skeleton outlined against the darkening sky. It stood in lonely isolation in the center of a grassy lea where nowadays only the occasional doe and fawn came to call.

She should have remembered the dilapidated gazebo, she told herself, by now almost beyond coherent thought. In happier times Madeline and her sisters had visited here often, bringing baskets filled with sandwiches and berries and flasks of lemonade.

Today the structure offered an almost-whole roof to

protect against the rain that descended in torrents, soaking her light muslin dress and chilling her from head to toe before she could stumble inside. But the pain in her temple drowned out the other less significant discomfort, bringing her to her knees on the cold, shattered tiles of the floor.

How long would it be before anyone thought to come searching for her? Her father had warned her about walking alone through the woods and moors, but now that their servants were few, she had thought they were needed more—

Oh, the pain!

She put both her hands to her head, clutching it, trying to contain the physical torture that spiraled always to greater heights, like a pot boiling over, spilling huge drops that would burn and blister everywhere they touched. The pain wouldn't stop, wouldn't slow. Oh, dear God, why had she chosen to walk to the village today—why must she fall victim to this assault today—

Everything around her spun into a pulsating whirl of unbearable unending torment. Death would be easier than this.

Pain was everywhere—she curled into herself—and if someone sobbed, she no longer noticed.

The first drops of rain fell when he was only a few miles past the village. Adrian wondered if he should have stopped there for the night after all. But he'd seen no decent inn, and he had no time to spare with a would-be murderer, who had an uncanny knack for finding his trail no matter how determinedly Adrian tried to hide it, hard on his heels.

No time to spare—a good jest, that. They could inscribe it on his tombstone.

He lifted his lips in a grim smile that might as easily pass for a grimace. The last man who had smiled back rested now beneath a marble slab, presumably at peace although still bearing Adrian's bullet.

As Adrian did his.

Inconvenient things, duels. They interrupted one's life so easily . . . as did dying.

Self-pity was an indulgence he would not allow himself . . . did not have time to allow himself.

He glanced again at the lowering sky, the dark clouds heavy with rain that would not be put off much longer. As if the thought had opened heaven's floodgates, he felt another large droplet smack his cheek. Adrian turned up his collar, pulled down his hat, and resigned himself to a wet and miserable ride.

His horse—an iron-mouthed, surly gray—seemed to take matters under its own control. Snorting, the gelding plunged into the trees that surrounded the narrow lane.

"What the hell?" Adrian tightened his grip on the reins and tried to turn his mount back toward the road, but it was too late. The horse had taken its head and seemed, as the damned beast sometimes did, to have been momentarily possessed by a devil. Or else, it wanted out of the wet, not being fond of rainstorms.

"And what makes you think this way leads to a stable, you fool?" Adrian demanded, as if the dumb brute could understand. But the insane thing was that the animal had, now and then, been right about which road to take when its master had lost his way.

After a moment Adrian realized that they were, in fact, following a narrow but discernable trail through the woods. Was this some local gentry's parkland? Perhaps they would find a house and stable at the end of this overgrown pathway, after all.

If it was a park, a gentleman's property, someone had come down in the world, Adrian told himself. The narrow path was poorly maintained, and—

Just then he saw the first sign of habitation. A servant's cottage? It was very small. No, he saw now that it was only a roof and frame, a gazebo set out for shelter on a nice summer day, now half derelict but still offering some shelter from the elements. This time, as the rain fell more steadily, the gray turned willingly under his hand and trotted toward the new goal.

Adrian dismounted and led his steed under what was left of the roof, pulling off a blanket from behind the saddle to throw over the horse and giving it handfuls of the oats that he carried in his bag. Only then did he turn and make out the body lying motionless amid the shadows.

"Good God!" Adrian exclaimed. He tied his horse to one of the roof supports a safe distance away, then took several long strides to see who lay so ominously still.

It was a young woman, her muslin dress sodden and sticking to her body—a very nicely made body, he could not help but notice, beneath the clinging fabric. She had golden brown hair, wet, too—she had obviously been caught in the storm—and her eyes were shut. Had she been injured in some way?

She lay sprawled on her side, curled in a semicircle like a babe. Something about the way she lay or the expression on her face—such suffering it seemed to show—caught at his heart. She looked so vulnerable, so helpless. Her cheeks were damp from raindrops or tears.

What had happened here?

Her face was very pale. He knelt beside her and leaned over to touch her hand. It was as frigid as a mountain stream. He drew a deep breath.

Was she dead?

Too alarmed to worry about propriety, he put his hand against her chest, searching for a heartbeat. He was relieved past measure to detect a steady rhythm beneath the skin and then to feel the slow rise and fall of her chest.

At another time his hand might have lingered, if she had been well and interested in flirtation, but she was not well at all, and he was still not sure what had caused her current distress. One thing was sure, she could not continue to lie against this cold tile floor in a wet gown. Whatever her other problems, if he left her in such a state, she would end up with a fluid on her lungs and die of a congestion and fever, as his own mother had done too young.

He had no idea where her home might lie. He could continue down the path and search for a likely structure or retrace his path to the village, but the sunlight was fading rapidly and the chill in the air deepening. He hesitated to leave her here in such an isolated location, with the temperature dropping and without anyone to watch over her.

Pausing only for a moment, Adrian made up his mind. He walked back to his horse and, with an ironic grin, stripped off the blanket he had only just put over the animal. "Sorry, old man, a greater need!"

He shook off as many horse hairs as he could, then came back and lay the blanket on the floor next to the unconscious woman.

Leaning closer, he unbuttoned the back of her wet gown—he'd had some practice removing women's apparel, though never before on a female who could not give him permission. Lifting her as gently as he could, he stripped off the soaked clothing. The gown stuck to her arms and clung to her full, well-shaped breasts, and he ripped one of the sleeves before he could pull it off, but finally she was free of it. He found that her shift was little better, dripping with cold water, so, with the ruthless determination that his friends, and his enemies, would have recognized, he stripped it and her other underthings off as well.

Her body was lovely, pale as alabaster in the blue of the fading light, with no bruises or obvious injuries. Drawing a deep breath, he put aside the surge of passion that threatened to rush through him.

Bloody hell, she was beautiful.

He laid her very carefully upon the blanket, pulled off his coat, and covered her with it, or as much of her as he could, hoping that removing the soaked clothing and putting dry wool over her would allow some heat to return to the young woman's body.

He knelt beside her and took both her ice-cold hands in his, rubbing them and trying to return some warmth to them, but she still seemed ominously chilled. He could not allow the life to seep out of her, not without a struggle, damn it!

"Wake up," he said into her ear. "You must fight!"

He took one hand, than another, into his. She seemed almost like some nymph out of an oft-told fairy tale. She seemed so slight, so delicate next to his large-limbed frame. Ironically, he had never felt so healthy, so full of life.

He gently rubbed her hands, her arms—feeling how soft was her skin, how delicate the clean lines of her forearms. The rest of her body . . . no, she was helpless and in his care. Even in his thoughts, he could not trespass, not now. Nor did he have the leisure for idle fancies, he told himself. He must make sure she survived this ordeal some cruel fate had thrust upon her.

Bending closer, he muttered, "Live!"

She drew a breath more labored and more palpable than before. He felt a moment of encouragement.

"Stay with me," he told her. "Lady with no name, stay with me. Surely if I can just make you warm again, bring back the heat of human blood and bone . . ."

Her skin was still so cold, especially her hands and feet, which had been as frigid as a corpse's from the beginning, as if the joyless grip of the grave already reached up to claim her. No, he would not consider such a possibility!

He continued to chafe her hands, gently but firmly, trying to force some hint of warmth back into her limbs. But the air around them cooled even more as the sun dropped behind the horizon, and everything seemed to conspire against him. The breeze had picked up, and as the wind whipped through the trees, the mournful sound made the horse toss its head.

Adrian pressed his lips together. Even he shivered, and he had not been soaked to the bone to start with. Whereas the woman on the ground . . .

He would not give up! How could he improve her condition?

Could he start a fire?

The trees and bushes around them were drenched, and the rain still fell, rattling against the leaves. He saw no way to find any brush dry enough to use as tinder, and he had no time to waste wandering through the dark in search of kindling suitable for immediate burning. What else could he do?

Try to ride with her in his arms as he sought help? He did not think he could balance her safely atop the fractious horse—he pushed the idea aside as wild and impractical.

He had to do something. He would warm her if he had to strip off his own skin to do it!

The madness of that notion made him smile grimly once more. Without thinking about the wisdom of his actions, he slid to the tile floor, wrapping his arms about the young woman, gathering her closer and pulling her naked body into his embrace.

Her slight body offered no resistence. It seemed as light as an eggshell. Smooth and finely made, its softness and pleasing curves were as exquisite as God could ever have created.

She was female in her essence. Her breasts were round and soft as they pressed against his chest, and he wanted badly to cradle them within his hands, knowing that they would fill his palms so sweetly. Her hips made a natural curve, and they would match his own body—he pulled his thoughts back with an effort.

He could not take advantage of her in such a state. But dear God, it was hard to hold her so close, knowing that this delectable body was bare and lovely against the inadequate shelter of his own patchwork of clothing, and not pull her nearer, closer, mold her hips into his and—

He could not think like this when she was unaware of their embrace. He had only meant to warm her, save her from illness or death. Feeling the sweat break out on his forehead, on his upper lip, Adrian tried to focus instead on the pale complexion of her face, the delicate blue veins that could be seen in her temples . . .

"You are so beautiful," he said softly. "If only I could woo you properly. If only I had met you before I started this journey toward death . . ."

Her eyelids lifted.

Startled, he paused and stared into her eyes. They were as beautiful as the rest of her, green with the faintest specks of gold sprinkled across the iris. Her lashes were long and blinked now as if she did not believe what she saw.

For one long moment, they stared at each other as Adrian held her close—held her naked body next to him, with only the barest layer of cloth to separate them. He was acutely aware of how it felt to be this intimate, this near to the unknown woman from the damp wood where mist now rose in foggy fingers—but how did it feel to her to wake thus, in the arms of a stranger?

"Don't leave me," she murmured.

"I won't. Don't be afraid," he said quickly. "I was only—"

And as quickly as she had come to herself, she fell limp once again.

Adrian sighed.

A few feet away, the gelding snorted.

"I didn't ask you," he snapped. "At least she's still alive. That is, if I haven't scared her to death."

But her body was growing warmer, he was sure of it, and even though he might have caused her alarm, at this point he decided to remain close to the unconscious woman. Night was upon them, the air was colder than ever, and he dared not allow her to become chilled again. If she woke once more and railed again his ungentlemanly behavior, he would explain and, if she insisted, give her a more proper space. Until then . . .

He didn't want to let her go, dammit!

How long had it been since he had held anything so precious in his arms? Hellfire, *had* he ever held anything so precious as this lovely woman with the look of pain etched onto her face?

A brief look—he was not sure what her expression had meant—but he would dearly like to convince her to stay, convince her to know him, allow him to know her . . . for as long as she might.

For now, he only wanted to wrap his arms about her, enfold her, hold her tight, hold her close.

Rain spattered beyond the roof, the cold wind whistled, the gelding stamped its feet and snorted its opinion of these drafty lodgings and lack of proper provisions. The trees beyond were indistinct, cloaked in the fog that made the moors beyond the small pocket of woods too dangerous to travel tonight, even if he had wished to dare the dark road. He would have had to stop, regardless. But who could have predicted such a find?

Adrian lay as close as he could to the woman whose name he did not know, tried to endow her with every scrap of warmth that he might, and waited for dawn to break.

For a long time he lay stiffly, afraid to relax in case in his slumber he allowed his arms to slacken and drift away from her, permitting the cold to seep in and envelop her in its killing shroud. But eventually sleep overcame him.

When the faintest glimmer of light streaked the sky and the first bird calls rang through the woods, he opened his eyes.

One arm had loosened its grip, but the other still cradled the mystery woman, still held her close to his body. Her eyes were closed, but she seemed to breathe more easily, and she had shifted a little to lie with her cheek against his chest. His coat had slipped slightly, exposing her bare arm. He reached to pull it up so that it would cover her naked-ness more completely.

And as he did, he looked up to see, past the splintered column of the gazebo, a trio of staring faces.

Two

E *yes wide, the villagers—he judged by their dress* that these were likely inhabitants of the hamlet where he had stopped briefly yesterday to feed and water his horse and take a quick luncheon himself—stared at him as if he were an invading Goth, or one of the Vikings who had once overrun these shores. They, too, had savaged the Yorkshire women, he remembered from early history lessons, though the prim cleric who had taught him had sidestepped the grimmest details.

Had he saved the unknown young lady's life only to destroy her reputation? The way they gazed at her with mingled relief—to see her alive and not dead in some grasping boggy moor—and horror told him without a word spoken that she *was* a lady, not simply another village lass. Although he supposed village lasses had reputations to uphold, too.

All this flashed through Adrian's mind as the trio glanced at each other, replacing their first looks of astonishment, alarm, and horror with expressions of disapproval.

Two were women, and the lone man was a short, stout fellow of advanced age. Adrian had to admire his boldness as the man drew a deep breath and stepped forward. He had no weapon except a narrow walking stick, and only his righteous resolve to stiffen his backbone. He drew himself up and faced the ravishing blackguard.

"Sir! Explain yerself! How 'tis that we find ye thus? Thou hast attacked a virtuous lady of our shire, Miss Madeline—"

One of the women hissed at him.

He recovered quickly. "That is, Miss Applegate. Ye must unhand her at once!"

At least he now knew her name, the ravishing blackguard told himself. This would take some delicate handling . . . if it could be done at all. His mind was blank as an empty card table beneath the scorn of the two goodwives who gazed at him as if they knew his type, oh, yes . . .

Rapidly, he shuffled through a dozen explanations, including the unmarked truth, and he knew that the most strenuous effort would slide off shuttered minds as quickly as any of the others. These three had already made their judgments, and so would the rest of the shire.

Miss Madeline Applegate's good repute was doomed. No one—absolutely no one—was going to believe that they had spent the night together in this lonely place, that she had lain naked in his arms and not surrendered her maidenhead.

Such was his reward for the most difficult feat of self-control he had ever maintained!

Still, Adrian had to at least try to save her good name. Drawing a deep breath, he dropped caution into one of the soggy Yorkshire moors that surrounded them. It was not as if he had much to lose.

"Last night I discovered Miss Applegate alone in the woods and in obvious distress," he said, keeping his voice calm. "I felt it unsafe to attempt to move her unassisted, so I tried to warm her so that she would not take a deep chill. She is still in a poor condition, and I am quite concerned. If one of you will go to her home, reassure her family of her safety, and bring back a carriage so that I can return her there without risk, she can receive proper care."

They gazed at him, and their collective scorn, if not banished, perhaps wavered just a bit.

"A likely story, sir!" The man, who seemed to have taken on the role of spokesman, replied, while one of the women sniffed. "And who be thou that we should accept such a fardingle?"

"I," Adrian said, his voice cool, "am Viscount Weller, Miss Applegate's fiancé. And this is no time to stand about with mouths agape. If you would, step lively, please!"

The man dropped his walking stick. All three showed expressions of pure astonishment.

"B-but we have not heard the banns read!" one of the women stuttered.

"Miss Applegate was waiting for me to join her for the occasion," Adrian said, his voice smooth. "Why are you standing there? Miss Applegate needs assistance!"

"I-I—yes, sir—I mean, ye lordship, sir," the man stuttered. He turned and took out his bewilderment on his companions. "Ah, get a move on, Maud, Sil, don't jest stand here!"

They departed as abruptly as they had come. Adrian looked down to see that Madeline Applegate had opened her lovely eyes. How much had she heard?

"Help is on the way," he told her. "How do you feel?"

"My head hurts," she said, her words a little slurred. If she had been some young buck, he might have suspected a late night and too much wine, but he could smell no wine on her breath, and it seemed out of character for a young lady.

"What happened? Did someone attack you?"

"No." She shut her eyes again. "My mouth is so dry. I'm cold."

He tried to pull the coat more securely around her. Now that she was awake, he didn't dare put his arms about her and pull her close to him, though he would have dearly liked to do so. He went to his saddlebags and took out his silver flask, bringing it quickly back and kneeling beside her.

He offered a sip. She took it, swallowed, then coughed.

"What is it?"

"Wine," he told her. "It will be good for you. You've been asleep for a good while."

She blinked at him, then shut her eyes again. "It's too bright," she murmured.

Indeed, the sun had risen above the trees. Sunshine slanted across the floor of the gazebo, and the fog seemed to have burnt away.

He sat down beside her and allowed himself the luxury of putting one arm lightly about her to hold the layer of clothing closer to her body, trying to keep her warmer. In the daylight the air was not as chill, but the breeze was still brisk.

Miss Applegate opened her eyes again at the unaccustomed touch, and a look of alarm crossed her face. "Where are my clothes?"

"They were drenched in the storm last evening," he told her, his voice matter-of-fact. "I feared you would be very ill if you lay in the wet and cold."

"But . . ."

She looked dazed, as did soldiers who had suffered blows to the head during a battle. He kept his voice low and soothing. "Help is coming."

"My father—he will be very worried—"

"It's all right. I have sent word to your family."

The tenseness in her face eased, and she shut her eyes

again. "You're being very kind," she murmured. "I'm so sleepy."

"Then rest. I will not leave you," he promised, remembering her whispered plea.

She shut her eyes again, and he sat beside her without speaking. Around them, a manic chorus of birds trilled in the treetops, the sun rose higher in the sky, and a deer ventured out of the edge of the copse to drop its head in the tall grass and sample the greenery.

It had been a long time since Adrian had experienced this sense of harmony, as if all were right with the world, even for just a golden moment. Whatever had happened to Miss Madeline Applegate, she seemed to be recovering, and that brought him a feeling of joy he had not known in years.

And his lie—when she learned the deception within whose deep folds he had felt compelled to enshroud them— it could well shatter the brief accord of this moment. So he might as well enjoy it while he may.

Within the hour, Adrian heard a heavy tramping of footsteps, and then an elderly manservant appeared on the path between the trees, followed closely by a maidservant, also of advanced years. They both wore expressions of mingled hope and anxiety.

The man paused when he set eyes on Adrian, but the woman—either more anxious or simply more stubborn— plowed ahead and didn't stop until she could fall to her knees beside Miss Applegate.

Their noisy passage had given Adrian time to extricate himself from close contact with the sleeping young lady, so this time the scene that met their eyes was not quite so scandalous. Even so, the sight of their beloved mistress lying on a horse blanket beneath a stranger's clothing, bereft of her own, made the maid suck in her breath.

Not wanting the woman to fall into hysterics, Adrian said quickly. "Do not shriek! I found her unconscious and soaked to the skin in the storm last night. I feared for her health if she lay in her wet clothes. She has not been harmed in any way, I give you my oath as a gentleman."

"Of course I wouldna scream out, noises 'urt her poor 'ead at such times as these," the serving woman said, to his mystification. They both stared at him with distinct suspicion.

"Ye told the baker that ye were Miss Applegate's betrothed," the man said now.

"I did," Adrian agreed, meeting the man's narrowed eyes.

"Miss Applegate," the elderly man continued stubbornly, "has na betrothed."

"I would suggest that you speak to Miss Applegate about that," Adrian said, his tone firm.

The man pursed his lips together and hesitated, and Adrian hoped he had the chance to speak to Miss Applegate first.

"Did you bring a carriage so that we can convey her to her home?"

The man nodded slowly. "It be there on the byway." He motioned toward the road that Adrian's mount had left before plunging into the trees. "We will ha' to carry her there."

But first, the maidservant insisted on making her mistress more respectable, taking up the damp clothing that Adrian had stripped off the night before. So Adrian turned his back and walked over to his gelding, patting the sulky beast and promising it a proper breakfast soon.

"Unless we are both of us fed first to the Yorkshire lions,

of course," he added beneath his breath. Playing Good Samaritan might become a dangerous pastime.

But Miss Madeline Applegate had, with her wistful green-eyed gaze and alabaster clean-lined body, already taken hold of him in a way that was hard to explain. He could mount his bedeviled horse and ride away, he told himself, now that the mystery lady of the moors had a name, had others to aid and succor her—he told himself that, but he knew it was not true.

She had already woven a spell about him, even though he knew she was no sprite, no changeling, but a real woman in real distress, and in some ways he had added to her problems when all he had meant to do was help her.

Although he had a would-be killer riding behind him—although time was slipping away—he felt the tiny bulge in his waistcoat and resisted the urge to pull out his watch with the tiny charm attached.

Adrian bit back an oath.

The die was cast.

When the maid indicated that masculine eyes could once more be properly cast in the direction of her mistress, he and the elderly manservant returned to the gazebo. The male servant, whose name it appeared was Thomas, hesitated.

Adrian walked over and leaned to pick up the still sleeping woman. He lifted her easily in his arms, carrying her cradled like a child.

"If you would lead my horse?" he suggested.

He would not have been surprised if the man had argued, but instead Thomas looked relieved. The man took the blanket from the floor of the gazebo and tossed it over the gelding, and the two servants walked just behind as Adrian followed the path back to the public road. He could feel their gaze upon his back, as if making sure that he did not abscond with their mistress.

Miss Applegate seemed to inspire loyalty in her staff, at least, he thought wryly. And now he would have to face her father and the rest of her family . . .

When they reached the road, he saw that the Applegate carriage was like the gazebo, once well made, now somewhat run down, although not as ramshackle as the structure in the clearing. He suspected that Thomas worked hard to maintain the vehicle and the single elderly mare who pulled it.

He placed Miss Applegate carefully into the carriage, and the female servant climbed in, as well, to make sure that her mistress did not fall out of the seat. Thomas clambered up to take the driving reins and clucked to the mare. Adrian mounted his own horse and followed at a slow but steady pace.

As he had suspected, his "fiancée's" home was of similar cast as the rest of the Applegate property. Her family was making a brave effort against looming penury, he thought, wondering what had brought them down—a father addicted to cards or a fast life of drinking and womanizing or all three?

The maid bustled to open the front door, and it seemed to be left to Adrian to again lift Miss Applegate from the narrow seat and carry her inside.

She opened her eyes once more. Blinking, she seemed to recognize him.

"Where—"

"You are home, now," he told her. "Do not fear."

She smiled up at him, a smile so sweet and untrammeled by any care that he ached for the approaching storm that full knowledge of their unchaperoned overnight stay would incite.

He tried to fix the sweetness of that look in his mind's eye as her eyelids drifted shut, and he carried her inside.

He had expected to meet a noisy crowd of family members awaiting the lost lamb's return. Instead, he saw only one figure in the entry hall. An older man, his expression concerned, sat in a wheeled chair.

"How is she?"

He was not very like her in the face, but this must be her father, Adrian thought, the head of the Applegate household. An invalid—perhaps that was the reason for the family's downward spiral of fortune.

"Your daughter is very weary, sir, but I think she is recovering. If you will permit me, shall I take her up to her room?"

The man nodded, albeit reluctantly, but no one else seemed hardy enough to lift the still slumbering woman. The maidservant led him up the stairs to Miss Applegate's chamber. Adrian laid her gently down after the maid hastened to turn back her covers, then the servant fussed about to bring a damp cloth to lay on her forehead.

With no excuse to linger in the lady's bedchamber, he could only cast one last glance from the doorway. Adrian thought that Madeline might have opened her eyes again for an instant, in time to look up at him before he left the room. Did she smile just slightly?

He came slowly down the stairs.

Mr. Applegate was waiting, as Adrian had been sure he would be.

"I believe we have matters to discuss," he said, his tone formal. The older man's body might be weakened by whatever accident or illness had wasted his legs and twisted his hips, but his expression showed resolve. "If you would accompany me to a more private setting?"

"Of course." Adrian followed him down the hall to a small room lined with bookshelves.

Rolling across the wood floor, his host poured them both glasses of wine.

"I am John Applegate. And you are?" Mr. Applegate wheeled his chair behind a small desk and circled to face him.

"Viscount Weller, at your service, sir." Adrian accepted the glass and took the seat that the older man waved him toward.

"First, of course, I must thank you for giving aid to my daughter and for bringing her home. She is my eldest and very dear to my heart. I spent a sleepless night, concerned that we did not know where she could be or what could have happened. The moor is a dangerous place, and even more dangerous men sometimes roam the land. A young lady unprotected—"

"I would have done no less for anyone I found in such distress," Adrian said. "Certainly I would always render aid to a young lady, alone and unconscious and in such need."

Mr. Applegate winced, no doubt at the picture of his daughter in such straits.

His voice firm, Adrian continued, trying to stop the accusations before they began. "And no doubt you also wish to ask me if I have taken advantage of Miss Applegate while she was in such a vulnerable condition. I came across your daughter in the woods, lying unconscious on the floor of the gazebo. Wanting shelter from the rain, I had turned in when I saw the structure. Fearing she would fall ill from cold and damp, I tried to help her. I did nothing that a gentleman would not, should not do. I have no way to prove it; I can only give you my word as a gentleman, sir."

He met the other man's gaze and held it for several long moments, then continued into the silence. "The problem, of course, is that I understand that the world is not given to accepting such explanations on faith—even when they happen to be true."

Mr. Applegate's expression was grim. "Indeed." He took a gulp of his wine. "Which leads us—"

"To my comment to the villagers," Adrian finished for him. "About being your daughter's betrothed."

"Aye," the older man said, his eyes hard. "So you admit it was—is—a lie? Because I happen to know, for a fact, that my daughter is most certainly not betrothed."

"I'm afraid I knew that the local gossips would put the worst interpretation on the circumstance, no matter how many oaths I swore," Adrian said. "I admit it was a concoction of the moment. But I am willing to make it the truth, if your daughter will agree."

His expression hard to read, the man behind the desk stared at him.

"I am a man of good character," Adrian continued, his voice steady. "I have an old and respected title, an estate of some value, and I will make sure she would have a considerable and comfortable inheritance when I am not around to take care of her."

"You are a stranger. I do not think she would easily leave her home for a man she does not know," Mr. Applegate said slowly.

"I can understand that," Adrian said. "I could make provision for her to stay here. We would think of some story to explain it to the neighborhood."

"You would make a most accommodating—and unusual—husband," the other man said, his expression frankly puzzled now. "Why would you be willing to do this to save the reputation of a young woman you don't even know? If you are one of the—the lovers of men and need a wife to cover up your other activities, then I must tell you I would not sacrifice my daughter even—"

Adrian tried to push back a slightly hysterical snort of laughter. "Certainly not!"

"Then why . . ."

Seeing that only the truth would serve, Adrian gave it, even though he knew that in the end, he would face what he dreaded most—that horrible look of pity that rose in others' eyes when they learned the fate that rode always behind him, dogging his footsteps like some ancient gypsy curse. But at least the elder man now knew why it was easy enough for Adrian to offer his hand in marriage . . .

And then Mr. Applegate sent the maid upstairs once more, to see if his daughter was awake.

Now Adrian had to face Miss Applegate herself and persuade her that this was the curse she would be fated to share, and yet at the same time her best chance for salvation.

Three

*M*adeline opened her eyes to see the familiar flowered coverlet pulled pristinely up to her chin. An
extra blanket—the faded blue one with a patch at the bottom right-hand side—was folded over her feet, and the
draperies were drawn, so the room was dim. Her room, her
draperies, her patched blanket and faded flowered coverlet.

She blinked.

She was at home in her own bed. She looked down. She
wore one of her own linen nightgowns, and the ties at her
neck were tied securely.

It must have all been a dream, born of pain and light-
headedness—of being stranded alone on the path through
the home wood, of being overcome by pain, drenched in
the storm, then—then waking briefly to find herself naked,
lying next to a man of dark hair and dark eyes with such
fire in their depths, a man who had looked at her with an
emotion she did not even know how to describe but which
made her thrill just to remember.

He had touched her gently, held her when she shivered with the icy cold that came with the pain, covered her and held her close when she almost couldn't move or speak. He had not fretted her with stupid questions, as most people did who didn't know about her wretched ailment. He had been a marvel.

But it had been a dream, she told herself. If he had been real, he would have been a marvel. It would also have been a scandal, and an unspeakably embarrassing imbroglio—having a man, a stranger, see her naked. No, impossible to even contemplate. She blushed now, just considering such an unthinkable, unbearable contretemps.

The door opened. For an instant Maddie hoped it would be her sister Juliana, come to share hugs and sympathetic wishes, but Juliana was married now and sailing off to distant shores with her animal-mad zoologist husband. Their newly widowed middle sister still dwelled with her grief-stricken father-in-law. Even the twins, Ophelia and Cordelia, had recently married. Now only Madeline was left at home. She was happy for all the new brides, of course, only the house seemed so empty sometimes, and she missed them acutely.

Bess, their elderly maidservant, came inside, unaware that she trailed phantoms of happier family times behind her. The maidservant carefully balanced a tray with tea and a bowl of hot soup. Steam rose from the broth, and the aroma reminded Madeline that her stomach was very empty. She sniffed cautiously and decided that the nausea had abated, and it would be safe to eat a light meal.

"'Ow's yer poor 'ead, Miss Madeline?" the servant inquired.

"The pain's fading, slowly," she said, putting one finger cautiously to her temple. It was tender to the touch, and she winced. The anguish, unbearable twenty-four hours past, had now dropped to a low pounding, the ache still a familiar foe, one she had lived with her entire adult life.

"Ye shouldna 'ave gone to the village." The maid shook her head. "I tol' ye a storm was brewing. You know 'ow fast yon storms come on, as do yer sick 'eadaches! And ye going off on yer own like that, leaving us worried sick, we were, and yer father 'aving conniptions, 'e was, thinking ye lost out on the moors!"

"No, you were right," Madeline agreed, her tone doleful, "and I paid the price. Next time I will listen. I thought I could slip to the village and pay my respects to the new Widow Talbot, but the storm hit so abruptly, my sick headache, too, and both were severe."

In fair weather her headaches occurred only rarely, mostly once a month before her courses, but sudden hard storms would bring one on with swift and severe results. She could do little except go to bed and wait out the agonizing pain.

She knew that her father worried about her a good deal. Several physicians had been consulted; one had advised drinking vinegar mixed with wormwood—that had made her nausea ten times worse. Another had wanted to bore a hole in her temple where the pain was the worst— fortunately her father had shown that surgeon the door right away.

Maddie knew that she simply had to endure the attacks; other people had worse scourges to bear. So now she listened to her longtime servant's lecture without complaining, knowing it was well meant.

"Yes, indeed, Bess," she said when the maid finally stopped for breath. "I will not do it again."

Bess grumbled a bit more, but went off to fix a fresh cold compress for her mistress's head. Madeline was able to sip a good portion of the broth and drink some of her tea before lying back on the pillow, exhausted by the slight efforts. An attack always left her feeling as if she had struggled through a rainstorm—except this time she had.

"Who found me out in the woods?" she asked. "Was it you and Thomas? I hope it wasn't too hard to get me home. If Thomas has thrown out his back again . . ."

Her expression hard to read, the maid stared at her.

Maddie had a sinking feeling inside. "What is it? *Has* he thrown out his back? I'm terribly sorry, Bess."

"Donna ye remember, Miss?"

"Remember?" Madeline felt her heart seem to skip a beat.

"The stranger who found ye in the gazebo?" Now Bess's tone was frankly accusing. "Did 'e do anything 'e oughtna? If 'e did, I donna care what the master says, I will scratch out 'is eyes like a cat—"

It wasn't a dream!

For an instant she felt as if time shifted, and she once again lay in the gazebo. She could almost feel his warm skin against her own clammy flesh—enjoy the firm touch of his muscle supporting her own limp limbs as she lay cradled in his embrace, barely aware. . . .

Madeline swallowed hard.

It was not a dream.

Oh, my lord. She had lain naked with a man, alone in the woods after dark . . . for how long? Surely only for a brief time before help had arrived. Oh, if only she could remember more.

That was another thing her headaches often stole from her—clear memories of the time that elapsed. It was easier to try to sleep away the pain—to shut her eyes and try to push away the rest of the world. Noises were too loud, lights too bright, smells too intense. So Maddie withdrew from it all, curled into a ball, and tried to escape the pain that dwarfed all else.

Now she put down her spoon. Why had she been naked? Had the man—had he—surely he hadn't. She swallowed hard.

"What—what did my father—what did he say about—about the stranger?" Her voice sounded peculiar to her own ears. "Does he—who knows?"

"Since the baker and two of the biggest blatherskites in the whole village were the ones who found ye," Bess wrinkled her brow as she picked up the tray, "I'm feared the whole shire will know soon enough."

"Oh, Bess!" Maddie wailed, too loudly. Her head throbbed harder and she groaned, regretting her cry at once.

"Now then, too late for that," the serving woman said matter of factly.

She sounded almost as if Madeline might deserve some punishment for her wanton behavior. If her own maid could harbor even a tiny bit of—no surely, not, Maddie tried to tell herself. Yet, the rest of the village was bound to be thinking—and saying—much worse.

Oh, God, she was ruined.

What was her father going to say?

A knock sounded at the door.

She pressed the cold cloth to her head. The pain had increased. She could feel the worry and distress pulling at her shoulders and neck. If her body stiffened with tension, a new cycle of headaches might start.

"Yes?" she said, hearing her voice wobble.

Bess hurried to open the door, and her father wheeled his chair inside.

"How are you?" he asked.

Madeline searched his expression for condemnation or anger. To her relief, she saw only concern and the usual affection that softened his blue eyes. She had to blink hard.

She cleared her throat, then was able to say, "I'm all right, Father."

He rolled up to the bed and pressed her hand. "I doubt you're all right, but I'm very relieved and happy that you are safe, Maddie."

Blinking against treacherous tears, she nodded. "I'm sorry I worried you. You know I didn't mean to."

He smiled at her, but his next words made her eyes widen in surprise.

"The man who brought you home to us has something he wishes to say to you. I would like you to listen to him, my dear. It would be to your advantage, I believe."

His tone was grave, and she had never seen him look so serious. What was this about? Surely, surely, he did not think she had encouraged this stranger to take such liberties?

"Father," she said, "I did not—that is, I did nothing that was not proper. I don't even remember meeting this man!"

"I know," he told her, his eyes rueful and loving and yet troubled, too. "Just give him a fair audience, my dear."

And while she watched him in astonishment, he went out of the room, leaving the door open. Then a stranger stood in his place—his frame tall and broad in the doorway, seeming to take up more room than any one man had a right to.

She blinked up at him before she realized that she was still in her nightdress, still lying in her bed. Blushing, Maddie pulled the coverlet up to her chin.

"May I come in?" His voice was deep and pleasing.

How could she allow a strange man into her bedchamber?

But her own father had sanctioned this interview. Besides, this same man had already seen her naked as a babe. The memory made her flush deepen and she looked away from his gaze, studying the faded roses on her bed hangings. Madeline, whom her sisters had sometimes called high-and-mighty, seemed to have lost her voice. She nodded, and the man entered her bedchamber.

He looked about him, found the stool by her dressing table, and pulled it closer to her bed. Perching on it—he looked as incongruous as a stallion trying to balance on a half bale of hay—he nonetheless seemed to make himself at home.

"How are you feeling?"

As if a dozen small imps mined her temple for hell-cursed ore, she thought. "Better," she said. "I understand that I owe you thanks for bringing me home."

Something that she could not interpret crossed his face. "You don't remember?"

"I recall—bits and pieces," she said, her tone cautious. She looked away from his gaze, which all at once seemed too piercing. "It's hard to tell what is memory and what is—what is out of my—my illness."

"I see," he said. "Does this occur often?"

She stiffened. She didn't care to discuss her affliction with outsiders. Only her father and sisters, and the two servants, knew about her disorder. She didn't want the whole village to have even more to gossip about—the whispers would swirl and grow and they would have her on the verge of being sent to Bedlam next!

"I beg your pardon," the stranger said at once. "I should not ask such a personal question."

And then, because he had not demanded it, she felt the need to tell him. He had rescued her, after all, and she must have looked very strange, lying senseless in the woods.

"Not—not often, exactly," she said, not wanting to discuss feminine matters with a stranger. "But storms will bring them on—the sudden overpowering headaches, I mean. I thought I could get home by the shortcut, but, obviously, I didn't make it. Thank you for your help."

Then, remembering what his help had entailed, she felt the warmth rise in her cheeks, and again she looked away from his gaze.

"My mother died after being drenched in an unexpected shower. I could not allow you to be endangered just because of propriety's artificial taboos. However, when we had the

bad luck to be discovered, I realized I had put you in a difficult position. And in trying to protect you, I fear I may have
compounded the tangle."

For a moment, she could only think about his long,
well-shaped fingers—she could just see his hands, his
strong, capable-looking hands, without lifting her gaze—
removing her clothes and touching her body just slightly,
and the thought made a nearly imperceptible shiver run
through her. Maddie had known for a long time that she
would not marry, so she had never thought that a man
would touch her so.

Then the sense of his words penetrated her thoughts and
jerked her back.

"What—I'm sorry. What did you say?"

"I'm afraid I may have the situation worse by trying to
make it better," he repeated.

She raised her brows.

"When I told the villagers that we were betrothed."

Madeline felt as if one of yesterday's lightning bolts
had drilled right through her. She sat straight up in the bed.

"What!"

His smile looked rueful. "It was a decision of the moment, as I told your father."

She stared. "But they will know that it is not true. The
banns have not been read, for one thing."

"Yes, they pointed that out. I told them you were waiting for me to join you for the momentous occasion."

His lips curved upward, and a hint of a dimple showed
at one corner of his mouth. For a face that she suspected
could look downright ruthless, it was unexpected, and she
felt a moment of corresponding warmth before she remembered to erect once again her wall of righteous affront.

"But—we cannot expect anyone to believe—"

"I have told your father—I have permission from your
father to make the lie truth."

Again, it took a moment, several moments, for the sense of his words to sink into her pain-befuddled brain. Madeline put one hand to her head and tried to push away the lethargy, the persistent ache, desperate to summon her usual quickness of intellect. "I don't—don't understand," she stammered. "What—what kind of trick are you playing at?"

He frowned suddenly. "I'm sorry, Miss Applegate. With you so unwell, this is a terrible time to thrust all this upon you. It's just that we must act quickly to save your good name, to avoid any outcry of public condemnation. I do not wish to see you hurt, whether in body—as I first thought you were—or in spirit, as you might be if the village thinks the worst of our night together."

She must have paled, because he stared at her with a concerned expression.

They had spent the whole night together, then? Oh, God help her. Yes, the village would be not just whispering; the gossips would be shouting it from the rooftops. Her reputation would be savaged, and no one would ever believe her blameless.

She swallowed hard. "I—I did not plan to marry, regardless," she said, her voice sounding hollow. "So really, it's—it's of no matter."

"And your sisters?"

"They are all married, some just recently," she told him. "Although my middle sister has been widowed at a young age, also lately. But surely it will not affect her."

He looked skeptical. "It could. And are you prepared to not be received by your own neighbors?"

She felt an emptiness in the pit of her stomach. Would their old friends turn their backs on her? She ran through a mental list. Some would likely stand by her, but yes, some would no doubt enjoy a chance to show their moral superiority, real or imaged. She would have to endure it, but—but her father would be so grieved.

Madeline felt her eyes fill with tears, and she blinked hard to hold them back.

"If you are imagining the worst, you are forgetting my offer," he broke into this abysmal daydream suddenly. "We can have the banns read. I am ready to do it."

"But—"

"My name, which I don't believe you have heard, is Adrian Carter, Viscount Weller, Adrian to my closest friends and family." He flashed her that sudden smile, which changed his face from handsome but somewhat forbidding, with its strong nose and chin and dark brown eyes, to purely irresistible. "I have a respectable name and fortune, and my character is also that of a decent man. I do have one main blot on my past, which I will explain in more detail later, but it will also offer you the solution to any disadvantage to our engagement, and I hope, marriage."

"Marriage?" Madeline, who was still breathless from the word *betrothal*, now felt downright giddy. She felt as she had as a small child when she'd slipped on the top of an ice-covered hill and every attempt to save herself had only added to the speed of her descent. The whole world seemed to be flashing past. "Marriage? No, no, I just tried to explain. I have to stay with my father, take care of my father. My sisters have all gone. Did you not see that he is an invalid—he must have someone here to take care of him—I promised my mother on her deathbed. I cannot leave him!"

"I will not expect you to leave him," the stranger said, his tone soothing.

She stared at him in bewilderment. What kind of man was he, and what kind of ruse was this, then? What kind of bogus marriage did he offer?

"It would be to both our advantages, Miss Applegate—may I call you Madeline?"

He had already seen her naked—he could call her anything he wished! Maddie drew a deep breath. She felt the heat rise inside her as that dark-eyed gaze raked her body, and she could not keep her thoughts in order.

"Let me tell you why we must marry."

Four

"*Have you lost your wits?*" *Maddie blurted.* "*Why* would you do such a thing for a stranger?"

It was his turn to raise his brows. "Do you think a gentleman would allow a lady to be compromised by his rash actions and not do the honorable thing? Or, even worse, do you doubt that I am a gentleman?" The hint of reproach in his voice made her blush even harder.

Dropping her gaze to the counterpane, she couldn't quite bring herself to add what was so obvious. But I am only a poor man's daughter, and you are a viscount! You could have your pick of so many more well-connected, wealthier, more pleasing ladies.

"I always thought that was rather—rather an extreme action to take" was all that she could manage.

She suddenly realized she had sat up in her shock, allowing the concealing bedclothes to fall away, and she wore only a thin nightgown. Yet it would seem very cowardly to crawl back between the sheets now.

She reached for her shawl and draped it around her

shoulders, pulling it about her to cover herself more modestly. Not that he hadn't seen everything there was to see already—the thought made her blush even harder.

"Extreme or not, it is the only thing we can do," he told her, his tone steady. "I must insist that you allow me to offer you the protection of my name, Miss Applegate—Madeline."

Her name sounded so natural on his lips. She found the sound of it so enticing that she hesitated too long, and he seemed to take her silence as assent.

"We could have the first reading on Sunday, and—"

"No, no, didn't you hear what I said?" she broke in. "I cannot leave my father alone!"

"Madeline, do not fear, I will never make you leave your father if you do not wish it," he said, his tone patient.

What kind of husband would allow his wife to linger in her father's house?

"Are you planning to reside here as well?" she demanded. Was he hiding out? Was he wanted for some crime? None of this made sense; there had to be something he was not telling her. In fact, hadn't he said there was some other part that he had to explain? Oh, if only her head would stop hurting so that she could think!

She put one hand to her right temple, pressing the spot where the deepest ache lingered as if she could push back the pain that refused to leave her. Becoming agitated would only make it worse, but it was hard to relax when this handsome stranger was ready to rearrange her future with such alarming alacrity.

His expression sympathetic, Lord Weller watched. "Don't fret about it now, Madeline. Lie back. Let me massage your temples. It might help the pain in your head."

The thought of those long, supple fingers touching her tormented head made a curious shiver run up her back, and if she were not feeling so wretched . . .

"Oh, I couldn't," she demurred, but he had already lifted her shoulders to move the pillows behind her head and before she could argue further, he had laid her flat on the bed and was smoothing her hair across the linen sheets. Did this man always get his way? When she was herself again, she would tell him.

"Shut your eyes," he was saying now, his voice soft. "Try to let it all go, let your thoughts fly away. There is nothing to trouble you, Madeline my dear, all will be well."

He said it with such authority, she could almost believe it would be so. And yet it was all nonsense, it must be, she argued with herself silently. Even that quarrelsome voice inside her mind faded as he touched her head.

She jumped, she couldn't help herself, but then the touch of his strong hands—at once pleasing and oh so soothing as he stroked her temples with a light but sure touch, then down her shoulders and over her forearms, up and down, back up to her shoulders and up into the hollows of her neck, kneading the sides of her neck until the hard knots wrought by her tension loosened.

Maddie felt as if she might dissolve into the bedclothes and slip away, yet she couldn't wish for that, either, because she could not bear to lose the wonder of his touch. . . .

It was such an intimate sensation, his hands moving easily over her neck, his warmth adding to her own, his sun-bronzed skin and slightly roughened fingers against the softer skin of her throat—she found her whole body reacting to his closeness. An unfamiliar tingling woke deep in her belly and she found her breath coming more quickly . . . and the headache did indeed seem to fade a little into the background. It was still there, but she was less conscious of it.

He continued to rub her shoulders, and now he eased her onto her side and rubbed her back as well, and Maddie felt even more languorous. Sighing, she felt old tensions ease, and she wondered if she might turn right into jelly. And if so, perhaps Lord Weller would scoop her up and—and what?

Who knew that her body could have such strange and wondrous feelings? If only her headache would fade completely, she could concentrate on the other.

"That feels so good. I fear you are taking advantage of—"

Too late, she heard the sound of the door opening, and the gasp and rattle of china as their faithful Bess took in this shocking tableau.

"I never! I'm fetching the broom and I'll dust yer backside meself, ye presumptuous no good—"

"Bess!" Maddie said, "You misunderstood! I didn't, he didn't—he was massaging my head because it aches so."

"I know where yer 'ead is, and it ain't what 'e was a'rubbing." The maidservant sat down the tray with a clatter of china and folded her arms in suspicion.

Blushing once more, Madeline struggled to find some dignity. Lord Weller had straightened, but she had a dreadful certainty that if she glanced at the viscount she would find him choking back laughter.

"Bess! You mustn't speak so. This is Lord Weller, our guest and—and my—my fiancé." There, she had said it, she was bound to this man, and she would indeed have to go through with this crazy plan.

Because, really, what other choice did she have? She could not shame her father and her whole family by having stories of their night in the woods together repeated throughout the village—through the whole shire, no doubt.

At least her announcement made Bess hesitate, and Lord Weller was wise enough to make a tactical withdrawal while the moment was ripe.

"I shall leave you to the ministrations of your faithful servant," he said, and slipped out the door before Bess could remember her earlier fury.

Unhappily, Maddie's headache throbbed once more, still very much with her. Sighing, she put one hand back to her temple.

The maidservant forgot her indignation in her haste to come to her mistress's aid. " 'Ere now, I got a fresh cold compress, and more of me 'erbal tea, what always 'elps yer stomach when yer 'ead is so bad."

Maddie agreed meekly and allowed the woman to bustle about until everything was settled to Bess's satisfaction. Maddie managed a few swallows of the liquid, then settled back with the cool cloth on her head, and the pain subsided once more into a low throbbing roar.

But she thought with a pang of Lord Weller's incredible hands and how they had felt stroking her neck and throat. Still, she should not allow such liberties—their engagement was only a ploy to save her reputation—and why was he doing it? Was it only to save her honor?

He had not told her the rest—why he would benefit, too, from this engagement. She could see no reason at all why he would want to marry a penniless and unimportant girl from the wilds of Yorkshire. Perhaps he had only said that to ease her mind. Or perhaps he didn't mean them to actually marry. Was the betrothal only to be a ruse? And what was it he'd said—something about a blot on his name . . . no, perhaps she had not heard him aright.

She could not imagine that he could do anything truly disgraceful. He was so kind and yet so forceful.

Sighing, Maddie shut her eyes and prepared to wait out the rest of this bloody headache. The same illness that had gotten her into this predicament in the first place made it hard for her to reason out what she should do about getting out of it.

She spent the rest of the day lying in the darkened room, moving as little as possible. By late afternoon, she was able to bear the light of one candle, and she wrote short letters to her sisters, although she was able to tell them only an abbreviated version of her ordeal.

To the twins, Ophelia and Cordelia, she wrote almost the same letter.

Are you back from your wedding trips? I yearn to hear about the South of France, and if Italy is as picturesque as it is said to be. Do write long letters, and I hope you come north soon to see us. I have missed you so!

Sighing, she put the pen down, blotted her somewhat messy script—they would know she had a headache just from her handwriting, she thought—then folded the pages and put them into the lap desk and pushed it aside. She lay back onto her pillow again and shut her eyes.

She slept off and on through the night, and by the next morning she woke with the pain gone at last, and only an overwhelming sense of fatigue and lassitude hanging over her, the last stage of her headaches.

Sighing with relief, she sat up gingerly and pulled on a robe. When she came back from the necessary, she found that Bess had brought warm water. She bathed and then was glad to sit back on the bed when the maidservant warned her not to do too much.

It was true that she still felt very shaky.

"I'll 'ave ye a tray up in a two shakes of a lamb's tail," the servant told her, casting a worried eye at her mistress.

"How is my father?"

"'E's right as rain," Bess told her. "Seems to 'ave taken quite a liking to the hoity-toity lord. And I will say the fancy viscount ain't above playing chess with our good master, nor talking for 'ours 'bout 'is books and stuff," she finished with reluctant approval.

Startled, Maddie stared at the servant's wrinkled face. "Really? That is a surprise—I mean, that's good."

It had not occurred to her before that her father, with his family of daughters and few male friends in the neighborhood, might be hungry for male companionship, but it was probably true. The local squire was interested in little beyond a day's hunt and the chance of a good harvest, certainly not in books or thoughtful conversation, and the gentleman farmers were mostly cut from the same cloth. Madeline suddenly felt impatient to be out of her bedchamber and back downstairs so that she could join them and see for herself if her father and Lord Weller had struck up an accord.

But her energy was still limited. Perhaps she would feel up to going down for dinner.

However, to her annoyance, she found that she would be seeing company much sooner than that.

She ate breakfast and then Bess helped her dress in a faded muslin day gown and put up her hair. Then Maddie lay back upon her bed, content to rest a little longer before venturing out. She thought with anticipation of a walk in the garden, and she found herself hungry for fresh air as well as her new fiancé's presence.

But hardly had Bess taken her tray away when the door to the hall suddenly burst open and Mrs. Masham, a stoutly built matron somewhat overdressed for a morning call in the country, stepped into the room.

Madeline blinked in surprise.

"Oh, there you are, looking so pale, too. I declare, poor Miss Applegate, I just had to come and see about you," the young matron declared.

"I beg your pardon," Maddie answered, knowing her tone was somewhat stiff. "I don't believe I said I am in to callers today, Mrs. Masham."

"Oh, so your maid said, but I knew you didn't intend that prohibition to stand for your *close* friends, such as I!" The woman batted pale lashes over slightly protuberant eyes and smiled coyly. "And there are such stories being passed around the village—well! I just had to come and see with my own eyes that you are not at death's door after your perilous night in the woods!"

Translation: she couldn't bear to wait another moment to ferret out more gossip, Maddie thought. Mrs. Masham knew perfectly well that it was people such as her that Maddie would definitely want excluded, which was why she had waited until Bess's back was turned and then nipped up the stairs.

But unless Maddie barred her from the house and caused a total scandal—and that might upset Papa—she would have to put up with her. No wonder Maddie's sister Juliana had once fled to London just to escape Mrs. Masham's arrival in their shire.

While Madeline hesitated, Mrs. Masham looked around for something to sit on and finding no chair, pulled the stool in front of the dressing table closer to the bed. "Now, you must not exert yourself in the slightest, just lie back and rest, and tell me everything about your secret engagement and how on earth you ended up in the woods overnight. I thought you were reasonably proper, even if you are so sad as to have lost your mother so young and to have had no one to teach you what it is to be a lady, but to end up so totally depraved, I mean, really . . ."

She fastened her toadlike eyes on Maddie, who felt as transfixed as a gnat on a lily pad, and as unable to flee.

"I beg your pardon . . ." Maddie began, her voice stiff, but she couldn't seem to finish the sentence. While she hesitated, she heard a light knock at the door, and another familiar face appeared in the doorway.

This time, it was someone she was actually happy to see.

Mrs. Barlow was a penurious widow who had moved into the neighborhood not too long ago. Some of the neighbors had turned a cold shoulder to the new arrival, feeling that her background was not sufficiently vouched for. No one seemed to know where the petite young woman had come from, or who her relatives might be.

The widow said little about her past and, indeed, did not try overmuch to insert herself into the social life of the shire, but Madeline felt sorry for her and had been friendly. The widow was hardly past her thirtieth birthday and often seemed pensive if caught in an unguarded moment, though she was always good company. She lived quietly in her rented cottage and, showing evidence of a sharp mind and a kind heart, enjoyed reading and quiet conversation, which pleased Maddie a great deal.

Like her father, Maddie did not always find sympathetic companions in her neighbors, especially since her sisters had all flown the nest. Of late, Mrs. Barlow and Maddie had taken to walking together now and then, and Maddie often invited her over for tea and lent her books to read.

She looked up to see the newcomer with a distinct feeling of support being at hand.

"I'm so glad to see you looking better, Miss Applegate," Mrs. Barlow said. "I heard that you have been under the weather."

"Indeed she has, and too much society may put her back into her sickbed," the first visitor retorted, her tone peevish. She showed signs of wanting to keep her pride of place. "In fact, Miss Applegate and I were having a quiet tête-à-tête."

"Oh, please come in," Maddie interjected, overriding this complaint. "I'm so happy to see you. Yes, I've been ill, but I am recovering. How nice of you to come and ask about me."

"True friends always remember you when you are ill," Mrs. Masham put in, glaring at the newcomer, "and I fear there is not another chair."

"Sit down on the end of the bed," Maddie said. "I don't mind."

"If it will not jar you," the other woman said. "I would not wish to intrude if the two of you are exchanging confidences."

"That's most observant of you," Mrs. Masham began. "In fact—"

But Maddie interrupted once more. "Of course not, more company is just what we should like! Is it not so, Mrs. Masham?"

Mrs. Masham looked as if she wished to bite something, or someone, but she could not openly contradict her hostess, so she murmured something that one might construe as polite, and the widow, her tone demure but her eyes dancing with mischief, sat down at the foot of the bed.

"I hope you are feeling better?" Mrs. Barlow suggested.

"Indeed, I am beginning to be more myself," Maddie agreed.

The door opened again, and to her relief—surely there could not be more visitors—it was Bess, whose eyes widened to see her mistress's bedchamber so invaded.

"Bring some tea if you would, Bess," Maddie said quickly, before the servant said something too blunt about the wisdom of allowing guests so soon after her illness.

Her lips pressed together, Bess went out again without comment, and Maddie turned back to her company.

"But you have not said a word about how you ended up in the woods overnight," Mrs. Masham complained.

"Perhaps that is a subject best left unexplored," the widow suggested, her tone light. "Surely, Miss Applegate's *friends* would not wish to press her on such a delicate subject."

Mrs. Masham bristled, while Maddie felt a rush of gratitude. She smiled at the lady whom she knew to be truly her friend, but she also knew that the other woman, a remorseless gossip, would worry the question like a bulldog with a particularly savory bone.

In the end Maddie knew she would have to say something and she might as well face the question head-on. "It's a simple enough tale. I fell ill, and Lord Weller was afraid to leave me to get help. So he sat beside me until the villagers found us and could send word to fetch the carriage."

"Of course," the widow agreed, her tone unruffled. "So often, the simplest explanation is the true one."

"And yet," Mrs. Masham shot back, the gleam in her eyes too bright, "while Miss Applegate's friends will, of course, believe this inoffensive excuse, one wonders if the villagers, being perhaps too suspicious in their habits, will accept such a tale?"

"If we all stand by her, surely they will, in time," Mrs. Barlow argued.

The other matron looked skeptical. "I fear they are too quick to see wicked behavior where there is the slightest chance of it!"

"Perhaps those who are determined to see evil have some acquaintance with it in their own lives?" the widow murmured, her expression a little too innocent.

The other woman shot her a sharp glance, while Maddie bit her lip to keep from laughing. Mrs. Masham continued to try to pick away at Maddie's reasons for her night in the wood, and the widow continued to head her off, and the conversation went on in this way until shortly the door opened again.

This time it was only Bess, with a tea tray that seemed to be hurriedly assembled. If the water was not quite hot enough, the tea too weak, and the cake sliced unevenly, Maddie was so exasperated with her unwanted company, she found she didn't care.

Her guests pretended to find everything as it should be and made a game effort to drink the sickly hued refreshment, then Mrs. Barlow stood.

"I'm sure we do not wish to tire you when you are just recovering, Miss Applegate, so we will take our leave. I hope to see you out and about very soon."

"Thank you for coming," Maddie said, keeping her tone pleasant with determined effort.

Her other guest was forced to rise and say her goodbyes, as well, though her expression showed resentment as she did so. The widow looked cheerful and unrepentant, Mrs. Masham sulky, as they both made their way out the door. Mrs. Masham threw one last glance back over her shoulder, as if hoping to catch Maddie in one more instance of improper behavior before the door shut. Did she expect her to dance naked on her bed?

"Miserable woman!" Maddie muttered beneath her breath, then she lay back upon her bed for a few minutes, giving them time to get down the staircase, through the front hall, and out the door before she rose from her bed and left her room. She had no desire to run into Mrs. Masham again today.

When she at last opened her door and ventured out, the house was very quiet. She knew she would find her father in his study on the ground floor, so she tiptoed down the staircase and, keeping an eye out for any more visitors, approached the stout oak door.

She was eager to speak to her father now that her mind was clear and also impatient to once more see the mysterious man who had so turned her life upside down by his mere presence. But perhaps that wasn't fair—it had been she who had so rashly gone into the woods and across to the village, despite the fact that the oncoming rain had threatened, and when she knew that her headaches could come on so quickly. At any rate, it was done, it had happened and now—now she was paying for it tenfold, and truthfully she could not even be sure if she was sorry or glad.

When she tapped on the door and it opened to show the tall, broad-shouldered figure of Lord Weller, she inhaled sharply, even though she had half expected to see him there.

"Are you here to see your father? He's inside," the viscount said. "I will not keep you." He stepped aside to let her pass.

Maddie was very conscious of his well-built body as she slipped so closely past him, his smell of clean linen and outdoor air and something inexpressibly masculine. For a moment the awareness of him made her almost dizzy, but she had to swallow hard and keep her expression clear because her father sat as usual behind his desk in his wheeled chair. He looked up now to smile at her.

"Ah, my girl, how good to see you up. How is the head?"

"Much better," she said automatically, ignoring the lassitude that always plagued her after an attack.

She waited a moment, then looked back at the doorway, but Lord Weller was too well bred to linger where he might appear to be eavesdropping. He had walked away down the hall. She came inside the room and closer to the desk.

"Papa, Mrs. Masham came to call. The woman is such an old cat—she's hoping for more scandal to repeat to the village!" she told him, the words rushing out.

"This is why we must be very cautious," he told her. "And why your betrothal is so important. I do not wish to see your good name destroyed."

"What do you think—really—of Lord Weller?" she asked him, dropping her voice. "Bess says you have spent time with him while I have been abed."

He smiled at her. "I cannot claim to know him well after only a few days, my dear. He has a good mind, that is obvious. He is nigh impossible to beat at chess, and he would not make a good enemy, I suspect. Yet I also think he has a compassionate heart."

Maddie nodded. She had a flash of memory—of lying with only a rough woolen blanket beneath her to cushion her against the cold ground while the viscount pulled his coat over her, the woolen cloth scratching her bare nipples as the chilly air rippled over her skin. They had lain together, so close. She looked away, hoping that she did not blush and that her father could not discern the direction of her thoughts. "Yes, I think he is kind at heart," she agreed, her voice low. "He tried hard to aid me, in the woods. I think he was sincerely worried about my plight."

"I would not allow any other type of man to court you," her father told her, his voice serious, "even in such circumstances as these."

She gave him an impulsive hug. "Thank you, Papa," Maddie said. "You are such a good father."

He tightened his arms for a moment and kissed her forehead, but then patted the frame of his wheeled chair and sighed. "A father with empty pockets and useless limbs? I rather think you could do much better, my child."

"No, indeed," Maddie insisted.

"And as for the other . . ."

She remembered that Lord Weller had spoken of a blot on his name, and curiosity stirred, sharp as a needle's prick. What was the transgression that darkened his reputation, even as the viscount fought to save her own? How could a such a thoughtful, kind man have a serious crime in his past? Or did she make too much of his words?

"Yes?" she prodded, impatient for her father to go on. But to her disappointment, the answer didn't come. "What is there about the viscount I should know?"

Her father shook his head. "I think he is the one who should speak to you about that."

They talked quietly for a few minutes more, then Maddie left the study and walked down the hall to the sitting room. It was empty.

Where had the viscount gone? Their house was small enough, with few public rooms, and she could not venture up to his guest chamber. She swallowed against her disappointment.

Had he gone outside? The day was fair; perhaps he was enjoying the air. She could check the gardens. But first Maddie paused to gather up scissors, a basket, and thick gloves from the pantry so she did not look so plainly in search of him. But obvious or not, she would find him.

It was time she uncovered the viscount's secret.

Five

*T*o *her satisfaction, she located him almost at once* in the small flower garden at the side of the house. The garden was certainly in need of her ministrations. To give herself time while she arranged her thoughts, she knelt to pull weeds from one of the flower beds, then selected blossoms to adorn the sitting room.

The viscount crossed the path in the middle of the garden and bent down to help her. He chose one long lilac stem from a nearby bush, cut it with a small knife from his pocket, and handed it to her.

"I'm glad to see you out in the fresh air," he said. "Your cheeks still appear somewhat pale."

He continued to select blossoms to give to her until her arms were full, and the sweet smell of the flowers drifted about them. Even so, she was still aware of his nearness, and his own fragrances, just as she had when she had passed so close to him in the doorway. How had she never noticed that men had their own scents, too, of clean linen and male skin and more that she hardly knew how to define—and they could be just as pleasing. It made her want to reach out and touch him—but what a very unladylike thought!

When he bent so near to her as he did now, she forgot, for a moment, what she had planned to say. If it were possible, Lord Weller seemed even more handsome in the clear light of day than he had indoors. His skin was slightly bronzed from the sun. He must spend a good part of his time out of doors, she thought. And his eyes were so well shaped, framed by their dark slashing brows, and with colors so rich and true–she felt herself gazing into them and somehow could not look away. She felt warmth flooding her cheeks and knew she must be blushing again.

He took hold of her elbow and helped her rise.

"Yes," he said, his tone lower and more intimate. "Being out in the sunlight does improve one's color, I believe."

He was teasing her, she thought, but before she could reproach him, he put one hand beneath her chin, lifted it, and leaned closer. He was going to kiss her!

He moved slowly and deliberately and she had more than enough warning to move away. More than enough time to tell him how improper it was to stand in the midst of the garden and share an embrace in the broad sunlight.

Except she didn't wish to move away, and she very much wanted him to kiss her!

His lips were sure and firm, and they seemed to fit against her own lips as if they had both been born for nothing else. And it was not just her lips that tingled from this touch. Amazed at the sensations that flooded through her, Maddie stood very still. His mouth was warm, and his arm was about her shoulders, now, and she felt enveloped, consumed by this man. She couldn't believe that her whole body seemed to quicken with flickers of sensation, quicksilver streaks of impulse that called to her—to deep-seated emotions, longings that had never before made themselves known to her.

Pausing, he drew back long enough to whisper against the corner of her mouth, laughter making his voice quiver. "You are allowed to kiss me back, you know, dearest Madeline."

Was she? Of course she was, they were betrothed.

She dropped the flowers without even thinking and threw her arms about his neck, overjoyed to think that it was perfectly fitting to share an embrace. So she pulled his head back down so that again their lips met, and she stood on tiptoe in order to press her lips even more firmly against his. This time she pressed her whole body into his firm torso without leaving any distance at all between them.

And was startled by his body's response. For a moment she didn't understand, then it came to her—she might not have spent as much time in the barnyard as her sister Juliana, who had helped Thomas with the sheep and the other animals, but she wasn't deaf and dumb, either. She almost pulled back, but Adrian had his arms about her now, and he held her inside his embrace, and really, it felt too good, pressed against him, and why be missish now?

So she clung to him, returning his kisses with a passion she'd never dreamed she might possess, and thinking with what little conscious thought that remained that on their marriage night, what wondrous new delights might unfold.

Then some small breath of sanity blew through the fervor that befogged her brain. Maddie straightened and pushed the viscount away so suddenly that she overbalanced and almost fell.

"What is it?" he demanded, looking about them. "Is someone here?" He frowned at this possible intruder, and his expression would have daunted a lesser woman.

But Maddie had her own demons to face.

"I can't!" she said. "I can't marry you! I can't leave home."

His eyes narrowed, the viscount was gazing about them as if he expected to find a dragon sitting in the stunted apple trees. He turned his attention back to her, and his expression softened. "I promised I would not expect you to leave your father, Madeline. I always keep my word."

"But—how can you want a wife who will not—will not . . ." She stared at him, not sure how to go on.

Adrian pressed his lips together. Before Madeline had appeared, he had been pacing up and down in the garden, feeling as confined as an eagle in a canary's cage. He felt exposed, vulnerable, and every time he paused, he seemed to feel the pressure of unseen eyes, as if his cousin peered at him from some secluded hiding place. How close was he this time?

How long before Francis appeared, before the shots rang out, again, before the trapdoor closed, yet again?

Adrian should be on his way now, fleeing once more. Yet, God's blood, how long could he go on this way?

What kind of miserable coward had he become?

And how could he leave her alone when he had promised . . .

When Madeline had appeared, with that small line of anxiety creasing her forehead that had smoothed away when she saw him, something inside him sparked the same warmth that always flowed through him whenever she was close by. Almost from the first moment Adrian had seen her in the forest, something about her had captured his heart.

It was more than the grace of her form or the vulnerable look in her eyes. Now it was her wit, her candor, her courage in facing her own private demons—oh, so many things about her. And he had given his word. He could no more leave her than could some medieval knight flee a bolt riveting him to a dungeon wall. Only Adrian's prison had a much more beautiful aspect, as long as Madeline was nearby.

And now he had to tell her the truth—well, most of the truth, anyhow. Best to get the worst of it over, he thought.

"Madeline, I want you to marry me, but there is something you should know first, before we are pledged to each other before God and your neighbors. I have killed a man," he said, letting the words fall like blows against the innocent silence of the garden. "Worse, the man was my cousin and my heir."

Her eyes wide, she stared at him. "An accident?"

Shaking his head, he braced himself for a look of disgust or even fear. If she moved away from him, he thought it might destroy him.

Instead, she looked at him seriously but seemed more puzzled than anything else. "Was he trying to kill you?"

"Yes. It was a duel, a most foolish combat," he told her, shaking his head at the inanity of it. "It began with a quarrel over a game of cards. Linley was drunk, I'm afraid, and quarrelsome, although he was often that, drunk or sober. I tried to joke him out of it, but to no avail. Then I tried to get his chosen second, his younger brother, Francis, to persuade him to change his mind.

"Not only did he not try to settle the quarrel peacefully, Francis allowed Linley to drink all night instead of taking him home to get some sleep. So he came to the appointed place still drunk. I had meant to delope, but he fired the first shot while I was still turning and it struck my arm, making my own shot go wild, out of control. He was hit and later died. Dueling is, of course, illegal, and I could have gone to prison or been executed, except the evidence showed that he fired first and improperly, before the time was called. In the end, I was released."

"So it was not your fault, not really, that he died," Madeline said, as if trying to reassure him.

"Ah, but his brother now blames me and has announced his intention to see me dead in revenge for his brother's demise."

"But you said—he is now the heir. It was to his advantage that his brother was drunk and fired against the rules." She stopped as if trying to puzzle out the connections.

Adrian nodded. "Yes, there has been gossip enough about that. Perhaps Francis planned to be next in line to my wealth and title. If we had both died, he would have been in prime shape, would he not? The gossip has not helped his temper, I must say. And since he is now my heir, you must see why I would be most happy to have a child to inherit, an heir of my blood."

"Surely the law will not allow him to inherit your property if he murders you!" she exclaimed, putting one hand to her face in horror.

"It would be a nice tangle for the solicitors," he agreed, knowing his tone was dry. "But keep in mind, they would have to prove that he is the one who had killed me. If we meet in a dark alley or on a distant moor, only the two of us, who will be left to give evidence?"

"But you must not be alone! And for goodness' sake, you must inform the courts of his evil plans, tell someone! You must not allow him to do this!"

Madeline looked deeply distressed. He wished he could simply kiss her again and forget this wretched story.

"I have hired Bow Street Runners," he told her. "They have eaten me out of house and home, annoyed my servants, and arrested my tradesmen. In the meantime, they have never been able to put hands on my cousin. Francis continues to dog my steps and has twice put a bullet much too close, once ruining a brand new hat, and another time creasing my side and breaking a rib. It hurt like the devil until it healed, not to mention destroying an almost new coat. I really should send him my tailor's bills."

"It is not a matter to laugh about!" she snapped, and to Adrian's surprise, he saw that her lashes had dampened.

"My dear Madeline," he said more gently. "I must laugh—otherwise, it is too depressing a tale."

"Then hire private guards," she suggested. "If you have the funds . . ."

He could not simply give in to this bloodthirsty relative, Maddie told herself. It was too unfair to allow such an evil man, with murder in his heart, to succeed.

She saw his lips tighten, but it was a moment before he answered. "I have tried that, too," he said, his voice low. "A servant of mine, a very good fellow who went through the whole war with me with only a few scars to show for it, the most loyal man you could ask for. He had taken to sleeping beside my bed, and when Francis bribed an innkeeper for the key to my room, John was there to intercept my cousin's knife. He saved my life, but he paid the price with his own."

Maddie gasped.

"Unhappily, Francis got away in the confusion as I tried to stop the bleeding from John's wound. Furthermore, he bribed his servant to say that he was elsewhere at the time, and we could not make the murder charge stick."

A crow called from across the garden, and a cloud slid across the sun. She shivered as the hitherto sunny day felt suddenly colder. Adrian looked up at her, and his handsome face seemed bleaker, his expression more austere. "I will allow no other man to die for me," he told her, his voice quiet. "I ordered enough men to their deaths during the war, Madeline. I cannot do it any longer. The next time I face my cousin, no innocent people must suffer. It has to be only him and me who face each other. That is why I can stay here long enough to have the banns read, to marry properly and legally, but then I must leave to keep you from harm. I dare not risk your safety."

Thinking of his lonely days and nights with an enemy always a few steps behind him, she swallowed. He took both of her hands in his. "Will you marry me, Madeline? For your sake, at least, if not mine."

His words hung in the golden air for a moment.

Her answer sounded husky. "Yes, I will."

Maddie reached to grip his forearms, as if she could hold him in place, keep him from confronting such an intractable enemy. "But there must be some way for you to stay. Your cousin is mad," she muttered. "Surely he is."

"Perhaps," Adrian agreed. "I think it quite likely. I have tried to simply stay out of his way, but he has a nose for my presence like some demented bloodhound, always sniffing out where I am."

He grinned at her, and despite herself, she laughed, although a moment later, thinking of someone lying in wait for Adrian, she had to blink against betraying tears. A man wanted to kill him, and he made silly jests. How could he?

But then, perhaps he was right; what else could he do? Moan and feel sorry for himself? Adrian would never do that, she knew it instinctively. He was too proud, too fierce to wallow in self-pity.

She wanted to hug him to her, cradle his head against her breast in sympathy. The thought of his face against her breast made her whole body tingle, and she blushed as her thoughts turned in a quite different direction.

He gazed at her, and his knowing expression made her glance away. He wanted an heir, she remembered suddenly. He wanted a baby. That meant a real marriage, in every respect. She blushed again, and remembered how it had felt to lean against him, pressing her whole body into his. She'd never expected to have that kind of pleasure, the unknown joys of the marriage bed.

Now she wished she had quizzed her married sisters in more detail. Why did they all have to be out of the country or in faraway London when she needed advice? She knew nothing at all about what role a wife should play when the wedding guests had made their good-byes and the servants had snuffed out the candles. What if she couldn't please him?

He was watching her with an uncanny glint in his eye. He couldn't discern what she was thinking—could he?

His deep brown eyes seemed much too knowing.

She had a sudden image of the two of them in bed, of Adrian pulling her gown over her head and seeing her naked once more.

Maddie felt her cheeks burn; she couldn't seem to stop blushing. "I'd better go back—that is—my father might think—I mean—I'd better—"

Losing her nerve entirely, she turned and fled back toward the house.

Once inside, she hurried up the staircase to her bedroom. She pulled paper and ink out of her bureau and curled up on her bed with a lap desk to write another letter. She'd sent the others out, but now she had pressing concerns to express.

Her widowed sister Lauryn was the one who had been married first, perhaps she was the most promising person to ask.

Maddie dipped her quill into the ink and wrote:

Dear Sister,
I know this will be an unexpected question, but many things in my situation have changed rapidly. In my last letter, I told you about the sad experience with my headache and how I was caught in the woods, and how the viscount tried to help . . .

It was still hard to work up to the questions she wanted to ask. Maddie stopped and frowned at the ragged end of the quill. She dipped the nib into the ink and tried again.

> *If we go through with the marriage, I fear I will not be . . . I don't know if I will know enough . . .*

Oh, dear. She couldn't even write out her anxious feelings. This didn't bode well for her marriage night. If she couldn't even speak about her worries to her trusted sister, how could she expect to face a husband whom she had acquired in such an unorthodox manner? And how could she hope to satisfy him as a good wife should?

Felicity Barlow walked briskly down the lane, wishing for the hundredth time that the cottage she let was not quite so isolated. But she had got it for a paltry lease, and given her small income, that was essential. She was lucky to have found it at all. It was, mind you, drafty and cramped. Some daft artist chap, as the locals described him, had had it built. A wooden frame cottage with a thatched roof, it was much more practical for the south of England than cold, damp Yorkshire.

When he had tired of it and returned south, it had remained empty for some time until she had arrived in the village. The rent was very cheap, and she had enough space for a small garden, so it suited her fine. Miss Applegate had been very generous about giving her extra eggs and milk from their animals as well, even though the Applegates had little extra to spare.

She was lucky to have found a friend who was so generous of heart, Felicity thought, sighing as she stepped around a bramble bush that had grown across the path. It was not easy for a woman alone. The rest of the gentry were suspicious of her, as no one knew her well enough in the shire to vouch for her background.

She brushed at her rusty, well-worn black skirts and shook them free of the other weeds that clung to them. No need to fret over things she could not change. It was a nice day, Miss Applegate was on the mend, and she herself had had a nice walk. She would have the last egg for tea and warm up the bit of soup that was left from the morning.

A blur of movement caught her eye, and Felicity turned her head sharply. But nothing was there, except a sparrow, which, startled by her movement, took flight suddenly from the hedgerow. She was being silly, she told herself. She drew a deep breath and walked on. She would not panic; it was just such a lonely path. Her steps were quicker now, but she controlled herself and would not break into a run. One had to have some measure of dignity. Her cottage was just ahead, and she had locked the door—she always locked the door—and her ancient key was on her belt as it always was. She gripped the large copper key with its reassuring weight and kept moving.

Trying not to look back over her shoulder, but unable to keep herself from taking one more quick glance, which showed her nothing but an empty path, Felicity pushed the key into the lock and let herself in, then quickly slammed the heavy oak door and turned the lock again. The heavy silence of the empty cottage—she could afford no help, of course—settled around her like an old if capricious friend.

It was all right, just her nervous fancies. The cottage was just as she had left it, neat if rather plain of furnishing. She had enough wood inside and enough water. She would not have to go out again today. The thought was reassuring. She walked across to the hearth and added a small length of wood to the banked fire, using the poker to stir the coals and coax the flames back to life, then warmed her hands, which were colder than the day seemed to warrant. Her unsteady nerves, no doubt.

She was glad that her younger friend had never seen her like this. But then, Miss Applegate had no idea that there were parts of her friend's background that haunted her with fears unnamed. Felicity folded her best shawl and put it into the chest by the wall, found a plainer one to throw about her shoulders as she prepared a simple meal for the evening, and then sat down in an oak rocker close to the hearth to eat. A small gray cat came out of the shadows to wind about her feet and purr and push its head against her ankles.

"Yes," Felicity told the animal. "You know about being homeless and friendless, little one, do you not?" She rubbed the cat behind the ears and fed it a few bites of her meager dinner before finishing it quickly and putting her plate aside. The cat jumped to her lap, curled up, and purred itself to sleep. Felicity stared into the fire for a long while as if she saw more there than the jumping flames, but whatever scenes were painted in the glowing embers of scarlet and gold did not bring her comfort.

Maddie wrote two letters, one to Lauryn and one to Juliana, though she did not know if either would make it to her sisters and back before the wedding. She considered whether she should write to the twins, too. Both were just married, and deliriously happy, they often said, but they were the youngest of the Applegate sisters, and it was hard to contemplate asking them for advice, married or not.

She would, of course, invite them all, and their husbands, to the ceremony, but again, she wasn't sure if any would be able to travel to Yorkshire in time. Juliana and her baronet husband were usually in foreign climes searching for yet another wild beast for his collection. Lauryn, who had been recently widowed, was still with her father-in-law, feeling bound to him in his grief and loneliness.

As for the twins, they hadn't even returned from their own bridal trips. Cordelia's wedding had been the talk of the shire. Maddie smiled, remembering the dark-haired groom who had so obviously captured her younger sister's affections.

At any rate, all of her sisters, except for Lauryn, made single again by a cruel fate, had found their mates despite having no dowries, which no one in the neighborhood had expected. Certainly, the local gossips had been all agog. Even Maddie herself had been surprised. She'd always expected to have one, if not more, of her sisters left to share the house while she tended to their father as he aged.

Not that it would have changed her plans if she had known differently, she assured herself, remembering the pledge she had given her dying mother. And now—to be married herself—even briefly—no, she must not think like this. She couldn't assume that Lord Weller would not live long, just because an insane man intent on revenge was determined to kill him.

The viscount was intelligent, vigilant, prepared. But was he prepared enough, the other part of her mind argued, remembering the close calls he had barely survived.

The man must be captured, she raged silently. There must be something they could do. She closed her fingers into a fist and found that she had snapped her quill into three pieces. Sighing, she threw it into the fireplace and got up to change her dress for dinner.

Having a visitor in the house made even their simple evening meal seem like a party. When she came down to the dining room, she found her father and the viscount waiting. Lord Weller held out his arm to escort her in to the room and seated her at the table as if she were a great lady. She tried not to look self-conscious.

"Thank you," she murmured.

Her father rolled his wheeled chair to the head of the table, and their guest sat across from her. The cock-a-leekie soup was good as usual, a tribute to Bess's talents with the bare minimum of ingredients in the kitchen.

The viscount swallowed a spoonful and praised the cook's skill.

Bess, who was also serving the table, turned bright red. "Thank'ee, sir, I mean, me lord," she said. "Good plain cookin' is always the best, me lady always said so."

Then, perhaps remembering that she wasn't supposed to speak, she dropped a curtsy and, looking flustered, hurried back out only to return momentarily carrying a plate of warm, fragrant bread.

Maddie pressed her lips together so she wouldn't laugh at their servant's unaccustomed confusion. She saw her father raise a brow.

"She is indeed a very good cook, in the plain style, of course," he agreed, his tone grave.

The viscount nodded. "I never complain about the style of my food as long as the taste is pleasing," he noted.

"That is the mark of a wise man," Mr. Applegate said. The two men exchanged smiles.

The rest of the dinner was also simple but succulent, rabbit stew, a side of venison sent over by a neighbor who enjoyed shooting, several vegetable dishes supplied by their garden, and a gooseberry fool that her father was fond of, made from berries off their own vines. The wine was the best of her father's remaining bottles; she only hoped his supply held out for the duration of the viscount's visit.

The thought made her pause, fork in midair.

The thought of Lord Weller leaving—and yes, he planned to leave—sent a pang all the way through her.

You're being foolish, Maddie scolded herself. You heard what he said. Are you hoping for a miracle?

Better not to answer that question.

The men's conversation had flowed from topics as varied as their chess games, about which the viscount gave polite answers, to politics and history and literature, when the exchanges became more animated. Maddie found that Lord Weller could hold his own with her erudite father, and she admired him for it.

Not many visitors could match John Applegate for scholarship or wit, and she could see how much her father was enjoying the companionship of another gentleman possessing both intelligence and education. She and her father often enjoyed conversations about history, philosophy, or politics, but a new voice with new opinions to debate was always stimulating, and she could only be glad to see her father so animated.

"Where did you go to school?" she asked their visitor quietly, as her father took a bite of dessert.

"Eton, and then Oxford," he told her.

"You seem not to have wasted your time," she said, then afraid she had sounded wistful, looked down at her dish of dessert. "My sisters and I were tutored at home by our father."

"Judging by your contributions to the conversations, your time was also not wasted," he pointed out, dipping a spoon into his serving of gooseberry fool. "This is excellent, by the way. Your maid may be a woman ready to speak her mind—and I respect her for it—but she is also a good cook."

"A good plain cook," Maddie murmured. Bess had left the room to fetch a dish of nuts, but still, Maddie didn't wish the servant to overhear stray words that might wound her.

"And nothing wrong with that," he told her, his lips lifting just slightly at the corners.

"Of course not," she agreed, smiling, too.

"Yorkshire fare can be just as pleasing as French cuisine, or London dinners, for that matter," he assured her.

"No doubt," she said, not sure that she believed it. What was he trying to tell her? She wasn't sure, although she suspected there was more at the heart of this conversation than mere styles of cookery.

There was a slight pause, then her father broke the silence.

"So, has it been decided—are we going to have the banns read on Sunday?"

The viscount looked quizzical, but turned to Madeline and left it to her to answer. And oh, dear, she was blushing again!

Madeline licked the end of her spoon with careful deliberation; her mouth seemed enormously dry. She had to take a sip of her wine before she could answer.

"Yes, Papa," she said. "We are."

She saw her father smile, and when at last she dared to look toward the viscount, she saw him meet her gaze with a gleam in his eyes that she could not decipher.

But something inside her leapt in response.

So it was that on Sunday morning, she found herself sitting in the family pew, with her father on one side and Lord Weller on the other, conscious of the stares of most of the other churchgoers. With some effort, Maddie kept her eyes straight ahead and, with even more effort, managed to keep her thoughts on the service. Well, mostly on the service. After the second lesson, there was a slight pause, and then their aged vicar read the familiar words. But hearing her name read aloud gave Maddie the sensation of being assaulted, as though the words had somehow pummeled her like stones from a catapult.

"Madeline Margaret Applegate . . . to wed . . . Adrian Phillip Carter, Viscount Weller of Huntingtonshire. If any person can name any impediment to this marriage, let him speak now or forever hold his peace. . . ."

The church seemed suddenly full of sound as people shifted position in their pews, and the old wooden benches creaked in protest. Maddie found she was holding her breath.

But no one spoke out.

Of course they would not, why should they?

In a moment, the vicar went on with the service, and she exhaled with a long sigh, trying not to allow her unease to show. The viscount would think she was mad. It was just— she wasn't sure why she felt so restive.

She was glad when the service finally wound its way to a close. She took her rectangular cushion with its hand-some needlework design that her mother had done with her own hand and knelt upon it for the final prayer, glad to have the padding between her knees and the cold stone floor of the old church.

When the last "Amen" was said, she stood, still ponder-ing the mysteries of marriage, and lingered without speak-ing as the church emptied. Lord Weller waited for her father to turn his wheeled chair, and they headed for the front door of the church.

Adrian found that his shoulders ached with tension. He had been fighting the urge to look behind him ever since the banns had been read. He seemed to feel the eyes of every person in the church concentrated on the back of his head, even though the pews hid much of his tall frame. And without any rational reason, he kept wanting to turn and search the crowd of parishioners to see if he could make out his cousin's face amid the cluster of churchgoers.

"You're going as mad as Francis," he murmured to him-self.

Madeline glanced up at him, and he pushed back his worries with great effort, smiled down at her instead, and offered his arm. She smiled back as they made their way toward the sunshine outside the open church door.

The vicar stood at the doorway and gave cheery greetings to his flock at they all exited the church.

"Ah, my dear Miss Applegate, you too will taste the joys of matrimony, just as your younger sisters have done, having most unkindly preceded their elder sister," he said, his tone jovial, as they came out into the level ground. "I know I speak for everyone when I say that we are all happy for you."

Adrian felt his brand new fiancée stiffen. He knew that older sisters usually married before the younger; did she feel some hidden barbs beneath the churchman's comment?

"Thank you for your good wishes," he said, so that she did not have to reply. "I am the happiest of all, I think, having secured the promise of such a pleasing bride."

"Indeed, indeed," the vicar agreed. "The most beautiful of all the sisters, and that is saying something, I must tell you, Lord Weller, as there is not a plain face in the bunch. Mr. Applegate and his late wife, may she rest in peace, produced a most handsome family." The churchman leaned over to shake hands with the man in the wheeled chair, and they exchanged greetings, leaving Adrian free to speak quietly to Madeline.

"Are you all right?"

"Of course," she said, but she didn't quite meet his eye.

He would have it out of her later, when they were in private, he told himself.

Once Mr. Applegate had made his farewells, they walked at a leisurely pace back to the Applegate residence, pushing the chair along the wide path, leaving the

conversation confined to innocuous subjects of weather
and the church service.

But Adrian still glanced about him at the thick copses
and wondered uneasily which could hide a sharpshooter
taking aim.

Madeline saw her father to his own room on the ground
floor to take a short rest before the midday meal, then went
into the kitchen to see if Bess needed any help. One of their
neighbors had sent over a couple of pheasants newly shot.
Thomas had plucked the birds and prepared them for cooking, and the kitchen now smelled agreeably of roasting
meat. Bess handled the delicate matter of the plum sauce,
but she put Maddie to work on the potatoes. When the veg-
etables were ready for the cooking pot, Maddie was free to
take off her apron, wipe her hands, and become a lady of
leisure again.

Presently she returned to the sitting room and found the
viscount pouring himself a glass of wine.

He raised the bottle. "May I?"

Maddie started to shake her head, then paused. "Yes,
thank you, I believe I shall."

He poured and passed her the goblet.

She took a sip, then stared at the glass as if untold mysteries were hidden inside.

"Is something wrong, Madeline?" he asked, his voice
quiet.

"You told the vicar you would stay here the required
four weeks, making the reading of the banns in your own
home parish unnecessary. Is there some reason you don't
wish to have them read in your own church back in Huntingtonshire?"

He tried to guess at the direction of her thoughts, and what might have created the furrow of worry on her brow. "Such as another woman who might have claims on my affections?"

"Perhaps," she agreed, her tone even.

He thought of the spies paid by his cousin to send word of any news of his comings and goings, even as he shook his head. "I simply thought this would be easier and more efficient," he told her. "I make no claims to have lived my whole life like a Turkish eunuch, but for some time, I have been unfettered when it comes to matters of love. I assure you, no other lady—no other female, for that matter—has any claim on my attention, Madeline. I leave behind no brokenhearted squire's daughter, or innkeeper's daughter, or farmer's daughter. No lady of the evening expects me to call. I am free of entanglements, quite free to make a betrothal."

He sounded completely sincere, and some small knot inside her eased. What did she fear? She wasn't sure, only that she felt he was holding something back. And yet, he had stood beside her in church and listened to the banns being read—what more could she expect from him? Why did she still wonder?

Why could she not trust him completely? Was it something she sensed about him, or something lacking in herself that she found it so hard to trust? Perhaps it was only that their acquaintance was so new, their engagement so oddly made. Maddie bit her lip and looked away from him.

"I don't know why . . ." she started, and then paused again. "I'm sorry."

"Don't be," he told her, his voice gentle. "After all, we have found ourselves in a strange predicament." He reached across the space that separated them and took her hand before she realized what he was about. Adrian lifted her hand to his lips, kissing the back gently, with a soft precision that sent sparks of feeling all the way up her arm.

Maddie had to fix all her resolution not to jerk her hand away. It was like coming into contact with a leaping flame, except it was not a pain—no, it was more like an exquisite pleasure, but almost more delight than one could stand. How did wives endure so much joy, if their husbands pleased them so deeply with every touch? She almost moaned aloud but managed to swallow the sound before it emerged from her lips.

But instead of leaving her alone to sort out her very confused feelings, the confounded man leaned forward and kissed her hard on the same lips that had almost betrayed her. He tasted of port wine and warm sunshine.

"And you will stay here for four weeks?" She pulled away and tried to sound as if her mind was still alert.

"Since I've already been here almost a week, that's not such a long visit, unless you feel you will weary of my company?" That irresistible grin lifted the corners of his lips again.

She smiled back, unable to withstand him. "Of course not, I just meant . . ."

When he smiled at her just so, she couldn't remember what she meant. She took a sip of wine to cover her moment of confusion.

This was ridiculous, Maddie decided. They were betrothed. They were alone. She should enjoy the moment. She set her glass down up on the table. "And what did you wish to tell me?" she asked boldly.

"Just this," he murmured, taking her hand and once again lifting it to kiss. He brushed his lips over her fingers one by one while she shivered from the sensations that the warmth of his kisses produced. Then he turned her hand over and pressed a more distinct kiss upon the palm; this one Maddie felt deep within her. It was all she could do to remain still and not fling herself bodily upon him.

Was this flirting? She had heard of discreet flirtations between sophisticated ladies and gentlemen, but how did one manage the necessary self-control? She found that she was breathing quickly, and she thought that the viscount's breath was also coming more rapidly.

She watched the way his eyelids lowered over his dark eyes, and the veins in his temples throbbed; she could draw a map of his face, she thought. She ached to reach out and push an errant lock of hair back behind his well-shaped ear.

Now his kisses moved up her wrist, to her arms, and she felt the sensations inside her body deepen, the longings increase, and she fought not to slip down upon the settee and pull him down with her. She didn't even really know what she wished for, only that she wanted to be close, she wanted him to assuage these deep longings in a way that she instinctively knew that he would understand how to do.

Lord Weller looked into her eyes and kissed her palm one last time, then released her with reluctance. "We'd best stop for now, my darling Madeline. If your father comes in, he will take one look at your languorous eyes and know precisely what we have been about."

"Oh!" Maddie said, alarmed. She moved back a few inches and tried to straighten both her collar and her face before anyone could indeed recognize what they had been up to in their precious minutes of solitude.

But she couldn't wait until they could do it again!

Six

*N*ow that her neighbors knew that Madeline Applegate was betrothed to a titled and prosperous stranger, and—better yet—that it was an engagement made under possibly scandalous circumstances, the whole shire seemed to overflow with intense curiosity. Their volume of mail suddenly erupted to new heights. Bess came in on Monday with her apron nearly full of notes and letters.

She looked a bit stunned. "The post is 'ere, Miss Madeline."

"Good gracious," Maddie answered. "Is that all for us? Put them on the table, Bess, and I will sort through them."

Their usually quiet neighborhood seemed to have blossomed overnight into a veritable social playground. Their previously sedate neighbors were now planning a wonderful procession of tea parties, alfresco meals "before the good weather disappears altogether," shooting parties, small dinner parties, small dinner dances, larger but still intimate dinner parties, riding parties, card parties, and Lord knew what else, and to all of these no doubt enjoyable diversions Miss Applegate and her newly betrothed fiancé were cordially invited.

"You're well favored among your neighbors," the viscount said when he came down to find Madeline, feeling quite overwhelmed, sitting at the dining table sifting through the pile of invitations.

"I've never been this popular in my life," she declared with a wry smile. "I fear we must hold you accountable for the sudden demand for our company."

His dark eyes held the twinkle she had come to watch for, and she smiled back at him as he grinned. "Funny that, I never knew I was such a social lion. I shall have to practice my roar."

Just then her father wheeled himself in to the breakfast table, and she turned to him. "Can you believe this, Papa? All invitations, and most of these people haven't bothered with us since your accident. I've a good mind to write them back and tell them to go to the devil!"

"Now, now," John Applegate said, picking up his napkin and taking a piece of ham to put on his plate. He allowed the viscount to add a good-sized slice of cold venison as well, nodding his thanks. "We must allow for some normal inquisitiveness, my dear."

"Normal? They are as curious as cats!" Maddie allowed her disdain to show. "And I am of no mind to humor their need to meddle and pry. Why should we aid their rush to dig into our private affairs?"

"Why, indeed," the viscount agreed, filling his own plate. His expression was sober, but his eyes still twinkled with hidden laughter. "Our lives are none of their concern, I agree. We did not make our betrothal for their amusement."

Bess came in carrying a teapot swathed in a tea caddy and proceeded to pour hot tea into their cups. "Bunch of nosy parkers, all of 'em," she said, her tone brisk. "Best to watch what ye say out in company, a 'cause it'll be all over the shire a 'fore ye blink."

Maddie opened her mouth to reprimand her too helpful servant for offering advice when she was, again, supposed to serve quietly at the table, but paused, not having the heart.

She glanced at Lord Weller, whose lips were pressed together a bit too tightly, in that way he had when he was suppressing a smile. Her father simply looked resigned.

When Bess had left the room, John Applegate chuckled. "So, we are agreed that we shall have to keep our own counsel. But shall you not accept some of the invitations, my dear? Lord Weller will no doubt appreciate some amusement."

Maddie recalled their tryst in the flower garden and hastily pushed that thought away before she blushed again. Amusement, indeed!

"But you find it so tiring to go out in the evening, Papa," she pointed out, even as she glanced down at the pile of notes, knowing that she was tempted by some that came from genuine friends and that she could be sure were offered in the spirit of good will.

"Ah, but Lord Weller can help get me into the carriage, and I'm not as frail as all that. Or you could always find a matron who would be willing to act as chaperone, I'm sure." Her father took a sip of his tea.

Maddie thought of Mrs. Masham and repressed a shudder. Then she remembered her friend, Felicity Barlow. Would she consider going out into company with them? Surely Maddie could ask, tactfully. Besides, the viscount did deserve more entertainment than they could manage, not being able to entertain themselves. After all, he must be used to a more interesting nightlife than what passed as such in this rustic corner of Yorkshire.

If perhaps he found some genuine pleasure from her company—better not to consider that just now. It would bring another blush to her cheek, and with her father sitting close at hand, just as well that he didn't realize that his daughter was hoping that provincial dinners and dances were not the most amusing diversions that Lord Weller would enjoy during his time in Yorkshire.

"I will speak to Mrs. Barlow and see if she has any inclination to play duenna," she told her father.

"Ah, the perfect person," he agreed. "She is sweet-natured and always pleasant company."

After their meal ended, the two men retired to her father's study for a friendly game of chess, and Maddie helped Bess in the kitchen for a time, then set off down the path to the widow's small cottage.

It was a lovely fall day. The leaves showed their splendid autumn hues, russet and deep red and gold, as they fluttered in the slight breeze. The air was cool enough that Maddie was glad she had wrapped a thick shawl about her shoulders before she'd left the house.

When she reached the cottage, she saw a thin column of smoke rising from the chimney. Knocking at the stout oak door, she soon heard footsteps from inside.

Still, it was a moment before the door swung open.

"Oh." Felicity Barlow looked surprised, then she smiled quickly. "How nice to see you, Miss Applegate. Please come in."

The small residence, which seemed to be mostly one large room, was painstakingly tidy. The wood floor was swept clean, the small fire contained behind a screen, and the hearth clear of ashes. The table was free of crumbs and held a bowl of nuts and a pitcher of water. A small gray cat curled up near the hearth. The bed in the corner was neatly made.

Mrs. Barlow poured water into a teakettle and put it on a hook that swung over the coals while Maddie explained her errand.

The matron smiled a bit ruefully. "I would be happy to help out," she said, "but I'm not sure if my wardrobe is up to the challenge, Miss Applegate."

"Oh, do call me Madeline," Maddie told her. "We've known each other for months, now. And honestly, I'm not sure mine is, either. I'm going to go into our attic and dig through my mother's trunks and see if there are any gowns we can make over. I would be happy to share what I find with you."

"Oh, that's more than generous—but they are your mother's things! I'm not sure I should accept." Mrs. Barlow looked a little flustered. "And you must call me Felicity."

"What a pretty name," Maddie exclaimed, distracted for a moment from her train of thought.

"It means fortunate, in the Latin," her friend explained, glancing ruefully about the sparsely furnished cottage. "There have been times when it has seemed an ironic jest that Fate has played upon me."

"Which is why you must accept, and really, I have no idea if there is much to give," Maddie confessed. "I haven't looked at Mother's chests in years. The twins always turned up their noses at the idea of reworked gowns, and Juliana had no need as she disdained the local boys, finding no one who caught her fancy until she went off to London and was well and truly caught by her gorgeous baronet."

Felicity laughed.

"Of course, if you're still in full mourning . . ." Maddie hesitated, not sure how delicate this topic was. Mrs. Barlow, no, Felicity, had never shared any details about the death of her husband, and Maddie had respected her reticence and never asked.

"Oh, no, it's been much more than a year, I just—well, as you said, sometimes it's a matter of one's budget." The widow smiled again.

"Oh, yes, I know." Relieved, Maddie smiled back. "Then you must come over and help me dig through the dust and see what we can discover in the eaves. I know that neither of the men will be interested in our search for treasure troves of fabrics."

After a cup of tea, the two walked back to the Applegate house and went up into the attic where the flotsam and jetsam of past years had come to rest. With Felicity's help, Maddie moved aside the occasional broken piece of furniture, and they opened the trunks and examined full-skirted gowns of old-fashioned design. The trunks were heavy with the scent of lavender to ward off insects, so most of the fabrics were untouched despite their years and were still fit to be made over and refashioned for their benefit.

Maddie and her father had generally led a quiet life and had not gone into local Society all that often, so her need for gowns had never been as urgent before. But now she was very glad to have her mother's old dresses to call upon. She removed several silk gowns and a lined satin evening cloak that was wide enough to provide material for reworking. Before she shut the trunk, a book of receipts caught her eye. Maddie took it out, too, wondering if there were dishes here that perhaps even Bess had forgotten and which might be tasty to prepare for their guest.

They left the attic with their arms full and brought it all down to her bedroom to sort through. Their designs were too out of date to wear as they were, of course, but the material and trimmings could be salvaged and reused. They would simply pick out the seams and take the gowns apart.

"This lavender silk would make a good dinner dress for you," Maddie suggested. It would make Felicity's shift from full to half mourning less of a shock to the neighborhood.

"You are being more than generous," her friend told her. She stroked the sleek fabric with a sigh of appreciation. "I don't know how to thank you."

"Nonsense. I am thankful that you are willing to leave the peace of your quiet life to chaperone, so that Papa does not have to exhaust himself just because everyone in the shire suddenly wishes to take a look at my new fiancé," Maddie said, rolling her eyes.

"I suppose we are providing our neighbors with a genuine act of kindness, then," Felicity said, with the lilt of laughter in her voice. They both giggled.

"I hope, dear Madeline, not that it is my place to say, that you are happy with the betrothal," the widow added more soberly. "I mean, I hope that you have not been pressured into this arrangement simply for the sake of your honor, or for appearance's sake, as important as I know that always must be for a maiden of good family."

Maddie looked away for a moment, but then turned back and met her friend's eyes. "In the beginning, it was mostly for the sake of appearance—my and my family's honor, you are right. But I find—I find that I am becoming more and more pleased with the arrangement."

She remembered her uncertainties and the great chasm of ignorance that fueled her frustration and her fears that she might not make a pleasing bride. Could she ask an older and more experienced friend for advice? She drew a deep breath and gathered her resolve.

"You know my mother died when I was very young?"

"Yes." Felicity nodded.

"And I never planned to marry."

Her friend looked startled. "Why on earth not, my dear?"

Madeline looked away, thinking of the terrible time when her mother had fallen ill, and all the certainty in her world had crumbled. "My mother—my mother asked me to look after my father. And I promised her I would—that was the last coherent thing she said to me as she was burning with fever. I held her hand until she grew too weak to talk at all, but she gazed at us with eyes that grew too fever-mad to know anyone—anyone except my father. He was the only one in the last hours who could rouse her to a knowing, loving glance. She loved him so much."

Madeline found her own gaze blurring, and she had to blink hard.

Felicity put one comforting hand on her shoulder. "That had to be very hard on you, I know. Were you very young?"

Maddie nodded. "Hardly eight years old. But I promised, you see. And then as the rest of my sisters grew up, as we all grew up, I tried to mother them, guide them, comfort them—because I was the eldest. And there was so much I didn't know, and there was no one to ask."

"Oh, my dear, what a task you set for yourself." Felicity's voice was soft with sympathy. "You have not had the easiest life, either, and you forfeited your childhood very young, I think."

"Not that our father was not the best father in the world, you understand, but he was a father, and he could not be a mother, too, even as much as he tried. And then he suffered his own injury, and that made it all even more difficult." Maddie sighed and drew out her handkerchief so she could wipe her eyes.

"I never thought, without dowries, that we would be lucky enough that even half of us would find husbands, and it seemed clear that I must stay home and look out for my father and whichever of my sisters remained at home. That Lauryn should fall in love with the squire's son and he with her was wonder enough, and then Juliana going to London, and the twins running off—which could have been, really should have been, a total disaster—well sometimes miracles happen." Maddie shook her head, remembering how angry she had been at her feckless younger sisters. Honestly, if they had not been so amazingly fortunate—

She drew a deep breath and picked up the gown that lay across her bed to distract herself.

Felicity seemed to follow her thoughts. "Happily, that has all ended well. I was so pleased to see the twins married; they both looked so happy. I'm sure they have matured beyond their wild times."

"I hope so!" the twins' older sister said, grinning reluctantly. "If not, it's their husbands' problem now, not mine. The tales I have heard about their London escapades—"

"Um, yes, but I'm sure that much of that is exaggerated," Felicity said quickly, as if to change the subject.

"I do hope so," Maddie agreed, remembering what she had meant to ask her friend, and it had nothing to do with her younger sisters' dreadful exploits. If she didn't speak now, she would lose her nerve completely. "Felicity?"

"Yes?"

The change in Madeline's tone seem to alert the widow to a change in topic. The older woman turned to gaze at her. Almost wishing she had not spoken, Maddie ran her finger along a row of lace and tried to frame her question.

"When you were first married, did you know—I mean, how cognizant were you—that is, did your mother explain to you about—about . . ." Again her voice faltered, and she could not think how to word the question, as pressing as it was.

"About what to expect from the marriage bed?" Felicity smiled just a little, but her voice was serious.

"Yes!" Maddie sighed in relief. "Since I have no mother, and my sisters are not at hand, I have no one to ask, and I'm afraid I won't know what to do, or how to please my husband."

This time Felicity did smile. "I see. If I should to try to give you—ah—a lesson in lovemaking, we would both be somewhat abashed, I think. But I can tell you that if you trust him, if you have good feelings for each other, it can be a most wondrous experience. And I will certainly be happy to answer any questions, my dear, now or later. But most of all, having seen the two of you together, I can reassure you that you will have two big advantages."

"What are they?" Maddie asked, thinking that she really didn't know enough to know the proper questions to ask.

"First, Lord Weller does not appear, to my eyes, to be a green lad, so I suspect that he has sufficient experience to be a pleasing guide for your bridal night and will have no problems leading you smoothly into your introduction to lovemaking."

Maddie put one hand to her cheek—she suspected she was turning pink again—and wished she didn't blush so easily. "I think that is likely true," she agreed, trying not to giggle.

"And if you don't mind me asking, have you—ah—exchanged a kiss with your new betrothed?" Felicity picked up one of the gowns on the bed and appeared to examine its needlework with great care.

This time, Maddie was quite sure she had turned red. She told herself she was sure Felicity would be discreet and not repeat this conversation. "Yes," she said simply.

"Did you like it?"

"Oh, yes!" Maddie answered with a good deal more force.

The other woman laughed, and Maddie, after a moment of confusion, laughed, too. "Then there you are. Follow your own instincts, my dear, and you will have no problems."

"But do you think that he will—that I will be good enough—"

"I doubt very much that Lord Weller will have anything to fault you with, my dear," Felicity assured her, looking up. "Please do not worry about that. A bride should have brighter thoughts on her wedding day—and night."

Maddie nodded. "Very well, I will try."

"You have been attempting for too long to take care of your family, your sisters, your father," the widow pointed out, sighing. "Madeline, this is your time to enjoy someone else caring for you. That is your husband's province—allow him the privilege, the honor, of doing it."

She had not looked at it in that way. Perhaps acquiring a husband had advantages she had never considered. It was true that she was more accustomed to caring for others than to having someone look out for her. It had been a long time since she had had anyone to cosset her, except for faithful Bess taking care of her when she was ill. This was different.

Perhaps being married could be a good thing, even outside of the marriage bed.

They went downstairs. Felicity had put the lavender silk into a neat bundle to take home and work on, promising that she would also help Maddie with her own make overs. Maddie went into the kitchen and assisted Bess in putting out a light luncheon, and the two men emerged from the study, her father shaking his head.

Maddie felt a moment of anxiety. Had they had a quarrel? No, it appeared that her father was simply admiring a particularly adept move.

"He has bested me, Madeline," he told her as they sat down to the meal. "He kept his bishop waiting patiently, and when my knight was out of the way, it came swooping down to capture my queen and checkmate my king."

"Quite an accomplishment," Maddie said. She had played chess often with her father but almost never had she been able to beat him, and she said as much as she passed the dishes.

"Your father is a skilled player," the viscount said. "I merely had a moment of luck."

"Some moment," her father contradicted. "You set up that play very patiently, Weller; I give credit where it's due."

Despite having lost, he seemed in excellent humor; the pleasure of a good match was exhilarating, Maddie thought. She smiled at them both.

"That play reminds me of a particularly good move in a match I played with a visiting vicar years ago . . ." her father commented.

After the meal, her father retired to take his afternoon rest, and Maddie, too full of nervous energy to wish to go up to her room, and not sure she could maintain her stance as a demure young lady, announced that she was going into the garden. There were dark clouds to the west, but at the moment, despite a brisk breeze, the sun still showed its face.

"I shall come, too," the viscount agreed.

Inside the flower garden, Maddie put down a rough cloth so that she could kneel and pull weeds from a bed of flowers.

Lord Weller looked disappointed. "I am overthrown for the company of stray nettles?" he muttered, looking up as if speaking to a chattering sparrow in a tree that overlooked the flower beds. "How the mighty have fallen. That will put me in my place. Obviously, my kisses are of no value if they are rated so low."

She laughed. "I must point out, my lord, that this part of the garden can be seen from my father's window."

"Ah, I see, discretion is a worthy virtue." He glanced over his shoulder without making the movement obvious. "And where would we not be seen?"

"At the other end of the beds . . ."

"So why do we not move there?"

"We will," she told him, her tone calm. "When we have reason—when we have weeded the bed."

"I see." To her amusement, he pulled off his gloves and hat and knelt to attack the weeds with a vengeance. "Then I must add my labors to yours, so that we can finish with the infernal weeds more quickly. I have a more agreeable pastime in mind!"

His weeding was fast if not terribly accurate; she saw a few flowers tossed through the air along with the brambles, but she didn't scold, too amused and touched to see a peer of the realm apply himself to agricultural chores for the sake of a lady's favors.

Her favors.

Being courted was certainly an agreeable sensation. And the thought of being kissed again—she thought of Felicity's questions—oh, yes, she liked it exceedingly.

She quickened her own pace, and soon they did reach the end of the flower bed, and the more private side of the garden, where they were hidden from the house and the view of the windows by the privet hedge and the angle of the building.

This time, the viscount leaned over her, and she didn't try to move away. She looked at him instead of down at the ground, and as her fingers brushed a last bunch of unruly greenery, she felt a sudden searing pain.

"Oh!" Maddie pulled her hand up, but it was too late. She had touched a stinging nettle, and the plant's noxious touch had had its usual result.

"Wait!" the viscount said. "Don't touch anything else."

She certainly wasn't going to touch the nettle again, Maddie thought, frowning at him. She had to blink back tears. Amazing that such a small plant could inflict so much pain. She should have been paying more attention, not gazing into the viscount's dark brown eyes. Really, she was acting like a lovesick girl, and she was too old and sensible for such behavior—or she should be, she scolded herself.

But while she admonished herself, and tried to blink away the tears—she knew better than to rub her lids and transfer the oil from the plant into her eyes—the viscount was several feet away, bent at the waist and scanning the long grass past the garden in search of something.

"Found it!" He announced in triumphant tones. He pulled up a broad-leafed plant and came quickly to rub it gently over her reddened and still burning finger. Almost at once, the pain in her blistered skin eased.

"Oh, thank you," she said, sighing with relief. "You are as adept as Thomas in knowing the plants and their properties."

"I grew up on my family's estate, and my manager made sure I spent plenty of time outdoors," he told her, "learning my way around the property and getting to know as much as any good farmer would know."

He led her to the wooden bench beside the beds of flowers where they could sit, safe from any more assaults from treacherous flora.

"Your manager? Did your father not spend time on the estate?" she asked a bit hesitantly, not sure how he would respond to a question so personal.

For a moment, her fiancé's face closed, then he drew a deep breath and looked across the garden and into the surrounding trees. "Like you I lost a parent young, but more than just the one. My father died when I was ten, my mother when I was fourteen."

"Oh, I am so sorry," Maddie exclaimed impulsively, putting one hand on his arm. Having touched him, she was then not quite sure what to do—to withdraw it at once seemed unkind, yet to continue the contact . . .

He solved her quandary by laying his hand over hers, then lifting it and turning up her palm, despite the dusting of soil that remained from her gardening, and kissing it lightly.

"You have a kind heart, Madeline. Yes, it was hard. I felt very—very adrift. I had one grandparent still alive, who made her home with me until I went into the army. I served with Wellington during the conflict against the French . . ."

His voice trailed off, but his expression tightened, and she felt this was not a subject that he wished to pursue. Many men had fought against Napoleon in the long years of war; some spoke of it often, some not at all. Nodding, she let the sentence die away.

Perhaps that was why he seemed to genuinely enjoy spending time with her father, she thought, since he had lost his own father so young.

"Papa has relished your company," she told him, speaking the rest of her thought aloud.

"And I, his," Lord Weller said quickly. "But even more, I am enjoying my time with his daughter."

Yet he spoke as if the time were limited, Maddie thought, feeling a pang of foreboding. Four weeks . . . he had to stay four weeks to have the banns read before they could have their wedding, and over a week and a half had already gone . . . was that all the happiness she was to be allowed?

Despite the story of the drunken duel and the man who was determined to kill him, surely there was something that could be done, some way a madman could be stopped . . . there had to be a way.

Now the viscount was running his hands down the slope of her neck where it met her shoulders, and the small movement sent a shiver down her spine and woke a quivery sensation inside her body. All the feelings inside her body seemed to jump to life.

How did he do it?

She forgot the sting of the nettle, and instead, her whole body poised itself for pleasure, for the delight that his touch always brought. She lifted her face to his, hoping for another kiss, but for the moment, he seemed to concentrate on his hands, on running his fingers lightly over her arms, bare on this sunny day below her short sleeves, skimming her forearms down to her wrists, lifting first one hand and then the other.

"But I am dusty from the garden," Maddie tried to protest.

He shook his head. "Good honest English dirt," he said, grinning.

He kissed one hand, then the other, then put her hands behind his head. Maddie clasped her hands around his neck and came willingly, more than willingly, into his embrace.

A drop of cold liquid hit her cheek, then another. Was the viscount weeping? Confused, she blinked, and felt more liquid touch her face.

Oh, blast—the contrary English weather had turned against them.

"We'd better run for it," Lord Weller said, his tone as frustrated as she felt. He clasped her fingers, and hand in hand, they pelted for the house, as the clouds—she had been too engrossed in his lovemaking to notice the clouds thickening overhead or the sunlight dimming—released their burden of rain.

She was thoroughly drenched by the time they made it through the doors. Even then, shivering, she would have lingered to gather warmth from his embrace, but Bess was there with well-worn linen towels to throw about their shoulders.

"Mercy, Miss Madeline, my lord, ye'll catch yer deaths! Yer both dripping like fountains. Better get upstairs and change at once!"

Maddie glanced at her fiancé, and he gave her a rueful smile in return. It seemed they were checked at every turn. He gave her a slight bow. "We will finish our gardening another time," he told her, his intimate tone making the ordinary words a promise that warmed her.

She flashed a smile in return and climbed the stairs feeling more cheerful. She had a feeling that Lord Weller always honored his pledges.

Bess came upstairs right behind her, fussing like a broody hen about young ladies who did not keep an eye on the clouds.

"And it's not like ye donna know the weather—yer na some fine London lord who donna know better!" Her long-time servant pointed out darkly.

"You're quite right, Bess," Maddie tried to soothe the maid's feelings. "But I'm inside now, and I'm sure I shall be fine." She did shiver as she peeled off the sodden cloth-ing, but with Bess's assistance, she was soon dressed in another gown, with a warm shawl pulled around her shoulders.

She thought of the viscount, with no one to help him dress—he must have a valet at home—but presumably he managed on his own. When she went back downstairs with her sewing basket and one of the lengths of silk she was re-fashioning, she found him already in the sitting room.

He stood when she came in and gave her a bow and a slightly penitent smile. "I trust you are none the worse for your unexpected wetting?"

"I'm sure I am just fine," she told him, "despite all of my maid's grumblings. Bess is making us some hot tea, to complete our recovery, no doubt. Please sit down."

They had to sit a proper distance apart, with the servant popping in and out, but at least she could relish the sight of him, smile at him, listen to the rich tones of his voice.

"Tell me more about your life, your boyhood, growing up on your estate," she suggested.

He shrugged. "Not that much to tell," he said. "I missed my parents, of course, after their early deaths, but it was not a bad life. I had my grandmother to look out for me, and the estate manager, a worthy man, to provide guid-ance. I went away to school not long after, and that kept me occupied, I can tell you."

"You had no brothers or sisters?"

He shook his head. "My mother had a hard time having me, and there were no more to follow."

"Then you must have been very precious to her," Maddie suggested as she sewed a neat seam into the length of silk in her lap.

He smiled. "I believe so. She was a fond parent, and my father, too."

She smiled back, not quite brave enough yet to tell him that she could see the love he had received reflected in him, in the capacity that he possessed for gentleness, for displaying love and compassion, just as he had done that night in the gazebo when she had been in such pain. It made him amazingly attractive, even if he had not been so handsome in his face and body.

"And after Oxford?"

Something changed in his expression. "After university I went into the army, as so many men did . . . and there was the war with France."

She knew even without further queries, that he would not wish to speak of the war. Turning, he was spared the necessity of coming up with an excuse when Bess entered the room with a tea tray.

"Some nice 'ot tea, Miss Madeline, and crumpets and 'oney, always good for the constitution on a cold day," the servant said, surveying the full china plates with a satisfied air as she pulled up a low table and set down the tray.

"Thank you, Bess," Maddie told her, "I'm sure this will do us a great deal of good."

The maidservant nodded in agreement and left the room.

Maddie poured them both some of the steaming tea and handed the viscount his cup. He took it without meeting her eye.

She did not mean to pursue the subject of the French war; it obviously made him uncomfortable. Instead, she gestured to the tray. "Please, help yourself. We must not disappoint Bess. She is on a mission to save us from lung fever, and besides, her crumpets are indeed the best for miles around."

Chuckling, he filled a plate and then covered one of the flat pastries with honey and took a bite. "Certainly the best," he agreed before sipping the hot tea cautiously. "Now it's your turn. Tell me about you."

"I'm the oldest sister," Maddie told him. "You know about my mother's early death, and the promise I made to take care of my father. Juliana is the next sister, and we are close; I do miss her since she has married. Her husband is a zoologist and always, it seems, off after new animals, so they live an adventurous life. Her letters keep me either in a constant state of alarm or paroxysms of laughter. Juliana does tend to get herself into scrapes. Lauryn is the sister who married the squire's son; she is very sweet and pretty and biddable. And the twins, oh, lord, they keep the whole shire talking."

She told him several funny tales about her sisters, and then, to her surprise, he repeated his direction.

"Now, tell me about yourself."

"But, my lord, I did—"

"No, you told me about your sisters, Madeline. And don't you think you should call me Adrian? You've allowed me the privilege—which I cherish, I assure you—of calling you by your Christian name, and you should do the same."

She glanced into his dark eyes and then away again, a little flustered by the gleam she saw there. She felt that stirring of feeling inside her, and he only held her hand. Amazing the response he could invoke inside her.

"Adrian," she said tentatively,

"Yes, nicely done," he agreed.

She laughed despite herself.

"You are a wretch," she told him, forgetting to feel shy.

"Better yet," he said, smiling, "you must tell me off whenever I become too dictatorial, my dear. I'm sure it will be very good for me."

"I'm sure it will," she agreed, trying not to smile as she kept her tone stern, but fearing that she could not quite manage it. "Anyhow, what do you wish to know? I've had a very boring existence, you know. Growing up in this quiet bit of Yorkshire, tending to my family, trying to fill the space left vacant by my dear mother, trying to look out for my father and my sisters."

"No secret lovers?" he demanded, his tone half-teasing. "No passionate squire's sons riding up at midnight to throw stones at your window?"

"That would have been for my sister, but as for throwing stones at her window, Robert would never have dreamed of doing anything so improper." She giggled at the very idea. "And the squire had only one son, poor man. He is quite bereft, as is Lauryn, of course, at his heir's sudden death.

"And no, I had no secret passions for anyone in the village, either, or for any neighbors—and oh, speaking of our neighbors, we are bidden to the Callestons for dinner and just look at the time." She glance at the small mantel clock and shook her head. "I have been nattering away like a washerwoman. We had best go up and change!"

She put down her teacup, pushed back her plate, and gathered up her sewing, gave a quick smile and curtsy to the viscount, who bowed in return, then hurried out.

What had she been thinking? It was so unusual for them to go out at all that it had been easy to forget that they had plans for the evening.

At least the Callestons were old family friends, and a good thing, too, as Maddie had not yet had time to put together any of the revamped dresses she was planning.

Upstairs, she pulled the bell rope for Bess, then looked into her clothespress and selected the most presentable of her dresses. She had already shed the muslin she had worn for daytime and was pinning her hair back when Bess came in with a pitcher of warm water.

"Thank you, Bess," she said. "Is Thomas going to help Lord Weller?"

"In due time," her servant answered, her tone brusque. "When 'e finishes with the master."

"Of course," Maddie agreed. She thought of Thomas with his calloused farmer's hands and matter-of-fact speech playing valet and bit back a grin. But he was totally faithful to the family, and they would have a hard time doing without him, and Bess, too.

When Bess departed, Maddie went over to her bureau and glanced at the book of receipts she had found in the attic. She still had not had time to look through it, but the pages of faded ink drew her; she recognized her mother's hand in these carefully written lines.

As she skimmed past pages of careful instructions for puddings and pastries, she saw something she had not noticed at first. A packet of folded pages had been tucked into the back of the book.

She paused, her hand on the packet.

What was this?

Seven

*T*hey were letters, tied together by a blue ribbon and tucked away with obvious care. With her hand on the top sheet, Maddie hesitated. She felt as if she were breaking into a sanctuary. These were written by her mother; Maddie shouldn't pry.

But there were so many questions she wanted to ask her mother—had wanted to ask her mother for years, and now she never could. If reading these pages would tell Maddie more about her mother, wouldn't her mother have wanted Maddie and the rest of her daughters to read them?

Not sure if this was logic or simply temptation speaking, Maddie bit her lip. Then she slipped the first letter off the top of the pile, and—her heart beating fast—unfolded the fragile and creased paper.

The date at the top showed that her mother had been hardly eighteen when she had written the note. "My dearest," the letter began. "My head is still spinning from our last dance tonight. Just being so close to you made my heart sing!"

Oh, my, they were letters to her father! Why were they here, and not in a private place in his study or bedroom, Maddie wondered. Now she felt twice as invasive—she could not read love letters from her mother to her father.

With great reluctance, she refolded the letter and slipped it back beneath the ribbon. She put the slender stack in the back of the book of receipts where she had found it.

What were the letters doing here? she thought for the second time. Perhaps when her mother died, they had been too painful a reminder of happy times, and her father had put them away from his sight. And now, even if he had wanted, he could not climb to the attic to retrieve them. Should Maddie ask him if he wanted them back?

But she hated to have to admit that she had looked at them.

She would decide later. But now she knew that her mother had already been courting, and being courted by, her father at seventeen, Maddie thought. She had a delightful picture of her mother happy and so much in love. That was almost worth the guilt she felt at reading the hidden cache of letters. It was if she had been given access to her mother's voice from beyond the grave. She shook her head at herself—such a thought. Hearing the men talking in the hallway below, she made her way downstairs.

After imagining her father as a dashing young man, it was almost ironic to see him in unaccustomed evening dress. Since his accident, he had rarely ventured out in the evening. He looked very fine, she thought, even if the cut of his jacket was a trifle old-fashioned. Adrian, on the other hand, wore what was surely the latest London style and appeared very polished and urbane, his dark eyes and hair set off superbly by his dark evening jacket and pure white linen.

Her father smiled when she came into view on the stairs, and Adrian bowed as if she were a grand lady, not an impoverished gentleman's daughter wearing only an out-of-date muslin with twice-dyed ribbons for trim.

The viscount and Thomas put her father carefully into the carriage, and Thomas tied his wheeled chair onto the back. Then the viscount helped her up, and he climbed in, too, and they set out for the short drive to the Callestons' residence.

The Callestons' home, while not as large as the squire's, was bigger than their house, and it was lit up tonight with more candles than usual, denoting a festive occasion. Despite a nervous flutter in her stomach, Maddie smiled when she was handed down from the carriage, and she watched anxiously as her father was lifted out and put carefully into his chair. When the lap robe was tucked around his wasted legs and his three-corner evening hat put into his lap, the footman pushed him carefully ahead of them into the house.

Due to his higher social rank, Adrian should have had precedence, but he had waved her father to go on ahead. Another thing she loved about him, Maddie thought. He did not stand on ceremony. Hadn't he fit right in at their home, with no footman, no gentleman's gentleman to wait on him, except for a rough farmhand? Many London gentlemen, much less titled lords, would have raised a fuss or refused to reside under such primitive conditions.

But Mrs. Calleston was coming forward, and Maddie pulled her thoughts back to the present moment.

Holding out her hands in welcome, the matron said, "Here is our newly engaged pair, and what a handsome couple they make. My dear Miss Applegate, we are so happy for you. Your dear mother would be in ecstasies!"

Maddie felt herself flushing and cursed her tendency to blush easily. "Thank you," she muttered. Even though she was fond of the portly and sweet-natured Mrs. Calleston, who had been a close friend of her late mother's, just now she wished their neighbor would not be so voluble in her praise of the engagement. Maddie felt a bit like the beggar maid who has snared the prince in the fairy tale. Adrian seemed to sense her discomfort.

"As I'm sure my own late mother would be, also, if she could know what a wonderful bride-to-be I have secured for my future happiness," the viscount put in, his tone smooth.

"Oh, of—of course," Mrs. Calleston stuttered, then recovered quickly. "You are fortunate, indeed. Our dear Miss Applegate is the prize of the shire, I assure you, Lord Weller. Only her dedication to her dear father, which has kept her close to home, has prevented her from attracting suitors from all over Yorkshire. Why, her beauty, her sweetness, her quickness of wit, her skill in housekeeping—not that you will need to worry about that, of course."

Barely pausing for breath, she allowed the viscount to offer her his arm and took him off to introduce to the other guests, thankfully sparing Maddie, now blushing in earnest, more details of her own virtues.

She wondered if it was too late to go home and hide in her bedchamber? Oh, this betrothal business was more complicated than she had imagined. A footman came up with a silver tray holding wine, and she accepted a glass, then saw her father speaking to Mr. Calleston at one side of the fireplace. On the other side two matrons eyed her with open curiosity and motioned with their fans for her to join them.

And be questioned further on the subject of the engagement, or worse—the night in the gazebo? Oh, no!

Maddie pretended not to see their signal and headed for her father's side instead. She tucked his lap robe in more securely—her father gave her a smile—then she hovered nearby as he and the other man talked about the newest types of plows.

Her own thoughts were not on farming. She saw that poor Adrian had been turned over to the inquisitive matrons. But he looked quite calm, and she was sure that he could handle himself better than she would have, so she gazed into the fire and watched the darting scarlet and gold flames leap and crackle.

She thought about the letter and her mother's joy. It was so nice to think that her parents had been happy when they had been young, since her mother had not had many years to enjoy that contentment.

Deep in thought, Maddie jumped when someone walked up beside her.

"I must apologize for keeping your fiancé from you, Miss Applegate, but everyone here wishes to talk to him," Mrs. Calleston said. "The women are overcome by his looks, and the men by his rank, so you will find it hard to find a moment for yourselves, I fear. I should have thought to plan some dances in the sitting room, later. We could have rolled up the rugs, but the room is really too small, and I have no one to play for us."

"No matter, Mrs. Calleston," Maddie said. "Although dancing is a romantic pastime when one is—well . . ." Drat, she was turning red, again, she just knew it, and her neighbor had a knowing look on her face. Maddie tried to change the subject, and blurted out the one thing still on her mind. "Do you remember my mother and father dancing when they were young and still courting? Did they particularly enjoy any special dance? It would please me to know that Adrian—Lord Weller—and I were dancing it as well."

"Oh." Mrs. Calleston looked thoughtful. "Elizabeth did much enjoy dancing, that was true. She was as light on her feet as any girl I ever saw. We were all envious. But your father—he had many strong points, my dear. His style on the hunting field was excellent, and such a good rider—and he could read aloud with such feeling—why, when he read poetry, the ladies would almost swoon!"

Maddie giggled, trying to imagine her father as a romantic young swain, sending the ladies into transports. "But, dancing?"

"Ah, yes, dancing. He knew the steps, but even before his accident, he had a slight slowness in one leg that made him perhaps not the best dancer in our little group." Mrs. Calleston stared into the distance as if she were indeed looking back in time. "But Elizabeth was a delight to watch on the dance floor, and every young man clamored to be her partner. Even when—ah, well." She sighed, but at what, she didn't say. "Such a shame," she said beneath her breath.

"What was?" Maddie demanded, too curious to be tactful. After all, it was her own mother they were discussing. Did she mean when her father had had his accident and been confined to the wheeled chair? No, that was long after her mother's death. So what had suddenly made Mrs. Calleston pause in her reminiscences?

"Oh." This time, to Maddie's surprise, it was the matron who flushed. "Nothing, my dear, nothing at all. Your mother was my dear friend, and I would never speak ill of her."

This made no sense at all. Their hostess had just been praising Maddie's late mother's dancing—how could that be construed as speaking ill?

"Excuse me for just a moment, I should check on how the dinner is progressing," Mrs. Calleston added and made a somewhat less than graceful exit, her expression hard to decipher.

Now what had Maddie said to upset their neighbor? While she puzzled over the answer to this, she glanced across the room to find Adrian surrounded by an even larger circle of women, and some men as well. When she met his gaze, she saw him nod and turn aside to say something she was too far away to hear, then he somehow made his way through the group and came to her side.

"Finally, you give me an excuse," he said, keeping his tone low. "I was rapidly being overcome by the cordiality of your neighbors, my dear Madeline."

She tried not to grin. "You are too much preferred, Lord Weller. Everyone begs for your company."

He gave a muffled groan, sending her into giggles, which she hid as best she could behind her fan. She knew that many of the company were watching them, covertly or openly.

"I told them you had an urgent need for my presence," he continued. "If they wish to know why, you will have to come up with the reason."

"Oh, good," she told him, trying to make her tone cross, but finding it hard to succeed. It was impossible to be angry when he was beside her, looking down at her with his dark lustrous eyes and pleasing features. Just being close to him sent a rush of happiness through her. "You give me the harder chore."

"They are your neighbors," he said reasonably, just as their hostess returned to the room, followed by the head footman, who paused in the doorway, waiting to draw the eyes of the guests.

"Dinner is served," he proclaimed.

Mrs. Calleston began to pair up partners to go into dinner together.

Adrian turned and gave Maddie his arm.

"But you will be assigned a lady to escort," she argued.

"I have chosen my lady," he said firmly. "Come along."

"Oh, gracious," Maddie muttered. "At this rate, we shall furnish even more grist for the gossip mill."

With a smile of apology for their hostess as they passed—she appeared too startled to scold—they headed for the dining room.

Perhaps she would attribute it to the eccentricities of a viscount, Maddie thought wildly. Perhaps titled guests were allowed some mischief making?

Once in the dining room, however, Maddie insisted that they heed proper decorum, so they found their place cards and took their seats. Lord Weller was at their hostess's right, as his rank demanded, and Maddie had been put further down, between an elderly neighbor and a beaming, slightly spotty young man just up from university and very full of his own ideas.

She resigned herself to a dinner spent in polite if unexciting conversation. But she could watch Adrian from the corner of her eye, while she enjoyed Mrs. Calleston's cook's undoubtably tasty dishes.

However, she found that viscounts were not the only ones who could disregard the most basic tenets of good manners. The older man on her left side spent the first course expounding on the problems arising from the lack of good breeding stock in local rams, and then suddenly switched course. "And prices are all akilter, too. Now, during the war we got good prices for wool, but the government needed material for uniforms, didn't it? Doing our duty, we were, as well as making a good profit."

The man had a naturally loud voice, and the other conversations at their end of the table faded as the other guests listened or just found it too hard to compete.

The man's wife looked a bit flushed at all this attention to their financial practices. "We never charged more than a fair price, you understand," she told the other guests.

"Of course not," Mr. Peetwee agreed. "As I said, doing our duty and making a just profit, that's all."

"Always a pleasure when the two go hand in hand, Peetwee," her father noted wryly from their hostess's other side.

"And thank God, we trounced the bloody French as well. Not that it came easily, never does in war."

There were murmurs of agreement, and Maddie hoped that he might be silent for a while; the man seemed to have the handy talent of being able to talk clearly despite a mouthful of food.

"My nephew was in the thick of it, told me about the worst of the fighting." While he sliced his rare roast beef, Mr. Peetwee proceeded to describe a particularly bloody engagement.

Maddie watched the red juices run out of her roast beef and felt her stomach twist as her dinner companion went on about the many wounded who had lost limbs and whose mangled bodies had littered the field. She swallowed hard.

This surely was not the most felicitous of dinnertime conversations. Poor Mrs. Calleston, Maddie thought, seeing her delicious dinner dishes go uneaten all because the heedless Mr. Peetwee, who seemed to have a digestion of iron, would bring up a topic at such an inopportune moment.

Then she happened to glance at the viscount and was startled by what she saw. His face had paled, and his expression was set, as if he kept it under control only by great effort. He also had stopped eating, though she saw that his wineglass was empty.

Feeling as if she had caught him in an instant too private for anyone, even a fiancée, to share, she looked away quickly. But as bad luck would have it, Mr. Peewee seemed to follow her glance.

"I know you were in the war, my lord," he said, looking up the table to Lord Weller. "One of my other nephews is in the War Office; he's heard some good things about your regiment. I heard you were particularly effective in the

Peninsula. Your regiment had some deep casualties, though, I'm told—a pity, that."

Maddie held her breath. A footman bent to refill the viscount's glass, coming between him and his interrogator. When the servant straightened, Adrian seemed to have composed himself—or perhaps she had imagined the strain she'd glimpsed in his face.

"Yes," he answered the older man, his voice quiet. "We did take some grievous losses more than once, perhaps more than our share." His tone was somehow final, and no one had the nerve to ask more.

With relief, Maddie motioned to the footman to take away her plate—she could not face the meats and sauces tonight—and applied herself instead to some simple blanc-mange with candied fruits.

She did not look at the viscount again; perhaps she was making too much of one glance of strained countenance. She tried to turn her thoughts to more innocuous topics. When the footmen passed around the table with more port, and Mrs. Calleston took the ladies away, leaving the men to their wine and male conversation, Maddie thought of their two hardworking servants at home. At least with the family gone, Bess had gotten a night off, with only Thomas and herself to feed. Right now Maddie needed any good thought to sustain her because she had a sinking feeling she was about to face the most difficult part of the evening.

And indeed, in the sitting room she found the air charged with suppressed tension, and the other women waiting to attack. She felt her whole body stiffen as she sat down near the fireplace. She saw the worried glance that Mrs. Calleston gave her, but there was little her old friend could do to help. Now she was in for it!

"I hope you are quite recovered from your illness, Miss Applegate," one matron said, fanning herself vigorously even though the room was not overly warm.

"Yes, thank you," Maddie said, keeping her tone calm. She would not allow them to see her quail.

"Miss Applegate has suffered from these sick headaches for years, poor thing," their hostess put in. "We have all worried about her condition."

"You're very kind," Maddie said. "But I am recovered. Your dinner was excellent, Mrs. Calleston. You must give your cook my compliments."

Their hostess smiled. "Thank you, dear; she will be most pleased. I did think the white sauce turned out exceptionally well."

But their effort to turn the conversation to another topic was to no avail.

"That night in the woods—it must have been quite an ordeal," a second lady said, her tone arch. "How fortunate that Lord Weller should have come to your rescue."

"Yes," Maddie said. She allowed the word to hang in the air, folding her hands demurely in her lap and refusing to give in to the pressure she felt from the other women to continue.

"I suppose Lord Weller is a most *compassionate* man? It was certainly most fortuitous that he should be in the little wood at just the right time, in just the right place," the first woman said. "How strange that your paths should cross."

They thought it was a planned tryst? That was the gossip that had spread through the shire? Maddie struggled to control her temper.

"Not so strange, since there is only one path through the trees and the moor," Maddie said. "The viscount was looking for shelter from the rain, as I was. We met in the shelter of the gazebo; the only shelter for miles around."

"And stayed there all night, alone, together"—the matron flung the words like blows—"instead of asking him to escort you home, which was only another mile or two away.

And you managed to lose all your clothing during the night hours. Really, Miss Applegate—"

"Mrs. Gates, that is too much!" Mrs. Calleston interrupted. "Miss Applegate is my guest—her mother was my dearest friend. You must not—"

Her inquisitioner let out her breath with an irate hiss. "I didn't know your mother, my dear, but I must believe it's just as well she is not here to see what a disappointment you have turned out to be."

Feeling a flash of pure rage run through her, Maddie jumped to her feet and glared down at the other woman. "My mother would have found nothing in my conduct to disappoint her! I could not direct Lord Weller to take me home, as I was unconscious by the time he found me. He was nothing but a gentleman, trying to save me from more serious illness. And yes, he is compassionate, which is more than I can say for some of my lifelong neighbors!"

"Well, really," Mrs. Gates said, fanning herself briskly again, but her tone had lost some of its self-righteous resolve.

"Really," Maddie repeated, knowing that her face was flushed, but this time with anger rather than any other emotion.

The other two ladies looked embarrassed, and Mrs. Calleston grim. "I will call for a tea tray," she muttered, and went to the bell rope.

Maddie walked away to look out the window into the shadowy garden. Her hostess came to gently touch her arm.

"Are you all right, my dear?" the older woman spoke quietly.

Maddie nodded.

"The alarming thing," her hostess continued, "is that these are the neighbors I thought would be the most—the least—"

"I know." Maddie sighed.

"It will all die down eventually, my dear. After your wedding, it will soon be forgotten." Mrs. Calleston patted her arm.

"I hope so," Maddie said.

She was more than happy when the men rejoined them, and the ladies became more circumspect in their comments. Soon after, she and her party said their farewells, as her father looked gray with fatigue.

"Are you all right, Papa?" she asked as they made their way to their carriage.

"Quite all right," he told her, "just a bit tired."

"What about you?" the viscount asked her quietly. "You look done in, yourself."

"I'm somewhat fatigued, as well. We are not used to such late hours in our quiet routine, my lord."

Her father chuckled. "You see what effect you have on our quiet and boring life, Lord Weller."

"I hope to the good," Adrian said, but even he seemed somewhat more subdued than usual.

Her father showed more signs of strain by the time they reached home and got him back into his chair. His complexion was pasty, and he sighed as Thomas pushed him back to his room to get ready for bed.

Maddie shook her head. "I know he enjoyed getting out of the house, but he doesn't have the energy to do this very often. I shall have to call upon Mrs. Barlow to serve as chaperone, and be thankful for such a good friend."

He didn't respond, and she looked at him quickly. "Are you all right, my lord?"

"Of course," he said. "A slight headache, nothing like the ones you sometimes endure." He smiled down at her. "But I think I will retire, also, if you will forgive me."

"Certainly," she said. "Shall I send up some tea or a glass of port?"

"No," he said. "But thank you."

Maddie wondered if the talk of the battle had somehow upset him, but surely he was accustomed to hearing the war with the French discussed.

So she kept her own council and merely bid him a polite good night, then went to the kitchen to drink one last cup of tea with Bess. She knew her longtime confidant would be eager to hear how the dinner party had gone.

"I think Papa had a fine time," she told Bess, who grinned in delight.

"I do hope so, as Thomas said 'e was proper wore out, the poor man." Bess took a hearty gulp of her own tea, which was strong enough to stand a spoon in.

Maddie watered hers down and added a tiny bit of sugar, which was too fearfully expensive to use with abandon. "I know; we must not allow him to go out too often. I don't want to see him exhausted. But Mrs. Barlow has offered to chaperone for me, so that will serve."

"Do ye think all the fine ladies of the shire will accept 'er as proper enough to 'ave in their parlors?" Bess demanded, wrinkling her long nose as she pondered the intricacies of social rank.

Maddie made a face. "They jolly well have to if they expect to see me and the viscount, as we will not grace their doorsteps except accompanied by Felicity!" And perhaps the widow's quick wit would help her when she had to face more verbal duels, Maddie thought, sighing. "Oh, and Lord Weller was a big hit tonight," she added. "He charmed the ladies and delighted the gentlemen, which comes as no surprise."

Bess wiped the already spotless table, apparently trying not to show her vicarious pride in her charge's new acquisition. "Aye, I always said 'e wasn't such a bad 'un."

Since she had said nothing of the kind, Maddie swallowed a smile with some effort. She put down her tea. "And I am as wearied as the gentlemen. Good night, Bess. If you'll just unbutton my back buttons now, you don't have to come up."

The maidservant protested, but Maddie was firm, and she carried up her own pitcher of warm water to wash with. In her bedchamber she was soon in her nightdress, pulling out the pins that had held her golden brown hair into the neat coil behind her head and sitting down to brush out its lustrous waves.

The house was quiet and peaceful. Bess and Thomas had gone up to their room in the attic, the door downstairs was bolted and latched, her father was surely asleep by now, and she assumed their guest must be, too.

She had turned back the bedclothes when she heard the slight sound in the hallway.

Maddie paused. Had Bess come back downstairs to check on her? Ready to scold her too conscientious servant, Maddie listened and waited. Her door didn't open, yet she could swear she had hear the shuffle of footsteps.

She picked up a shawl to toss about her shoulders and eased her door open. A short distance away, a tall figure loomed amid the shadows of the hall. She blinked in surprise.

"Lord Weller?" she asked, keeping her voice low. Surely he did not mean to offer a secret assignation; that is, surely he would have at least asked her permission before, or taken in account if she had any inclination toward—

She'd done nothing to give him permission to sneak into her bedroom!

She did not know whether to be offended or just puzzled, or even frightened—they were on the floor alone, the servants were a floor above, and her father, even if he could do anything to come to her aid, the floor below. The viscount had not seemed the kind of man who would offer her insult or do anything she did not wish. So why this sudden out of character action?

"Lord Weller?" she asked again, a little louder.

Still there was no answer.

She could not see his face in the darkness of the hall. She slipped back into her room and lit a candle, then returned to the doorway with the light. Strangely still, the figure remained in the same place.

What could be wrong?

She lifted the candlestick and came closer.

His expression was—she wasn't sure what he was thinking, but, even though his eyes were open, he didn't seem to see her. He looked straight ahead, his eyes a bit out of focus.

She took another step closer and put her hand lightly on his arm, and since the situation was strange, took refuge in formal address. "Lord Weller, are you ill?"

He still didn't seem to notice her presence, but in a moment he spoke, his voice low as if he feared for someone to hear. "Do not speak," he said, his tone urgent. "The guns are firing."

"My lord?"

"The guns are firing, the French guns in the left side of the embankment. We must be very quiet, or they will discover just where our forward lines are deployed."

"Of course we must," she murmured. Could one have a waking dream: she wondered. No, she thought, with a moment of inspiration, he was sleepwalking! Despite the fact that his eyes were open, he was asleep and in the grip of some nightmare left over from his years of soldiering. Perhaps the talk of war tonight at the dinner table had brought back more memories than he cared to recall.

"Let us go back to your room, my lord," she told him.

"I do not have a room." He shook his head slightly. "My bivouac—"

"Then let us go back to your bivouac," she said quietly. "This way, my lord."

"Major," he corrected.

"My lord Major," she said, not quite sure how one addressed military men. "This way."

He didn't move until she took his arm and pulled him along with her. To her relief, she found that he accompanied her without fuss, turning and walking beside her, only cautioning her again to go noiselessly.

"Yes, we will take care to make no noise," she agreed.

She found his guest room door standing open and led him inside, pulling the door shut behind them, just in case he should begin shouting or acting even more irrationally. She had lost any fear for herself. She simply didn't want anything embarrassing to occur.

"Now," she said, "you are safe, Major, and you need have no fear for your troops."

The furrow in his forehead appeared to soften. She had an irrational urge to touch it, rub it away completely, but she couldn't do anything so personal. He wore only a dressing gown and—well, she didn't know what beneath, but it wouldn't do to allow her thoughts to roam that way. "Would you not get back into your bed, my lord?"

This he was less amenable to. She was able only to get him to sit down upon the edge of the mattress. He seemed tense and ready to bolt again. He turned his head as if he still listened to the boom of ghostly guns.

She could not have him roaming the house, perhaps falling down the stairs and doing himself an injury. "My lord—"

He jerked. "The cannon—the big guns—they are firing, now, too. We must be sure that our men are dug in as far as must be, or the casualties—I had two men lose limbs already, and the blood—the blood—the blood follows me—"

He gave a massive shudder, once again. He could not seem to stop.

He seemed only barely aware she was there. She stopped

worrying about the impropriety of the situation and concentrated on trying to talk him out of his nightmare.

"My lord, please."

His teeth were chattering. "There—do you see it? That pool of blood—it is rising—it will pull us beneath it and drown us beneath the waves."

She could not suppress a shudder at such an image. No wonder he could not sleep peacefully.

"Major. I must insist!" She tried to push him down upon the pillow. "The blood is only in your mind. It is not real. The blood is fading; it is seeping away. I promise you."

He put his hands to his face. "It is falling away?"

"It is, it is." She put one hand on his arm. "Come, now. Lie back against the pillow. You must rest."

After her repeated pleading, he lay back against the mattress, but his head barely touched the pillow and his body was still stiff, as if he only awaited the next round of the guns, the guns only he could hear, and then he would leap to his feet again. How could she pluck him from these nightmares?

It had been years since the French wars had ended, yet in Adrian's mind, they seemed as fresh as if the last shot has just been fired and the scent of gunpowder still lingered in his nostrils. How many other men who had served in uniform still suffered from nightmares of blood and mangled bodies long after they had put away the gilt-trimmed jackets and military boots?

She felt a deep welling of compassion for him, much more than mere pity. He had given his youth to his country, and now he might never have his dreams unsullied again. Was it not enough to have his life complicated by deranged killers, living his life on the run after the impromptu duel? Must older wounds haunt him as well? And yet, he would still go out of his way to help a lady found helpless and stranded in the middle of a wood.

He was really an incredible man, she thought. She ran her hand over his shoulder, trying to get him to relax. He was, she told herself, still caught in his own tormented vision; it was not as if he even knew that she was so improperly here, in his bedroom in the middle of the night.

"Here, you are still shivering. Please, get beneath the blankets."

"My men—I cannot leave my men—"

"I promise you that your men are safe. You may rest now. Shut your eyes, allow your body to rest. Then you will be able to lead them on the morrow with much more stamina, with a clearer mind, a stronger body." She ran her hands over his shoulders, touched the taut tendons of his neck and throat, and felt him swallow hard.

"Yes," he said, "yes. I must rest, or I will not be able to think clearly. You are right."

"So shut your eyes," she whispered. "Pretend I'm not here. You will go back to sleep and sleep quietly all night, and tomorrow you will not remember any of this. Just allow your body to rest easily."

She stroked his rumpled hair, ran her hands down the sides of his jaw, feeling the weather-hardened skin at the side of his face and then the slight prickle of his shadow of beard. How different men felt from women! Something inside her stirred to life, aroused by his very maleness. It was just as well that he did not know that she was there, just as well that she was going back to her own bed—any second now, she told herself.

"That feels very good," he muttered, and at last some of the tension in his muscles seemed to ease. He lay back against the mattress and drew a longer breath. She pulled the blanket up to his chest and tried to arrange it so that he would be warm. He had shut his eyes, and she thought that he was breathing more naturally.

For a few moments she continued to run her hands easily

over the soft wool of his dressing gown, to massage his shoulders, and even more daringly the firm, warm skin of his neck and his strong jawline, although touching his skin made her insides quiver. It seemed more prudent to go back to his shoulders and upper arms, which were very nicely shaped, corded with muscle. He must be very strong.

She was about to slip back off the bed—it was more than time to leave; she knew she was tempting fate to stay this long—when she learned just how strong he was. She had turned to go when his hand shot out, and she found that she was anchored to the bed.

"Don't go," he muttered. "Don't leave me alone."

"But—"

"Please," he said.

Was he awake, she wondered in alarm, or still in one of his dreams?

"You are the most beautiful woman I have ever known," he said, very softly.

He must be dreaming, she thought. Of which woman he had these memories, she could not know, and she certainly would not ask. Some European courtesan? A long lost lover? This was not a subject that a lady *could* ask about. Maddie told herself she would certainly have to forget she had glimpsed this part of his dream; she was looking into his private life, and she really hadn't meant to take advantage of him. And she had no right to feel the smart of jealousy, which despite her best intentions pricked at the corner of her thoughts.

He reached out with his other hand and ran it softly over her face.

Startled, she forgot to be envious of whatever female he was dreaming of, since she seemed to be standing in for the phantasm of his memory. If the viscount had touched her this gently, Maddie feared that she would indeed be jealous, however. The soft brush of his fingertips over her eyelids . . . the way his hand lingered over her lips and then stroked the soft skin of her throat . . . her body was responding in ways she had not been aware that a lady could even feel.

Oh dear, oh dear.

She really must get out of here and back to her own bed. She was living someone else's fantasy—this whole thing was wrong.

But it was *her* fiancé, part of her mind argued back. He should be courting *her*, not some figment from an old memory!

Do you really want to wake him and tell him that, she told the rebellious part of herself. Oh, heavens, what if he waked himself?

No, as intoxicating as these small touches were, she really had to get away.

"Major?"

"Mmmm?"

"My lord? Adrian?" She tried again.

"Yes?"

At least he sounded calmer now, she was glad to hear. The frantic tones that he had used during the agitation of his nightmare had faded. At least the image of the unknown woman—as much as Maddie might want to pull out her hair—had given him some peace.

"I have to go." Unable to resist, she leaned over and kissed him on the cheek. This was a tactical mistake. While she still touched his cheek, he pulled her closer and turned her mouth toward his lips so that the kiss became a real one.

Oh, god, his lips were firm and warm, and they tasted of port wine. He pulled her close against him, and she felt his dressing gown fall away, his chest bare beneath it. And the kiss—his tongue pushed through as her lips fell apart—there were so many sensations she felt that she was drowning in them, but unlike Adrian's nightmare, this was heaven, a cloud of pleasure that almost overwhelmed her. She shut her eyes and gave herself to the kiss, to his embrace, and the rush of feeling that swept through her body made her cling close to him and forget everything.

Only when he was pushing aside her shawl and kissing her breast through the thin fabric of her nightgown, reaching to slip his hand down to fondle the soft skin of her thigh did Maddie remember where she was—perhaps even who she was.

Gasping, she pushed his hand away, and slid back from the tempting pleasures that had almost made her forget every precept of propriety.

"I have to go," she whispered, even though he surely could not hear her. She scrambled out of the bed, and, her nightgown unbuttoned and her hair in her face, grabbed her candle, now near to guttering. She hurried across the floor, then for a moment paused in the doorway, one hand on the door handle.

Breathing hard, she glanced back, almost afraid she would find that he was pursuing her. Instead, she saw that he had turned over in the bed and now sighed heavily. But he still slept.

With one last restless motion, the viscount pushed the bedclothes away. In the slanting moonlight where the draperies allowed one ray of light through, she had another look at his handsome—and bare—chest. He lay back against the disarray of the bed, but he did not wake.

She thought she heard him breathe a name as he settled into a more restful sleep.

"Madeline."

Eight

$\mathcal{M}$ addie stood transfixed for several long seconds, then she shook her head and eased the door shut. She hurried back to her own room. Only when safely inside and leaning against the back of the door did she release a gusty sigh.

She must have been mistaken. She could not have heard what she thought she—no, it must have been her imagination, wanting to put her own name on his lips. They had agreed to a friendly marriage of convenience, a binding that would save her reputation and aid him by possibly giving him a heir. It would benefit them both, and he was certainly appealing, but no one had mentioned love . . . she had no right to assume that he might dream about her. Still, she was seriously shaken.

Going back to her own bed, she pushed off her slippers and crawled under the covers, but it seemed so chill and cold. Lying next to Adrian's warmth had been so different. . . . Never had she been so aware of how alone she felt in the solitary bed.

Turning on her side, she pulled a pillow into her arms and hugged it to her, thinking what a poor and puny substitute it was for the firm, hard body of her fiancé. But in less than three weeks, he would replace it, if all went well. She felt a rush of sensation just thinking of lying in his arms and clutched the pillow tighter, pounding it several times in frustration.

He was only down the hall, and yet he might as well be on the other side of England.

Sighing, she tried to compose herself for slumber, but she lay awake in the darkness for what seemed like an endless time. Not until the first faint trills of the dawn birds could be heard outside her window and a few streaks of gray light appeared on the horizon did she finally drift into an uneasy sleep.

When she woke, the morning seemed far advanced. Maddie felt as if her eyelids were sprinkled with sand, and she still felt almost as tired as when she had laid her head upon the pillow. Yawning, she sat up slowly. She found that Bess had left warm water on her washstand, and she made a leisurely toilette. When she came downstairs, she found her father also looked heavy eyed, and even Adrian not quite as energetic as usual.

Her father looked around the table. "We do seem to be laid low by our small attempt at frivolity."

Maddie smiled at him. "I believe we're out of practice, Papa. I'm sure Lord Weller will think us very provincial."

"Not at all," the viscount said, taking a gulp of his tea. "It seems that your neighbors are giving you every chance to practice until you are thoroughly at ease again." Grinning, he nodded toward the stack of notes and invitations that sat on the tablecloth at Maddie's elbow.

She grimaced as she scanned the correspondence. "I believe you are right, my lord."

Her father made a face, too, but he kept his tone upbeat. "Then I fear we have no choice but to devote ourselves to satisfying the vulgar curiosity of our neighbors, Lord Weller. I regret you are put to so much fuss, though I suppose it is worse in London?"

"Oh, much worse," Adrian agreed, his eyes twinkling. "And as you said, I suspect I have aggravated the situation, so I have no right to complain about it. They are curious about the stranger in your midst, and I'm sure they want to offer their good wishes to Miss Applegate on her betrothal."

Maddie thought about the near savage assault last night and bit back a rejoinder; no need to upset her father. Instead of telling them what the neighbors really wanted to find out, she only smiled and nodded. "We do not mean to exhaust you, Papa," she added. "My friend Mrs. Barlow has offered to chaperone whenever I need her, so you do not have to go with us on every engagement. Not that I mean to accept all of these, I hasten to say."

She thought that Adrian looked relieved. "An excellent plan," he said. "And what would you say to a ride into town today, Miss Applegate?" He nodded toward the blue sky visible through the window. "The day looks very promising. If your father would allow the use of the carriage, we would take your friend up on her offer, and have an excursion into Ripon."

"Oh, that would be nice," she agreed. The thought of seeing strangers who had no idea of her history sounded like a positive relief. "I will send Thomas over to Mrs. Barlow's cottage with a note while I go up and get ready."

Since trips further than the village were rare, she stopped in the kitchen long enough to confer with Bess and get a shopping list of provisions that needed to be obtained from the better-provided shops in the larger town. Then she whisked upstairs to find a shawl and the most decent bonnet she owned, wishing that one of her refurbished gowns was further along. She really had to stay home long enough to finish her gowns.

By the time Felicity came hurrying up the path from her cottage, looking pleasantly excited, her cheeks pink, wearing her black dress and shawl and a plain bonnet with a black ribbon, Maddie was ready.

"Oh, I'm so glad you are willing to accompany us," Maddie told her when Bess showed the guest into the sitting room.

"My dear, I'm delighted to be asked. Such an excursion is a rare treat," Felicity said as they exchanged a quick hug. She curtsied to the viscount as he bowed to her.

Maddie felt a surge of pride in her fiancé's kind heart and excellent manners. He always treated the impoverished widow with just as much tact and consideration as if she had been a duchess.

"I believe the carriage is ready, ladies," he told them. He helped them in himself, and took his seat across from them.

"Did you have a nice evening out at Mrs. Calleston's?" Felicity asked. Maddie had told her earlier about the planned engagement.

"It was an agreeable evening," Maddie said, her tone noncommittal. "They have a highly skilled cook, and her hand with sauces is very fine. The dinner had much to be enjoyed."

Seeing that the viscount was gazing out the window of the carriage, she raised her brows slightly, but said no more. Her friend pursed her lips and nodded.

Maddie would tell Felicity more when they were alone, but she did not intend to allow Adrian to know that gossipy neighbors were still tormenting her, despite all his efforts. As Mrs. Calleston said, the scandalmongers would eventually choke on their own ill-natured lies—or at least, she hoped they would!

It was a most pleasant day; the sky was blue and a few high wispy clouds floated overhead. For the rest of the drive, they chatted about matters of little consequence, and it was a delight to be among friends and to fear no unexpected verbal attacks.

In Ripon they left Thomas and the carriage at an inn and posting house, where he and the horses could seek rest and refreshment, and the viscount ordered a luncheon set out for the three of them in a private dining room when they returned.

"In a few hours or so," Adrian told the innkeeper.

Maddie raised her brows. "I have a list of foodstuffs to obtain, if you do not mind me looking into a few shops, but it should not take that long, my lord. Of course, we might walk about for a bit and look into the shop windows, but—"

"You may look into any shop you like, my dear," he told her. "I have some shops I wish to investigate, as well."

"Oh, of course," she said. How silly. It had not occurred to her that he might have items to buy, too, but of course he would. He had not come to Yorkshire planning for a lengthy stay.

After she had found the lemons sent all the way from London's wharfs and some spices that Bess had not been able to buy in the village, along with other various items, she directed the merchants to wrap and send everything to the posting house, to be placed in Thomas's charge.

"Now, my lord, we are at your disposal. We will follow you to your shops. Or," thinking that he might wish to buy his underwear without female eyes upon him, she added quickly, "we will go and have a cup of tea at some nearby tea shop and allow you to select your merchandise at your gentleman's shops undistracted."

His eyes glinted with humor as if he guessed the direction of her thoughts. "I will see to my needs in a moment.

First, I have obtained the name of the best modiste in town, and I shall require your presence for some time longer."

Mystified at why he would wish to visit a dressmaker, Maddie could only nod and accept his arm. Felicity followed just behind them. Glancing over her shoulder, Maddie saw that her friend was grinning. Did she know something that Maddie did not perceive? How provoking!

When they entered a handsome shop with an alarmingly august sales assistant waiting to aid them, the viscount inclined his head and asked to see the modiste, a Madame Alexanderine, herself.

"And whom," said the clerk, in icy tones, "shall I say is calling?"

"The Viscount Weller, his bride-to-be Miss Applegate, and Mrs. Barlow." Adrian had never sounded so grand, and his usual easy demeanor was not at all in evidence.

Maddie stared at him in surprise, but the effect of his pronouncement on the modiste's assistant was even more marked. Her eyes widened, and her manner warmed from December to June.

"Of course, your lordship. Madame Alexanderine would be honored, your lordship. If you and your betrothed and her friend would be so good as to step into an inner room, your lordship, you could have a seat just here . . ." Almost stumbling, she backed through one of the doors on the other side of the room and showed them into a small room that held several gilt-edged chairs with a round table piled with ladies' magazines, a tall looking glass, and little else.

"I'll just go and inform Madame," the young woman said, her voice a little breathless. She managed to get out of the room without falling and shut the door.

For a moment, no one spoke, then Maddie gave a nervous chuckle as she sat down. "Oh, dear. Why do I think that poor girl has not come across very many viscounts? You must be nice to her, Adrian."

"You think if I raise my brows, she will go into hysterics?" he asked, very quietly.

"Please don't try it," Felicity begged him. She had claimed another of the gilt chairs. "I could barely keep from laughing myself. The poor girl is so overcome, although I know she simply wants to secure your patronage."

"But I can't—that is, this woman must be quite costly, Adrian, and really—"

"You would rather go home and work on redoing the dress you were taking apart yesterday in the sitting room?" he asked, his gaze tender.

She flushed. "You are altogether too observant," she pointed out. "The gown was my mother's, and the silk is still good. There's no need to waste it. I don't mind at all, and—"

"And I admire you for it. But I take great delight in providing for you, you know, and since I will soon be your husband, it is my privilege. Can you not allow me to start?"

"But we're not married yet," she noted, trying to make her tone stern and having a hard time doing it when he looked at her with such a gentle expression.

He lifted one hand and kissed it. Maddie found herself blushing even more deeply. Felicity had picked up *Godfrey's Lady's Book* and turned away from them, seeming to absorb herself in the fashions depicted in the journal.

"I'm all too aware of that," he told her, keeping his voice low. "But since your neighbors are determined to fete us, you are in need of your trousseau sooner rather than later, and since I would like to be of use to you, why not allow me the pleasure? It is a small thing you can do to make me happy, Madeline."

"But I'm sure it's not proper—not yet," she tried to argue, distracted by the fact that he still held her hand, by the warmth and strength of his grip, by how her pulse raced when he held her so close.

"Oh, fie. It's only a few weeks. Can you not allow me the enjoyment? I want to see you in new dresses and see you savoring them now, not later!" He smiled at her, and suddenly she heard him again—*time is rushing past—time—time—time is not my friend.*

Oh, God, she thought, please don't take this man away from me!

They were interrupted by the sound of footsteps. The viscount dropped her hand just in time, and Maddie blinked and tried to compose herself when the modiste, Madame Alexanderine herself, swept into the room, wearing a marvelous gown of gold-embroidered violet silk.

Her assistant, coming in behind her, made nervous introductions, and the modiste bowed as to a king.

"And I understand we have the betrothed couple, yes? My lord, Miss Applegate, how wonderful! And what a beautiful young lady—to dress her will be to gild the lily, and such a joy! It will be an inspiration, my greatest joy in all my years of dressmaking," the lady declared in heavily accented English.

She gestured with fingers covered in rings and continued to declaim about Maddie's merit, the viscount's wisdom in choosing such a consort, and how much her gowns would accent the beauty of the bride.

If she sewed half as well as she talked, the modiste's dresses would be successful indeed, Maddie told herself. She gave up arguing and allowed herself to be put upon a stool and measured. Then she and Felicity looked through swatches of material and trim and pored over books of patterns. There were even two dinner dresses that another patron had ordered and then canceled, and the gowns were close enough to Maddie's size to be altered on the spot—a piece of rare good fortune.

Which only went to show, the beaming Madame Alexanderine proclaimed, that it was Fate herself who had sent

Maddie to Madame's door. While the changes were made, Maddie and Felicity were served tea in the fitting room, while the viscount did at last depart to see a tailor and haberdasher for some needs of his own.

Maddie was feeling guilty to receive so much when she knew that Felicity's wardrobe was also very meagerly furnished. When she tried to intimate as much, her friend shook her head.

"No, indeed, you are the bride, my dear! You should be the one who receives such good fortune, and from your magnanimous fiancé." She took a sip of tea. "I am making good progress with the gowns you have kindly given me to redo, and that is a great gift. I'm only delighted to see that Lord Weller is so generous. I believe that he may make a very good husband for you."

Maddie smiled. "I don't believe I will be able to fault his generosity, at any rate." She still felt a bit dazzled.

When Adrian returned, he directed the modiste to send the dresses on to the posting house when the alterations were completed, and they strolled leisurely back to the luncheon that awaited them.

The sunlight was now dappled, with clouds obscuring the blue sky, and a wind that tossed the ladies' bonnets made them shiver. Maddie was glad to reach the inn and go upstairs to the private room and the handsome meal that waited for them. What fun it was to have an outing like this, she thought.

Felicity must have found such an occasion even rarer, as she was bright eyed and obviously enjoying herself. Maddie was so glad they had become friends; the widow's means were so straitened that she had no hope of getting out of the village on her own. When Maddie and Adrian entertained . . .

Again her thoughts came up against the brick wall that his doubts always erected. Did she have a future after her wedding—or, more properly, did they have a future? It was all very well to say that he would marry her to protect her good name, but if he feared the man who pursued him all across Britain, how long before the lunatic located him in Yorkshire and destroyed the happiness that Maddie increasingly had become to believe that they could create together?

There must be a way to eliminate the danger . . . Adrian could not keep running all his life.

The day suddenly seemed darker, and she was not sure if it was the sunlight dimming or her mood. She had to bite her tongue to keep from snapping at a maidservant carrying a pitcher who spilled water on Maddie's lap when she moved too abruptly away from the table.

"Oh, miss, I'm that sorry!" The girl looked both embarrassed and frightened. "I'll just get a cloth and dry your gown."

Maddie was ashamed of her moment of temper. She hadn't said a word, but her expression must have been black indeed, judging by the girl's recoil.

"It's quite all right," she said.

The food arrived, and they all applied themselves to the meal. But Maddie's appetite seemed to have left her, and presently she was alarmed to see that the candles' flames seemed to waver before her eyes, and a familiar feeling of pressure was growing in her right temple.

"Oh, please God," she whispered. "Not now." It had been such a lovely day.

She put down her fork, and glanced at Felicity. "I believe I shall have to excuse myself."

"I will go with you," her friend said at once.

"You don't have to go," she told her. "It may not be—ah—pleasant."

"You've gone quite pale, my dear. I think I should be with you," the widow said, her voice firm.

"Are you ill?" the viscount said, standing as the two women stood up from their chairs. "Is there anything I can do?"

"Just leave this to the females," Felicity advised him.

He bowed and said no more, but he watched them go with an expression of concern on his face.

Maddie was concentrating on not losing her meal until they made it to the necessary. Afterwards, when Felicity had bid one of the inn's servant to bring them water and a towel, and she had washed her hands and face, she groaned.

"Is it bad already?" the widow asked, keeping her voice low. She knew from conversations earlier that noises were painful when the headaches started.

"It's just beginning," Maddie said. "I don't know—oh, this is wretched luck."

"I believe storm clouds are coming up; the weather may have caught you again," Felicity told her. "Come, let's go back to the room. The viscount will be worried."

Indeed, they found Adrian pacing up and down. "Is it your head?" he asked at once. "I see clouds rising outside."

Felicity nodded. Maddie could not move her head without pain lancing through her temple. She braced her head and tried to contain or slow the pain, though she knew it did little good.

Adrian took both her hands in his. "My dear Madeline, tell me what you wish. Would it help you to summon a local physician?"

"No," she answered, her voice a little hoarse. "They can do nothing helpful, except give me laudanum, which leaves me heavily sedated. It makes me ill in itself, and it helps the pain only briefly. When I wake, I am very nauseated, and the pain seems to have grown more than it usually does. It can cause cravings for the drug, and unless you are careful, you can end up like some pathetic opium eater sleeping your life away. So I do not care for it."

"Would you wish to engage a room here, so you can sleep? The rain will start before long. Or do you wish to leave at once and get ahead of it if we can? I hate for the carriage to rock you about when you are feeling ill, but we will do whatever you wish."

"Aside from giving the scandalmongers more fuel," she began, her tone rueful.

"To hell with the old cats," he interrupted. "No, my dear, as I said, we will do what makes you most comfortable. Do not even consider anything else!"

She smiled up at him, for a second even forgetting her growing discomfort. "You are a wonder. I would truly rather be home, my lord. If I have to suffer, I would rather do it in my own bed."

"Then that is what we shall do," he said. "I have already ordered the carriage made ready and all our parcels packed and tied on beneath a canvas, just in case that was your answer, so that we did not lose a minute."

"You begin to know me well," she told him, smiling a little despite her feelings of illness.

He offered to carry her down, but Maddie insisted that she was still well enough to walk, although she did accept his arm to lean on.

When they reached the courtyard, she found that he had had a brick warmed and put into the vehicle for her feet to rest on, and another warmed and wrapped in a towel for her hands.

"I remember how icy your hands and feet were, that night in the gazebo," he told her when he helped her in. "I have a blanket to wrap you in, as well. I think you should take this side, and Mrs. Barlow the other, and I will sit up by Thomas."

"And be drenched when the rain starts, no, no, I am not that sick yet," Maddie said. "I will be much more affected by my worry about you; you must not."

She was insistent, so the viscount remained inside with them. She did find the hot brick very pleasant beneath her feet, and the extra warmth of the blanket also a welcome touch.

It was true that the day had changed swiftly. The blue skies and balmy air of the morning had been replaced by brisk, cold winds and dark clouds. They were able to cover almost half of their journey before the rain began, at first a slow patter against the carriage, then a harder rain with occasional crashing thunder that slowed the horses since poor Thomas, wrapped in his heavy cape, had to watch for holes in the road that might be disguised by puddles of rainwater.

Inside, Maddie braced herself against the jolting of the carriage and felt the pain in her temple grow with every passing minute. The smells of the rain outside, the horses, the damp clothing, all seemed too harsh in the small, contained space. Her stomach roiled, but she pressed her lips together, pushed her fingers against the stabbing in her temple, and tried not make the pain worse by becoming stiff with tension. The viscount sat beside her and gently rubbed her shoulders and neck. She leaned against him as they covered the last miles.

At last the carriage approached the Applegate residence and slowed. She heard Thomas's cry to the horses, and when they rolled to a stop, Adrian, who had been watching her with an increasingly worried gaze, did not wait for Thomas to open the door. He unlatched it himself and jumped out to lower the steps, then returned to gather her into his arms and lift her out, carrying her with long strides straight into the house.

Maddie felt she should protest, but the pain was too strong. She lay her face against his chest, comforted by his masculine scent, while he drew the blanket over her to protect her from the pelting rain. Once inside the house, Adrian allowed the blanket to fall away, and she sighed with relief.

She saw that her father waited in the hall, and his tone was anxious.

"How is she?" He looked up from his wheeled chair, trying to see her face. Bess hovered nearby.

"As might be expected," the viscount said. "I shall take her straight up to her room, if I may, sir."

"Of course, of course," her father said.

For a moment, she felt a strange sense of déjà vu. The viscount had brought her home once before, much like this.

As Adrian rapidly ascended the stairs, she heard Felicity comforting her father in the hallway below. "We came home as quickly as we could. He took very good care of her, Mr. Applegate . . ."

In her own room, Adrian lay her upon the bed, and Bess swooped in and removed her pelisse and bonnet. "I'll make ye some of me 'erbal tea, and then I'll 'elp ye into yer nightgown, Miss Madeline." The servant cast a stern look at the male in the room, as if warning that, lord or no, he should remember his place, and then bustled out the door.

Adrian pulled up a stool to sit on and took her hand in his. "Can I do anything to help you?" He kept his voice low.

"You have done a great deal already," she whispered.

"It grieves me to see you in pain."

"It will pass," she told him. "Bess will take care of me, do what can be done. Thank you for the wonderful day."

"I'm sorry it ended like this," he said. "If you had stayed home—"

"The headache would have come, regardless, with the storm and the change of weather," she told him.

"Are you sure we—I—did not make it worse?" he asked.

She smiled at him. "I am most thrilled at the prospect of my new gowns, Adrian. New clothes give no one a headache." She would have laughed, but the pain was growing too severe, and she winced instead.

He sighed for her and sat silently, holding her hand while rain and high winds lashed at the windowpanes and a crash of thunder made the frames shake. When the maid returned, she brought a cup of bitter-smelling tea, a cold compress for Maddie's head, and a silent but definite command that it was time for menfolk to depart so her mistress could change clothes.

"If I can do anything, I am yours to command," he said softly, then kissed her hand one last time and took his leave.

Maddie managed a smile, then, when the door was safely shut behind him, sighed and with Bess's help struggled out of her clothes and into a loose nightgown, curled up with the compress on her aching head, and shut her eyes, trying to think of the pleasing images of the day, anything except the waves of brutal and overwhelming pain.

Three mornings later she woke, as tired as if she had been laboring in one of the coal mines that dotted the Yorkshire mountains. A lingering soreness afflicted her temple when she rubbed it gingerly, but the worst of the pain had gone, and—please God—would not return any time soon.

And she actually felt hollow with hunger. She had only been able to swallow a little tea and dry toast during the worst of her attack. Feeling slightly dizzy, she pushed herself up just as Bess came through her doorway.

"Ah, Miss Maddie, 'ow are ye?" The servant looked at her hopefully.

"Better, hungry, and much in need of a wash," she told her.

"Oh, that's good," Bess said, beaming. "I'll bring up some breakfast, and then some warm water. Just don't ye take it too fast, Miss, remember the time ye fell and busted yer chin open."

Maddie nodded, then wished she hadn't, as it made her head spin again. But she managed to sit up in the bed. By the time Bess was back with a full tray of eggs and ham and buttered bread and hot tea, Maddie found her stomach rumbling. She could set to with a ready appetite.

"'Is lordship sends 'is regards," Bess said, "and 'e picked ye a bouquet." She had brought the flowers up. They had obviously been picked from the Applegates' own garden, and Bess had crammed them into one of the older vases, but still the autumn blooms were pretty.

Maddie felt a wave of pleasure. "How sweet. Thank you, Bess, and tell Lord Weller I was very pleased. I hope to be downstairs soon."

"No, no, ye won't." Bess's tone changed at once. "'Aven't we already turned aside Miss Nosy Parker to keep ye quiet and peaceful, like?"

"Who?"

"Mrs. Masham, 'o else," Bess said, with a jerk of her head.

Who else indeed, Maddie thought, grinning, as she took a bite of her eggs, which were as light and delicious as usual. Bess was a fine cook.

"Yer papa sent a note that ye weren't able to go to 'er dinner two nights ago—"

"Oh, heavens, I forgot all about that engagement—I'm so glad he remembered!" Maddie almost dropped her fork.

"Well, 'e did, so not to worry," Bess said, her tone matter-of-fact. "And just as well, I'd say."

Maddie thought it more prudent not to answer aloud, but she was quite glad to have missed the Mashams' dinner party. "So she has already come to call?"

"To see if ye were really ill, I'd say—and not just sloughing off 'er dinner party—such a suspicious one I never saw!" Bess shook her head as she straightened the bedclothes. "She was all set to nip up to yer room again, but the viscount caught 'er and maneuvered 'er into the sitting room and 'ad a cup of tea with 'er. All politeness, of course, but sharp, 'e is. She couldn't get away from 'im."

She made it sound as if Adrian had cornered a rabbit in the garden trying to get into the peas. Maddie had to concentrate in order not to laugh.

"Then I am doubly grateful to Lord Weller!" Smiling, she finished her breakfast, drank some of her tea, and then, although still feeling shaky on her feet, bathed and dressed.

After even that slight exertion, she was glad to sit and rest for a few minutes. Then, after checking with Bess to be sure no unwanted visitors lurked below, she made her way down the stairs.

She found Adrian in the sitting room glancing through a book. Standing when she entered, he put down the volume.

"My dear Madeline—I am so glad to see you on your feet. At least, I hope you are not up too soon. How are you?"

"Much better," she said, smiling at him. "Thank you for the flowers. That was a very sweet thought."

"The day is mild," the viscount noted. "Would you like a stroll in the garden? If that is not too much exertion. You look a bit pale, still. Would the air do you good?"

"That sounds lovely," she told him, smiling still. Just seeing him standing there, smiling in return, made her happy, she realized suddenly. When had he become so essential to her well-being?

"You might want something to put about your shoulders. Shall I ask Bess—" the viscount had begun, when the maidservant herself came to the door.

"Yer father is asking about ye, Miss Maddie," she pointed out, her tone somewhat astringent.

"Oh, of course," Maddie said, abashed. She had not even stopped at her father's study to tell him she was recovered. She'd never forgotten to do that before! "I'll go down to his study right now. And would you go up to my room and bring down my shawl, please?"

"Yes, miss."

With a smile for the viscount, Maddie left the room and hurried down the hall.

After spending half an hour with her father, she felt free to return to the front room to rejoin the viscount and then make her way outside. The sky was clear again after several days of rain, and the puddles almost gone.

Adrian offered his arm for support, and she was happy to lean on it, and not just because she still felt a little shaky. Truth was, she also enjoyed being so close to him. She didn't have to be on the verge of a headache to enjoy his touch, his masculine scent, the intoxicating awareness of having him so close.

She was jarred out of her pleasing thoughts when she looked up at the big oak in the center of the garden, the one they had leaned against the last time they had been out among the flower beds. Then it had still been in the height of its golden autumn glory, full of riotous color.

The heavy rains had brought down the better part of the tree's leaves, which now littered the ground below. The golden leaves were turning brown and brittle, their splendor only a memory, and the limbs overhead were mostly bare, outlined against the blue gray autumn sky in stark lines.

Maddie felt her heart sink. Somehow, this was too oppressive a reminder of how swiftly time was going by. Two more days and they would be sitting again in their family pew, and the vicar would read the banns once more. Then only two weeks would be left, two more readings, and they would be free to marry. And Adrian would be free to leave, if circumstances should demand it.

He still kept his eyes on the woods around the house, she noticed, still watched dark shadows at the edge of the treeline, or scanned tall trees that someone might climb to get a good shot upon an unwary passerby.

How long would he feel like someone's quarry?

How long could she keep him here?

And if she could not keep him, how could she bear to lose him?

Nine

$\mathcal{M}$ addie felt her heart contract at the thought of losing Adrian. She paused, and the viscount turned his attention at once back to her.

"Are you fatigued? Shall I take you back inside? I can carry you if you are too tired to walk."

She shook her head.

"It would be no trouble. You are as light as a newborn lamb, Madeline."

She smiled ruefully at that. "I doubt it. But I'm fine, Adrian. Although we might sit a while on the bench up ahead."

"Of course," he agreed. The bench was still damp, but Bess had sent along an extra throw, and he spread it on the seat then steered her to it and sat down beside her.

"I just—I just had a moment of melancholy, that's all," she told him. "Time is passing, and nothing can stop it, slow it. I don't want you to go, Adrian."

He pulled out his watch and she saw the small charm, a miniature hourglass with sand that poured from one side to another. He twirled it, and the sand slid too quickly—much too quickly—from the top to the bottom.

For a moment, neither spoke.

He looked away, down the swath of green lawn to the trees beyond, where one could not see the hidden undergrowth. "Nor do I wish to leave you, dearest Madeline. But if I stay, if my pursuer finds me, I cannot risk putting you in danger when bullets fly. After this madness is ended, you know I will return."

If you can, if you are still whole, or even alive, she thought, wanting to hurl the words at him, shout, scream her frustration, but knowing she dare not.

Today, she did not even have the energy to discuss it. He slid the watch back into its pocket and put his arm around her, and she lay her head against his chest—she didn't care who saw—and they sat quietly for a long time, as she listened to the quiet pounding of his heart.

Later, they returned to the house. Maddie was glad that dinner tonight was a quiet, pleasant one at home, with just the three of them. But it seemed Bess was destined for many more evenings with less work, as the invitations continued to pour in.

With distinctively mixed feelings, Maddie accepted a dinner invitation for Saturday, but she enlisted the support of Felicity so that her father did not have to go out, as he had had more aching in his poorly healed broken bones than usual since the last rainstorm.

Since they would be returning fairly late, Maddie wrote a note asking her friend to spend the night at the Applegate house, so Felicity walked up the path Saturday afternoon carrying a modest carpetbag.

"You should have waited," Maddie scolded. "Thomas was coming down to accompany you back; he could have carried your bag."

"It was no trouble. And I have my gown completed and ready to wear. I'm so excited," Felicity told her. She had also done her hair slightly differently, with a smooth twist instead of the usual severe bun, so she was going to look very fine, and Maddie told her so.

"And look," Maddie said. "When I got the first part of my packages from the dressmaker in Ripon, she sent an added present since we ordered so much—two reticules, and with such lovely trim. I want you to have one of them."

"Oh, I couldn't," Felicity said.

But Maddie insisted, and Felicity gave in, with suspiciously damp eyes. "You are very kind."

Maddie, who had wanted her friend to have something new, was satisfied. "This one will match your outfit very well. Now, we are both ready to go!"

She was feeling very festive herself, with one of her new dinner gowns from the modiste. Bess and Felicity helped her with the new silk, a soft green that made her skin look clear and her eyes bright. Maddie added her mother's pearl eardrops and wove some fresh white asters into her hair, and was pleased with the result. She only hoped the viscount would be, as well.

When Maddie came down the staircase and saw his face, she judged that he was. The sparkle in his eyes made her blush.

"My dear Madeline," her father said. "You look particularly fine tonight. You will outshine all the young ladies!"

"Thank you, Papa," she said, leaning over to kiss his forehead.

Adrian took her hand and kissed it lightly. "You are a vision," he said simply. "The modiste could have no better person to show off her talents."

She blushed even more deeply, and turned to say, "Look, Papa, doesn't Mrs. Barlow look very handsome?"

"I assure you, I had already noticed," Mr. Applegate said. "I am pleased to see you put aside your black, Mrs. Barlow. The lavender becomes you splendidly."

Felicity seemed startled to be complimented, and she blushed just as readily as Maddie had done. "Oh, thank you," she said, her voice a little breathless. "Your daughter, that is, Miss Applegate, has been so magnanimous—"

"Oh, yes, Madeline has a kind heart, takes after her mother," he agreed, beaming on them both. "Have a splendid time tonight, now. I'm sure Lord Weller will take good care of you."

Maddie gave her father another quick kiss good-bye.

Adrian grinned. "I am pleased that you come with such a testimonial," he said in an aside to Maddie, which made her giggle as she put on her shawl.

"Wretch," she said beneath her breath. "You will see what a termagant I can become."

"Ah," he offered her his arm as they started for the carriage, giving his other arm to their chaperone, "I tremble at the thought."

Maddie rolled her eyes at him as she stepped into the carriage.

The first part of the evening was pleasant, the meal sumptuous. Once again the most difficult part of the evening occurred when the ladies withdrew, and the female guests seemed to feel freer to offer more sharp-tongued observations without the men around to make note.

"You're looking very well tonight, Miss Applegate," Mrs. Terrence remarked as the ladies settled into the sitting room.

"Thank you," Maddie answered cautiously. "As do you."

"That's a new outfit, I believe. Most becoming."

"Perhaps she needs it to make up for the clothes she lost in the wood," a younger lady, Miss Jeets, muttered just loud enough to be heard. Several of the women tittered, although some of the older ones looked shocked.

"A pity about the lack of good morals these days," Mrs. Jeets, the mother of the young lady who had spoken, added, her voice loud.

Maddie felt her cheeks burn, but could think of no retort that would not make the situation worse.

"A pity about the lack of good manners, these days," Felicity said clearly and just as loudly, looking Mrs. Jeets straight in the eye.

A couple of nervous laughs came at this, although Mrs. Jeets *harrumped* in displeasure. Felicity kept her expression pleasant and quite composed. Maddie wanted to shout with laughter and didn't dare, but she felt better.

"It's a shame they are letting just anyone into Society these days," the matron shot back, glaring at Felicity.

"Yes, isn't it?" Maddie snapped, scowling at Mrs. Jeets.

By this time the tension in the sitting room was as thick as treacle. But Maddie was losing her nervousness, although she felt sorry for the hostess, who looked decidedly woebegone. Having Felicity beside her made all the difference.

"I understand acorns do not fall far from the tree," Mrs. Jeets declared.

Not sure what this referred to, Maddie had no good retort ready.

One of the other ladies seemed to think this might make a more inoffensive topic. "My mums are doing quite well this season. How is your garden, Mrs. Bright?"

But her attackers were not done.

"You'd think that a lady—I mean, a female—who was conscious of her misdeeds, who had been so obviously compromised, would have enough awareness of her shame not to flaunt herself by going about in Society before she was decently married!"

"Oh, dear, dear," their hostess, Mrs. Bright, sputtered. "That's hardly fair when it was I who invited—"

"I wouldn't know," Maddie said, keeping her tone mild with some effort. "Perhaps in your family, you do?"

Gasping, Mrs. Jeets dropped an almost full cup of tea into her lap, with not good results for her rather loudly hued purple satin gown.

At the same time, her daughter wailed, "Mother! You didn't tell them about—"

"Lavinia—hush!" her mother snapped, dabbing her napkin ineffectively at the spilled tea, which was now running in rivulets onto the carpet.

Mrs. Bright waved to a maid in the doorway to bring a linen towel, while several of the other guests goggled at this unexpected revelation, and Maddie tried not to giggle. She'd had no idea that her chance remark would produce such results. At any rate, her tormentors seemed to have forgotten about her in their own embarrassment.

Next another matron remarked on a group of gypsies that her husband suspected of camping on their estate.

"Dangerous, those vagabonds, best watch out for your valuables, and I wouldn't go out alone," she said darkly.

"I should say not," Mrs. Bright agreed, happy to have a new topic to discuss. "They will cut your throat as soon as look at you!"

This at least kept the conversation going until the men rejoined them, and before too long, Maddie and her party could excuse themselves and start home before the moonlight faded and the road became too dark for Thomas and their team to see.

"I hope you enjoyed the evening, Lord Weller," Maddie asked, her tone formal, as they all rode home.

"Oh, yes, your neighbors are a cordial lot."

To a visiting peer, a man who appeared rich and powerful, they were, she thought, sighing. Amazing how men were not attacked for their social sins, only women.

At least the war did not seem to have come up, unless it

had been discussed during the men's conversation, and she thought it best not to ask.

When they reached home, her father was waiting to see how the evening had gone. They all had a last cup of tea and then went up to bed. Felicity stayed the night in a guest room. Maddie told her how much help she had been, and the widow laughed.

"It was a pleasure; some of the same old cows have turned up their noses at me, you know. They are so quick to criticize and yet such hypocrites! When you are a viscountess, they will forget it all soon enough, you'll see."

"I hope so." Maddie shook her head.

The night passed quietly, without any evidence of sleep-walking. The next day they all went to church, and again, the banns were read.

Maddie felt time rushing by, as palpable as a winter wind that shakes the eaves and makes the shutters knock against the house. What if these were the only weeks she might have with Adrian? It was almost enough to make her stand up and object herself, if it would give her more time. Oh, what was she thinking—they would all judge her mad, and rightly so!

Of course she didn't want to object. The longer she knew Adrian, the more time she spent with him, the more she truly wanted to marry him.

But if he had to leave her . . .

She glanced toward the viscount and saw that his expression seemed set. What had caught his attention?

At the front of the church a lesson was being read from the book of Numbers.

"So ye shall not pollute the land wherein ye are: for blood it defileth the land: and the land cannot be cleansed of the blood that is shed therein, but by the blood of him that shed it."

Always blood and killing, she thought. It seemed to haunt them, to haunt him, everywhere they went.

She was very quiet as they returned to the Applegate residence, as was the viscount, and her father seemed content to chat with Felicity, who sat beside him.

They enjoyed a luncheon, and then Felicity said her good-byes and continued home, with Thomas to escort her and carry her bag. Before she left, she told Maddie she had enjoyed her evening out.

"All of it?" Maddie couldn't help asking.

"Indeed," Felicity answered, grinning. "I must keep in practice, you see. Just know that you can call on me at any time."

"You were a great help," Maddie said, keeping her voice low. She still did not want her father to know that some of their neighbors were not offering great examples of kindness and forbearance.

Felicity found her cottage just as she had left it. Why had she expected otherwise? But it was a comfort to have Thomas with her when she opened the door and crossed the threshold, looking quickly about to check that everything was in place and no surprises lurked.

She thanked the Applegate servant, and when he took his leave, she latched the door behind him and sat down on a stool. She had to get water and firewood in, but she could rest for a moment and think about how pleasant it had been to get out of this tiny cottage and pretend that she still had a life.

Her cat came and wound about her ankles, brushing her skirt and purring.

"Did you miss me, little one?" Felicity murmured. She leaned over and stroked the soft fur of the cat's head and behind its ears, and the purring sounded even more loudly. "Yes, we all appreciate someone to love!"

Sighing, she lifted the cat into her lap and stroked its fur again, while her thoughts ranged widely, back to memories she had sworn to put behind her forever. Should she—dare she trust her new friends with the truth? Madeline Applegate had been so good, so generous, that Felicity felt very guilty about not being completely open. Or was it better to leave it all behind her, as she had sworn to? Surely that was the safest way?

A shadow flitted past the window. Felicity blinked, and her hand stopped moving. The cat ceased its purring and raised its head from its paws as if wondering what was wrong. Staring at the small window set high in the wall of her cottage, Felicity tried to see what had caused the moment of dimness.

Was it only a cloud obscuring the sun? A bird flying past? She strained to hear any suspicious noise, anything out of the way, but nothing peculiar met her ears. A crow cawed from a nearby field. An insect sounded from beneath a leaf; these were the only noises that floated through the open window.

She found she had been holding her breath, and she was so rigid that her back ached. She made herself draw a deep breath and release it slowly. Nonsense, she was being too vigilant; no one would find her here. Surely not!

Yet, to be sure, she sat very still for at least half an hour, and listened and watched the two windows—the cottage had no windows that looked north—and waited with a terrible patience. Nothing presented itself except the sounds of the fields and meadows beyond her small home. At last she reminded herself that darkness would be upon her soon, and she must make a fire—the cottage was growing colder by the moment. She also needed water.

So, despite the small hollow of fear that lingered in the pit of her stomach—a fear that these days she was seldom totally free of—Felicity changed back to her rusty black dress, tied her oldest shawl about her shoulders, and put on an apron to protect it. Then she put the small but very sharp dagger that no one, not even Madeline, knew that she owned into the waistband of her skirt where it was effectively hidden. Heart beating fast, she picked up her empty pail.

She eased back the latch on her door, opened it slowly so it would not creak, and peered out, looking both ways, still seeing nothing but quiet landscape. She needed a dog, she thought, more than a cat—a large, fierce dog that would growl if a stranger, an intruder, came near. She'd considered that many times, but she knew she could not afford to feed such a beast.

She shut the door behind her and walked steadily toward the spring. After climbing a small incline to the cleanest part, above where the cattle came to drink, she knelt to fill her bucket. Waiting for water to flow into it, she gritted her teeth—it seemed to take an interminable time. At last she could pull up the now heavy pail and stagger to her feet. When a twig snapped nearby, she jumped, almost dropping it and spilling some of the water, leaving a big damp stain down her apron.

When she whirled to see where the sound had come from, she observed only a single brown cow, staring back at her with big round eyes.

"Shoo," Felicity said, almost limp with relief that it was nothing more alarming. "Out of my way, please."

The cow ambled on, and Felicity walked as quickly as she could with her heavy burden, trying not to slosh the liquid over the edges of the tin pail. When she reached her doorway, she pushed open the door and stepped over, glancing about her. All looked the same. She set the water on her table then, before her dread could grow any deeper, picked up her small ax and set out toward the woodpile.

There were some lengths of wood already split from her

last session with the ax, and she put those into a pile, cracked a few more into kindling, and hacked a larger limb into pieces suitable for her small hearth. She set down the ax long enough to wrap her arms around the stack she had prepared, then retrieved the ax with one hand and, grunting a little, straightened and turned back toward the house.

And stopped, her heart in her throat.

Whose footprint was that?

It was surely not hers. The toe was the wrong shape, and it was much too large. It looked like a man's imprint, and from the depth, it seemed to come from a person of some weight.

Had it been there when she came out of the house?

She glanced around her. The sun was sinking behind the trees, and the light was dimming rapidly. She could not see anything out of the ordinary. Perhaps someone had walked past the cottage while she was away. . . .

At any rate, this was not a good time to meet a stranger, with her hands full—she took rapid steps toward her cottage, feeling her heart pounding in her chest and glancing back often. She reached the building without seeing anything else, and hurried through the doorway.

She dropped the wood into her woodbox and held on to the ax while she ran to latch the door and push the bar across it to secure it more firmly.

Then, feeling foolish but better safe than sorry, she knelt to check under her low bed. Seeing nothing but a few dust balls, she felt better. Her cat came to rub against her, and she petted the animal a bit absentedmindedly.

"Yes, I know. Perhaps I'm losing my mind," she said, sighing. Shivering—the air was certainly growing colder—she went back to the hearth and took kindling and small logs and arranged them to start a fire. When a small flame burned, she warmed her hands, and put on a kettle to boil water.

She would brew a cup of tea, and after drinking something warm, she would feel better, Felicity tried to tell herself. Madeline had sent a fresh loaf of bread home with her, and a tub of butter and some slices of ham, a rare delicacy on her budget. She could treat herself and take her mind off these fears. She was being silly, imagining danger like a child seeing a bogeyman in the dark and scaring herself over trifles.

Surely, that was all it was. But she shivered and drew her shawl closer about her shoulders. When her cat purred at her feet, Felicity picked up the animal and stroked the soft fur and wished her world was as uncomplicated.

After a dinner of cold meats and bread and fruit, they went up to bed early. Maddie was still tired from Saturday night's festivity, she thought ruefully, or more accurately, from bracing herself against her more judgmental neighbors' criticisms.

Although she fell quickly to sleep, she woke again later to hear a slight sound in the hallway. Somehow she was not surprised.

As the clock in the hall downstairs struck one, she grabbed a shawl and eased her door open. Sure enough, there was the familiar figure of her betrothed, again standing and staring into space, looking as if he existed in his own world, as he almost did.

He wore his trousers and his white shirt, and his untied neckcloth trailed in two long bands from either side of his throat; he must have been in the process of undressing when he'd thrown himself into a chair or on top of the bed and fallen into uneasy sleep.

What had set off his anxieties this time?

"Come along, dear heart," she whispered, hoping his

dreams were not nightmarish, and that the lakes of blood were not pursuing him once more.

But his words made her heart sink.

" 'For blood it defileth the land'," he muttered. "Blood, blood, blood—I have brought blood to this house. I must leave before she is harmed, too."

"She?" Momentarily nonplused, Maddie stared up at him. She had come out of her room so hastily she had not put on her slippers, and the floor felt icy against her bare feet. She tried not to shiver.

"Madeline—she must not be distressed . . ."

"Nonsense!" she retorted, louder than she had intended. Then, afraid someone would hear them, she whispered, "Come, my lord. Madeline will not be troubled. There is no blood here, but the night is cold and you will catch a chill. Come back to your bed."

"But the tracks—"

"You have not tracked any blood in, I promise you. There is no blood," she said firmly. "Here, take my hand."

She pulled his arm gently, and in a moment he followed her toward his room. When she got him safely inside and could shut the door behind them, Maddie breathed a long sigh of relief.

Now there was a new problem.

This time, he did not want to climb back into bed.

"The linen is spotless, and I am stained with blood," he protested. "I cannot."

"Adrian!" She was tired and cold, and the thought of crawling next to his warm, hard body was more than she could resist. But he wouldn't even sit down on the side of the bed. "You are not stained with blood, I promise you. If I get into bed, too, will you—where are you going? Wait!"

He walked across the room and she ran after him.

Grabbing his arm, she stopped him near the window. Silver moonlight poured through the panes, and the cold seemed more piercing at this side of the room. She shivered again.

He seemed oblivious to the cold.

"If Madeline knew how many men I have killed, how much blood is on my hands, she would never marry me, never love me, never choose to be close to me." His voice wavered.

Hearing him, Maddie thought her heart might break. He spoke of love, she thought, not just of a convenient marriage. He gave her hope and at the same time snatched it away.

"What do you mean, Adrian? The war? You were fighting for your country—you cannot feel guilty for every life you took in the midst of a war—you had no choice."

"But the blood," he repeated, his voice low. "The blood everywhere. And now . . ."

He hesitated, and held out his hands.

"The duel?" Madeline guessed. "You didn't plan to kill him, did you, Adrian?"

"No!" he said, his breath coming out in an explosive rush. "The bullet hit my arm, and the shot went wild."

"Then it's not your fault," she told him yet again, then shook her head at herself. How did you reason with someone locked in an unending nightmare?

He stared at something she couldn't see.

Madeline gave up trying to use logic and went to his bureau, taking up a linen towel and dampening it in his washbasin. Holding the bowl in one hand, the towel in the other, she came back to him and took one of his hands. "Look," she said. "I'm wiping away the blood, Adrian. It is gone, now."

She did the same with his other hand, and only hoped the touch of the moist cloth would penetrate his dreams.

He jumped at the dampness of the touch, and she almost lost her hold on the heavy china bowl. The water sloshed over him.

"Oh, no," she muttered. Now his shirt and trousers were covered with large wet spots. Would he wake from the touch of the cool water?

No, but he shivered.

"Now you really must get into bed." She put the bowl back onto the bureau and drew him to the bed. "Please, Adrian. The air is frigid, and you will catch a chill. I am cold, too. Come into the bed with me."

She drew back the bedclothes and pushed him gently, crawling up onto the bed and hoping he would follow. This time he hesitated only a moment, then sat down on the edge of the mattress.

She leaned closer to him and pulled off his neckcloth, tossing it to the foot of the bed. "Here," she said. "Take off your shirt, Adrian. It is soaked."

Mutely, he obeyed, and with her help, pulled it over his head. That too was tossed aside. In a moment he was naked from the waist up. Maddie did not feel brave enough to tackle the issue of his trousers and underwear so she simply patted the pillows.

"Come," she said. "Lie with me, Adrian. You need to get warm."

Without saying another word, he lay down in the bed and she was able to pull up the sheet and blankets and try to cover his torso, afraid he would indeed take a chill. The viscount lay passively, allowing her to wrap him in the bedclothes . . . for a few moments. But when she tried to tuck the covers around him, he moved suddenly, pulling her down against him, holding her tightly.

Maddie gasped in surprise, but she did not struggle, thinking it best to lie still until she saw what he was about. He might go on to another phase of his fantasy and forget what he had been dreaming of, all on his own.

Although he kept her inside his embrace, he simply lay for a long moment holding her close, and she found it very pleasant. Feeling his strong arms wrapped around her, the firm body pressed so tightly to her own, almost at once she found she was no longer shivering with cold.

Indeed, the warmth spread pleasantly through her whole frame, from the top of her body all the way down to her toes, and in the center of her belly, she felt a strange craving that made her want to press herself even closer, feel him hard and undeniably male as he—

Now what was he doing?

To her disappointment, he put her aside again. Ah well, while she was free of his embrace, she had best slip away and get back to her own bedroom before he woke and discovered her in such a compromising position. She blushed just considering it. Somehow, the viscount in a dream state was less intimidating.

Perhaps because he seemed more innocent, more vulnerable, even though he was still highly desirable. She stared at his face for a long moment, then shook her head at herself. No, no, this would never do. She was the one who had wagged her finger at her sisters, lecturing about self-control and upholding the family honor.

Not that they had necessarily listened. Lauryn had married too early to have caused any concern. Her sister Juliana had grinned and, aside from some boyish escapades chasing birds or animals on the moors, pretty much stayed on the beaten path. The twins, however; the twins had carved their own paths and seldom were they what one would expect of ladies of quality. In fact, one might as well give up trying.

But now she was the one who had set the whole shire atwitter, and she was sure her sisters would never let her live it down. Nor could she blame them, Maddie thought, her reflections dark.

She tiptoed toward the doorway, then jumped in her turn when she found that the viscount had left the bed and whirled to grab her, lift her nightgown, and pull it over her head—much as she had done for his soaked shirt—and pull it off.

"Adrian, wait!" she tried to object, but her protest was muffled by the cloth that surrounded her face.

Then the material was lifted away, and she found herself wearing only her drawers and a deep blush that spread all the way down her throat.

She folded her arms over her chest. "Pardon me, I would like my nightgown back." She sounded ridiculously prim.

He didn't seem to hear her. Instead, with the same economy of movement, he lifted her and tossed her lightly onto the bed.

Too startled for an instant to try to scramble off, she lay there and found that he had come right behind her. He put one strong arm across her chest, effectively holding her in place in the center of the bed, and then he kissed her.

Afterwards, she would remember it as *the* kiss.

His lips were so firm and warm and so insistent that she couldn't seem to think of anything except how it brought her whole body to life. She gave up any thought of remonstration. Instead of trying to slide away, she came of her own accord closer to him, pressing her breasts against his chest, her legs closer to his hard thighs. His arm slid to pull her into him, and she put her arms around his neck and clung to him, fears of consequences forgotten.

As before, he tasted of port wine, strong and heady, and his tongue slipped now between her lips and dared her to open further. Maddie thought she might drown in this wine-tasting cloud of unfamiliar sensation, but if Adrian, awake or asleep, wanted her, she would give herself, body and soul, into his keeping and fear nothing . . . so she opened her lips and allowed him entrance.

The strong thrust of his tongue made her feel as if even her spirit was being consumed, an exhilarating illusion. He pulled her whole body closer, and she almost lost her awareness of where she ended and he began. When he moved to kiss her cheek and her neck and nibble her ear, that, too, sent blood rushing to her head in dizzying spirals until she thought she must soon touch the ceiling.

Hoping to give him some of the same exquisite sensations she was experiencing, she ran her fingers along his naked back. He made a small sound deep in his throat. Encouraged, she did it again, and then moved her hands to his chest, and up his neck, tracing hard ripples of muscle.

Mercy, how strongly forged were his arms, and how she loved to have them wrapped around her. She traced them lovingly, then dropped her hands to his hips, but found she lacked the courage to go lower. He put his hands over hers, and pushed them down, down.

She felt the firm lines of his stomach, the hard muscles there, and then, curling hairs and—she gasped and tried to draw her hand away, but he brought it gently back.

This was his male member. How firm it was, just like the muscles in his arms and chest—and, well, she knew about the animals in the farm . . . Maddie gave herself a shake. Stop being a ninny, she scolded herself. This would go inside her? She felt another tremor of anticipation or nervousness, she wasn't sure which.

She felt a strange yearning in her body at the thought. Wishing she had had answers from her letters to her sisters, she thought of Felicity's advice. She should follow her instincts, the widow had said. What did her instincts tell her to do now? She put both her hands around his shaft and felt him quiver as she stroked it gently—yes, he liked that—and she stroked his thighs and the soft dark hair around the base; he moved with small thrusts, making deep sounds in his throat.

She hungered for more herself, without knowing just what it was that she wanted. He reached to push the last piece of her clothing down, and she shivered, not from cold because by now they were providing their own heat, but from expectation of the enormous step she was about to take.

Yet she did not wish to stop, either. Every ounce of her body wanted him, wanted to join with this man, wanted to meld with his body—a body so finely made and so beautiful, holding a spirit so loving and true.

She reached down to help him rid her legs of the cumbersome underwear, and then they were both naked. He pulled her to him, and she delighted in the warm, intimate touch of his skin against her own, from her head to her toes. It was a voluptuous sensation, both completely satisfying and at the same time causing her to want so much more, and she reveled in it!

Once more she threw her arms about his neck and pressed herself against him, thinking nothing was as good as the feel of his body against hers. She kissed him, loving the touch of his lips when he returned the embrace even more forcefully . . . and when he moved his body, placing himself so that he was poised to enter her, Maddie's eyes widened, but she did not protest—but despite herself, she tensed.

And she knew, somehow, even in the darkness, when he blinked and opened his eyes.

Ten

His eyes had been open before, as they usually were when he sleepwalked, but not really seeing. This was different, and she knew it.

"Madeline?"

Oh, dear heaven, what would he think of her? Would he call off the betrothal? He might think her too wanton to be his wife, Maddie thought, belatedly realizing all the implications of suddenly finding your fiancée naked in your bed. Glad he could not see her surely flaming face in the dark, she ducked her head.

"Madeline, did I force you to my bed? Or hold you here against your will?"

She could lie, of course. She could not read his tone, or tell if he was displeased or shocked. He sounded—he sounded—what did she hear in his tone? She could not dissemble.

"No, Adrian," she said, her own voice flat. "You were sleepwalking again. I brought you back to your chamber to get you safely back in bed, and—and—it came about that—"

He lowered his face and kissed her ear.

Surprised, she jumped.

He dropped his face even lower and kissed the skin just beneath her ear, and then the delicate skin of her neck. Shivering at the delicious sensations, Maddie could barely lie still. "Adrian!"

"As long as you are here of your own volition."

"You are not shocked?"

"Shocked? My darling girl, I am ecstatic. I have wanted to do this since the night I found you in the gazebo. But I had to be sure you wanted it, too." He kissed the sensitive skin where her neck joined her shoulder, and next she felt the soft touch of his tongue.

Unable to lie still beneath such provocative behavior, she moved restlessly on the sheets. "Adrian! You were not—I mean—were you really—you were not feigning?"

"Was I really sleepwalking? Sadly, yes. It's an unfortunate habit I had as a child, and it has returned since the war. But I do admit that for the last several minutes I think I have been half awake. At any rate, I was aware of a very lifelike and delightful dream . . ."

She blushed again, but now his hands were roaming over her body even as his mouth still lingered at her shoulder. He touched the tender skin of her breast, and Maddie knew that she gave a silent gasp as his supple fingers ringed her breast, circling closer and closer in lazy motions until they touched the nipple, easing it into a taut alertness that made her feel as if she might shout into the night. When he put his hand on her other breast, she clapped her hand over her mouth, afraid the spasms of pleasure might burst past her lips despite her best intentions.

He leaned over her and kissed her again, his lips hard and firm, and Maddie thought she might be drowning once more in sensations so deep and languorous that it hardly seemed they could get any better.

And then he moved one hand down to the soft vee between her legs, and Maddie found that yes, there was more, and she wanted it, and she was so ready for him that her body arched on its own accord.

"Yes," Adrian murmured, "yes, beloved." He slipped his hand lower and pushed his fingers into her inner self, and the resulting ripple of pleasure took her breath.

"Oh, Adrian," she said, not expecting this. When he stroked, she gasped at the sensation and found herself pushing against his hand. She discovered that she was wet with wanting, and now he moved himself again, positioning his body over her—she could just see him shift in the moonlight from the window.

"I think you are ready, my love, more than ready," he said, and he sounded breathless too.

Maddie couldn't even think of speaking; she was biting her lip to hold back the moans of pure need. Suddenly he thrust deeply into her, and she gasped. There was a twinge of pain, but only for a moment—then he pulled back, leaned to kiss her again, and before she could even wonder about the discomfort, pushed once more. This time, the blissful tide of feeling carried her deep, deep into the rushing ecstasy of their joining. It was so intense and delightful that she almost moaned aloud. Perhaps she did—she was aware only of diving forward into a sea of wonderful sensations.

They rose and fell together, their bodies naked, haloed by the faint golden glow of moonlight. The harder he thrust, the harder she pushed against him, and the more exquisite were the waves of pleasure that washed over her—and surely, him, too? They were one, they were one being, joined at the heart of their existence with a pulsating core of energy that sent back ripples of pleasure to rebound and wash over them again and again as they found the rhythm that their bodies demanded.

This was everything she had dreamed of and more. He rose and fell above her, and each time they met, the ripple of feeling that rushed over her skin seemed to ignite feelings of exquisite joy—she felt she could barely contain them. Together they seem to sizzle and spark until she thought that from the friction of their fevered union, the sheets, the bed, the room might catch fire. Yet she would not have stopped for anything.

What had ever been so sweet, so delicious, so deeply resoundingly pleasurable? This was beyond thought, beyond reason, when they rose to the highest peak—to the final crest of the utmost pinnacle, Maddie felt giddy from lack of breath till she thought she might not be able to bear the pleasure it was so intense. Then, like shooting stars, like meteors bursting from the sky, like a heart filled past contentment with love surfeit and true—at last Adrian fell back against the bed and gathered her into his arms, both too exhausted to speak.

This, then, was love between a man and a woman.

Maddie lay her cheek against Adrian's chest and marveled.

Filled with the delicious languor that came after joining, it seemed she had only allowed her eyelids, which had felt so heavy, to close for a moment. Then suddenly she was aware that Adrian was kissing her again. When she opened her eyes, she saw with alarm that outside the window, she could make out faint streaks of grayness. A lone sentinel tweeted the first notes that would soon be joined by scores of birds in trees all around the house.

"My dearest, I would be delighted to resume our lovemaking, but I fear your faithful maidservant might start her rounds soon, and—"

"Oh, heavens, if Bess should find me here!" Just the idea had Maddie sitting straight up in bed, then grabbing her nightgown to cover her bare body.

"Yes, that was my thought." He grinned, looking quite unrepentant.

"Wretch!" She made a face at him and leaned over to give him a quick kiss. She pulled her gown quickly over her head and turned toward the door, almost falling off the bed.

"'Ware the edge!" Adrian leaned over to grab her just in time.

Feeling foolish, Maddie managed to get her head through the neck of her gown, then pushed her arms through. "I have to go." She ran for the door, opened it, and checked the hall, then looked back and smiled ruefully at her fiancé—and lover.

Eyes tender, he smiled back.

She ran for her room.

*She was in the wrong house. It was too big to be the cot-*tage and too old and drafty to be the house in London. While she tried to think where she was, Felicity smelled the smoke. No, no, she had lived this before—how could it be happening again? The smoke was in her nose and throat and mouth—she could taste it, smell it, and it made her cough as she fought to breathe. The hair on the back of her neck prickled with an awareness of danger. She had no time to worry about how or why this was real, she had to get out.

She stretched out her arms for something to grasp, but she felt only the threadbare sheets of her bed. She tried to push back the bedclothes but they seemed to be wrapped too tightly around her body, clutching her like reeds pulling down a drowning man. Feeling more frantic with every moment that passed, she scissored her legs against them, fought and kicked again and again, and at last the heavy covers gave way. She half fell, half jumped off the bed, lurching to her feet.

The air was murky with smoke, and drawing in the foul air, she choked. She couldn't breathe. She caught up a shawl lying on the chair near the bed and held it over her mouth to filter the air as she groped for a candle to light so that she could see through the gloomy darkness, but there wasn't time.

She had to get out.

"Help me!" she called, her voice choking in the smoky air, but no one answered.

She remembered that she was alone; everyone she knew had been left behind—when she had been disgraced, when all the other ladies she had once known had turned their backs.

This was no time for memories. The smoke was growing thicker. Her head had a strange buzzing inside it, and her lungs hurt with the constant struggle to breathe.

She stumbled over a three-legged stool that loomed out of the darkness and fell to her hands and knees. Closer to the floor, the air was cleaner, and for a moment her head cleared a little. She pushed the stool aside and crawled toward the outer door. It was her last chance, she knew instinctively, her last chance to live before the smoke became too dense and she passed out and died in the conflagration.

Pushed by a desperate will to live, she crawled inch by inch toward the door. She could feel the heat of the flames at her back, hear the crackle of the blaze. She was so very afraid, and so tired of gasping for breath. If she could just lay her head down on her smoke-stained hands and rest for a moment . . .

No, no, she shrieked at herself from some distance above the small figure in the grimy nightgown, already streaked with smoke and falling cinders. Don't stop now!

Get up, get up! Somehow, she continued to creep toward the heavy wooden door. She reached it, ready to pull it open and tumble out into the clean outer air.

But the door wouldn't open—

Gasping, Felicity sat straight up in bed.

This was the way the nightmare always ended.

There was no reason for her eyes to be filled with tears, she told herself, rubbing away the treacherous liquid. She had survived, the door *had* opened. . . . But if the person who had set the fire—for she had never believed it to be an accident, as the villagers had judged—had thought to secure the door somehow, she could never have lived to move and try to hide her identity once again.

Shivering as she pushed away the memories, Felicity rubbed the small burn scars on her forearms that she usually kept hidden beneath long sleeves. As she did, she looked up at one of the small windows in the cottage wall. Blinking, she made out a man's face staring down at her.

After their wonderful night of lovemaking, Maddie thought it best to be extra circumspect, so she and the viscount met again only at the breakfast table, where she barely had the nerve to look at him. She felt as if her change in circumstances must be printed upon her forehead.

Could her father tell that she was no longer a maiden? Surely not, but still she fought with her treacherous too-ready blushes and strove to keep an even complexion, concentrating on her toast and porridge.

She shot Adrian only an occasional veiled peek from beneath her lowered lashes.

But he *would* send her those mischievous glances— with that glint in his eyes that made her want to giggle at all the wrong times, when her father was discussing the men's chess game and the viscount's excellent gambit . . . excellent, indeed!

She could remark on some excellent gambits, she told herself, and had to bite her lip to keep from collapsing into a fit of laughter. She took a sip of tea so hastily that she almost sloshed the liquid onto the tablecloth.

It was just as well that her father took Adrian off for yet another game of chess after breakfast.

"You don't mind, do you, my dear?" he said to his daughter.

"Of course not, Papa," she lied, smiling at them both.

"Chess is *almost* my favorite pastime," the viscount added, giving them both a cordial smile and, when Mr. Applegate had turned away, adding a wink for Maddie's benefit.

"Oh, is there another game you prefer? Perhaps we can try it instead," her father suggested.

She had to pinch herself when her father didn't see to keep from giggling, and she gave Adrian a reproachful look for his teasing. He immediately sobered and gave her a repentant bow.

"No, no, I like chess very well indeed," he said, "and we cannot stop our tournament at such a time; I am almost catching up."

They left for the study, and Maddie went to the kitchen to help Bess clear away the breakfast dishes and get some of the dinner menu started. Then, unable to be still, she climbed the steps to her room and, drawn once more to the neat bundle of her mother's letters, sat on her bed and held them to her heart.

Had her mother known such delights as Maddie and Adrian had shared last night, after she had married her father?

Maddie wished her mother had lived long enough so that she could talk to her now, ask her questions, request advice on her upcoming marriage.

She looked down at the letters, and the temptation was too strong to resist. She decided she could take another quick look. She drew out one of the letters and found that her mother was remembering a stroll they had taken through the garden.

"Our favorite rosebush is blooming, my love, and every time I see a new blossom, I remember how carefully you trimmed it, and now your care is being rewarded. In just the same way, I know my heart is safe in your loving hands."

How sweet, Maddie thought. She had not known that her father had ever been interested in the garden; he had not shown much concern for flowers or ornamental bushes in recent years. Perhaps after her mother died, he had lost his inclination.

She tucked the letter back into the pile, and, with a look at the sunlight and how the morning had advanced, realized she should go back to help Bess with the luncheon.

When the meal was on the table, and the men had left their chessboard behind and joined her in the dining room, she managed to work a question about the garden into the conversation.

"Did my mother have a favorite rosebush, Papa, that you remember?"

"Eh?" He paused with a slice of venison on his knife, and looked as if he were trying to recall. "Really, my dear, your mother liked all the flowers. She was quite a hand with the garden, always out working with the plants. I'm afraid it's never looked quite the same since she left us." He sighed, and Maddie found she hadn't the heart to ask him any more.

Perhaps it was as she'd thought; he simply had lost his zest for horticulture without her mother there to share his interests.

She let the conversation swirl back to other topics, but when they rose from the table and her father retired for his afternoon rest, she and the viscount wandered outside once more, and this time, hand in hand, they headed for the weathered bench at the far end of the garden.

Adrian sat, and she moved to sit close beside him. Remembering the passion of the night before, she leaned against his body, delighting in the firmness of his torso, the strength of his arms and legs.

"My love," he murmured, putting one arm around her shoulders. "What a joy you are!"

She slid across the bench until she was almost sitting in his lap. He pulled her even closer and scooped her up until she was indeed sitting on top of him—and, oh my, she could feel him suddenly hard against the underside of her legs.

"Do you think we dare?" he murmured.

She glanced around, not sure how much someone could see. But the hedge protected them from view, and she knew that Thomas was inside the house having his meal in the kitchen. How could she be sensible with the blood racing through her veins? She leaned into his kiss and threw her arms about his shoulders.

He shifted so that she could lift and rearrange her skirts—Maddie found she was becoming shockingly profligate at this business of lovemaking—and if they could not quite complete the act, it was still most pleasurable to feel him hard against the tender skin between her legs. She found she could rock slightly back and forth and bring forth exquisitely delightful sensations. She was not the only one who had to bite back moans. It was the viscount who made small sounds deep in his throat, now.

"Sweet girl, what you are doing to me—"

"Should I stop?" she paused for a moment.

"Good lord, no!" he said hastily.

She resumed her back and forth motion, and again, the sensations induced were deeply gratifying.

In a moment Adrian slipped one hand beneath her body. He inserted two fingers inside her, and the intensity of her pleasure grew once more. She gasped, and almost rose to her tiptoes, but he pulled her back down.

"Now, now," he said very low. "We must keep up appearances. Or lie low with them."

This struck Maddie as funny and she would have laughed if she had not been so consumed with feelings of pure physical fervor. She thought she might melt away as he continued to stroke and pulsate her soft inner folds in just the right places, and her response grew greater and greater till she thought that the shivers of delight that ran through her might literally turn her inside out. The feelings grew and circled and exploded outward.

At last she gave a soft cry, stretched upward once more, then fell into his arms. Adrian held her tightly and kissed her lips, her cheeks, her eyelids, and even the top of her head.

For a few minutes she lay in his arms with her eyes shut, totally sated, limp, and happy. She discovered that there were tears on her cheeks—tears of total physical and emotional completion. It was an amazing feeling, yet she felt rather selfish.

When she opened her eyes at last, she looked at him with concern. "But what about you?" she whispered.

"I'm all right, my sweet. Another time, when we have a more private space," he told her, grinning ruefully. "At least I could make you happy."

He seemed sincere, so she put away her concern. It hadn't occurred to her that it could be done like this. So many things to learn, Maddie thought. She wished that they could have years together to teach them to each other.

Afraid that Thomas might come out of the house, she reluctantly sat back beside the viscount, and he sat with his arm about her. They talked in low voices.

"Do you also enjoy the garden, as your mother did?" Adrian asked her, as they gazed over the late-flowering plants.

She looked over the flower beds. "I'm afraid I lack time to give them the care they deserve. They are not what they once where, as my father pointed out."

He lifted her hand and kissed her fingers gently. "I know that you work very hard, Madeline, and you could not put more effort into aiding your father, inside and outside the house. You are a dutiful daughter."

Feeling a sudden rush of renewed anxiety, Maddie stared up into his face. "You do understand why I feel I cannot leave him, Adrian? He could not cope on his own, and with only two elderly servants to aid him. But even if there were more, I could not leave him to suffer a lonely existence with only servants around him."

"I know," the viscount said, his voice tender as he looked down at her. "You have a very kind heart, my dear, and also a spirit—and a body—meant for love. I honor you for it."

"But the more I know you and the more time we spend together . . ." she tried to tell him. "I wish that we—that I . . ." If we had had a chance for a real marriage, she thought as she held his hand tightly. If you were not already cursed . . .

She could not go, and he could not stay. How could they find a way to keep their love alive, to have time to nurture it, to have the time to delight in it?

"I don't want to lose you," she murmured. He tightened his grip on her hand, but didn't answer.

The air was cool but pleasant, and with his arm around her shoulders, the familiar feel of the bench beneath them, the bronze and gold and white of the autumn flowers and the glory of the last leaves on the trees making a pleasing show all around them, and the gilded rays of the sunlight, it was a golden hour, and she wished she could hold on to it forever.

If she concentrated, could she keep them inside this bubble of time—stop the clock's clicking hand? Keep all evils away?

But most of the leaves had already fallen; the flowers were already dropping their petals, one by one. It seemed to Maddie that she could almost see one white petal detach itself and drift away in the breeze.

How could she slow—no, stop—time?

She did not want him to leave—she did not wish for Adrian to go away—she knew suddenly that he had captured her heart—she had no doubt at all.

Adrian had taught her not just passion, but love. She had fallen in love when she had least expected it. The convenient marriage, the contract for the sake of propriety, had transformed into an emotion that stirred her to the depths of her soul, and the sudden illness that had trapped her in the middle of a stormy night might turn out to be the dearest blessing of her life.

She lay her head against his chest where she could hear the comforting beat of his heart—his vigor, his vitality, the reassurance that he was here, now—and felt him wrap his arms about her.

Stay, she thought, stay. Dear Lord, ward off all ills.

If only they possessed some old wizardry—a magic wand, or a fairy godmother who would grant a deepest wish—anything that would guarantee a boon.

But the sunlight was already changing its angle. The air was cooling, and she heard a call as someone came up the path in front of the house. It was Felicity, come to chaperone as they had another dinner party to attend tonight.

Maddie raised her head, and they had to slip apart.

"I begin to see the many advantages of marriage," the

viscount muttered. "Oh, for the privilege of the shut door and the right to place all the world outside!"

She gave him a reluctant grin, then went to welcome their guest.

That night when they were ready to leave, Felicity wore her remade lavender gown and carried her new reticule and an Italian fan and looked very fine; even Maddie's papa commented, which made their guest turn pink.

Maddie was delighted to see how pleased her friend was to have a new outfit to enjoy. She found that her own new gowns from the dressmaker in Ripon were a great lift to her spirits, especially when with every dinner party, she felt as if she faced another gauntlet to run.

She admitted as much to the viscount when she met him on the landing upstairs before they went down.

"Then say no," he told her at once. "Send your excuses. We do not have to indulge these provincial hostesses who think they are so lofty in their entertaining. I would not have you be distressed, Madeline!"

"But I will not have them thinking they have bested me, either, Adrian," she pointed out, her tone even. "They are only a minor annoyance, really." Which was not quite true, but they were and would continue to be neighbors, and she would have to live here after the viscount had departed again, which was too painful to discuss out loud. At least her father did not know how she was distressed by some of her more vindictive neighbors' petty attacks.

To her chagrin, the first person she saw when they walked into the hostess's home tonight was her least favorite neighbor, Mrs. Masham. Maddie knew just who would lead the charge of belittling observations, disguised as they might be as kindly inquiries.

The matron didn't even wait till the ladies were alone to start her commentary. "I'm so glad you are quite recovered, Miss Applegate," Mrs. Masham said, in her usual sharp tones. "Since you were too ill to come to *my* dinner party last week."

"We are all happy that Miss Applegate has recovered," the viscount agreed, his tone amiable. "She had another of her headaches, which as you know, make her totally unable to function."

"As *you* know, at least, since it led to the two of you spending the night alone in the woods—but, dear me, how clumsy of me to bring up such a subject," Mrs. Masham retorted, fanning herself as if disconcerted, though her eyes looked as hard as always.

Adrian met her suggestive stare with an innocent look of his own. "Just so."

Maddie had to swallow a slightly hysterical giggle.

"All of Miss Applegate's friends are distressed by her sad tendency toward these unfortunate headaches, and her inability to control their timing," Felicity added. "Tell us how your dinner party went, Mrs. Masham. I'm sure you are a notable hostess?"

She allowed her remark to end on just a hint of a question mark, and that prompted the other woman to plunge into an indignant description of her party and how delicious were her many dishes and how lively her dinner conversation and how spirited her playing at the pianoforte when she entertained her guests afterwards (which made Maddie reflect that missing such a "treat" was almost worth her suffering).

"I suppose it's just as well that the two of you will be married soon. This coming Sunday will be the third reading of the banns, if I am counting correctly, will it not?" their inquisitioner demanded.

"I believe your counting skills are quite adequate," Adrian murmured.

This time Maddie did giggle.

"What was that?"

"Ah," their current hostess, a plump, good-natured lady, Mrs. Fritzwell, jumped courageously into the fray. "I remember when my own banns were read. That excited, I was, and a bit worried, too, that we would not get my wedding dress finished in time. I supposed you are sewing madly, Miss Applegate?"

"Oh, yes," Maddie agreed. "Although we have made a trip into Ripon to a dressmaker there, which will aid in the effort considerably."

"Indeed." Their hostess looked impressed. "Now that is good news. You will not be so anxious. I used to dream that skeins of thread and bolts of silk were chasing me around the bed. Not the best way to start off one's married life, I can tell you." She turned quite innocently to gaze toward the viscount, who had suddenly put on a blank expression.

Maddie was trying hard not to laugh once more. "No, indeed, how unfortunate."

"No, however, dear Mr. Fritzwell assured me that he would wed me in my petticoat, if necessary, didn't you, my dear?" Their hostess looked fondly at her husband.

He had been discussing last week's shooting with a couple of male guests and glanced up with an absent expression. "Right you are, old thing." He turned back to the men. "A splendid rack, twelve points, at the least."

"Such a romantic, he is," his wife concluded.

"After the third reading, you can wed any morning you choose," Mrs. Masham continued, like a dog that will not let go of a bone, "a quiet ceremony is no doubt most appropriate under the circumstances."

"On the contrary," the viscount said, his tone quite pleasant, and his smile unblemished, although Maddie at least could make out the adversarial gleam in his eyes. "It will not be quiet at all. In fact, I take the opportunity forthwith to invite you all to come and witness our ceremony."

"You do?" she murmured to her fiancé, but he simply smiled at her.

"Of course, should not all your friends be a party to our happiness?" he murmured back.

And such friends they were, too, she thought. But she could see he was too exasperated at the annoying Mrs. Masham to take back his blanket invitation, even if he could without being impossibly rude. Oh, well, she didn't mind. In fact, the whole world could come and see them wed—the blazing joy she would be feeling might flash across the whole orb itself, outshine the sun and blind the heavens!

Except, if it meant that the viscount would leave, would feel compelled to continue his wanderings in order to protect her from . . . no, she mustn't think about that just now.

Mrs. Masham had a sour expression on her face. She turned to locate Mr. Masham, who was standing in the corner of the room drinking a large glass of wine, and crooked a finger to summon him. He frowned and affected not to see her signal.

His hairline was receding, and his stomach expanding, Maddie noted. And he had a stain on his waistcoat. Her sister Juliana, who had once been courted by Masham, would be more than happy that she had not seriously considered his suit; Maddie would have to remember to mention that in her next letter. Not that Juliana's husband was not already a thousand times more preferable in every respect.

They were called in to dinner, and Maddie gave Adrian a quick smile before they had to separate. "You are a magnificent champion, my lord," she said, keeping her tone formal. "Thank you."

"Thank you, my lady," he responded, his own tone as stately.

She laughed. "I am not your lady yet."

"Perhaps not to the rest of the world," he interjected. "But in my heart, you are."

This sent her into the dining room in such a good mood that she hardly minded that her dinner partner on one side was over ninety and spent the meal extolling the virtues of Dr. AllGood's Miraculous Lotion for Arthritic Pain and her partner on the other just out of the schoolroom and too shy to speak at all, keeping his face almost in his plate.

No one monopolized the conversation and took over the table, and no one—to her relief—brought up the topic of the recent war.

When the ladies withdrew, leaving the men to their wine and conversation, she had Felicity by her side, so even with the poisonous Mrs. Masham among the women, Maddie did not feel alone.

She was not even dismayed when the waspish matron made a point of sitting down across from her. Happily, Felicity had taken the chair beside her, so Maddie could not be completely ambushed. She kept thinking in terms of savage peoples, Maddie thought, hiding a grin. But then Mrs. Masham, despite her new gown with its latest most fashionable trim, which she spent the first ten minutes telling everyone in the room about, had the most barbaric heart of anyone here.

"I suppose you will soon outshine us all, will you not, Miss Applegate?" The barbarian herself suddenly turned back to Maddie, who jumped slightly. She had made the mistake of taking her attention away from her formidable neighbor.

"Pardon me?"

"When you become Viscountess Weller?" another lady explained, her tone arch.

"Yes, indeed. I'm sure your clothing allowance will be much increased," Mrs. Masham almost purred. "Why, if such a thought had occurred to me, I might have gotten lost in the wood on a stormy night myself."

The silence in the room was suddenly tense.

Maddie raised her brows. This was a truly nasty cut—to suggest that she would deliberately fake her illness in order to trap the viscount into marriage and thus improve her standard of living, enrich her place in life.

For a moment, she thought she was literally seeing red. She opened her mouth to blast this insufferable woman—

"Money is not everything," another voice, cool and in command, cut in. It was Felicity, sounding detached and hardly interested. "Taste is even more crucial. For example, that color of blue in your oh-so-fashionable trim does not *quite* clash with the sea green in your gown, and I would not be so rude to point it out if it did, but if so, it would, of course, quite ruin the effect of your lovely and I'm sure quite costly new gown. But it does go to show that having sufficient funds does not, in itself, guarantee the final effect of one's couture."

"My outfit is perfectly matched!" Mrs. Masham snapped.

"Of course it is," Felicity agreed, her tone tranquil.

The other ladies simply watched, their expressions exhibiting every emotion from fascination to horror.

Maddie, quite forgotten, had the chance to pull herself together before she made a total fool of herself. To bite the odious woman's head off, as much as she longed to do it, would only convince Mrs. Masham, and many of the others, that the charges might have some truth in them. She had to look unmoved, perhaps even amused. Thank goodness for Felicity. Maddie drew a calming breath.

Mrs. Masham sputtered a bit more about her dressmaker and how dear were her prices, and how perfect her feel for color and hue and fashion. No one had the inclination to argue. When at last she spun to a halt, Felicity spoke again.

"Has anyone else seen more evidence of that band of gypsies still lingering in the neighborhood?"

This topic brought immediate response.

"Oh, my, yes," their hostess answered, fluttering her fan and looking relieved at the change in subject. "They stole a lamb from one of Mr. Fritzwell's tenants, and the poor man was quite agitated, as well he might be."

"They snatched a whole day's worth of clean wash from behind my gardener's cottage, clothesline and all!" another lady said.

"And they not only stripped my best cherry tree of all its fruit but dug out the tree," another lady said, putting down her teacup so abruptly that it clattered. "What on earth they will do with it, I cannot think, as everyone knows they never settle, but only wander about."

"Oh, they'll sell it, the next village they come to," another woman said darkly. "But you'll never see it again."

The other ladies nodded, and as more complaints were exchanged, Maddie said quietly to Felicity, "Have you had anything stolen, Felicity?"

Her friend shook her head. "But I've seen footprints around my cottage. And this morning when I woke, I thought I saw a man staring into my cottage window."

"Oh, my dear! How alarming," Maddie said.

Felicity looked grim. "I wasn't sure, at first, if it was only part of my dream—I had just opened my eyes. But later, I went outside and saw footprints in the dirt beneath the window, and I'm sure they are not mine; the size is wrong, for one thing." She shivered. "It does make one a bit—well, they can be a rough lot. One hears about attacks that are most disconcerting."

"You will certainly stay with us tonight," Maddie told her. "And perhaps you should stay for a while, till we know that this band is gone out of the neighborhood."

Here she was worried about sharp-tongued gossips, and Felicity was living alone in an isolated cottage, subject to wandering vandals, who might be even more dangerous than they knew, Maddie thought.

The men were joining them now, and their hostess was making up card tables. After a few rounds of cards, the party broke up, and Maddie was happy enough to say her farewells.

In the carriage ride home, they could talk softly, and when they reached home, she found her father still up. She told him about the gypsies and their transgressions, and he agreed at once that Felicity should remain with them for the time being.

"As long as you like," he added. "You are certainly not safe down that isolated lane all on your own."

Felicity's smile was tremulous. "You're very kind," she said, her voice husky.

"You have enough with you for tonight, I think," Maddie said. "Tomorrow, Thomas and I will go with you to help bring back what you need for a longer stay."

Felicity gave her an impulsive hug, then Maddie showed her upstairs to the guest chamber next to the viscount's room. If there was a drawback to having another guest, Maddie thought, it was that it made it more difficult—or even impossible—to slip into the viscount's room for more forbidden trysts. But perhaps having a full-time chaperone would remind Maddie that she must behave.

Too bad that behaving properly was not at all what she wished to do!

She saw Adrian watching her from his doorway and knew from his impish grin that he was almost certainly reading her thoughts.

"Are you sorry?" she paused to whisper to him as Felicity went inside and closed her bedroom door.

"What must be, must be," he answered, keeping his voice low. "It's true that she was not safe where she was, all alone. And as for us—"

"Yes?"

"I suppose we should be chaste in thought and deed, as the vicar would advise," he answered.

She must have looked most disappointed because he laughed silently at her expression and leaned to give her a sudden hard kiss.

"Or else," he whispered into her ear, "very very quiet."

Grinning, she kissed him back and walked with lighter heart to her own room.

Once inside, she washed and changed into her night-gown and climbed into bed. But the impression of the kiss lingered, and she hungered for more. Her bed seemed very empty. She wished for some way to signal Adrian to come and join her. She could tiptoe her way back down the hall to his room, of course, but every step was a chance to be seen, and she would blush indeed if they were caught in their illicit lovemaking . . . not that Felicity would tell her father, but still.

Sighing, Maddie tried to redirect her thoughts—not easy with her body craving the viscount's practiced and loving touch. She reached over to the table beside her bed and picked up the packet of her mother's letters, once again reaching into the pile and selecting one at random.

Just a glimpse, she told herself, just a few lines. Somehow that made her feel less intrusive than reading the whole letter, the whole stack.

When she unfolded the paper, her heart seemed to skip

a beat. The handwriting was different! This letter was not written in her mother's flowing soft script. Perhaps her father—no, no, nor was it in her father's more compact hand.

She had seen his writing in his household budget books, and in short notes to merchants and other business letters she had sometimes had reason to add her own notes to or carry to the village for him.

What could this be?

She should close it and put it back, one part of her mind said.

Maddie knew she should not read it, but now that she had seen it—now that she knew her mother had kept a letter from some unknown person—she could just as easily have stopped breathing.

Perhaps it was only a fond female friend, Maddie tried to tell herself. Yes, it was only a dear friend from some other shire . . .

But a quick glance at the salutation ended that theory, as the letter began:

> *My dearest love:*
>   *How did I ever survive without knowing that you were in the world? My world has been so much the richer since you entered it, my universe so much more golden since you eclipsed the sun!*

Oh, heavens! Someone else had written her mother a love letter?

She felt sick, as if her own world had suddenly been shaken, as if her foundations had crumbled.

She could not bring herself to read any more.

Perhaps she was wrong about the handwriting; perhaps it was her father's. Perhaps the carriage accident, even though most of the damage had been to his legs and hips, had nonetheless changed his style of handwriting, she told herself desperately, perhaps—

She turned the page over and scanned it for the signature.

James

Who in heaven's name was James?

Eleven

People could be in love with more than one person,
she tried to tell herself. It was just that her mother
had married her father quite young . . . she had had little
time to fall out of love with one man and into love with another. And her papa had always said that they had known
each other since childhood and always been fond of each
other. She had pictured their relationship as two childhood
sweethearts growing into a more mature romance as they
had reached adulthood.

When did that leave time for another man?

Perhaps this was some poor young man whose unre-
quited love had not been returned. Just an acquaintance carried away by her mother Elizabeth's pretty face and sweet
nature? That thought gave Maddie a space to still her fast-
beating heart and clasp her shaking hands together. That
could be why her mother had kept the letter, out of pity.

But she had to know. She found she was out of bed
reaching for her shawl and pushing her feet into her slippers. Her father might be already asleep, but if not—

She could not bear to lie awake all night wondering what this piece of paper meant about the mother she thought she had known, about her parents' marriage, their deep love that she had assumed had been so true and untroubled.

Easing open her door, she ran as noiselessly as she could for the stairs, tiptoeing down, avoiding the steps that she knew would creak. On the ground floor, the hall was shadowy and dim, but a light still burned in her father's bedroom. She could see the brighter glow in the crack beneath his door.

She hurried to his doorway and tapped lightly on the panel of the door.

"Yes?" came the voice from inside.

She turned the knob and pushed open the door.

His expression surprised, John Applegate lowered the book he was reading and looked up at her from his bed. "My dear, is something wrong?"

Then she was kneeling by his bed without even knowing how she got there. "Papa, who is James?"

From the change in his face, Maddie knew that this was not a slight acquaintance of her mother's, not at all.

She felt her heart sink, and wondered too late if it would have been better not to have asked, never to have known. Once the apple was bitten, would Eve have chosen to put away all knowledge? But how could one choose ignorance when the choice is given?

"If I have distressed you, Papa . . ."

He had put one hand to his face, but he lowered it and shook his head. "No. I had thought perhaps your mother had told you, but you were still so young when she died." He sighed. "What makes you ask, now?"

"I found a packet of letters in the attic, when I was going through a chest of some of her dresses, looking for material to remake. I haven't read them, just looked at a few passages. But I saw the name, and . . ." Her voice faltered at the expressions that flickered across his face. "You don't have to answer, Papa."

"Better that you hear it from me, my girl," he said, his mouth firming. "If your grandparents had not already passed, if—but there are always rumors, you know. I would not have someone in the shire throw out a harsh remark, someday when least expected, and wound you. Better to be prepared."

She thought of the acid-tongued Mrs. Masham and nodded slowly.

"Pull up the stool, my dear, the floor is cold, and I do not want you to catch a chill," he said, and when she obeyed, pushed a knitted blanket toward her to wrap around her.

Maddie found that she was shivering, but she thought it more from nerves than from the cool of the night. The cold seemed to have settled inside her. To find that her beloved parents that she thought she knew so well had such secrets—it shook her to her core. Now she waited, impatient and at the same time terrified, to hear about the great enigma that had been hidden from her all this time.

"What I told you was quite true." Her father spoke slowly, not quite meeting her eye. "I had known your mother since we were children. We grew up on estates, both not terribly large, which were not that far apart. She was a sweet-natured girl, pretty and kind, and I always liked her. But as she grew, and I went off to university, I had the chance to go to London for a year or two, and you know about my misadventure there." His mouth hardened for a moment, and Maddie waited.

Recently she and her sisters had learned, to their shock, of the existence of their half brother, Lord Gabriel Sinclair, when he had tracked down their father. At that point the long-ago affair between John Applegate and Gabriel's mother had been brought to light.

"When I returned home, after I'd agreed that I must give up my forbidden love, I was depressed and lonely, and—I'm sorry to say—given to bouts of self-pity, thinking only of myself. At first I didn't notice that Elizabeth was also in something of a state.

"But we both attended an alfresco party, dining at tables brought out under the trees. We had walked a little apart, and she passed out almost at my feet. I carried her to a nearby stream to revive her, and only then did I find out what had happened. While I was gone, Elizabeth had fallen in love with a young ensign visiting his cousin, who lived on a neighboring estate. The pair had made a secret betrothal, and the young man had planned to return to elicit her father's consent so they could be wed. But he had been sent back to sea earlier than he'd expected and was killed in a sudden engagement. Then Elizabeth discovered she was—ah—with child."

Her father paused, and Maddie knew her eyes had widened. Her mother had made love before she was married?

Good heavens!

Of course, she'd done so herself a mere few hours before, but her own mother? Somehow, one didn't imagine one's parents to be so—so human! First to find out that her father as a young man had been so fallible as to fall in love with a married woman in peril from an abusive husband and to try to come to her aid, in the end to no avail, and then to find her mother in such straits for being so precipitant as to make love before she was wed . . . and then for Elizabeth to learn that she was increasing and unwed, a situation always totally unacceptable.

"Oh, my goodness, what was she going to do?" Maddie asked, putting her hands to her cheeks, thinking what a panic her mother must have been in.

"Yes, that was the question," her father agreed, his tone grim just from the memory. "You can imagine what her father, what both her parents, would have said. And the community would have turned their backs on her. She was almost sick from considering it. Her condition was not yet obvious, but soon would be. She had not meant it to happen, of course. The poor young man had not meant to leave her in such sad straits, either, I assure you, Madeline; he had every intention of coming back to be wed. The French had the devil's luck—the wind on their side and a good aim with their cannon—and managed to end his life before he could get leave again, that was all. Poor James McInnon."

James—her father! Maddie felt a strange pang shoot all the way through her. She had to blink hard.

"So I offered her my name and my protection," her father—oh, no, not her father—continued. "What else could I do? As I said, I was always fond of Elizabeth, and at the moment, for myself, it hardly mattered as I didn't expect to ever fall in love again. And she was so distressed that I felt for her . . ." He sighed.

Maddie blinked; her eyes were filling, and her throat ached with a strange pain. "That was very good of you," she managed to croak out.

"No, no." He put his hands down and shifted in his bed. "Not at all. She was a dear friend, you know. And she was so grateful, it pulled me out of my stupid melancholy. I felt that I was doing something useful, at last. As it turned out, we were most content together; that was not a lie, Madeline, so I don't wish you to consider anything different."

He looked at her anxiously, and when he saw the tears on her cheeks, he made a distressed sound and reached out to touch her face. "We ended up loving each other, I want you to believe that. We lived together very happily. I'm sure I never regretted our marriage."

She nodded.

"Nor did your mother, I am confident, even though she

could not have her first love. She had been so frightened of what would occur—and she was so thankful—and we were two people who were much of a kind, she always said, soft-spoken and amiable, and we did know each other well, so it was a good match. You came along a bit soon, of course, but these things happen, and if there was talk, it died away. We didn't care."

He smiled at her, but this time, she couldn't contain her tears. She had to lean forward and hide her face on the bed.

"Oh, my darling girl, do not cry," he said, his tone anxious. "I am so sorry to have to tell you such shocking tidings."

He patted her shoulder, but it was a few minutes before she could control the spasms of sobs.

Her father—no, Mr. Applegate; she couldn't think what to call him—found a large white handkerchief beneath his pillow to hand her, and she wiped her face.

"I don't know very much about the young man. I believe he came from the Lowlands, but we can make inquires if you wish to locate his family and find out more—"

This time she shook her head vigorously. "No! At least, not yet. I do not know what I wish. I must—give me time to think about it, please."

"As you wish," he said quickly. "I didn't know if you would wish to know more. That perhaps that was part of your distress, learning that you had a father who was quite unknown to you, and then losing him at the same moment you had first heard of him?"

Again she shook her head. She thought, No, you—this is the father I have lost. But she could not speak the words aloud.

She wanted to reach out for his hand. Only a few moments ago, she would have, easily, naturally, but now something stood between them.

He was not her father.

She was not his daughter.

She had been living a lie, and no one had told her . . . they had not trusted her enough to tell her the truth.

Why had they not told her?

Her own mother had not told her . . .

Reeling inside from the stunning blow, she felt curiously light-headed. She managed to straighten her shoulders.

"I must get back to my room," she said, her voice a peculiar croak even to her own ears.

Mr. Applegate watched her with an anxious expression on his face. "Are you sure you will be all right? Should I call for Bess?"

Even though it was a falsehood, she shook her head. "No, I am fine." The servants likely knew more than she did! She had no inclination to discuss the subject any more just now. She wanted her own room, she wanted to be alone, her thoughts were all ajumble.

"Madeline, you must know that I could not have loved you any more than I do. You will always be my dearest girl, my first and most cherished daughter, no matter how you were engendered."

She felt a strange ache in her throat. She had to get out of the room before she fell apart completely. Maddie backed away, one hand holding her candle and one on her throat. "I must get back to bed," she said, avoiding meeting his eye.

"If you wish to talk again later, I will be happy— anytime—" he called after her, his tone still anxious, as she fled out the door and eased it shut behind her.

The hall was quiet and cold.

How quickly could your life change, she thought. Yes, to the world she was still Madeline Applegate, but now she knew that her surname should have been . . . McInnon? No, they had not managed to marry. How was a bastard styled? That was a bitter thought!

Perhaps that was why her mother had not told her, one part of her mind noted, with cold clarity, but it would not do. She deserved to know her own history, surely, she did.

Overwhelmed—it made her limp trying to absorb so much—she climbed the stairs slowly, feeling more lonely than she ever had in her life. The rooms on the other end of the hall were dark, and the house echoed with quiet. Her candle sent shadows quivering down the long hallway.

In front of the guest chamber where Adrian slept, she hesitated, then reached to touch the knob. She wanted to turn it. She knew instinctively that it was not locked, that it would turn beneath her hand. Inside, the chamber was dark, there was no line of light beneath the door, and its occupant must be asleep.

She should go back to her own room, she thought, and not disrupt his slumber. Besides, somehow, though she longed for his presence, for his comforting arm about her shoulders, another part of her wanted no man near her just now.

No man to hurt her, as her mother had been hurt . . . no man to walk away just when she needed him the most . . . and worse—he did plan to walk away.

Maddie lifted her hand from the doorknob and continued her slow pace down the hallway till she could climb into her own lonely bed, her heart frozen and her body cold, where she shivered beneath the bedclothes, all alone.

In fact, she woke early, when the darkness was only just graying. She tried to sleep again, but her newfound knowledge all came rushing back. All she could do was lie still against the pillow and stare up at the curtains of the bed.

Her mother, grieving for her lost love, panic-stricken over her state of impending motherhood with no husband ready to marry her. How grateful she must have been to her old friend when John Applegate had offered his hand . . . and how like him to come to the rescue, Maddie thought. He did seem to like to rescue damsels in distress, first the marquis's wife, which had led to their illicit half brother in London, Lord Gabriel Sinclair, and now, Maddie knew, he had rescued her own mother . . . but why hadn't they told her?

She felt her eyes dampen again. No, she refused to start up again like a regular waterworks, so she rubbed her eyes and turned over, pounding her pillow and trying to redirect her thoughts.

Today she had promised to walk to the cottage with Felicity and help bring back more of her clothes and personal belongings so that her friend could make a longer stay, and not worry about being alone and too out of the way with a band of gypsies wandering about the countryside. Having more people in the house should take Maddie's mind off herself, surely. Take her mind off the fact that soon it would be Sunday, and the final reading of the banns. Then she and Adrian could be married, and then—what?

Surely he would not seek to leave, so soon?

Her stomach lurched at the thought, and her mouth felt dry. She must impress on him how necessary his company was to her comfort, how important his nearness to her happiness. She could not bear it if he went away. She would take her chances with the mad assassin, wherever he might be.

Sighing, she tugged at her pillow again; it seemed determined to knot itself under her head instead of lying smoothly. As if she could sleep.

When the birds were singing in chorus outside her window and the sunlight could not be denied, she gave up and pushed back her covers, rose, and washed in tepid water. She would go down and help Bess with breakfast; Papa— that is, John—oh, she might as well call him what she had always called him; she would never break the habit! Papa always liked his food early, and her guests might be up at a prompt hour, too.

She took the time to wind a white ribbon through her brown hair so it would look its best, and to arrange a few curls on her temples so that they might look artlessly pleasing. She hoped that would draw attention away from her swollen eyelids and pale cheeks. When she was dressed, she went quickly down the stairs. Only Bess was stirring, and the maidservant was in the kitchen, rattling pans and stirring the coals of the fire.

"Yer up early, Miss Madeline, sleep all right, did ye?" Bess asked. "Yer head not paining ye, I 'ope?"

"No, I'm all right, Bess, thank you," she told her, and sat down at the wide kitchen table to help knead the bread. Putting her hands into the dough helped her work out some of her frustration as she pushed and pulled. *That* for the villain who could take away their time together, *that* for men who didn't listen . . .

Several loaves had been put aside to rise, some earlier ones that Bess had prepared were put into the oven at the side of the brick hearth. Maddie rubbed the flour off her hands and helped Bess carry dishes of food into the dining room.

She found John Applegate at the table having a hot cup of tea.

"Ah, my dear. I hope you slept well?" He glanced up at her, his expression anxious.

"I am well, thank you." She attempted to summon a smile. Despite the calm facade she tried to present, it was hard to be as usual. The worry lines on his forehead pinched at her belly and increased her guilt.

But her reply seemed to ease his disquiet. He patted her hand and looked more at ease as Felicity came through the doorway to join them.

"Good morning," their other guest said, and Adrian was just behind her.

"I seem to be the lie-abed this morning," he suggested, grinning.

His entrance gave Maddie an excuse to move to the sideboard and pour him a cup of tea, beating Bess to the chore.

"Good morning, my lord," she said formally, as Bess poured for their other guest.

They all filled plates from the sideboard, and then sat and ate, chatting easily. Adrian offered to accompany the women on their stroll back to the cottage, but Felicity declined, saying she could not steal Mr. Applegate's chess partner.

"We will have Thomas to help us; I think he is planning to take the handcart, and I have not that much to bring back," she told them. "Just a few clothes and a book or two. I do appreciate your kind offer of hospitality, Mr. Applegate."

"Think nothing of it," John told her. "We should have thought of it long since; how dangerous to leave you down the lane all on your own, with no close neighbor at hand to run to if anyone threatened. Quite a scandal, if you had been harmed—I should never have forgiven myself!"

He looked distressed at the idea.

Felicity thanked him again. "You're too kind," she said, appearing moved at his concern.

Immediately after the meal, although Felicity insisted on first helping clear away the dishes, she and Maddie and Thomas set off with the handcart.

Maddie and Felicity were in the lead. The day was a bit misty, but the sun tried hard to push its rays past the morning fog, and the dawn's early coolness had warmed. Yet as the lane dropped away toward the slight valley where the cottage was located, the mist looked thicker, and a smell hung in the air.

It looked like—

"Miss," Thomas said from behind them. His voice sounded alarmed. "'Ware that—"

"Oh my!" Maddie said at the same time. "It's smoke!"

Twelve

Maddie turned to ask Felicity what she thought might have happened, but Felicity was running, and Maddie picked up her skirts and hurried after her.

"Felicity, wait!"

Her friend paid no heed, so she could only scramble and try to catch up. Felicity ran as if her life depended on it; her bonnet flew off and she almost fell once, turning her ankle on a loose stone. Maddie thought she would tumble to the ground, but Felicity recovered her balance and ran on.

She didn't seem to hear Maddie's calls, so all Maddie could do was to run after her.

Thomas left the cart in the road and loped after them, but his three score and two frame was not as agile, and he was soon several lengths behind them both.

Now they rounded the last curve of the road and could see where the thick column of smoke originated. Felicity's cottage burned.

Maddie gasped. She had not quite believed until she saw

it. She was as close as the burning heat of the thatched roof allowed her to go, and the inferno spewed up a thick, nauseous smoke that surely would have suffocated anything living. The glass in the windows had cracked and split, and the partially stone walls had already fallen in at several spots where the wood frames had burnt and twisted.

"If you had been asleep there, last night . . ." Swallowing, Maddie almost choked on the smoke in the air.

Felicity had both hands to her face; she looked stunned. "My books," she said. "And, oh, my poor little cat!" She wiped her eyes and didn't seem to notice that her hands were trembling. "Who could have done this?"

"You do not think it was done on purpose?" Maddie felt as if the words were another shock, like an adder striking. "Surely, a spark from the fireplace—"

"The fire was out when I left," Felicity said. "I made sure of it, Madeline. I never take chances with fire."

"Then perhaps, a lightning strike . . ." Maddie's voice died away. Except the night had been clear. But who would seek to kill—because setting such a fire would have to lead to death. Could anyone not fail to realize that?

Had the gypsies rifled the house, stolen what they could, and then sought to cover up their crime? If they had known the house was empty, they would have known there was no one to kill, Maddie thought. That would still make it an awful crime but not quite so heart-stopping.

Poor Felicity, who had just lost all she owned, except what she wore on her back, looked pale with shock.

"You know we will help you," Maddie said now. "You will not be allowed to go without, Felicity."

"I do not wish to be a charge," her friend said, her chin up, although she shuddered again. She reached to touch the small silver necklace that hung around her neck. "At least I still have my locket . . ."

Felicity needed hot tea, perhaps some brandy, Maddie thought, wishing she had had the viscount come along with them after all.

The fire burned high into the air, and the crackling of it was so loud, the heat so strong, they had to step back to avoid the fierceness of the blaze.

"Look!" Felicity pointed at the earth in front of the windows. "You see; there are even more footprints there than when I left the house yesterday. There have been more men here, I swear, Madeline."

"I believe you," Maddie told her, "but it does no good to stay here just now, Felicity. I do not believe the fire will spread into the trees; there is enough bare ground around the cottage and the wind is not blowing. Let us go back to the house. We will come back later with more witnesses, with the viscount, I promise."

Felicity nodded, but still seemed to turn away with reluctance, as if it was hard to let go of the ruins of her life. The cottage had had little of worth, but it had been her home, and its contents were all she had. She pressed her lips together and braced her shoulders, wiping her eyes, and turned resolutely back toward the village and the Applegate residence.

They could not hear noises because of the sounds of the fire, but Maddie, too, saw the bush move just beyond them, and she stiffened.

Felicity threw up her hands as if to defend herself. It was not a gypsy dagger that came flying out of the greenery at her heart, but one small, slightly singed, and very frightened cat.

"Oh, my sweetling," Felicity cried. "Here, here, come to mama."

She wrapped the animal in her shawl and cradled it in her arms, speaking softly and trying to soothe it.

"Is it hurt very badly?" Maddie asked. "What a wonder it was able to get away."

Felicity was stroking the smoke-darkened fur. "It has some burns on its paws, but I don't think they are severe. Let us get it back to your house," she said. This time she set off at a swift pace toward the Applegate home, without any more backward looks at the conflagration behind them, as the last bits of the roof collapsed into the ruins of the cottage.

When they reached home, Maddie went to inform Adrian and her father, while Felicity bathed the cat's wounds in the kitchen.

"Good Lord," her father said. "How dreadful to lose everything that she owns at one blow. Thank God she was not there! And you don't think it's an accident?"

"Felicity—Mrs. Barlow—does not." Maddie explained about the footprints, and the man that her friend had seen about the house.

The viscount frowned. "If you will excuse me from finishing the game," he told her father, "I think perhaps I should walk down to the cottage and take a look at the scene."

"Yes, indeed," Mr. Applegate said. "I only wish I were in shape to go with you. Take one of my pistols when you go, Lord Weller."

He rolled his chair over to the gun cabinet and unlocked it, and Adrian selected one of the two antique dueling pistols that had belonged to her grandfather. Maddie felt even more alarmed, yet how could they not take this seriously? It was true that Felicity could have died.

Adrian had the gun loaded and tucked away out of sight inside his jacket before Felicity reappeared. She had left the cat, apparently happy enough with its change of residence, sleeping beside the warmth of the hearth, she told Maddie.

"My dear Mrs. Barlow, do sit down and have a glass of wine. You must be most overset," Maddie's father told her.

Felicity sank down into a chair at the side of the room. "I admit, I would not be adverse to a glass."

Adrian poured it for her, and she took a quick sip, then another.

"I was so glad to see my poor feline friend safe, and I have my locket with the miniature of my mother." She touched the silver charm at her neck and sighed again. "But my books—"

"You are welcome to use my small collection," Mr. Applegate told her, "and anything else we have that can help you."

"You're very kind," she said, her voice quivering just a little. "I think perhaps . . ." She paused and Maddie jumped up and went to put one arm about her.

"Perhaps you would like to lie down for a space?" she finished for her friend.

Struggling for composure, Felicity nodded and wiped away a trace of moisture on her cheek.

"Come, I will go upstairs with you," Maddie said. They both took their leave of the gentlemen, and Maddie accompanied her friend up to the guest room now put aside for Felicity's use. There, Maddie was pleased to see that Bess had brought up warm water for Felicity to wash off the smoke stains, and fresh towels had been put out.

"If you need anything that I can supply," she began.

Felicity's eyes were welling over with tears she could no longer contain. "I–you have been more than generous," she answered, wiping her cheeks with the back of her hand. "I think I just need some time to compose myself."

"Of course," Maddie said. "Please lie down for as long as you like. If you need anything, just let us know." She hugged her friend one more time, then left her to lie down.

After shutting the door gently behind her, Maddie shook her head. What heartless ruffian would burn down the home of an almost penniless widow, just to steal a few pounds? Felicity had lost everything she owned; it was so unfair!

She had not lost her friends, Maddie told herself. They were the most valuable commodity that one could possess, and she would make sure that Felicity knew it, too.

She descended the staircase in time to see the viscount about to go out the front door.

"Wait!" she called. "I will come with you."

He half turned to look at her. "I'd rather you did not. It's too dangerous. If the person who set fire to Mrs. Barlow's cottage is still in the area, who knows what villainous outrage he might be capable of?"

"Then are you taking Thomas with you?" she demanded.

He hesitated for a moment, then shook his head. "I think it best that your manservant stay here."

Startled by something in his voice, she looked closely at him. "Why? Surely you don't expect the gypsies to assault our house? That's far outside their usual sort of behavior."

"So is burning down a cottage," the viscount pointed out, his tone grim and his expression boding ill for the person who had torched Felicity's home.

"True," Maddie acknowledged. "Which makes the whole business so odd. But you should not go alone, either, Adrian. I am going with you. If you leave me behind, I will simply follow, which is surely more dangerous for both of us." She spoke calmly, without any bravado, and thought that he took her more seriously as a result.

The viscount raised his brows. "Blackmail?"

She grinned at him, but continued to tie her shawl around her shoulders. "If you like to call it such. But I am still coming."

So they set off together down the path that was the quickest route to the cottage, or what was left of it.

The heavy tread of the handcart could be easily detected, its impression still visible in the dusty path. And their own footprints from their passage earlier, somewhat jumbled but still there, could also be seen.

It was possible that other villagers had been down the path, drawn by curiosity, although so far she saw no signs of other passage, and at the moment, the byway was quiet. The birds had stilled in the afternoon hush, and peace hung over the woods.

Wondering what he was thinking, she glanced toward the viscount. He scanned the trees around them; he always seemed alert for any untoward observer. How many times did one have to be attacked to become this vigilant? Chagrined that she could forget so easily, Maddie tried to keep her eyes open as well, and looked around her for any trace of strangers. After all, she had come on this walk to be a help, not a hindrance.

Now the ruins of the cottage were coming into view. The fire had burned down by now. The roof had fallen in, and only parts of the walls were still standing. Maddie wrinkled her nose at the strong smell of smoke; a few spots still smoldered so she did not think that they could get inside to investigate the fire from close at hand.

They had to content themselves with walking around the outer perimeter of the cottage and peering into the ashes and shattered remains of the building. The furniture, simple as it had been, had all been destroyed, and the chest that had held Felicity's small collection of clothes, and her much loved set of books, had also burned completely. Maddie sighed as she looked over the corner where her friend had kept her most precious belongings. What a blow!

Meanwhile, Adrian had wandered farther. She gave up trying to use a long, narrow branch to reach a lone shoe that seemed to have escaped the worst part of the fire, though it did not seem to have a mate, and hurried to catch up.

"What do you see?" she asked, when he narrowed his eyes.

"Footprints that are not ours," he told her.

"Oh, where?" she asked.

He held out his hand and pointed, and she followed the direction of his hand. She could see them, too, now that he had suggested where she should look. A solitary man had been standing back where several other prints converged, perhaps taking cover behind a flowering shrub as the owners of various prints had walked to and fro.

"These are in the way," she complained. "If all these people had not trampled about like African elephants—"

"These elephants are you and Thomas and your friend, Mrs. Barlow," the viscount suggested. "I believe he was standing just behind and watching when you discovered that the cottage had been set afire."

"Oh, how unpleasant," Maddie exclaimed. She could not hold back a shiver at the thought of being observed and not knowing it. "How do you know?"

"Just examine the footprints. You have obligingly worn the same boots as you did earlier; you are making the exact same print."

"Oh, of course." She blushed at missing such an obvious clue. "We must take care not to change our footwear too often, and our detecting will go much more smoothly."

Bending over to examine the marks in the dirt more closely, he grinned up at her. "Just so. And I'm quite sure this is the widow herself. Her foot is a bit wider and longer than yours."

"I haven't noticed, but it's quite likely, if you say so," Maddie agreed.

"I have noticed that your foot is a neat one, much like your shapely ankle, and—ah—other parts of your anatomy," Adrian noted, his tone serious, but a teasing glint in his eye.

Maddie found her ready blush staining her cheeks. "Now, that has nothing to do with"—then she saw that he was teasing, and she frowned at him—"We must pay attention to the matter at hand."

"Of course, I stand rebuked." He didn't stand at all. He had crouched in the dirt, as he scowled at the last set of prints.

"You do remember that Thomas walked down to the cottage with us?" she reminded him. "Could they be his prints?"

"I do, but he stood back from the cottage with the cart. You will see Thomas's honest yeoman's prints back a ways up the lane. These are most dishonest footprints, and they are taking shelter behind a bush to remain out of sight."

"Is that why you make such a face?" she asked, coming closer, though walking carefully so as not to disturb the line of prints he was paying such close attention to.

"I am trying to make out why our lone gypsy—not a band, you will note, even though the Romany brethren usually move as a clan—is wearing such well-cut shoes."

Startled, she looked at him, then down at the footprints. "Perhaps the shoes were given away. Perhaps he stole them."

"They are not much worn to be secondhand. Of course, if he snatched them from someone's doorstep where the household boy left them to dry after blacking them for his master, that would explain it," the viscount agreed. "But somehow—"

"You are not satisfied," she finished for him. "It could happen, however."

He walked around the edge of the cottage, finding the stranger's prints again at the far side of the cottage, where he also noted the faint smell of sulphur, as in cheap matches. That comment made Maddie's eyes widen.

"But that would be truly evil, to think someone might have deliberately started the fire that destroyed Felicity's home!"

The viscount didn't answer. He only turned and followed

the footprints back into the trees. She trailed along after him, too, afraid that he might find the maker of the prints, if the gypsies still lingered near to the cottage.

If the band were indeed nearby, however, she and the viscount would be very much outnumbered.

They picked their way through the trees, following the trail until the footprints vanished entirely when the ground became too rocky to hold any impression of who had passed over it. At that point the viscount muttered a few words that Maddie pretended not to hear.

He leaned against a large rock, scanning the countryside. They appeared to be alone, but Maddie no longer trusted in appearances.

Who could be watching? The thought of unseen eyes and lurking evildoers made her shiver again.

The viscount saw the motion and held out an arm to pull her closer. Maddie made to step inside his embrace, then, remembering last night's revelations, hesitated. Her new loss of trust was still an open wound, and she had not had time to find the way to allow this hurt to heal.

"What is it?" he asked, gazing down at her.

She wasn't ready to share her somewhat unsavory family history—not all of it, at least. "I—I don't like to think of someone watching us, when we least expect it," she said. It was part of the truth, anyhow.

She reached for his hand and clasped it. It was a poor substitute for relishing the feel of his arms about her, but it was something. Adrian nodded and held her hand in both of his. If he thought her reluctance to be close came from the fear of someone watching, so be it. She could not bear to explain it all just yet.

They rested for a few minutes, then made their way back. When they reached the path, they made better time back to the Applegate residence. Inside, they parted, and Maddie went to check on Felicity.

She was not in her guest room. Alarmed, Maddie came back downstairs to seek out her friend. She was not sitting with Mr. Applegate. At last, Maddie found her in the kitchen, helping Bess complete preparations for their dinner.

"You must not feel you have to work all hours of the day, Felicity," Maddie told her. "It is kind of you to assist us, but—"

"It is another person for Bess to attend to, and I know how hard she works," Felicity told her. "I certainly want to do my part."

Maddie could see that Bess approved of their new guest; the maidservant beamed at the widow. "A nice light hand she has with the sauces, too," the maid said, approvingly. "But we're almost ready now, Miss Madeline."

Maddie ran back upstairs to wash the dust off her face and hands and push her hair back into place. At dinner she and Adrian explained what they had found.

Mr. Applegate looked grave. "I hate to think that the fire might have been deliberately set. Are you sure?"

They recounted the details, and John shook his head. Felicity had gone quite white.

"I apologize if I have alarmed you," Adrian told her.

Maddie felt contrite. "It may be that we are mistaken," she said, glancing at the viscount and hoping he would not contradict her.

Her friend shook her head. "No, it is better to know the truth and be prepared," she said, a bit cryptically. She pressed her lips together and stared down at her plate, as if not liking what she saw, although she had just praised Bess's excellent apple dumpling.

When the ladies withdrew from the table—a formality that normally Maddie didn't bother with when only she and her father dined together—she and Felicity went back to the kitchen and helped Bess clear away and begin the washing up.

When the two men retired to the sitting room, they did, as well, with Bess shooing them out of the kitchen and pantry.

"I can finish up, Miss Madeline. Ye both get along, now, do."

Maddie suspected the men had still been discussing the gypsies, but they changed the subject when the ladies rejoined them.

"Come, let's make a game of cards and think of something more pleasant," John said, smiling at Felicity.

She smiled back, although she pointed out, "We will have to play for imaginary points, I fear, as all my pennies went with the dastardly gypsies."

While the viscount got out the cards, Maddie and Felicity agreed that they would go into the village on the morrow and look for some personal items that Felicity needed for herself. Maddie assured her friend that she should not worry about money for such small notions.

"I will repay you when my quarterly allowance comes in," the widow promised. "And I do need to post a letter to my cousin."

"Of course, you will need to let him know you are well, and where you are situated," John told her. "Most understandable."

Maddie thought that the viscount flashed her friend a keen look for just a moment, but Felicity looked away and didn't meet anyone's eye.

When they finished their card game—Maddie found her mind wandering and her choice of cards therefore somewhat erratic—Felicity went to the side table and, with her back turned to the rest of the room, composed her letter. John told them about other fires in the village and how the grain mill had once burned, while the villagers had made a bucket brigade and managed to put out the fire before total destruction was achieved.

By the time Felicity had rejoined them, Bess brought in a tea tray, with some of her good scones, and after the tea was drunk and the baked goods consumed, three of them were ready to climb the stairs for bed, while Mr. Applegate went down the hall to his room. Although she saw the gaze that Adrian sent her way, Maddie was not yet ready to attempt a tryst with another guest in the next room.

Nor, if the truth were known, was she in the mood, as yet, to once more trust him totally. The memory of her mother, left alone and friendless, in dire straits after the death of her sweetheart, still haunted her.

So, without pausing at his door, she went straight on to her own room and prepared to retire. Her bed had never seemed so lonely, it was true, now that she knew the joys of a pallet shared with a man that you loved, a man who could pull you close and tempt your body into joys hitherto unknown but delightfully glorious. No use thinking of it now, Maddie told herself, pushing her pillow into a better shape as she tried to find a warm and comfortable spot in a cold and lonely bed.

It was impossible. She was here, and he was there, and there was no crossing the gulf between them. While she might blame their separation on the new guest in their house, on the rigors of propriety and her need to be circumspect, the truth was that she was afraid, afraid of being left alone. She was being ruled by fear, just as Adrian was—he was afraid of the madman who stalked him and could hurt innocent people in his insane quest to destroy him. She was afraid of being left alone and unprotected. Both of them lay in lonely beds because they allowed fear to rule their hearts.

She cradled her cheek on her pillow and wept.

The next morning, everyone seemed subdued when they met at the breakfast table. Felicity at least had an obvious reason. Adrian looked somber, but made no attempt to explain, and Maddie herself—well, did she need to explain? She poured tea for her guests and brought her father hot toast when Bess brought a new plate from the kitchen.

When conversation languished, Maddie looked from Felicity's wan face to her father's pensive expression.

"I'm taking Felicity into the village to look for a few items she needs for herself," she told her father. "Is there anything you wish?"

He looked up from the toast he had been buttering.

"A new bottle of ink, perhaps. And be sure to take Thomas with you, my dear. I don't wish either of you to be out alone just now."

"No need to take Thomas away from his chores," Adrian said easily. "I will accompany the ladies."

"I wasn't sure," Maddie began, glancing over at the viscount. For some reason she felt less at ease with him than she had, and perhaps he sensed it. He regarded her with a slight crease between his brows.

"It will be my pleasure," he assured her, his tone formal, as if he had felt her withdrawal.

She inclined her head and gave him a smile that she tried to make as natural and welcoming as it would have been a week ago. Inside she wanted to weep, that she had to go to the effort—why did all this have to come between them?

After the breakfast dishes had been cleared away, the three of them set off for the village.

It was a beautiful autumn's day, and Thomas was harvesting a field of grain with the Applegate's one horse, and the viscount's beast would not carry three, so they had agreed that a walk into the village would be a fine jaunt and just what they needed to brighten their spirits after the shock of the cottage's destruction.

Felicity was trying hard to be her normal, sunny self, and if her friend could make such an effort, when she had suffered such an overwhelming blow, Maddie thought she herself must try harder. So they talked and laughed and on the surface, all seemed well. But Maddie wasn't sure that the viscount was completely fooled.

When they reached the village, Felicity saw her letter into the post and Maddie took care of her father's request. Then Felicity went into the draper's shop to look for some personal items.

Maddie hung back a little in the doorway, while the viscount stood just outside.

"What's wrong, Madeline?" he asked, his voice quiet.

For a moment she considered pretending not to hear, but she couldn't be such a coward. How could she explain? She gazed up at him from beneath her straw bonnet, and the look of concern on his face pierced her to her heart.

"Oh, Adrian," she said very low. "If only—"

Then she heard Felicity calling her name. Looking around, she saw her friend signaling her from inside the shop. Excusing herself, she went inside and found that the other woman had a serious question about a matter of undergarments.

"You have bought these before, I imagine," Felicity whispered. "Which do you think is likely to hold up longer?"

She helped Felicity pick out bloomers and chemises, and when the parcel was made up, they both returned to the street and she and Adrian could not continue their private conversation.

"Perhaps we should have some tea and refreshments at the bake shop at the end of the lane," the viscount suggested, "before we start our walk home?"

"That sounds pleasant," Maddie agreed.

By this time it was past noon, and the street was more crowded than usual. On a Saturday, the local farmers were in town to visit the few shops that lined the one main street, and they had to dodge around men leading heifers brought in to sell or barrows piled high with cages of clucking hens.

They walked single file for convenience, the viscount going first to make room for them through the crowd, with Maddie behind him and Felicity last, carrying her parcels—she had refused Adrian's polite offer to take them from her. She had fallen a step or two behind when Maddie heard her exclaim.

Fearing she had stepped into a puddle, Maddie turned to see what had vexed her friend when she heard a note of real fear in her next words.

"No, no!"

"What is it?" Maddie cried, trying to find the widow as a group of young lads separated them momentarily. "Adrian!"

He turned and came back at once to see what had alarmed her. "What's wrong?"

"I don't know—where is Felicity?"

They both plunged through the crowd, pushing their way through a group of slightly drunken apprentices making good use of their half day of freedom.

Her heart beating fast, Maddie saw a brown paper-wrapped parcel lying in the street and recognized it as one of Felicity's. She stooped to pick it up, and hurried in that direction. "Here, over here."

There, at last she saw Felicity, cowering inside the slight depression of a shop window as if to efface herself from notice.

"Felicity, what's amiss?"

The widow's face was white and her eyes wide. "I saw— I saw a man I thought—I thought might be the man I had seen at my window."

"The man you saw before the fire?" Maddie demanded. "Which way did he go?"

"I'm not sure; I just wanted to get away."

"Tell me what he looks like," Adrian charged the widow.

"Black shaggy hair, a scarf obscuring much of his face, blackened teeth." Felicity shuddered.

"Stay with her, better yet, go inside this shop and wait for me. I will be back," the viscount told them, then he disappeared into the crowd.

Maddie put one arm about Felicity's shoulders; she could feel her friend still shaking. "Come," she said. "We will get out of this crush and out of sight of anyone on the street."

They went into the greengrocer's shop, which smelled musty with scents of earth and farmers' wares. There was nowhere to sit, but if they had to spend some time pretending to weigh the merits of bins of cabbages and turnips, so be it.

Meanwhile, Adrian slipped around the groups of farmers and farmwives that seemed to increasingly take up space on the cobblestoned pavement. He wished he had his horse. If the other man had a steed nearby, Adrian would lose him in the end, but he could but try.

He half walked, half ran along the edge of the street, pushing his way past more and more groups and singles, men and beasts alike. He saw more men and women who had been tasting the grape and the brew on their half day away from field and workbench. The level of noise in the open air rose as well as the earthy fragrance of the human and animal traffic, which often made him wrinkle his nose.

He paused long enough to look into the local pub, which was as dark and smoky as he remembered from his first trip through the village, but he saw no one similar to the widow's description. On his way out, he was halted a few feet from the door.

"Have a pint with me, friend!" a jovial farmer with graying locks said, trying to put one stout arm around Adrian's shoulders.

"Ah, no thanks, friend, my errand is an urgent one," Adrian told him.

"What, ye've no appetite for me ale—or me comp– comp–comp'ny!" The man looked affronted.

"Indeed, I should much enjoy your company," the viscount assured him. "But my urgent business calls me away, I'm sad to say. But let me buy you a round—no, two rounds more to show my regret." He pulled a half crown out of his pocket and tossed it to the bartender, and his new friend brightened at once.

"Well, then," he said, "thou's more friendly like." And he sloshed his way back toward the smoke-stained bar.

Adrian made good his escape. As he pushed open the door, he heard something whip past his head. He ducked instinctively.

He jumped toward the street, taking shelter behind a large man who led a fat cow behind him.

Neither of them seemed in the least perturbed.

Had someone taken a shot at him, or was he dreaming in the daytime, too? Adrian looked about him and felt a little foolish.

The street was full of people coming and going, and no one seemed to notice that he had bent double to avoid an imaginary assault.

When nothing unusual followed, he at last straightened and heard nothing but the blare of talk and animals bleating and mooing, feet stamping, wheels turning.

Shaking his head, he headed back toward where he had left the ladies.

❧

When Adrian returned, they finished their shopping.
Felicity looked often over her shoulder, and the viscount
also seemed on edge.

Maddie had picked up their nervousness, so she thought
they were all more than ready to set out for home.

The very last chore was a stop to see the vicar. Tomorrow would be the third reading of the banns. They found
the churchman not at home, but his housekeeper offered to
take a message.

It gave Maddie a strange feeling inside to think that
soon there would be no further impediment to their marriage. How could the weeks have flown by so quickly? The
stranger she had awakened to see embracing her naked
body in the gazebo was now the man she could not consider allowing out of her life.

When she looked up at the viscount, he met her gaze as
if he were reading her thoughts.

"When would you like to schedule the wedding, my
dear?" he asked, his tone still formal. "Did the dressmaker
in Ripon deliver your wedding gown as promised?"

She wished she could have claimed that the modiste had
been slow, or the skirt had been improperly sewn, or her
shoes did not fit. But in fact, the packages had come yesterday, and only the commotion over the fire had kept her
from enjoying them thoroughly. She had merely had time
to glance at her wonderful new possessions.

"They have arrived," she said, biting her lip and not
quite meeting his eye.

"Are you pleased with the result?"

"I have not yet had time to examine them closely, but
I'm sure I will be," she said honestly.

He nodded as if in understanding. "Then what morning
shall we tell the good vicar to plan for the ceremony?"

Not yet, she thought, not yet, if marriage means that you
shall feel no longer compelled to stay.

Feeling helpless to hold him here, she met his gaze without knowing how to answer.

"Wednesday, perhaps?" he prompted, when she didn't answer.

Her expression curious, the plump housekeeper looked from one to the other.

Maddie nodded.

"I'll tell 'im, me lord," the servant said. "Anything else 'e needs to know, ye just send a note over."

"Thank you," the viscount said.

They turned to head at last for home, but Maddie heard a whining noise, and something buzzed by her head and stung her skin. She jumped and slapped at her neck.

"What's wrong?" Adrian said sharply.

"I think—I think a bee has stung me," Maddie said, still holding her neck.

"Oh, 'ere, miss. Let me get you some cool water. You'll need to take out the stinger," the housekeeper said. "Why don't you come into the kitchen?"

While the viscount waited in the sitting room, Maddie, with Felicity and the housekeeper, went back to the kitchen. The housekeeper set about fetching what they would need, and after Maddie took off her bonnet, Felicity examined her neck.

"Madeline, this does not look like a bee sting," her friend said slowly, "and there is certainly no stinger."

Maddie looked into a small looking glass that the housekeeper had brought out for her use. She held it up by the handle and examined the streak of reddened flesh on the side of her neck. "No," she said slowly, glancing toward the housekeeper, who had gone to prepare a basin of water and clean cloths. "I believe you are right. Perhaps a wasp."

"But"—Felicity began—"I don't think—"

Maddie sent her a warning glance. She took the cloth

that the housekeeper held out and bathed the reddened skin, wincing at she touched it. "Thank you."

She put a small pad of cloth over it and arranged her bonnet so that when she tied the ribbon, the wound would be hidden. "This will do, I think. No need to make a big fuss."

When they had turned down, with thanks, the house-keeper's offer of tea and were ready to leave, she muttered to Felicity. "I don't wish it commented on."

"But don't you wish to tell the viscount?" her friend asked.

"Especially not the viscount!" Maddie raised her brows in emphasis.

The widow looked concerned, but she nodded.

All three of them were quiet as they walked home. Maddie noticed that they set a smart pace as they hurried through the trees toward the Applegate residence, and none of them inquired as to why they walked so quickly.

When they reached the house, Felicity went up to put her purchases away. Maddie went to help Bess with dinner, as she usually did, but presently she found that Felicity came to take her place, and Bess and the widow seemed united in shooing her out of the kitchen.

"Go and spend time with your fiancé," Felicity suggested. "Don't waste a minute."

"He's likely chatting with my father," Maddie argued.

"No, indeed, your father is taking an afternoon rest," Bess said.

"And I'm sure the viscount would rather have you to visit with than me," the widow said, dimpling. "So out with you!"

Maddie untied the apron she had put on to protect her dress and hurried down the hallway. It was true; time was flying by, and there was so little of it left. How had their three weeks, which had seemed like such a relatively long time, in the beginning, gone by so fast?

She found the viscount in the sitting room, but he looked up at once when she came in the door.

"There you are. Would you like to take a stroll around the garden before dinner?" His smile was mischievous, and remembering what they had done during their last stroll in the garden, she blushed.

But the garden gave them more privacy than the small sitting room, so she nodded and they headed out of doors.

"I cannot believe it is already another week gone by," she said as they entered through the gap in the tall hedge.

He put his hands on her waist and swung her lightly around, then stopped and put his arms about her. "No, nor I," he admitted. "My darling Miss Applegate . . ."

Bending his head to kiss her, he pushed her bonnet back, reaching down to untie the ribbon and free her of the tight-fitting headgear.

At first she lifted her face eagerly, anticipating the delight of his kiss. Then, remembering the reddened strip of skin on her neck that she had not wanted him to see, Maddie paused. "Wait!"

He stopped at once. "What is it, Madeline? Or should I say Miss Applegate in truth?"

She flushed, not sure how to explain her change of heart. But if he saw the marks and understood what had happened, she would lose all hope of persuading him to stay.

His eyes had narrowed, and he gazed at her. "Have I offended you?"

"No, no, it's not . . ." Her voice faded. She could not think what to say.

"Are you feeling guilty? If I have pushed you too far, too fast, then I am most sorry, my dear," he told her, his tone serious. He allowed his hands to drop, and he stepped back a pace.

It was as if a great gulf suddenly yawned between them.

Maddie wanted to weep. "There is nothing I have done with you that I regret," she whispered, "please believe that."

"Then I don't understand."

"Adrian." She paused again, not knowing how to explain.

The day was fading into twilight, and candles were being lit inside. She could see the soft glow behind the curtains. When the silence stretched, he spoke. "Perhaps we should go back to the house. But, Madeline . . ."

"Yes," she croaked.

"Do you still wish the banns to be read tomorrow?"

Unshed tears made her throat ache and stopped her voice. She swallowed hard; all she could do was nod her head.

"Very well," he said, and offered his arm as they turned to walk back across the uneven path toward the house.

It was just as well that the sunlight was fading; perhaps he would not see the teardrops on her cheeks.

Thirteen

*T*hat night Maddie slept very ill, and when Bess brought a cup of tea before she had to rise and dress for church, she saw a pale face staring back at her from the small looking glass above her dressing table. The other parishioners would think that she was dreading her own wedding, she thought, sighing as she picked up her cup.

In a way, she was, since the ceremony would release Adrian from his self-imposed promise. Once the propriety of her social status was assured, he would be free to leave.

She could not bear it if he walked out of her life!

She dressed quickly, but was human enough, or female enough, to try to make herself look as nice as she could, though there was little she could do about the dark circles under her eyes. As a result, she barely made it down the stairs before Thomas brought the carriage around.

She and her papa and Felicity crowded into the small vehicle, and Adrian rode his own steed the short distance to the church. Thomas and the viscount saw her father safely down and into his wheeled chair and they went into the building and found their usual pew.

Adrian excused himself for a few minutes before the service began. She opened the prayer book and tried to read from it, but she could not bring her thoughts under control. They darted here and there like the bees outside that hovered over the late-flowering autumn shrubs.

Even when the viscount slipped back into his seat just as the vicar began to speak, Maddie found that she could not focus on any of the readings or the hymns. But the reading of the banns made her sit up straighter. She glanced at Adrian from the corner of her eye, especially when the vicar repeated the viscount's invitation to the parishioners to come and witness the "happy event."

Did his expression appear somewhat grim today? What would the rest of the people in church be thinking—the future bride looked as if she were troubled, and the groom looked severe. The villagers would suspect they had been quarreling. They were almost correct, Maddie thought, miserable that she could not explain to Adrian her confused emotions. She simply wanted him to stay, but she had told him that, and it had done no good. He was so sure he knew what was best, but it did not mean it was best for her, for pity's sake!

Was it more than that? He did seem very reserved today, and he'd hardly glanced her way the whole morning. He held his prayer book out now, but did not stand as close to her as he usually did.

Did he regret having pledged himself to her? If he was sorry that he had proposed too quickly, too rashly, that would break her heart. She was probably imagining things.

She had to talk to him, Maddie decided. This guessing game would drive her mad. But what could she say? The service seemed to last forever. At last the final prayer was said, and they were able to slowly make their way toward the front of the church and speak politely to the vicar, who spoke jovially of the coming ceremony.

"This will be a memorable week for the two lovebirds, eh, Mr. Applegate?" the churchman commented as he leaned over to shake hands.

"Yes, indeed," her father said, with a polite smile. But he, too, glanced at her with concern in his eyes.

She tried to smile naturally, but she said nothing. When at most other times she would have regretted the viscount's absence from the carriage, today she was glad he was riding. She gave a pleading glance toward Felicity, and her friend, interpreting it correctly, at once begin to talk about the trim on her wedding dress and how it must be carefully pressed before Wednesday.

"Because it would never do to walk down the aisle with wrinkled lace, of course," she said cheerfully. "I would be happy to help. I have a steady hand with a flatiron, if I do say so."

"You're very kind," Maddie told her, and she meant her thanks for more than just chores with her new clothes, as she was sure Felicity was aware.

They were able to keep up the innocuous chatter until they reached the Applegate residence and were out of the carriage and had gone inside for Sunday dinner.

The viscount was quieter than usual even during the meal. Although he kept up a polite conversation with them all, she could tell that his thoughts were elsewhere.

When her father had retired to his room for his usual afternoon nap, she found her courage had sunk to a new low, and she could not face a private chat. She decided to stick close to Felicity, but that strategy was doomed to failure as Adrian quickly separately the two of them. If he had been this skillful in his maneuvers on the battlefield, she thought wildly, he must have been much feared by his foes.

"Perhaps we could take a stroll outside, Miss Apple-gate?" he asked her, with great formality.

"Ah—I should help Bess with the clearing away, first," she faltered.

"I'm sure Mrs. Barlow would not mind helping out," he said firmly. "And I do need a word."

Maddie gave Felicity a stricken look, but could hardly protest.

"Of course, I will," the widow said. "I had meant to, anyhow."

So Maddie had no excuse but to take the viscount's arm and accompany him out once more to the garden at the side of the house, where they had their best chance for privacy. This time, she did not think it would be for a brief bit of il-licit lovemaking. His forearm felt tense beneath her hand, and the side of his face again looked more severe than usual.

Was he terribly angry at her?

She felt her stomach go hollow. Maddie never did well when people acted wrathful. She felt the telltale tension in her temple that preceded her sick headaches, and thought, No, no, not now. That was the last thing she needed!

Without speaking a word, they walked side by side to the bench at the side of the garden. Then he stopped, and Maddie sat, a bit abruptly. She thought he would sit, too, but to her surprise, after a careful survey of the surrounding trees and shrubbery, he stood before her instead. His hand went inside his jacket.

"I have recovered your 'bee,'" he told her as he with-drew his hand.

"What?" For an instant, she was quite bewildered. Then she stared at the small metal object he held inside his palm, and she felt her cheeks go first hot and then cold.

It was a bullet, slightly flattened on one side where it must have hit the stone wall of the building.

Was that what had struck her neck yesterday at the vicarage? While she stared in horror at the bullet, he spoke again.

"This is why you did not want me to take off your bonnet, was it not, Madeline? Or should I say, Miss Applegate?"

"Oh, my lord, do not be angry!" she pleaded. "I wasn't sure!" Without thinking, she put her hands to her face. Then, afraid he would think that she was dissembling once more, she hastily lowered them back to her lap.

"May I?" He reached to untie, very gently and slowly, the plain bonnet she had donned before going out, and then pushed down the high neck of the dress she had chosen to wear this morning.

He touched the reddened streak on her neck, and she winced. The spot was still tender.

His expression made her flinch again.

"Madeline—if this had been an inch or two further to the left, we would planning your funeral service today, not your wedding!"

"But—we don't know that it was your enemy—"

Again, the fierceness of his countenance made her shiver. "Madeline, you are being nonsensical! How many times have you been shot at before during a quiet walk through the village?"

They both knew the answer to that, so she had no easy reply.

She blinked hard against betraying tears, and at last, he sat down beside her. But he did not touch her, and the small distance between them seemed as wide as the length between York and London.

Just when she thought she must break into sobs, she must plead, she must beg—he spoke very quietly. "You must know that I do not want to leave you, Madeline. You have given me more reason to want to stay, to want to live, than I have had for years."

Unbidden, hope sparked to life, only to sputter and die miserably when he spoke again.

"I cannot put you at risk." His voice was husky. "You are too valuable to me, Madeline, my love."

My love—he would call her that now, when he was preparing to leave her? Madeline bit her lip. "I cannot bear for you to go!" she exclaimed. "I think I have the right to decide if I wish to risk my life beside you!"

He gazed at her for a moment with what she thought must surely be admiration. But he shook his head. "My darling, now it is my turn to tell you I have not been honest."

"What?" That was the last thing she had expected him to say.

"I have another foe who threatens my life, more dire than even my deranged cousin."

She stared at him, afraid to hear what other threat could be out there.

He lifted her hand, which she had unknowingly clenched into a fist, smoothed out her fingers, and put it inside his jacket, inside his waistcoat, and allowed her to feel the beating of his heart. She could feel the warmth of his skin beneath the fine linen of his shirt, and she leaned closer, wanting to press her cheek there, as well.

"This," he said.

She blinked at him, not sure what he meant, then she realized what she was meant to feel—a fine line that seemed to lie very close to his heart. A scar? It was so thin that she had not even noticed it in the heat of passion the one night they had made love.

Not sure what to think, she looked up at him.

"It's a fragment of the bullet from the duel," he told her, his voice steady. "The surgeon tried to extract it, but decided it was impossible, as the shard lay too close to my heart."

Something too studied about his tone warned her. "Isn't that dangerous?" she asked.

For a moment he didn't answer. "He said it would not be, immediately."

"Immediately? What does that mean?" she prodded, when he seemed reluctant to finish.

"He said that the shard would eventually travel toward the heart and—and the result would be—ah—unfortunate."

She gazed at him in horror.

"So—"

"Adrian!"

"So," he went on, "I seem, one way or another, to be a poor bet for a husband, but I thought I could be of use to you at the moment, at least. When my attempt to aid you, that night in the woods, appeared to cause you even more distress, Madeline, it was the least I could do."

Trying not to weep, she could not answer. She had thought he had only one slightly mad would-be assassin to outwit, not that his own body would eventually betray him.

"I have written to my man of business and my solicitor, sent a new will," the viscount went on. "You will be well provided for, I give you my word. I have a handsome estate in Huntingtonshire—I wish I would have the opportunity to show it to you myself, but"—he hurried on, because she had made a small sound of distress deep in her throat—"the point is, you will have an ample income. You can stay here or move your father there, anything you choose, Madeline."

She could no longer hold back the tears. "I choose—if I could choose," she told him, "I choose for you to live, Adrian."

He put his arms around her and gathered her close, and this time, neither spoke. He held her tight against him, and at least for this moment, she could hear his heart beating against her cheek, and know that he was alive, very much alive.

The autumn sunshine flowed in golden rays about them, and a few trills of birdsong sounded from the trees. Once more, she wished desperately for the power to stop the moment and hold it still in her hand.

After holding her in silence for a space, his cheek against her hair, Adrian straightened and asked, "Do you still wish to marry me, Madeline?"

She frowned at him, wanting to box his ears, wanting to hold him close and never let him go, and exclaimed, "Don't speak nonsense, Adrian. And never, ever speak less than the full truth to me again!"

"Yes, my lady," he answered, his tone meek.

Maddie wiped her cheeks and hoped she was reasonably composed before they went back inside. They could not speak of the subject inside the house, of course. Maddie was sure Felicity was brimful of curiosity, but this time, she could not indulge her good friend by telling her the topic they had discussed.

After a light supper, they played a few rounds of cards, then all went up to an early bedtime.

But that night Maddie could not sleep. Thinking of Adrian so near and yet so far, and soon about to slip away from her completely, she lay miserable and wakeful in her bed. She wrapped her arms about her sides, clutching herself tightly, wondering how she would ever go on without him.

It was only a short time ago that Adrian had ridden into her life, yet now he seemed so necessary to her comfort that she knew that she would feel as empty as a hollow rind when he had mounted his horse and ridden away. And to think of him in such danger twice over . . .

Just the thought of it made her weak with misery.

Could Fate really deal him—deal both of them—such an unkind blow? To have her find the man she loved and then to take him away at almost the same moment? She would mourn him for the rest of her life.

The house had fallen silent, and only one candle burned on the table by her bed. A floorboard creaked in the hall, and she lifted her head, refusing to hope. It was only the house settling as the air cooled. Yes, now all was quiet again. She blinked. Hoping did no good, hadn't she told herself—

Her door opened, and the viscount slipped inside on stockinged feet, shutting it noiselessly behind him.

"I will stay only if you wish it," he said very low. "But since we have so little time remaining to us, I thought perhaps you might wish . . ."

Knowing her face was alight, she held up her arms to him, and he came quickly to her.

For a few minutes he held her, and it was enough for her to cling to him, cherishing the knowledge that he was real and solid and alive, breathing, whole. She cried a little, her face against his chest, still trying to cope with the overpowering blow of the information of his double threat.

"Madeline, my love," he told her, kissing the top of her head, then lifting her face and kissing away the tears on her cheeks. "All men die when their hour comes. We are alive now; this is no time to think of sadness. Let me show you how to celebrate life, instead."

"Yes, please," she said.

He bent to kiss her lips, and she tasted the salt of her own tears. Without speaking again, he lifted her nightgown and pulled it over her head, tossing it away. Because she had hoped he might come to her, she wore nothing beneath.

His dark eyes glinted with appreciation. "My darling, what a beauty you are," he breathed. "More than Aphrodite herself—if we dwelt on a classical isle long ago, the Greek goddess would be jealous and no doubt drive us into the sea or send monsters to devour us."

She laughed at such nonsense, but it warmed her, too. She was emboldened to sit and pull his linen shirt up over his head and fling it aside to follow her abandoned nightgown.

And below the waist—she blushed to consider going farther, but he pushed down his trousers and kicked them away, and then he lay back upon her bed and waited for her to join him. She climbed back onto the bed, eager for their lovemaking to begin. But this time, Adrian seemed to wait—for what? Was she supposed to start, do something? She still had so much to learn!

"What should I do?" she whispered.

"What would you like to do?" he asked. He lay back against the mattress and grinned up at her.

"I like to touch you," she told him.

He raised his brows, but he smiled, so this seemed acceptable. She curled up on her side and dared to run her fingers over him, relishing the freedom to explore what would shortly be her husband, her new property. His skin felt different than her own, that was true, but she liked the feel of it, the coarse touch of his dark body hair, lightly sprinkled over his chest, growing in a thicker vee that reached down to his private area—she still couldn't quite manage to stare at that without feeling shy.

She jerked her gaze back and ran her hands over his chest, touched the muscles that shaped his shoulders and upper arms and felt her blood heat even warmer as she marveled at what a well-made male animal he was.

Adrian made a contented sound, more a groan than a sigh. "You're teasing me, but I love it," he said, very softly.

Happy that this felt good to him, too, she leaned closer and kissed his neck just beneath his chin, then snuggled closer and kissed him again and again, on his neck, on his shoulders, on his chest where his flat nipples seemed to call to her.

He made an inarticulate sound.

Maddie put her arms about his neck and pulled their bodies closer together so she could press her breasts against his chest; they seemed right there, their softness felt good against his firmer muscled torso, and her stomach against the hardness of his. She moved against him again as he groaned once more.

"There are limits, my lady," he told her, his voice hoarse, as he reached for her hips to pull her even nearer into him. She could feel his maleness growing harder, and she couldn't keep from moving a little against it.

"Are you heavy with need for me?"

"Yes, my love," she whispered. "I want you—at once!"

She kissed his neck again, and when he lowered his head, she found his mouth and they met as eagerly as hungry men granted access to a king's banquet. His tongue slipped through her open lips, probing and impatient. and she met him with her own, feeling as fevered as he.

And even as the kiss continued, and their passion grew and climbed, she felt him pull her hips close and position her so that he could slip inside her, and the delicious pleasure of that touch made her the one to moan aloud this time.

"Oh, yes, my love," she muttered, not very clearly as they still kissed, then broke apart briefly to shift position. She found that Adrian had again pivoted to lie on his back. She was startled to find herself atop him, although they were still joined.

What—was this possible?

Her lover grinned up at her. "Do just what you like, my love," he said.

And she found that she could. Sitting over him, her legs bent, she held onto her knees and discovered she could control just how deep he was inside her, and in this position, the pleasure seemed even more intense. So she moved her hips with greater and greater speed and abandon—it was wonderful, it was freedom, it was the two of them released to ease each other into transports of delight.

The circles of pleasure ran over her body as intensely as before, and more, deeper and greater, rings of fire and ice that tingled through her, carrying her along with sensations she had never imagined. Her skin felt as if it were on fire, and the ecstasy was inside her and out, almost too much to be contained. Who had designed such joys—had the angels spun such feelings over thousands of years?—Maddie thought dimly in some distant corner of her mind. Surely this was too great to be merely made of flesh and bone. This feeling, this soaring lifting, intense and exploding ecstasy—

She gave a wordless cry, just as Adrian's hoarse exclamation came, and then he grabbed her hips and held her, held them together as she felt him spasm, again and again, and then they both collapsed into a heap of tangled arms and legs. She felt as boneless as a bowl of blancmange quivering in the summer's heat, and just as quivery as the pudding.

Every muscle of her body was relaxed, at ease, and their lovemaking seemed to have given her more than physical release. Somehow the rest of her doubts had drifted away, as well.

When had Adrian ever done anything except look out for her well-being, anything except try to protect her? Yes, he was stubborn and tended to make decisions too quickly and then inform her, but didn't most men? Give the two of them—please God—a lifetime together and she might teach him to better involve his wife earlier. But in the meantime, how could she rage at him for trying to keep her alive?

"I love you so," she told him, as he held her inside his arms.

"I love you more than life, my sweet Madeline," Adrian told her, looking down at her with his gleaming dark eyes. "That is why I must not allow my own special doom to touch you."

"But, Adrian—"

"No, Madeline, try to understand," he told her, his tone quiet, but firm. "When the war ended, I swore I could never again order another man to his death. Such were my dreams that . . . well, you have heard of the pools of blood that follow me."

Expression bleak, he shut his eyes a moment, and she shivered, just to think of such an image.

"So I must keep you safe. When I know that can be done, I will be able to consider another alternative, but first, you must allow me that."

Looking into his eyes, she saw there the overpowering need, and she had to nod, reluctantly, and touch his cheek.

"It's just—you hold my heart in your hand, Adrian," she whispered. "I will not be whole until you return to me. Remember that, as well!"

"I won't forget," he told her. "Ever."

Then they lay close and did not speak, but words were not necessary.

When dawn neared, Adrian kissed her one last time and left as quietly as he had come. Her body eased, if not her mind; she slipped into an uneasy slumber. When she woke again, the sunlight slanting in her window showed the day much advanced. She blinked at the light, and it all rushed back—the glories of the love they shared, both the exquisite joys of the physical pleasures they could give to each other, and the aching pain of her fears for him, and herself, the pain she would feel when he had left her.

The melancholy she felt was held at bay only with great effort, but she knew she could not allow it to paralyze her now. Time enough to mourn later, she told herself, one arm over her eyes—once he was gone, there would be endless time. Just now she must treasure every moment they had together. Maddie hurried to wash and dress, and when she came downstairs, she found everyone else had already finished breakfast and gone about their morning routine.

Going down the hall, she heard the murmur of the men's voices in her father's study. She found Felicity and Bess in the kitchen. Bess was rolling out a pastry for dinner later, while Felicity stirred a pudding, also to be steamed for the main meal.

"Are you all right?" her friend asked. "We didn't wish to wake you. Bess thought your head might be aching."

"No, I'm fine," Maddie lied. "Just a restless night. No, don't stop what you are doing. I can get what I need."

She made herself a cup of tea and some bread and butter and sat down at the plain wooden table to eat. The everyday routine going on about her should have been soothing. But Felicity looked a bit wan, as if her thoughts might also be troubled.

Maddie was keeping enough secrets of her own to know better than to pry into her friend's thoughts. So after she finished her light repast, she made no attempt to inquire, merely making light conversation while she helped with the cooking. When the dinner preparations were well underway, she and Felicity left Bess to take care of the rest, shed their aprons, and went back to the sitting room.

"I need to make sure of the fit of your wedding gown," Felicity told her. "I've pressed the lace and sewn the ribbons onto your best petticoat. While the men are still at their game, why don't we go upstairs and you can slip on the gown?"

Maddie agreed and they climbed the staircase again. When she shed her day dress and carefully donned the white silk gown, it was strange to stare at her reflection in the looking glass. She seemed a stranger—and she looked pale, ashen from head to foot.

"The gown is lovely," Felicity said. "The seamstress did a wonderful job. It's most becoming."

"Thank you," Maddie said, her voice faint. The person in the glass seemed foreign, a stranger. She, a married woman . . . and how long till she was a widow, and the white replaced by black? Oh, she could not bear it!

She put her hands to her cheeks.

"Madeline, what's wrong? Are you regretting that you said yes?" Felicity asked.

"No, no." Maddie covered her face, breathing deeply and trying to compose herself. Briefly, she told Felicity about the viscount finding the bullet.

"It was my 'bee,'" she explained. "He has an enemy who is trying to kill him—it's a long and complicated story—the man is quite mad. The viscount feels he must leave until—if ever—the man is no longer a threat to Lord Weller and those around him, especially, just now, me."

"Oh, how dreadful!" Felicity said, looking shocked. "Of course I understand that he does not want to see you hurt—I most certainly agree with his caution. But surely there must be another way?"

"So I have tried to argue, but without success. The apparent murder attempt at the vicarage has only strengthened his resolve to leave as soon as we are wed. So you can see that I view my fast approaching wedding with very mixed emotions!" She swallowed a sob, determined not to weep again.

Felicity hugged her briefly, but Maddie, although she appreciated her friend's support, sniffed and said, "Yes, but let's be sure of the fit. I want to take off the dress; I cannot bear to think about this."

"Of course." Felicity checked the gown and the cape that went over it, and then Maddie shed her wedding costume, somehow feeling it unlucky to wear it too long before the actual wedding day. She had enough portents of bad fortune, already.

They hung the gown up carefully. While Felicity carried the cape back to her own room to fix a few loose threads, Maddie took her mother's letters and made her way to the attic.

She had wanted to visit her mother's grave by the church, but the viscount thought that too dangerous just now, so she had decided that this would have to do. In the attic she knelt by the trunk where she had found the ribbon-bound packet in the first place. She kissed the thin stack and put it back in the very bottom of the trunk where she had first seen the book of receipts it was hidden in.

"Mama, I'm glad you had the chance to love, and I'm glad you took it," she whispered against the dusty lid. "I'm not angry at you, I promise. I understand."

Then she rose. Wiping her eyes, she descended the steps and began an orgy of cleaning, as if that might take her thoughts away from the jumble of anxiety that filled her mind.

The afternoon was rainy, and since Adrian had already decided it was better that they stay indoors while the shooter was somewhere in the neighborhood, it gave them an excuse to miss their usual stroll through the garden. They played spillikins with Felicity, and the viscount made silly jokes, trying to lift her spirits, Maddie knew. She tried to keep up her end of the game, and as she did, she asked questions about his childhood. She had suddenly realized there was so much she didn't know about him, and time was running out. She would have little opportunity to ask, to hear stories such as these about his first pony, his first trek out of his own courtyard.

"I thought I was a prime adventurer," Adrian told them while he tried to extract another straw from the pile. "I made it all the way up the hill before my nanny found I had slipped out and she raised the alarm. A stableboy came running to bring me back, thus ending my adventure on a depressingly ungallant note."

Both the women laughed. Maddie had a mental vision of Adrian as a five-year-old, his handsome face cherubic and innocent, and her heart melted. She smiled at him across the small table they had gathered around.

"Were you punished?" Felicity asked, practical as always.

"Oh, yes, I had to sit in the corner for the rest of the morning, which I thought most unfair," Adrian told them. He pulled out two more of the long straws.

"A mere bagatelle," Maddie told him. It was her turn next. She reached for a straw, but she was looking at Adrian instead of the pile, and it collapsed.

"Oh, dear," she said belatedly. "Meanwhile, you have beaten us again."

Although she cared not a whit about the game, Maddie kept her tone cheerful with the greatest effort. She would lock him in the corner if she could, she thought, but that would hardly serve. And anyhow, he was no longer small and innocent, but an adult, and much less amenable to taking orders from anyone, no matter how well-meaning that person might be.

She glanced at him, and his gaze back was rueful, as if—as so often—he understood the direction of her thought.

Felicity shook her head. "You two," she said. "You're not attending to the game at all. I'm going to sit in the corner and read. You might as well hold hands and bill and coo; it's obviously where your thoughts are."

Maddie blushed, and Adrian laughed. Maddie put away the game as Felicity picked up the book of ancient history that she had borrowed from Mr. Applegate and took a chair in the far side of the sitting room. Then Maddie rejoined the viscount and settled down to hear more tales of his juvenile misdeeds. Just hearing his voice was a comfort, much more so sitting next to him, holding his hand. She would take any part of him she could get.

At dinner that evening conversation was light, and they all were careful to keep the flow of talk cheerful. If she watched Adrian covertly, observing small details and adding them to her mental library, no one had to know. Perhaps she was going mad, too, Maddie thought ruefully. But it was a madness made up of love and a surfeit of coming loneliness, and she did not know any other way of coping.

Later, when they had all come up to bed, and the house had quieted, she washed and blew out all but one candle. Sitting up in bed, she waited, almost holding her breath, until at last the door to her bedchamber opened, and she could smile at her lover, her dearest love, when he came over the threshold.

The next morning, despite the fact that she had dropped off to sleep only a short time before dawn, reluctant to sleep away the precious hours spent in his arms, Maddie woke early. She also did not mean to miss any of the day before the wedding, the last day she knew for sure that he would be with her. After the wedding was solemnized, who knew how soon Adrian might feel compelled to leave?

They had argued about it in the middle of the night, after more glorious lovemaking. "If we roused the neighborhood and gathered all the men to search for your cousin the would-be assassin," she proposed, "surely with a large group of men, we could find him and confine him."

Adrian argued, "I would be loath to have you subject to that kind of gossip, Madeline, and besides—"

"What is gossip compared to your life!" she interrupted, throwing herself upon his bare torso where he lay on her mattress after their lovemaking, as if she could shake him into compliance. Then, remembering the particle of metal in his chest, she shivered and slipped down to lie beside him instead.

Frowning, she saw that he noted the motion, but he did not comment on it.

"He's too sly to be that easily trapped," the viscount continued. "As we spread the word to gather your neighbors together, he would be bound to hear and suspect our plan, and he would simply slip away, coming back later when the good folk were tired of lying in wait for him."

Adrian sounded too depressingly pragmatic. Maddie lay her cheek against his side, feeling the warmth of his skin, the slight sheen of sweat, which they had well earned. Every night he showed her something new. Every night she found that she could enjoy loving him even more, and every night she thought how much more she would miss him.

Today she washed and dressed quickly. Almost running down the staircase, she found the viscount still before her in the dining room. Bess was setting the first plates of food on the sideboard.

"Morning, miss," she said. "All excited, I guess ye are, about the big day tomorrow."

"Yes, indeed," Maddie said, but she looked at the viscount as she spoke, smiling into his eyes.

He gave her an answering smile back. When the servant left the room, he bent and gave her a fast, hard kiss before anyone else came into the room. They parted just in time; she heard the faint creak of wheels as her father's chair came down the hall, with Felicity soon behind him.

Her cheeks a little warm, Maddie spun to put eggs and bread on her plate and to give her color time to cool before she turned to tell her father good morning.

"A lovely day outside," Mr. Applegate said, greeting them all.

Maddie poured her father a cup of tea and then fixed him a plate, putting on his favorite foods.

When she set it down, he gave her a slight pat on the cheek. "Not much longer now," he said, smiling.

"No, Papa," she said, smiling back at him, though her heart dropped a little at his words with their double meaning.

One more day.

The eggs had suddenly turned tasteless in her mouth. After tomorrow, if the shooter tried again, would Adrian pack up and ride away?

Could she persuade him to take her with him?

No, then who would tend to her father? She had promised her mother she would take care of her father. How could she break a deathbed oath?

She had never thought *all* her sisters would marry. Of course, poor Lauryn had been widowed so young, but she would likely marry again.

So it really was up to her. Since Papa's accident . . . and it didn't matter if he wasn't her birth father, he had saved her mother from scandal, brought Madeline up, and treated her lovingly; she loved him like a father—he was her father!

She couldn't walk away and leave him.

But her heart was going to break in two when Adrian rode away.

Oh, God, why did this have to happen?

Maddie put her fork down. She couldn't see her plate. She blinked hard—she could not disgrace herself, nor upset her father, by crying over her eggs and ham.

The ridiculousness of that drove a little of her melancholy away.

She sipped her tea to avoid having to make conversation

and let the talk flow around her. Her father was talking about a neighbor's cow, it seemed. She had nothing to add to that.

Felicity chatted about the best way to churn butter, and Maddie nodded absently, though she had few thoughts on that subject, either.

When everyone had finished eating, the two men disappeared in the direction of her father's study, and she and Felicity helped Bess clear away. When Maddie came back to the sitting room, she was surprised to see the viscount there with her father's chess set arranged upon the small card table.

"Have you moved your game to the sitting room?"

"Your father suggested you might like a lesson in chess," Adrian told her, grinning.

"I can't imagine why," she said. "He tried to teach me when I was twelve, and I drove us both to a nervous frenzy."

She sat down across the table from him nonetheless, happy for any excuse to gaze at him. "And where is Felicity?"

"Ah, I suggested that Mrs. Barlow might like to discuss with your father the book of ancient history that she borrowed earlier from his collection. She was happy to agree. I wanted to assure him some congenial company, so she is sitting in his study with him just now."

"Thus leaving us alone in the sitting room?" she suggested. "I begin to see why you are so good at chess! You are a master of strategy, my lord."

"That, too," he agreed, his eyes glinting with laughter. "And while I fear we shall have to be—ah—prudent in our behavior, at least we can have a few minutes of private conversation."

So he, too, wanted any scrap of comfort he could get, Maddie thought. In an odd way, that cheered her. Adrian was also dreading their approaching separation.

Quite without thinking, she leaned forward toward him over the board.

"The white pawn always moves first," the viscount said. "Do you have any faint interest in chess, by the way?"

"Not the slightest," she said.

"Good, then I will tell you instead that your breasts look quite lovely from this vantage point," he pointed out.

She blushed and straightened. Her neckline was not very low, but still she had been bending over the table.

"No, no, that removes them too much from my view," he said, his tone teasing.

"Very well." She leaned forward again. "Anything else you like about the vista?"

"Everything," he said. "You didn't do that half-braid thing with your hair today."

She was almost surprised at how observant he was. "No, I was rushing, so I just pinned it up, and not very well, I'm afraid. I'm sorry it's a bit untidy."

"I think it's lovely any way you do it. But I admit, my fingers are longing to pull out those pins that are showing themselves so temptingly." He gestured, and she was surprised to see that he was gazing dreamily at her long hair. "I'm thinking I could release it and let it fall free about your shoulders. I have just realized that even at night, I've only seen you with your hair—and it's a lovely golden brown hue, you know, soft and gleaming and wonderful to touch—I've only seen it braided or somehow restrained. I'd love to see it free about your shoulders."

For some reason, this made her blush again; the thought of her hair flowing unrestrained seemed very sensual.

If her father came in . . .

Oh, for heaven's sake, she told herself. It was only hair. If he wanted to see her hair flowing . . .

She reached back and found the first pin.

"Oh, no, let me!" Adrian said. He stood and reached

across the small table, and his eyes danced. She smelled his clean linen and the scent of male flesh as he brushed her cheek with his arm; she shut her eyes and enjoyed his closeness. Very gently, he pulled out another pin, and another until she felt the weight of her hair shift, and the knot of hair gave way and slipped free of its mesh. She shook the snood and the rest of the pins away.

"Oh, fair lady," Adrian said, his voice low and husky, almost a caress. "You look as if you've just swept out of some fairy tale, as you did that night in the gazebo when I thought you might be a wood nymph, come to tempt me into faery land. You stole my heart then, and you've never let it go."

"I never want to let you go!" Although she felt her throat ache, Maddie smiled up at him, and he leaned to kiss her lips, firmly, sweetly, his tongue probing and lingering for a faint delicious moment.

Then he stroked his fingers through her thick locks, weaving them through her hair and holding her head back so he could kiss her again, and again, and kiss her yet once more, while Maddie put her arm behind his head and pulled him toward her so that she could kiss him back properly.

"You are so incredibly lovely, sweet Madeline," he murmured. He touched her cheek, and the light touch of his fingertips caressing her skin sent goose bumps up and down her spine.

She swallowed as he moved slowly away, but he traced his hand lightly down her cheek, around her lips, over her chin, each touch sparking sensations that warmed her, chilled her, thrilled her.

He moved one hand down to cradle her breast, straining through the thin muslin and aching for his touch. Deep inside her, other parts of her body were wanting him, wanting completions they could not achieve in her sitting room in clear daylight.

Oh, dear, they should never have started this, she thought. She would be aching all day until he could come to her tonight.

He grinned at her. "We shall drive ourselves into Bedlam at this rate," he told her. "But it's a better game than chess, you must admit."

She laughed aloud.

Then he turned his head, and she heard it, too: the slight creak of her father's wheeled chair in the hallway, and then Felicity, bless her, speaking rather loudly.

"Of course, the Greeks were much more accomplished architects, don't you think?"

She would be trying to give them warning.

Maddie hastily grabbed some hairpins from the chessboard and twisted her thick mane of hair back and up into a hasty knot once more, untidy though it might be.

She was so concerned with that—thank goodness nothing had been unbuttoned, she thought—that only when her father and Felicity were actually inside the room did she remember that she and Adrian were supposed to be playing chess. They had never moved a game piece.

She looked down at the board, expecting it to give them away. She saw instead that several pieces were arranged across the squares, and Adrian sat with his hand on a bishop as if he had been seriously contemplating a move. Trust her fiancé to remember the details, she thought with relief.

"Who is winning?" her father asked jovially from across the room.

"Not me, I assure you," she said. "I fear that my skill at chess remains the same as it was the last time I tried to learn." And that was the literal truth!

The viscount smiled at her. "You are too harsh on yourself," he said. "I think you have many skills."

"Thank you, my lord," she said, trying to keep her tone

demure and not blush. "You're too kind." And when her father turned his chair and his attention away, she favored her
mischievous fiancé with a playful kick under the table.

He grinned back at her.

They were soon drawn into a general conversation
about the history the other two had been discussing. Madeline found once again that the viscount was as informed on
as many subjects as her father, and conversant on all her
favorite topics.

Suddenly it seemed the day had flown, and they were
sitting down to dinner. As she looked out into the gathering
dusk, her heart seemed to contract. Time had defeated her
again. She had wanted to stop it, gather it together, hold it
back—and always it ran before her. Soon it would take
Adrian away.

After dinner, they were about to bring out the cards
when there was a knock at the front door. Bess went to answer, and Maddie heard the sound of men's voices. She
moved to the doorway of the sitting room and looked out to
see what was happening. The viscount had already brushed
past her; he seemed to be listening to a couple of villagers
who stood with hats in hand and eager expressions. Eyes
bright with anticipation, they talked quickly.

What was this about? Maddie watched as Adrian took
coins from his pocket and handed over an unseen amount
to each man, to their obvious satisfaction. Then he spoke to
them again briefly and shut the door behind them when
they turned on their heels and hurried out.

Wearing a thoughtful expression, he turned, too, though
he seemed headed for the stairwell instead of back to the
sitting room. When he saw her waiting in the doorway, his
brow cleared.

"Good," Adrian said, "you are here. Please excuse me to
your father and Mrs. Barlow. I have some news I have to
check out."

"What is it?" she asked, alarmed.

"While not as extensive as your idea of rallying the neighborhood, I did try to do what I could to find our mysterious intruder, my love. I have hired a dozen villagers to watch at selected points around the area ever since we have had reason to suspect that my cousin was here. I hoped they might note an unknown person lurking, one preparing to execute a surprise attack."

"Oh, wonderful," Madeline cried, "and they have located him?"

"They think they have found traces of an outsider, a man whose appearance matches the description given by Mrs. Barlow," Adrian told her.

"Oh?" Maddie paused, puzzled. "But I don't see the connection between your mad cousin and Mrs. Barlow's gypsy."

"Nor do I, frankly, but right now, we can't wait until we figure it out," the viscount pointed out. "I have to go; I will be back as soon as I can."

"Oh, take care," she said, wanting so badly to reach out and hold him back that she had to curl her hands into fists to keep herself from grabbing him.

He leaned forward and gave her a quick kiss, turned and opened the front door, and stepped into the darkness.

And he was gone.

She went back to the sitting room and told her father and Felicity, and then, unable to sit still, went to the kitchen and helped Bess make tea. She felt numb inside. If the viscount could find his cousin and, with the help of the men he had hired, bring him to the local magistrate and see him arrested, they might at last be free of his long-standing threat, the cousin's enormous, unbalanced hatred. Then she and Adrian would be free to live together as man and wife and enjoy their love for each other—at least until the pieces of the bullet in his body migrated to his heart and killed him.

The idea of a silent killer biding its time within his own body made her want to weep. Even if they found the traitorous cousin, now there was a second and more deadly enemy. How could they defeat the unbeatable foe he carried within him?

Deal with one enemy at a time, she told herself. She couldn't think about more than that, not now.

She paced up and down the threadbare rug in the sitting room. Her father and Felicity watched with pity in their eyes. But she could no longer attempt to cloak the anxiety that filled her mind and overflowed her body until she thought she might pound her fists against the wall and scream until in far-off London, the poor mad king himself—deaf or no—could hear her.

"Would you like more tea?" Felicity asked, her voice anxious and her forehead creased. She looked ready to wring her hands, too.

"No, thank you." Feeling guilty about inflicting such distress on her friend and family, Maddie tried to sit down and not try her friend's composure as well as her own, but she found it impossible. In a moment, she popped up again, unable to sit quietly when she had no idea what was happening to the viscount. Was he safe? She could picture Adrian gliding up to surprise his cousin and being waylaid himself instead. Shots ringing out, blood flowing, Adrian in distress, his lifeblood slipping away. She put her hands to her head trying to prevent these horrible images from flooding through her mind.

"Perhaps a sip or two of brandy?" her father suggested. He also sounded concerned as he watched her wander up and down.

When she shook her head, he added, "I'm sure the viscount is proceeding with courageous and intelligent caution, Madeline."

She smiled, knowing that her father was trying to soothe

her. But she could not be still, and she continued to pace, looking out the windows into the dark night, going now and then into the hall to stare at the front door and listen for the sound of the knocker, which remained adamantly still.

When the eleventh hour struck on the clock in the sitting room, her father said, "I think we should all at least prepare for bed. You still have a wedding scheduled for tomorrow, my dear."

"To have a successful wedding, one needs both a bride and a groom," Maddie pointed out, trying to smile at her feeble attempt at a jest, but finding herself unable to lift her lips—they felt as if they were frozen, numb.

"Lord Weller will no doubt return soon," her father said, his tone firm. "But in the meantime, you should attempt to get some sleep."

Sure that she would never be able to shut her eyes, Maddie went reluctantly upstairs with Felicity. They separated on the landing and she went to her own room, where Bess had brought up warm water. She washed and changed into her nightgown. She had had hopes of one more night of lovely, if illicit, lovemaking with Adrian, and instead, here she was, alone and consumed with worry. At least tomorrow night— oh, please let tomorrow night be a wonderful wedding night of love and joy, she prayed as she braided her hair before bed.

Just let him be safe, she prayed. God keep him safe!

When she was ready for bed, she opened her bedroom door again so that she could more easily hear any sound from downstairs, nor could she bear to quench the candle on her bedside table.

She climbed into bed and sat there, her back against the pillows and a book on her knees, but she could not focus on the lines of print. Instead she listened hard to every small sound that resonated through the quiet house.

It seemed as if hours—no, days—had passed when at last, she heard the thud of the door knocker. Throwing a wrapper over her nightgown, Maddie ran to the staircase. As she hurried down the steps, she heard other doors open. Everyone had been listening for the knocker, too, it seemed. But she beat them all to the front door.

When she pulled back the bolt, she trembled with nervous anticipation until she saw that it was the viscount who stood in the doorway.

With a wordless cry of joy, she threw herself into his arms. He was icy cold and smelled of outdoors and sweat and horsehair, and she did not care at all.

"Here, here," he murmured. "I am cold and muddy, my love; you will be drenched through and through."

She could indeed feel the icy wetness of his clothes penetrating her nightgown and chilling her body, but she didn't mind. Just the fact that he was alive and apparently unhurt left her nearly delirious with happiness.

"I was so worried!" she told him, her voice trembling. "I was so afraid for you."

"I know." He stroked her hair. "Here now, you've bundled up that lovely hair again," he said into her ear.

She gave a shaky giggle.

Behind her, she heard her father's chair as he maneuvered it out of his bedchamber. Felicity had come to the head of the stairs, a shawl wrapped around her nightdress, and even Bess stood peering around the end of the hallway.

"Did you have any luck, my lord?" John Applegate asked.

"Sadly, no," Adrian said. "We thought once we had trapped him in a farmer's barn, but he slipped away before we could close all the entrances. The devil rode for dear life, and we lost him in the darkness. When our horses could run no further, we had to give up and return."

She looked up at him and saw how defeat creased his forehead. She could hear the bitter disappointment in his voice.

"It can't be helped." Her father sounded disheartened, too. "Best get some sleep. It will be dawn soon."

The viscount nodded.

There would be no private time for the two of them tonight, Maddie knew, sharing a glance with her fiancé. And tomorrow—or today, really—today was her wedding day!

Now that she was assured of the viscount's safety, she thought she might sleep at last. She went back to her bedchamber and shut the door, climbing into bed and pulling the covers up, trying to get warm again.

At least she had had none of her sick headaches to interfere with her wedding day, Maddie thought idly. Suddenly she sat straight up in bed and counted on her fingers.

Oh, good lord, surely not. She counted again.

It couldn't be. Could it? Perhaps it was indeed a good thing she would be properly married today!

Now she found it truly impossible to shut her eyes. She lay in the dark for an interminable time until at last her lids closed. She felt as if she had just dropped off to sleep when Bess came bustling into her room with a cup of tea and a plate of toast.

"Mustn't be late for yer own wedding!" the maidservant said, her tone cheerful as she set down the tray. "Ah, I just wish yer sweet mum had lived to see today!"

Maddie blinked. "Yes, so do I, Bess, so do I." She sat up in bed and took a sip of the hot tea. Her wedding day . . .

What was the viscount thinking? And where was his mad cousin—was he still lurking about? Had Adrian set guards against him? Surely he would think of precautions to keep the man from disrupting their wedding. She must talk to Adrian, about that, and—and other things.

"I must talk to the viscount," she said, thinking aloud.

Bess looked scandalized. "Oh, no, miss, not on yer wedding morning! That's bad luck to see the groom before the ceremony."

"I'll have to chance it," Maddie said. But when she rose and put a wrapper on over her nightgown so she could walk down the hall to the other bedroom, she found that the viscount had already gone downstairs.

Hesitating to go down before she dressed, she sent Bess to fetch the viscount. The servant came back with word that the groom had already breakfasted and left for the church.

Frowning, Maddie told herself that should mean he was going early to check out the building and its surroundings. Meanwhile Bess had gone to great trouble to set up a hip bath that Maddie wanted to enjoy before the water cooled. So she had her bath, washed her long hair and brushed it before the fire to dry, then Felicity helped her curl it and pin it up. Finally Maddie prepared to don her new wedding dress, so carefully sewn by the dressmaker in Ripon, and the matching cape and bonnet.

Felicity was there to help, and Bess popped in and out.

"Such a shame yer sisters are not 'ere," the longtime Applegate servant said.

"I know," Maddie said, sighing. "If it were possible, I would wait, but—"

Clucking her tongue, the servant raised her brows

"No, no, it's not what you think, but"—Maddie put her head under the skirt of her white gown to hide her reddening cheeks for a moment—"oh, there are too many things happening at once. Mad shooters and bees that aren't bees . . ."

"It's wedding nerves, Bess," Felicity said. "Pay no attention."

"I vow she's already been into the brandy!" The maid shook her head. "And it's ne eight o'clock o' the morn!"

"Before this day is over, I may need more than brandy," Maddie muttered, than hoped her impulsive words did not turn out to be accurate. "Help me with these back buttons, please."

"I will do them, Bess," Felicity said.

"Then I'll nip down and see about the beef," Bess told them, shaking her head at such goings on. "Thomas'll be up 'o the while to empty the bath."

"I truly am in a state," Maddie told her friend after the servant had departed. "Even though I haven't been into the brandy."

Felicity laughed, and Maddie managed a nervous giggle. "I understand," the widow said. "Here is your best handkerchief trimmed with new blue lace, and your mother's prayer book to carry. And you may borrow a sixpence from me. Mind you, I borrowed it from you to start with, but I think that will still count."

They giggled again, and one way or another, Maddie tried to keep her mind off what might be happening around the church.

When it was time for Felicity and Maddie to join her father in the carriage, Felicity brought her the small bunch of flowers she had prepared for her, and Maddie took them, trying not to hold them too tight. She still had not seen Adrian, but she had to have faith that he was keeping a sharp eye out around the church and its outbuildings. He would use the men he had hired. What else could they do?

Surely that would enough to outwit one half-crazed would-be killer?

Bess rode beside Thomas on the driver's seat, not about to miss the marriage of the last Applegate daughter. As they drove up to the church, Maddie saw a quite amazing crowd gathered for the occasion.

Which only went to show, Maddie thought, that all one had to do was be caught naked in the wood with a good-looking, titled stranger: that would draw a good crowd of neighbors to one's wedding!

Now if she and Adrian could just manage to be married before one or both of them were shot dead, all might yet be well.

When she stepped out of the carriage, the assembly gave a soft sigh of approval. Her dress was becoming, a silky cloud of white that draped nicely around her hips, falling to the ground in soft folds; the bodice also showed off her curves without being overly low cut. She hoped Adrian would like it.

Felicity went ahead into the church, to tell the vicar they were here. Maddie waited for her father's chair to be untied and lifted down from the back of the carriage and for him to be carefully placed in it, then they proceeded more slowly into the building.

A murmur ran through the church when they entered.

Maddie found the pews crowded with friends and neighbors. Even Mrs. Masham and her husband were sitting well up front where they would have a superior view. And yes, Adrian stood in his place to the side of the vicar, and his smile broadened when he saw her. The look on his face made her heart pound.

Keeping pace with her father in his chair, she walked slowly up the center aisle to join her husband to be.

Bess and Thomas, after leaving the carriage and horse with one of the boys to mind, had already made their way up to the gallery where the servants generally sat. The other pews were all full, and the parishioners whispered and chattered to each other as the bride passed by them.

They had made it halfway to the altar when she saw Adrian's aspect change. Unable to stop herself, Maddie paused, then whirled to see what had brought that expression of horror to his face.

In the back of the church just inside the door stood a thin man of middle years. He was clad in a well-worn riding habit, his dark hair was thinning, and his face plain. He looked so unassuming, so ordinary, that she would never have looked at him twice except for two things: one, he had caused such a reaction from Adrian. Two, he held a hunting rifle, and it was pointed at her heart.

"Who are you?" she demanded, even though she knew the answer already. Surprised that her voice was so clear and steady, she found that she was quite unafraid. The important thing was that Adrian remain unharmed. "And how dare you interrupt my wedding like this? You have no right!"

"Perhaps I am an avenging angel?" the stranger responded. His voice was curiously high, and it rang through the church like the note of a warped bell. "That gives me the right."

"Francis!" Adrian's voice sounded grim but in control. "Not here, with innocent people at risk! I am the one you want. Come outside, man."

His cousin laughed, a strange hollow sound. "Oh, no, too simple. It would hurt you more if I cut down your bride. Do you think I don't know that?"

"If you harm her, you are a dead man!" Adrian retorted.

This time Maddie felt a whisper of cold. "You truly are evil," she muttered.

Shocked at first into silence, the congregation now stirred and whispered once more, and several of the men began to rise.

The stranger turned and pointed his rifle in a sweeping arc. "Sit down and be still, all of you. I have no qualms about adding to my list."

The men sat down again with more haste than dignity, and several were clutched and held in place by frantic-looking wives. Further up the church, Mrs. Masham had also half stood, wanting only, as Maddie could have told the gunman, to get a better look at what was going on. Adrian's cousin turned the rifle toward her next.

"I said, 'Sit down,' you old biddy."

Shrieking, she sat, ducking her head below the back of the bench to get farther out of sight.

And served her right, Maddie thought, without sympathy. She herself still stood in the middle of the aisle.

She heard her father speak. "Get behind me, Madeline."

She looked down at her father; she had forgotten he was beside her. Even in his chair, he was a man of courage and stature, she thought, and she felt a stab of pride. But he must not be hurt, either, nor Adrian, nor any innocent person here.

She glanced back toward the altar, where the white-faced elderly vicar stood, clutching his prayer book and obviously trembling.

Adrian was gone.

Fourteen

*F*or an instant Maddie felt ice-cold with shock. Her tongue seemed frozen to the top of her mouth.

He had walked away?

"Where is your brave husband now?" his cousin taunted.

Then she understood, and the coldness left her. She drew a cleansing breath. "Braver than you, any day," she said. "He would not take the chance of flying bullets hitting an innocent person." She gestured toward the people filling the church. "Take your bullets and leave now!"

"And if I don't?" He lifted his rifle and pointed it again toward her chest. "I can make him feel the pain I felt when he shot my brother! If I kill his bride, he will know how I suffered!"

He did not sound like a grieving brother, Maddie thought. She tried not to allow her fear to overcome her, like treading water in a cold pond, attempting to keep her head from submerging. He sounded petulant, instead, almost annoyed as if she were not responding the way she was intended to. Perhaps the whole plan was not going the way he had designed it.

Where was Adrian?

Again, her father said, "Step behind me, Madeline."

She didn't want to put her father into harm's way. But when she glanced down to argue, she observed an expression on his face that she rarely saw there, had not seen there since she was very small. And she found herself obeying.

So it was John Applegate who next faced the would-be assassin, his wheeled chair protecting most of his daughter's person. Peeking round the top of the frame, Maddie held her breath—if they angered this madman, who knew what he would do?

"So now we have a cripple to argue for my murdering cousin? Who will the craven send next—his old nanny?" the man with the gun sneered.

"My son-in-law, my future son-in-law, is no coward, nor is he a murderer. Your brother fired on him before the time was called, and it was your brother who insisted on the duel. It was your job to set up the duel properly, and you who failed in your duty. Perhaps it is your guilt that drives you mad—I neither know nor care."

She had never heard her normally gentle father speak in such a tone. Maddie knew her eyes must be wide.

"So either fire, or leave this church. You soil our sacred ground," John Applegate snapped.

The stranger wavered, and some of his resolve seemed to leak away. "He owes me a great debt—he killed my brother," the man muttered in his curious voice, but he appeared to have lost some of his resolve.

John Applegate stared at him, and the other man's expression turned sullen. "I will find him!" he snarled. "I'll be Weller's executioner yet. You may tell him that!" But he suddenly looked ill at ease, glancing about as if he expected Adrian to slip in with a gun pointed his way, and as suddenly as he had come, he spun and stamped away. In a moment, the heavy church door slammed behind him.

Around them, she heard various sighs and exclamations as the other people in the church released their pent-up anxiety.

"Upon my word!" one of the men in a nearby pew snorted. "He's fit for Bedlam, or for hanging, and I'd like to pull the cord!"

"Are you all right, Applegate?" Another neighbor asked. "Damn impertinent bastard, I'd say."

"Oh, Papa, you were splendid," Maddie said softly, "I've never seen you so brave." She bent to hug him.

"I could hardly stand by and watch my daughter shot," He patted her hand. "But I think we should return home, don't you agree?"

Realizing that most of their neighbors were watching them with interest—they had certainly added to the local storehouse of gossip for some long time to come—she agreed. Felicity hurried to put a supportive arm about her, and they made their way, nodding to expressions of sympathy from friends, back to their carriage.

Of Adrian, there was still no sign.

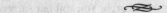

When they were safely back inside their own house, her father instructed Bess not to answer the door. Maddie realized with a sinking heart that he did not expect Adrian to return anytime soon.

"Did you know, Papa?" she demanded.

"What, dear?" he asked. "Now, I think we will all have some brandy." He rolled his chair over to one of the cabinets and poured glasses for all of them.

Felicity accepted hers silently and took a small sip.

Maddie made a face at the taste and swallowed only a drop, putting it down and preferring to wait for the tea that Bess was brewing in the kitchen. "Did you know that Adrian would—that his cousin might break into the middle of—what happened to the men who were supposed to watch out for him? And where did Adrian go? Is he not coming back?"

Her father sighed. "How many questions is that? We were not sure, no, but it seemed quite likely, since he seemed to have discovered the viscount's location. And Lord Weller had almost a dozen men around the church, but it was impossible to know exactly how his cousin might come. To ring the church closely with armed men would have made a scandal, and the vicar would not allow us to do it."

"The vicar got his scandal, anyhow," Maddie pointed out, her tone bitter. "I hope he is satisfied." His prohibition had ruined her wedding day, and she was not in the least happy!

Felicity looked sympathetic. Men were such unimaginative creatures, Maddie told herself. Here she was, wearing her wedding gown, and still not married. Bloody hell—just as well none of her sisters had been able to come up to her wedding.

Bess came into the sitting room and put the tea tray she carried onto the table.

"Now, don't take on, Miss Madeline," the servant said. "I'm sure me lord will be back soon. I'm just 'appy no one is 'urt. When I saw that madman pointing 'is gun at ye, and then at Mr. Applegate, I thought me 'eart was going through me chest, I did!"

"He is not a craven, Bess!" Maddie said.

"No indeed," the maid agreed. "Though, I must say, Mr. Applegate was that brave, I was so proud. Just like the old days, I told Thomas."

Her father looked a bit self-conscious, with all the women in the room beaming at him. Maddie wasn't sure whether to laugh or cry. What about Adrian—what were the rest of the parish thinking about him now? Would they think him a coward—how could they not—they didn't know the real story! It really was unfair.

When the tea had been poured and Bess had left the room, Maddie took her father a plate of cake, trying not to think what this was supposed to signify.

"Eat up, Papa. You are the hero of the hour, and we are eating my wedding cake, so we might as well enjoy it."

Later, they consumed a bigger than normal dinner, with roast beef, puddings, and cake again, although Maddie, at least, had no appetite at all. It was a relief to go up to her bedroom because it was becoming impossible to continue to maintain a brave facade.

It was her wedding night, and she would spend it alone.

She removed her gown, with some help from Felicity. "It will yet work out," her friend told her. "Would you like me to fetch you another glass of brandy? I think you deserve some help in sleeping."

Maddie shook her head. "Thank you, but too much strong drink could give me a headache, and that's not worth it."

"I forgot," Felicity said. "No, you're right."

Wearing a fetching new nightgown, and with no one to admire it, Maddie sat up in bed and hugged her knees, listening to the wind shake the trees outside her window and the sound of small creaks and groans as the house settled in the cooling night air.

At last, when the clock downstairs struck one, her door opened.

He came in quietly, his expression subdued.

"Oh, Adrian," she said, releasing her breath as if she had been holding it for the whole long, difficult day.

He came swiftly to her and wrapped her in his arms. "My darling Madeline. I was afraid you would never want to see me again."

"How could you think so!" she said, pulling him even closer and rejoicing in the solid feel of his body, the smell of cold night air on his clothes.

He leaned down and kissed her softly, then more firmly. Oh, his lips tasted of salt, as if he had sweated today, and he looked hungry and tired.

"You must be real," she said, running her palm over his chin, which felt prickly with beard stubble. She had never seen him so disheveled before.

"Because if this were a dream, I would look more like a hero?" he suggested, which made her smile just for a moment.

"You will always be a hero to me," she told him firmly.

That made him groan. "My dearest, I would not have left you, I promise you, except that I was terrified that he would start shooting, trying to bring me down, and you stood just between us in the line of fire."

She nodded; she had worked it out already.

"Although I had brought a gun with me, I didn't dare take the chance of a shot, because again you stood just between us. I had to make a split-second decision, and I thought it safer for you if I moved out of sight. It felt like pulling out my own heart to leave you there, exposed to a madman who is so unpredictable—I will always remember that moment when I had to turn my back. I shall have nightmares about *that* for years to come!"

"Don't!" Maddie cried, aching at the torment she heard in his voice. "Dearest, don't, I am here, unharmed, as you see. And I understand."

He pulled her even closer and held her so tightly that she could hardly take a breath. "Oh, Madeline, if I lost you I couldn't survive—"

"And how can I go on if I lose you?" she whispered into his chest, but she didn't think he heard. She didn't repeat herself; he was suffering enough already.

It seemed enough for the moment that they could cling together, like two children afraid of the dark, having seen the monsters that dwell there.

"Where did you go?" she asked him at last. "You disappeared so quietly and so quickly."

"I went around to try to get a fair shot at my cousin, but he left too soon. I wanted to track him, but it seemed more important to be sure that no one followed you. Much later, when I was sure that all was calm, I slipped out again and returned here."

"What do we do now, Adrian?" she asked, her voice husky as she waited for his answer, fearing what he would say.

"I shall have to move on, quickly, and try to find another hiding place where I can elude him for a time. It's clear that I shall have to confront him, but I do not want to kill the man in front of my new wife, if it must come to that," Adrian told her. "I will kill him—I know that now—before I allow him to point a gun at you again!"

"But our wedding?" she asked, knowing that anxiety colored her voice. "Must we wait?"

"We will have our wedding, but without more public announcements, and crowds," Adrian told her. "I was too rash, forgive me! I'm sorry that we must be so clandestine, but under the circumstances—"

"No, of course," Maddie agreed. "It's just that I do think that we would be better to make sure the marriage vows are official. Unlike my mother, I do not have a childhood friend waiting in the wings to rescue me."

For once, he could not follow her thought. Adrian raised his brows, and Maddie had to explain, smiling a little shyly.

When Adrian realized what news she had to share, his face lit up. "Dearest Madeline! Then we must certainly make sure our vows are unshakeably fixed and set down for all eternity. I would never have my son a bastard!"

"It could be a girl," Maddie pointed out, as he bent to put his hand tenderly over her still flat stomach.

"No, no, the next one will be a girl," Adrian predicted, "and as beautiful as her mother." He kissed her with exquisite tenderness.

It was much more satisfying to kiss him back than to argue.

The next morning, they all left before the sun was even up. Adrian set out by one path, in order not to draw any danger to them by his presence. Madeline and her father, with Felicity and the servants, traveled once more in the carriage, as quietly as they could manage, and they arrived at the vicarage to rouse the startled vicar, still in his gown and nightcap, out of bed.

"We'll have that wedding service read now, Vicar," Adrian told him. "Hopefully, without interruption this time."

"Ah, yes, yes," the churchman said. Rubbing his eyes and looking nervously about, he led them into the church by the back door.

Thomas and Bess stood watch at the windows, and the doors were bolted while the vicar read the service in record time, stumbling over some of the words as he rattled them off, glancing often toward the back of the church as if he expected the lunatic cousin to make another appearance at any moment.

While the ceremony might be lacking in grace and the pews empty of well-wishers, Maddie was simply glad that at last they would be legally husband and wife, and the child she was increasingly sure she carried would have a proper lineage. And that she would be Adrian's wife was a joy of its own!

"Lady Weller!" Adrian murmured when they joined hands at the close of the service and he had slipped on her finger a lovely gold ring he had bought during their shopping excursion in Ripon.

Still mulling over "to have and to hold, from this day forward," Maddie gazed up at him, love filling her like a golden liquid overflowing a too small goblet.

"Yes, my love?" she answered.

"You are that, too," he agreed, "but now you are indeed my lady."

"Oh," she said, flushing a little. "My lord." So she was—and she wondered how long it would take to get used to that.

Adrian insisted that they wait to see the vicar write their names into the parish book then and there—he didn't seem to trust the vicar's fractured nerves. After they turned down a somewhat unconvincing invitation to stay and have tea and breakfast, they left as quietly as they'd come.

By now the dawn was erupting on the eastern skyline, and the sun peeking over the treetops. It seemed a fitting image, Maddie thought as she began a new part of her life—Lady Weller, indeed. A whole new name, new life, new role—wife and mother—she'd never planned to bear such titles. How on earth would she do it?

Remembering that Adrian loved her buoyed her amazingly. But first of all she had to remain whole and evade the murderous cousin, she thought, sitting far back in the carriage and hoping no bullets came flying.

At home, Bess shooed her out of the kitchen—"On ye wedding morning, no indeed!" while the maid took the leftovers from their dinner last night—somehow no one had eaten very much, it seemed—and turned them into a quite decent breakfast. So even though they had no fancily-clad guests or long speeches, Maddie was just as happy with her wedding as her twin sisters had been with their more fancy event a few months ago.

She sat with her new husband beside her, her father across the table, and a good friend to cheer them. While she would certainly have liked to have her sisters there to join them, she was so happy to be wed at last and to have everyone unharmed that she could complain of nothing.

Now, if they could only find a way to rid themselves of the lunatic cousin and secure Adrian's safety.

They lingered at the table a long time, and when the sun was high in the sky, her father yawned and announced that he was going to retire for his afternoon rest.

When he had departed, Felicity said, "I think I will help Bess straighten up after the meal, and then a nap sounds just the thing. After all the excitement, this morning and yesterday, I'm still fatigued." And if she didn't meet anyone's eye when she said it, she managed to keep a commendably straight face.

Maddie looked down at her plate and tried hard not to break out into one of her too easily provoked blushes.

Adrian stood when Felicity rose. Maddie stood as well, and offered to help, but Felicity was as firm as Bess had been.

"You'll do no work on your wedding day. Go and discuss philosophy, read love poems to each other, or whatever takes your fancy."

She turned away quickly to take dishes out to the kitchen, and not until she was out of the room did Adrian laugh under his breath.

"Shall we retreat to the bedchamber, my love, and peruse some of that poetry?"

Maddie laughed, too, twining her fingers through his. "It seems we have no choice."

He grinned at her. "May all our choices be so grim!"

Hand in hand, they went up the staircase to her bed-chamber, and, with obvious satisfaction, Adrian shut the door behind them.

"Did I not say that this was a prime advantage of married life?" he pointed out.

Maddie giggled. She started to unbutton the back of her wedding dress, but had managed only the top buttons. "I need some help, here, my lord," she suggested, looking over her shoulder and smiling an invitation to her new husband.

He came at once, shedding his jacket on the way. The next button came easily out of its hole at the bidding of his nimble fingers, and he kissed the tender skin thus exposed.

The feel of his lips against her back made her shiver, and the promise of more wonderful sensations to come made Maddie's insides glow with the usual warm and quivery feelings of delight that Adrian always induced. "Don't dillydally!" she commanded. "There are more buttons!"

"Such a harsh taskmaster my new wife turns out to be," he muttered, as he released one more button, and kissed one bit of skin. Again, she shivered.

"Adrian!"

His fingers moved with lazy grace. One more button—one more kiss. The feelings inside her belly grew, and she bit back a moan of longing.

It was exquisite torture, especially as she knew there stretched a long line of tiny buttons down the back of her gown.

"Adrian, I shall rip this gown off myself if you don't hurry!"

"Ah, the lady grows impatient!" His tone was still teasing.

It occurred to her that two could play at this game. She turned and unwound his neckcloth, kissing his neck, loving the clean smell of male flesh. She pushed back his shirt and kissed his chest, as much of it as she could reach, until he groaned slightly and reached down to pull it over his head and toss it aside. His chest was bare to her touch, and she ran her fingers lightly over his skin, the light sprinkling of dark hairs, the firm muscles hard-ridged just beneath the sun-bronzed skin, delighting in the beating of his heart. She paused a moment over the faint scar that made her lips tighten as she remembered the other threat—how could she forget it even for a moment?

She kissed his neck and his chest and the firm skin above his heart—oh, God, protect his heart, protect all of him, she thought—forgetting all about her gown and buttons, kissed him again and again until he groaned and pushed her gently back.

"Wait," he said, reaching for the back of her gown. "I need to—"

He never had the chance to finish.

A sharp sound burst the quiet of her room. The glass in her window shattered and exploded inward as dust erupted from the wall just behind Adrian's head.

Fifteen

*S*he cried out as Adrian shoved her against the mattress, pressing his body against hers to hold her down.

"Don't move!" he exclaimed.

"What is it?" she demanded, although she knew the answer even as she said the words, adding, "How can he see us?"

"He must be in the top of one of the trees near the house," Adrian told her, his voice grim but amazingly calm. "Hold on, we're going to slide off the bed on the side next to the wall." Hardly had he spoken than they were moving, falling willy-nilly toward the floor.

She could tell that he tried to take the brunt of the impact of the fall, turning them as they fell. But the floor rushed up to meet them, and she still had the breath knocked out of her. It was a moment before she could speak.

"Are you all right?" he spoke into her ear.

Fighting for breath, she nodded.

"We shall have to crawl to the hallway," Adrian said. "You must not give him a clear target."

"I understand." It was difficult in her wedding gown, but she pulled up the skirt into a bundle and tucked the short train over her arm and managed as best she could.

Just before they reached the door, it flew open, and Felicity stood there.

"Get back," Adrian said sharply. "Do not show yourself to the view of the window."

Looking alarmed, Felicity did as she was told, just as another bullet came flying. With a high-pitched hum, this one went through the doorway and thudded into the other side of the hall, but again, thankfully, no one was hit.

Maddie crawled around the side of the doorway. Beyond the range of the window, finally, with Felicity's help, she could stand. Her legs cramped, she straightened with a jerk and waited anxiously until her new husband joined her.

"We'd best go reassure your father. I'm sure he's heard the commotion, and he will be most worried," Felicity said.

Maddie nodded, but she was watching Adrian.

He met her gaze. "I'm going out the front door and I'll circle around," he told her, his voice calm. "You go to your father. And all of you, stay away from the windows!"

"We will," she promised, "but, Adrian, be careful!"

They hurried down the staircase and found her father just coming out of his chamber, a frown on his face. "Madeline, what is the ado? I thought I heard shots!"

She explained quickly, and he looked grave.

"Then we must do as Weller advises, and most certainly stay out of sight of the windows." He looked at Maddie's worried face and reached to pat her arm. "Don't fret, Madeline. Your husband is not a green lad; he will proceed with due caution."

"I will go down to the kitchen and see if we can brew some strong tea," Felicity suggested. Madeline followed her to help.

The kitchen's windows were mostly high set, so by moving carefully, they were able to make tea and fetch bread and butter and slices of cake, and they gathered in the central hallway as the most prudent location. Everyone supped in near silence. Maddie, at least, had her mind solely on Adrian's safety, hoping that she did not become a widow before she had even had time to become accustomed to being a wife.

She had no appetite at all, but her father urged her to eat something, so she bit off a small portion of bread. Although Bess was an excellent baker, it seemed as tasteless and heavy as stone in her mouth. Just as she was struggling to swallow the morsel, she heard a shot ring out from behind the house, then another, and she choked.

Felicity jumped up and hit her sharply on the back.

Coughing, Maddie finally got the bread down, drank some tea, and was able to speak. "Oh, sweet heaven, please let Adrian be all right!"

Her father's lips had tightened.

She looked at him in entreaty. "Should we not go to see if he is wounded?"

"And walk straight into a bullet yourself?" her father demanded. "You'll do no such thing! I will go out presently if he does not return in a timely fashion."

What did he consider timely, Maddie wondered, wanting to rebel. She considered telling him she was a married woman now and no longer under his control, but thought that probably not the most prudent course. She could, of course, simply walk out the door—it wasn't as if her father could physically stop her—but that would wound him terribly. And there was the chance that he was quite correct. She sighed and had to content herself with pacing up and down the hall. But if Adrian did not return soon, she had to do something!

For the first time, she wished she had been more like her

sister Juliana, who when she was growing up had tried hard to be the son her father had not had, so that she could learn masculine skills and help run the farm. Juliana had climbed trees and herded sheep, but even Jules had never learned to shoot, and that was the skill that Maddie wished for just now.

She would have to do the best she could, but her father would never allow her to take one of his grandfather's dueling pistols out—she didn't even know how to load the weapon, for pity's sake. Although she could slip out one of Bess's large carving knives, that would be of little use against a gun.

So, plotting outlandish and probably illogical schemes to do away with Adrian's enemy, Maddie whiled away minutes that crept by like years. Every time she passed the sitting room doorway, she paused to look through at the clock over the fireplace. Its hands moved with amazing slowness. She began to think it must be broken. How could time have slowed to such a degree?

But even when she felt that time flowed as slowly as treacle from a pitcher on a cold day, still her father would not allow anyone out of the house.

"Weller knows what he is doing," he told her, yet again. "I know it is hard to wait, my child, but it is what he would want."

"Yes, indeed," a new voice said.

She jerked so hard that later she would find her neck sore for days. "Adrian!" Running the length of the hallway, she cast herself into his arms, feeling the cold air upon his person, and clinging to him, not caring that everyone was watching.

"Are you all right?" She could not see any obvious wound, no sign of bloodshed, but still she wanted to hear it from his lips.

"I am quite well, thank you," he said, managing a smile for her benefit. He looked cold and tired, despite his claim.

At once, she felt selfish, and she begged him to come inside and sit. "I shall warm up some fresh tea for you," she said, then discovered that Bess, bless her, had already gone to put the kettle back on. "Tell us, if you will, what has happened. What about your murderous cousin?"

"He has withdrawn for the moment. We exchanged shots. I think I have managed to wound him, probably not seriously. I found a trace of blood, but only a few drops," he told them.

"A shame!" Maddie exclaimed, then blushed as her father glanced at her in surprise. She had never been so bloodthirsty before, but she'd never had someone she loved threatened with violence. She found it made a great difference in her thinking.

"Do you think he has gone away for good?" she asked her husband. What a lovely word that was, she thought, brushing a leaf off his sleeve just for the excuse to touch him.

"I fear not," Adrian replied. "I'm sure he will return, after he has bandaged his wound and perhaps taken a brief respite to recover. Which means that I am the one who will have to put a distance between us. I must not allow anyone here to be threatened by my presence."

"I don't care for that!" Maddie exclaimed, unable to be silent while Adrian exiled himself from her out of an excess of caution.

He turned toward her, and with his back to the others glanced at her belly. "You know that I must," he told her gently, his look a silent rebuke, though he doubtless did not mean it so. It was a reminder that she was now responsible for two lives, not just her own. How could she risk their child's life so recklessly? Throwing away her own without thought, in order to stay close to the man she loved, was one thing. Putting their first baby in harm's way was quite another.

"It's not fair," she whispered, trying to blink away the sudden moisture that blurred her image of his face.

"I know," he said, putting one hand up to cradle her cheek, "but I have no choice, nor do you."

For a moment they stood thus and no one spoke, then he stepped back. "I must go up and pack," he said. "I will leave when it is full dark. There is a quarter moon tonight; it will be enough to get a safe distance from the village."

"Where will you go?" she asked, her voice sounding strange past the lump in her throat.

"I don't know," he answered. "As far and as fast as I can. The most important thing is to lead him away from here and those I hold dear."

Her father wheeled his chair closer. "You know I wish you Godspeed, and even more I wish this was not necessary, Weller," he said, putting out his hand. "If I can do anything to help, just send word."

"Thank you, sir." They shook hands.

"Thank you for all your help, my lord," Felicity told him. "I will pray for your safety."

He bowed to them and then headed upstairs. Maddie lingered only to take the tea when Bess brought it, and to instruct their maidservant to make up a packet of food for Adrian to take with him. Then she followed him up to the bedchamber.

Her heart aching, she did what she could to help, folding his garments and smoothing them with hands that sometimes trembled.

He told her again about his estate, his man of business, his solicitor, and gave her papers with all the names and directions written carefully down. The ache in her throat made it impossible to answer, but she nodded and smiled at him, trying not to allow the tears to slip out.

He touched her stomach gently, cupping his hand over it and leaning down to kiss it. "Tell your father when you judge the time is right. Put something in the Yorkshire papers when the babe is born, with what you have decided to name it, so I can hear," he said.

He did not plan to return even for the birth of his first child? His only child if he never returned, she thought with a strange formless panic.

Stammering and awkward, she tried to ask, "B-but, Adrian, w-will you not be coming back by then?"

He closed his saddlebags and set them on the rug, then took both her hands in his larger ones. She could feel the callouses from long hours of riding, the strength in his hands, reassuring when she thought of him riding out to face a killer.

"I will come back if I am able, Madeleine. When he threatened you in the church, I knew—nightmares of blood, or not—that I would kill him in a fair fight as soon as I was able. I must see his face; I cannot shoot him in the back."

She nodded.

"But before I risk a confrontation, I must lead him away from here. If by bad luck, he should best me—he doesn't always fight fair . . ."

That was an understatement, she thought.

"I cannot have my cousin coming back here, in his madness, to harm you. I want you to draw upon the resources of my estate and set up more servants and more protection for you and your father, do you understand?"

She nodded again.

"I will draw him away, then I will feel more assured about how we may proceed."

His tone was reserved, and she was not sure if he believed his own statement, if he really expected to see her again, alive, or not. And then there were the bullet fragments, waiting killers in his own body!

While she tried to think how to argue—they had not

time to waste—he pulled her quickly into an embrace, one arm about her shoulders while he kissed her. She put her hands about his neck and kissed him with all her might. For long seconds, the kiss took all her attention, and while he held her close, Maddie could forget everything else. Kissing Adrian was the world.

He pulled away, leaning back only to brush his lips against the top of her head.

"My darling, you are my deepest center," he whispered, "where the universe begins, and love is eternal."

And then he was gone.

Would she ever see him alive again?

Too weak with fear even to take two steps to the bed, she sank to the floor, put her face into her hands, and wept.

For several days Maddie went about in a fog, too dazed with grief and fear for her husband to worry about her own safety. The would-be assassin had undoubtably followed Adrian's trail; she was sure Adrian had made it obvious that he was leaving the village. Only when he was past Ripon would he begin to hide his footsteps, he had told her. If only he had gotten that far without incident, she told herself, tossing in her lonely bed at night as she worried and fretted.

During the day she wrote letters to his solicitor and man of business, as Adrian had instructed her to do, enclosing his own letters of instruction, and waited for the funds with which they would add more men to protect themselves. She did not intend to move to Adrian's estate. To go there without him would feel like encroachment, and she had not married him for his land or wealth—she had not even considered that he might have money or titles. The fact that she was now Lady Weller still seemed very strange. The only time she found it quite satisfying was when Mrs. Masham came to call.

Only on Felicity's urging did she even let their annoying neighbor in, that and the knowledge that she could not hide forever. She welcomed the matron with as much politeness as she could muster.

"Lady Weller is in," she heard Felicity say smoothly as she ushered their neighbor into the sitting room.

It was all Maddie could do to keep a straight face. She tried to smile naturally as she motioned Mrs. Masham to a chair. The ridiculous thing was that the woman looked impressed. Maddie had not changed a whit, nor had the slightly shabby chair to which their neighbor was now applying her broad posterior.

"I am so relieved to see you quite safe," their visitor said, sitting down primly. "I mean, the gypsies do seem to have left the area, although Mrs. Grey swears she has glimpsed a shaggy-haired stranger around their barn, but—"

"Really?" Felicity cut in, her voice sharp. "Is she sure? When was that?"

"That's what she said." Mrs. Masham was choosing a piece of Bess's shortbread. "Just three days ago, I heard. But it was only one man, and everyone knows that the gypsies travel in packs, like wild dogs, don't y'know?"

"I suppose so," Felicity said, but now she seemed to be looking at something over their visitor's shoulder. Perhaps it was Bess, who had just brought in the tea tray. Felicity stood and helped put the dishes on the round table.

"But one hardly feels safe in one's own home, I vow. And after that alarming episode in the church during your first attempt at a wedding ceremony. I know our poor vicar is still talking about it, poor man."

"Yes, it was frightening. I'm afraid the man who invaded the church must be quite demented," Maddie said.

She turned to pour the steaming liquid into cups. This allowed her to hide her face as she tried to think of a way to change the subject, but as usual, Mrs. Masham was about as easy to lead as a charging bull.

"That was obvious!" The matron rolled her eyes. "Imagine threatening me! Still, no one was hurt, thank God. And I was most sorry not to witness your actual wedding ceremony, but I'm sure it was quite proper."

Maddie thought of the vicar in his dressing gown and nightcap, but she nodded. "Just so."

"I do feel for you, however, deprived of the support of your many friends and neighbors." The matron gave a gusty sigh.

Since Maddie could not very well point out that she withstood that loss surprisingly well, she thought it best to remain silent.

"I do find it odd that your brand-new husband has departed the area already," the visitor said next, raising her brows and giving her arch smile. "One hopes that the bliss of married life is all that he has hoped for?"

That was too much even from the tart-tongued gossip.

"I'm afraid he had urgent business to attend to," Maddie said, keeping her voice level with some effort.

"It must be urgent indeed to take him away from his blushing bride," Mrs. Masham responded, almost purring.

"Oh, it is," Maddie told her, taking a sip of her tea and throwing all sense of propriety to the wind. "He is seeking diamond jewelry sufficient to drown me in."

Mrs. Masham almost dropped her teacup. "Oh?" she squeaked.

"Yes," Maddie said, unrepentant. "He is quite determined to drape me in jewels like an Indian rani. He says I am an empress in his eyes, so it will be only proper."

"Oh, my," Mrs. Masham said, her slightly protruding eyes open wide. She looked as if she was soaking up every word, which Maddie knew would be repeated at every house the matron had access to.

Oh, who cared, she was well into it, now. "He'll probably bring back emeralds and rubies, as well."

"And perhaps pearls, but no jade or lapis or coral, Lady Weller does not wish anything that might be considered common," Felicity put in helpfully.

Mrs. Masham put one hand up to the coral beads at her throat. "Oh, I see," she said. "And I suppose you'll be departing for London, soon, to stock up on the latest fashions?"

"When it suits me," Maddie said, her tone offhand.

"Ah, I should be going. I'm sure you have many plans to make," their visitor said. She stood almost too quickly and swayed a moment, in her eagerness to start spreading her newly acquired stock of gossip. "And I have a few stops to make on the way home."

"Good afternoon, then," Maddie told her.

Felicity said good-bye, and their neighbor hurried off as Bess showed her to the front door.

"I am a terrible person," Maddie told her friend after the sitting room door was safely closed.

Felicity laughed, but in a moment, she sobered. "I think those who know you will know better than to believe such nonsense as what she will be tattering about. But, Madeline, if the gypsies have departed—"

"Who is the man with the shaggy hair? Yes, I noticed that. Can you imagine that Mrs. Masham may have actually said something useful?" Maddie took a sip of her cooling tea. "Do you think it is the same man that you saw at your cottage before the fire?"

"I don't know, but it's an alarming coincidence." Felicity frowned at the fire in the hearth, which was growing low. She stood up and put another log on. "Perhaps I need to find another cottage to let, so that I can move out sooner rather than later."

"You know what Papa said about that. He likes having you here," Maddie pointed out. "He says you're almost as good a chess player as Adrian, and very intelligent to talk to, not to mention much prettier than my husband"—she grinned at the widow—"though you may allow me to differ on that last opinion."

Felicity looked self-conscious. "Your father is too kind. I was only trying to help him pass the time, Madeline, since Lord Weller had to depart. I didn't mean—"

"I think it's marvelous that you two get along so well, Felicity, truly. Papa would worry about you if you ended up in another lonely cottage. I certainly enjoy your company, and Adrian wants us to have more people here with us, not fewer. So please don't rush away just yet."

"Oh, I would certainly not abandon you," Felicity said, looking appalled at the thought. "When you have been so kind and done so much to help me! It's just, if I should bring more danger to you—"

"How on earth would you do that?" Maddie demanded.

"If "—Felicity gripped her hands together—"It's complicated to explain. When I hear from my cousin, I should know. Then I will tell you the whole story, Madeline. I never meant to deceive you, I promise you." And with that enigmatic statement, she turned and hurried up the staircase.

Good gracious, Maddie thought. But when she sat down again, as usual, her thoughts turned to Adrian. Where was he tonight? In an inn or alone in a cold forest, stalked by his mad cousin? Oh, my darling, she thought. What strange and lonely kind of marriage is this?

She had almost forgotten that the union had ever been meant only as a convenience, as a way to save her name and her reputation. Now she had that, true enough, and a title and easy wealth to boot. She would also, if all went well, have a healthy child—a little part of Adrian to keep with her—that thought did make her heart sing. Perhaps a boy who would have his father's strong good looks, or a girl with his dark hair and fair skin? Except for the child, she would trade it all to have her husband himself back with her.

Staring into the fire as it leaped and danced, she forgot everything else and allowed the afternoon to slip away.

A week after Adrian had left, Maddie and Felicity walked down to the village to buy some thread and see if the post office had any mail for them. The last few days had been quiet, and Maddie was hopeful that all dangers had flown. She was also hopeful that Adrian might send her a letter telling her that he was in one piece, still evading his cousin. Even a short note would make her feel so much better.

To her disappointment, the only mail addressed to their residence was a few bills for her father. Felicity, on the other hand, had a letter directed to her. The postmaster looked at her curiously, as the widow normally received very little correspondence.

"Got an admirer, have ye, Mrs. Barlow?" He gave her a leering grin.

"Lovely day, isn't it?" was her only answer.

They took their letters and swept out into the street where other shoppers moved up and down. Felicity broke the wax seal and unfolded the single sheet of paper, pausing on the pavement to scan the closely written lines of script.

"Oh, dear heaven," she muttered. "It is as I feared, Madeline. We must get home. I must talk to your father. I regret I am going to have to leave the village."

"Why on earth?" Maddie demanded. Then, glancing about them, she saw several nearby women, expressions inquisitive, slowing their steps to listen to this interesting bit of conversation.

"No, you're right, we cannot talk here." She put her own mail into her shopping basket with the skeins of thread she had purchased and turned back toward home. They set a smart pace. Maddie was impatient to hear what had creased Felicity's brow and brought such a look of concern to her face.

As they left the village behind and climbed a small hill, Maddie experienced a sense of unease, as if someone was watching them. She could almost feel the pressure of eyes boring into the small of her back.

Looking toward Felicity who was a few steps in front, Maddie wondered if the other woman felt the same. "Do you—" she began, when a sudden sharp whine interrupted. The leaves in front of her ripped and a few pieces of greenery floated to the ground.

Maddie gasped, and Felicity gave a small shriek. This time, Maddie knew what the sound and the near miss meant.

"Run!" she exclaimed. She grabbed her friend's hand, and they both dashed through the copse of trees, hoping to evade the shooter's angle of vision.

Fortunately, it was only a short distance to the Applegate residence, and Maddie had played in these woods all her life. She led Felicity off the path and over the grassy knolls. They traveled a slightly longer route than necessary, but it seemed prudent to take a less obvious path.

When at last the Applegate residence came into view, it looked peaceful and quiet, a refuge in every way.

"Thank goodness," Maddie muttered. "Surely we have lost him. I cannot believe he is still here—I thought he would have followed Adrian off. Perhaps if the mad cousin has returned, Adrian has come back to check on us?" She felt a moment of hope.

"It may not be what you think, Madeline," Felicity told her, holding her side and panting a little from their long run.

"Let us get inside where it is safe and get some tea, and then you may tell us what you wish. I warn you, Felicity, if it has to do with moving out, however, Papa is not going to take kindly to it."

Felicity threw her a troubled glance, but didn't try to explain just yet, and they both hurried to the front door. Maddie opened it without bothering to knock; she knew that Bess would be expecting them back and would not have the door bolted.

The front hall was empty and quiet, just as Maddie thought it would be. Her father might already be having his afternoon rest. Bess was probably in the kitchen. If they had missed lunch, Bess would have left some cold meat and bread and butter out for them, she thought. Then she heard a slight noise from the sitting room.

Her father rarely used that room; it was most often the province of the females of the family or used to entertain visitors. Had someone called?

She put her shopping basket on the hall table, glancing into the looking glass over it to make sure she was reasonably presentable. Her cheeks were pink from the brisk pace of their walk home, but she could do nothing about that, and the color would fade. She pushed a stray lock of hair back into place, then turned toward the sitting room.

"I will see about some tea," Felicity said. "Then I will explain it all." She turned toward the kitchen.

Maddie nodded. She walked into the room and stopped in surprise. Her father sat in his wheeled chair a little to the side of the fireplace, his expression hard to read. On the other side of the fire, standing back against the wall behind the edge of the brick hearth, stood a man.

Maddie's pulse jumped. His long hair was dark and shaggy and hung into his face, and his clothes were ragged and dusty. Beneath the mop of disheveled hair, she saw the gleam of cunning eyes. In his hand he held a gun.

"Papa!" she exclaimed.

"Be calm," her father said, his voice even. "It may yet be well."

The stranger lifted his gun, and Maddie held her breath, but he simply motioned her to the side. She took several steps toward her father, but paused inside the doorway. What about Felicity?

The stranger had turned back to watch the doorway again, and then it hit Maddie. This man wanted to kill Felicity! He was the one who had shot at them on the path, not the mad cousin. He had been shooting at Felicity, not at Maddie. This was the shaggy stranger who had peered at Felicity in her cabin—he must be the one who had burned down her home! But why?

She bit her lip—they could not just stand here and watch the widow be slaughtered! What on earth could they do? She looked around for something she could throw to distract him . . . and then what?

She heard footsteps in the hallway, and now Felicity appeared in the doorway. "I cannot find Bess, what do you suppose—"

She stopped when she saw Maddie's expression. Then she turned and saw the stranger, and her puzzled look turned to fear.

"No!"

The stranger lifted his rifle.

Maddie heard the sharp report of a gun firing, and she shrieked. But it was the gypsy whose expression faltered. The gun dropped from his fingers, hitting their floor with a clatter.

She turned to her father and was astounded to see that he had pulled a pistol from beneath the blanket that covered his knees. A faint vapor of smoke rose from its barrel.

Felicity screamed. She looked as if she were going to swoon; she had gone very pale. Maddie ran to support her.

When Maddie glanced back at the prone figure, she exclaimed, too. Had his head been blown off?

No, it was a wig that had tumbled loose; the disheveled black hair was a wig. Now the figure that sprawled across their floor looked much more ordinary, a man with brown hair of average length, an unremarkable round face, the spot of blood that stained his dirty clothes the only sign of the bullet that had ended his life.

Maddie felt a wave of nausea, but she swallowed hard and tried to be calm.

"It's all right, you are safe," Maddie told her friend. "Papa, how did you know? He shot at us on the way back to the village. He must have gotten ahead of us when we left the path and tried to lose him."

"I have been half expecting something of the sort," her father said, his voice grim. He looked at Felicity. "I am so sorry you had to experience such an alarming attack. Do you recognize him?"

"Oh, yes," the widow said, her voice faint. "That is— that is my husband, Jerod."

Sixteen

*F*elicity still looked as if she might faint. Maddie guided her friend to the closest chair and supported her until she sat, then looked to her father, but he seemed quite composed. Especially so, considering they now had a dead man lying across their sitting room floor!

At least, he appeared to be dead. She stared at the man, but she could not see that he was breathing. Maddie shivered.

"I suppose this is the shameful secret you were going to share with me?" her father suggested, his voice calm.

Her face crumpling, Felicity nodded. She put her hands to her face, her eyes filling.

"I don't understand," Maddie said. "You thought he was dead, and he wasn't?"

"No, I knew he was not," Felicity said, her voice tremulous. "I am so sorry to have told you a lie. You see, I was not widowed, but divorced."

Maddie was speechless. She had never met a divorced woman before. Not sure what to do, she glanced from one

to the other. She had a feeling it was her father whose reassurance the widow—no, not a widow, well, yes, she was a
widow now!—really wanted.

Oh, what a tangle!

"Can you explain it all now?" Maddie ventured to ask.

John wheeled his chair until he was close enough to
reach for one of Felicity's hands, which she had been hiding her face behind. He pressed it gently. "Do not weep,
my dear. You are with friends. We do not judge you."

Felicity drew a deep, gasping breath and tried to control
her sobs. "I am so very, very sorry. I should not have lied to
you. It was just, when I came here I told the village that I
was a widow because—because—"

"Because to admit that one is a divorced woman would
cause a great scandal, and you did not wish to be ostra-
cized," her father prompted. "That is easy enough to understand. How could we blame you for that? You did not know
us well at that time."

"And then later, it was hard to change your story," Maddie suggested.

Nodding, Felicity wiped her cheeks with her handkerchief. "Yes, but I have been feeling very guilty. When my
husband first began the proceedings, all my neighbors
stopped calling, and those who had been my friends would
not speak to me on the street or even acknowledge that they
saw me when I passed by—I felt like a ghost. So when I
moved away to a new location, I thought it best to say that
I was a widow." She sighed.

Maddie felt a strong wave of sympathy. "That's terrible!"

"Yes, but you know how unusual it is to be a divorced
woman, and usually it is for"—Felicity's fair skin showed
a wave of color—"ah, improper behavior. You must let me
tell you the circumstances."

"That's not necessary," Maddie's father said at once.

"No, but I wish to. I realize that having been lied to once, there is no good reason for you to believe me now, but nonetheless, I would feel better if I told you the whole story." Felicity drew a deep breath.

He nodded. "If you wish it."

Filled with intense curiosity, Maddie simply smiled encouragement and support and waited.

"It started during the French wars. My husband was an officer with our army, and I traveled with him. The living conditions were primitive, and when I became with child, I did think that perhaps it would be more prudent to return to England, but he liked having me near him, so I stayed. But the baby came early, and there was no doctor nearby. Things did not go well."

Felicity paused for a moment, and the pain in her eyes made Maddie ache for her.

"At any rate, after a long and difficult time, the child was born dead, and I barely survived. When a doctor finally did arrive, he told my husband that I had been so injured, I would never be able to bear more children."

"Ah," John said, as if that said volumes.

"Yes," she said, twisting her handkerchief between her two hands as if it were her lifeline. "It will explain even more if I tell you that my husband had a baronetcy and was determined to have a son to whom he could pass his title and estate. If I could have no children—well, he was fixed on finding a way to insure that he could have a legal heir. So he began divorce proceedings." Her voice wavered, and she drew another deep breath as if to compose herself.

Maddie exclaimed, "How unfair!"

"I understand his motive," Felicity answered, but she looked away as she spoke. "But, yes, it has been very hard. He said he would send me an allowance, enough to live on, but after a few months, that money first dwindled and then stopped altogether. I have a very small fund that comes from my late mother, and I have been surviving on that, but I had to move to a smaller cottage. And there is more. . . ."

She hesitated, then, when they both looked encouraging, seemed to gather the courage to continue.

"The first time I moved, it was only to the next shire, and I made no special effort to hide my change of location. I found a cottage for let in a small village, and I did not think that anyone would try to find me. Most of my friends had already dropped me"—she paused, obviously trying not to show her hurt—"and I lived there for several years. But one day I left the house early to get to the shops and home again before a rainstorm hit. I came home to find my cottage a smoking pile of rubble."

"You've had two cottages burn?" Maddie exclaimed, surprised enough to interrupt.

"Yes." Felicity pressed her lips together and shivered at the memory.

"That does seem more than your share," Maddie's father said slowly. "Was it decided what caused that fire?"

"There were gypsies in the neighborhood, then, too, and the villagers blamed it on an accidental or deliberate attempt to cover a robbery," Felicity told them, shuddering as she spoke. "But I wondered, even then. After that, I moved again, and much farther away. That was when I came north, and after several stays in various villages, I ended up here." She drew a deep breath and then continued.

"I took a different last name, and again, I said I was a widow. The only person who knew I was here was my cousin, who had to send on my small annuity, and I asked him not to share the location with anyone. I've been here for some time, and all was peaceful, and I thought I would be left alone."

She paused, and Maddie looked from Felicity to her father.

"Another fire. And now we find your divorced husband in disguise, trying to shoot you! Do you think he started the fire?"

"It seems that might be the most obvious answer." It was her father who spoke. "But if he had already divorced you, why would he want to kill you? Did he hate you so much?"

Felicity looked pale. "I think the letter from my cousin explains it. There is an impetus I had not known. You see, he has married again, and his new wife is expecting a child."

"So?" Maddie looked from one of them to the other. Felicity did not answer, and her father frowned. "Was that not why he got the divorce to begin with?"

"Yes, but, like most people, I knew little about divorce in the beginning, never expecting such a disgrace to touch my life," Felicity told them, her voice low. "Now I know more than I should wish. Jerod obtained our divorce from the Chancery Courts. We were divorced; the marriage was ended. I moved away. But that decree did not give him—or me—the right to marry again or have a legitimate heir."

"No?" Maddie said in surprise. "But—"

"It turns out that there are two more steps to a divorce if one wishes to marry and have children," Felicity explained, twisting her handkerchief again. "My cousin is a solicitor, and he has explained it to me. The final and necessary step is to obtain a Private Act of Divorcement from Parliament, and that can cost several thousand pounds! When I wrote the letter to my cousin, I asked him to check again and see if there was any record of such an act, of a final divorce, and he says there is not."

"So your husband was about to have a child, perhaps a son, who—if anyone discovered you were still alive—would not be his legal heir, after all," John said slowly.

Maddie looked at them both. "You mean, he decided to just see you murdered instead? That is horrendous, how could he be so evil!"

"Yes, but much cheaper than a divorce," her father pointed out, his voice dry.

Felicity wiped her eyes. "My cousin says that Jerod, apart from the cost of keeping up a new household, has been gambling heavily, and there was no hope of him having the money to apply to Parliament. Apparently he thought this was his only option."

Maddie shivered, now. "Definitely evil," she repeated. "Oh, Felicity, what a narrow escape you have had." She put her arms about her friend.

Giving a strangled sob, Felicity hugged her back. "Thank you for not holding it against me!"

"Certainly not," Maddie said. Privately, she thought that if someone had told her that a stranger, a divorced woman, had moved into the neighborhood, she would indeed have been shocked. That the "scarlet woman" should turn out to be gentle, seemly, kind-hearted Felicity—it just showed that one should not judge hastily, she told herself.

Her father wheeled his chair about just slightly to view the body again. "What shall we do with this big lump of trash? The squire, who is our local magistrate, is not even home to help us straighten out the legalities."

"How can you be at fault for shooting an intruder who forced himself into your home at gunpoint?" Maddie demanded, adding, "Although I do wish the squire would come home, and bring Lauryn with him. I know he misses his son, and it was dreadful for them both to lose Tom at such a young age. But Lauryn feels she must stay, since her father-in-law has no other children. We have not seen her in ages."

"We must not leave his new wife, legalities aside, in limbo. It would be too cruel for Jerod to just disappear and never be seen again," Felicity said, her mind still on the immediate problem.

"You are too forgiving," Maddie said. "I"m not sure I

could think of his second wife's feelings so easily, were I in your place."

"Then I think we shall have to put him into a wooden casket and ship him back to his home, since you know the location," John said practically. "Maddie, ask Bess to tell Thomas to come inside and I will put him to work on it at once. We cannot leave the body lying about."

"Ugh, no indeed," Maddie agreed, then suddenly remembered what Felicity had said at the beginning of their ordeal. "Oh, Bess—you said you did not see her? Oh, pray tell me he has not hurt her!" Maddie went flying for the kitchen, which at first indeed seemed empty, although filled with the smell of burnt meat.

Closer inspection showed that the pantry door had been jammed shut, and inside she found Bess, gagged and bound and lying on the cold tile floor half hidden behind the flour bin.

Maddie hastened to release her. She guided Bess to a chair by the fireplace and put on the tea kettle. Although dry mouthed and somewhat groggy, after a drink of apple cider, Bess told her in no uncertain terms about the intruder who had surprised her.

"While me back was turned, so rude he was, Miss Madeline! And we need to move that kettle of stew, if ye please."

"A dreadful man, Bess, and I'll do it. You sit still." When the sadly burnt stew was put to the side of the hearth, and after the water boiled, Maddie made tea. She gave the older woman a large cup sweetened with honey while she explained about the stranger's invasion of the house, and how her father had shot him.

"Serves 'im right," Bess said, with no regret at all. "Ruint my good rabbit stew, 'e did. Now our dinner will be light on the dishes."

"Don't worry about dinner; we'll manage," Maddie told her. "Oh, but I'd best go and check on Thomas. He might be tied up in the stables for all we know!"

Thomas's wife looked only mildly concerned. " 'E was supposed to be in the back pasture mending the fence, so likely 'e's been out of the way, Miss Madeline. And ye 'elp me up now so I can see about setting a good blancmange for yer father's supper."

Maddie still planned to go out and check on Thomas, her father needed him—but fortunately, their other servant came in the back door just as she was about to go search for him. He had indeed been at the back of the small estate and was astonished to hear about the attack and the shooting.

"It's from living in yon south," he said, shaking his head. "Muddles ther brains, it does."

Maddie took him to the sitting room, and John gave him his orders. The first thing Thomas did was bring a long piece of canvas, roll the body up, and haul it outside in his wheelbarrow. Then Bess scrubbed the floor beneath to get up the bloodstains.

Maddie had taken Felicity up to her room first so she didn't witness any of the macabre cleanup. As the floor was drying, Maddie rearranged the tables and chairs slightly to hide the darker stains just in case they did not come totally clean.

The dratted man would be a nuisance even in his death, she thought uncharitably. She recalled his efforts to murder Felicity and shuddered. Little did she imagine there could be more unpleasant surprises to come.

Later they had almost finished a light dinner, during which no one had been very talkative, when Thomas came to the doorway. Since the male servant never interrupted a meal, Maddie looked up in surprise.

Her father put down his fork and knife. "Is there a problem, Thomas? Or is there a visitor asking for me?"

He shook his head. "I found some'un in his pocket I thought you'd want to see, Master Applegate." Thomas brought a wrinkled broadsheet and handed it over, then touched his cap with his usual calm dignity and clomped out.

Maddie and Felicity both watched as her father picked up the grimy, creased sheet and read it, his forehead wrinkled. Then, frowning, he read it again.

"What is it, Papa?" Maddie burst out, unable to be patient any longer.

"First," he said, "let me explain that I told Thomas to empty the dead man's pockets so I could examine the contents before we put him into the temporary casket. It seemed quite likely that he might have written down Mrs. Barlow's present name and location, and I didn't wish the body to go back with anything on it that might connect it to her."

"Mercy, what an idea!" Felicity turned pale at just the suggestion.

"Oh, Papa, how clever of you to think of that," Maddie told him. "But what is this?"

"A flyer offering a reward for information on the whereabouts of Viscount Weller," her father told her, his voice grim.

"What!" Feeling as if she had been cuffed, Maddie pushed her chair back so abruptly that it almost fell over and rushed to read the paper for herself.

Sure enough, in big bold letters, it said:

20 pd for news of location of Adrian Carter, Viscount Weller

Below, in smaller letters, it told where to send the information—to his mad cousin, of course.

"But how did Felicity's husband come to have this?" Maddie wondered aloud. "Surely there is no connection between the two?"

Looking thoughtful, her father fingered the sheet. "This has been passed hand to hand many times, I think. There are many low dives in London, my dear, taverns and gambling hells, where denizens of London's underworld meet and conduct business."

Both the women stared at him. He smiled ruefully. "I was young once, and not bound to this damned chair, you know. I didn't go quite that far into its low life, but I did spend a year or more in London. I learned a thing or two about its seamier side. If Weller's cousin plastered the worst part of the city with these flyers, if he sent them out to other cities in England, which also possess criminal elements—I wondered how his cousin always managed to find him, you know, and often so quickly. The cousin does not appear as smart as all that."

Maddie gasped. "But if he has petty criminals all over Britain working as his eyes and ears, so to speak—oh, Papa, Adrian must know this! And I don't know how to get in touch with him!"

She clasped her hands together in frustration. No wonder Adrian was in such danger. It was worse than even he suspected. She must warn him!

"And Jerod picked this up, thinking that he might have the opportunity to make a few pounds—which he did, if he is the one who alerted the would-be assassin to Adrian's presence here. Oh, Madeline, I'm so sorry!" Felicity looked concerned.

"It's not your fault," Maddie told her. "You could do nothing to prevent it." But the fact remained, she had to find her husband. She looked down at her plate, but her appetite was gone. Adrian would continue to be in danger, even as they sat here at the dinner table. She had to find him, warn him—and then what?

He had to at least know what he was up against.

～～

She slept very little that night, and after hours of tossing and turning, she rose early and packed a bag. Her mind was made up. She could stay here and wait to hear that she, like Felicity, now was a widow, or she could try to do something. Even if her chances of finding her husband were not good, knowing that he was trying to cover his trail, she would rather be actively searching than going quietly mad at home.

Before she told her father, she sought out Felicity for a quiet talk. Maddie had told her friend in the past about her promise to her mother.

"So I am truly torn, Felicity. I do not want to feel that I am breaking my oath, but—"

"But you have sworn another vow to your husband, have you not?" Felicity said, her tone grave. "I will stay with your father, if you wish it, Madeline. After all you both have done for me, it would be a very small thing I can do to repay your many kindnesses."

"I would not think of it like that, exactly, but your presence would relieve my mind," Maddie confessed. "With you here, I would feel that I could leave without so much guilt. Thank you!"

"Please don't worry about your father," Felicity told her. "I will do everything I can to see to his welfare and comfort."

Her father frowned when she told him her decision, but she met his gaze with a firm one of her own.

There was a brief silence, then he nodded reluctantly. "I see you have made up your mind. You must take Bess and Thomas with you."

"No, you will need them," she said.

"I will not have you going off alone," her father said more sternly. "And what do you think Weller would say to you traveling unprotected?"

She rather thought he had a point, and as it turned out, Bess had a few words to say on the subject. "If ye think ye be trottin' about the countryside all on ye lonesome, Miss Madeline, ye best think again," the maidservant admonished, waving her wooden spoon at her recalcitrant mistress. "Just what do ye think yer good mum would 'ave said?"

"But Papa will need you here," Maddie tried to argue.

"I'll fetch the baker's two lasses and put them into the kitchen while I'm gone," Bess told her. "They'll not be so good a cook as me, but they'll keep 'em 'ere from starvin'."

Adrian's letter of credit from the bank had come through, and Maddie set up enough funds to keep the household comfortable while she was gone. She also drew out money for her own use. Fortunately, Thomas was not as insistent on escorting her as Bess. Since she suspected that their gray-haired, slightly bent coachman and farmworker would only slow them down, she did not regret the loss of his company.

She told Thomas to hire more men to have as protection about the estate, and more maids, as well, then she had him drive her and Bess into Ripon to catch the coach. She began her inquiries there, asking at the coaching inn about anyone who might remember Adrian. Since he preferred to ride his own horse, she didn't expect the viscount to have purchased a ticket, but she asked the ticket vendor anyhow. He remembered nothing about a tall, handsome man with a pleasing deep voice, who had left at the time that Adrian would have passed through.

This was going to be a difficult search. But she had known that from the start, Maddie told herself. She would not give up just as she was beginning!

The first lead that seemed promising came from an inn and posting house near Yarm. She heard a tale of a mysterious dark-haired man who seemed to want no one to know his name or where he was headed.

"Perhaps it is his lordship, Bess," Maddie told her maid. She hired a private chaise and followed the trail to a smaller town, where she almost lost the man completely. But after asking everyone in town, and then casting out to several villages in the surrounding areas, she at last picked up news of a stranger staying in a small house near a lake up "by the vale where the mill used to be, afore the laird built his new boathouse."

After interviewing two more farmers, she finally found the right road, and just as night was falling, the hired chaise took Maddie and Bess bumping along a truly dreadful lane.

When they came to a stop at a small, dilapidated manor house that looked as if it had been abandoned for years, she couldn't believe this was the right place. But when the hired postboy came to consult with her, he told her it was the only habitable residence along this lonely road.

Maddie stared at the house again. Obviously, they took the term *habitable* loosely in this northern shire. But now she could make out the faintest sheen of candlelight reflected within, even thought the windows were covered by patched draperies that seemed to be carefully drawn.

"Very well," she told the boy. "Have the driver hold the carriage ready. I shall try to see if this is the man I am seeking."

He touched his cap and took the news to the driver, then returned to lower the steps and help both the women out.

Maddie knew that both her two hired employees were keenly curious about her mysterious mission, but she was not of a mind to enlighten them. Instead, she pulled her pelisse and her long muffler closer about her—the wind was howling around them—and picked her way along an overgrown path to the front door.

She pounded on the door, at first to no avail.

"Mayhap we should come back on the morn, Miss Madeline." Bess had to almost shout to make herself heard. The wind was growing even stronger.

Maddie shivered, but she had no wish to come back to this godforsaken spot again. Her hopes were fading—somehow, she could not imagine Adrian hiding out in such a spot as this, but it would be folly to have come this far and not make sure. "I will see who is here, first," she said grimly. "And I'm sure someone is here!"

"But what if it's a robber, or a murderer?" Bess asked, the whites of her eyes showing.

Maddie had never seen her intrepid servant afraid before, so she felt a tremor of apprehension herself. The darkness around them was truly dark, and now it was going to be hard to see to drive their hired vehicle back to the nearest town. She had not been thinking very wisely when she had decided to come this far tonight.

Just as she was castigating herself, however, a gleam of moonlight showed through the thick clouds overhead, and she drew a deep breath.

"There, the moon is coming through," she said. "We will leave in just a minute, but first, I will see who is here."

She pounded again.

"There, my lady!" her driver suddenly called. "'E's getting away out the back."

"What?"

To her astonishment, she stepped to the side of the house and saw a figure bent over, a shawl pulled over his—its—head and running across the shadowy heath.

Just as she debated the wisdom of trying to follow, through the darkness, the moon went behind a cloud and the fugitive seemed to hit a low spot or a rabbit hole. The shadowy figure went down and a howl went up.

The moon reemerged, and Maddie could not resist circling the building quickly and running to catch up with the now downed man, who was clutching his leg.

"I think I've broken my ankle!"

"Who are you?" she demanded, stopping a few feet short, just in case. It obviously was not Adrian, who would never have run like a rabbit. The voice was wrong, and what she could see of the man showed no resemblance at all. She swallowed hard against her disappointment.

From the house, another face looked out the back door. "Are you hurt, Terrence, dear?"

"Get back inside, Celie, didn't I tell you to stay out of sight?" he bellowed. To Maddie, he retorted, with no less change of tone and a sad lack of civility, "Who the bloody hell are you? I thought you were my wife!"

"Ah," she said. That did explain a lot, probably as much as she needed to know.

Beside her, Bess had swelled up like a broody pigeon. "Ye donna talk in such tones to me lady, I'll 'ave ye know, ye common bit of no good dog spit—"

"Come along, Bess," Maddie interrupted hurriedly, trying hard not to laugh. "This is an—ah—honest mistake."

They reentered their carriage as quickly as they could, especially as the man in the field has suddenly changed his tone and called after them, "Wait, you could give me a lift over to—"

The postboy slammed the door and Maddie, who had no desire to share her small carriage with the philandering couple, didn't wait to hear the rest. He had gotten himself there; he presumably had a plan to get himself home again.

And she was no closer to finding Adrian than she had been when she left her own home. The slightly hysterical laughter on her lips faded quickly, and, as they made their way slowly along the rocky road before the moonlight faded, she tried not to feel discouraged.

The house seemed very quiet after Madeline and Bess had departed. Thomas drove them to Ripon where they could catch a stage, and he reported they had gotten off without incident. Felicity kept an eye on the new girls in the kitchen, and, as Bess had predicted, their cooking was adequate, if not exciting. Felicity lent a hand now and then, although John told her not to feel obligated.

"You should not feel like a servant; you are a guest in this house," he told her gently when they sat together at dinner.

It felt strange to her to sit alone with him at the table, only the two of them.

She looked down at her plate, and when Livvie, the girl who had been serving, retreated to the kitchen, Felicity met his gaze. "You've been so kind, Mr. Applegate—"

"I did ask you to call me John," he reminded her.

"I don't want the servants to talk," she said, smiling a bit shyly. "They will think I'm taking too much liberty. And you know I would do anything I can to help the household run more smoothly. I had thought of offering to fill the position of housekeeper, if that would ease Madeline's mind; she does worry about your comfort and your ease."

"Madeline is a loving daughter," he agreed, with something in his expression she couldn't quite read. "But you are a lady born, Mrs. Barlow—and I cannot call you Felicity if you will not call me John! And as I said; you are a lady. You are not suited for the position of housekeeper."

"But—"

"If you mean to speak of—what you do not wish to speak of in front of the servants"—he paused as Livvie returned with a new dish to place on the table—"that was not your fault and does not come into the discussion. And there is another problem."

"Oh?" Puzzled, she glanced back at him.

"Perhaps we can finish this discussion later?" he said, his tone polite as Livvie served them a new offering of lamb and mint sauce.

"Of course," she assured him. Then she looked back at her plate, dipping a spoon into the concoction there. Gracious, she would have to show these girls how to make a decent sauce, or everyone here would be thinner before Madeline returned home.

When the meal had been cleared away, and she had retreated to the sitting room, John soon came to join her.

He wheeled his chair to a comfortable distance in front of the hearth, and motioned to her to take the chair next to his, so she did.

"What is the problem?" she asked. "If there is something I can mend, I promise I will see to it at once."

He smiled at her, and she thought, not for the first time, what a handsome man he was, and how kind and wise were his deep blue eyes, no matter the fine lines about them that the passage of years and the pain of his accident had engraved there.

He was an honorable man, and there were few enough of those in the world, as she had cause to know!

"I said there were problems that would prevent you from taking the position of housekeeper," he told her.

She flushed. "Oh. I should not have mentioned it. If you prefer that I leave the house, I will understand, Mr. Applegate. I do not wish to cause you or your family any embarrassment, and your daughter is so kind-hearted—I mean, she did not know about my divorce when she offered to be my friend, and—"

"Hush," he said, his voice firm. "Leave Madeline out of this; it does not concern her."

"Oh?" Now she was more puzzled than ever. "But—"

"And please call me John. We are alone now, you will note. I told the maids to go to bed after they finished in the kitchen. If we need any more tea, you will have to make it, I fear."

"I don't mind," she assured him, not sure what this was about. "Indeed, I am happy to do anything—"

"Except what I most want you to do." he interrupted.

"What?" This time she stared at him, nonplused.

"Felicity, my dear, I realize that I am only half a man, and it may be hard to see me as the man I once was."

The pain in his voice made her wince, but she looked into his eyes and did not blink.

"Even so, I am going to risk the ultimate rejection. I know that you have not been treated well by one of my sex. So I can understand your hesitation if you have doubts . . . but nonetheless, my feelings for you have been growing ever since you have come to stay with us, and they demand that I dare to ask the question."

Her heart was pounding so loudly that she could almost doubt the meaning of his words. He could not be about to say what she began to think he intended.

"I don't want you to be my housekeeper, Felicity. I love you, my dear. I very much wish for you to be my wife."

"Oh!" She adored him so, and to hear such words . . . She jumped to her feet and almost walked into the fire, then stepped back just in time. For a moment, she almost could not see.

John could not stop her, but he watched her in concern. "If it causes you distress to consider it—"

"No, no, I mean, your wife would be a most fortunate woman, indeed. It's just that after the stillbirth, it was not just—not just more children that I was unable to consider in my future, John. I could not—I was so injured that—that I could not come together with a man without much pain. And my husband, my husband–"

She knew she must have flushed. She put one hand to her cheek. "He was most unhappy with the situation."

"I see. If I had not already shot the bastard and shipped his body south, I think I should do it again," John said, his tone dry.

She was so surprised she sat back down on her chair again.

"Felicity, do you recall that I am unable to walk, that my legs are useless to me? My injuries did, I fear, affect other functions of my body as well," he pointed out, his tone gentle now.

"Oh," she said, feeling very foolish. "Yes, I did realize that, John. I just—how thoughtless of me. I have been so aware of my own—my own inadequacies that for a moment I forgot that you have your own—your own unique circumstances."

He said, watching her, "That's putting it tactfully."

She felt a great weight lift. "So—so you would not mind that—you would not mind?"

He smiled. "I think we would suit, my dear."

She had never expected to find any man, much less anyone as kind and wise and pleasant to be with as John Applegate, who would ever want her again. Blinking against sudden happy tears, she smiled back at him. "You make me very happy."

"Oh, that is yet to come, I think," he told her, his eyes glinting with the mischievous gleam of a much younger man.

He put out his hand and she extended her own eagerly, expecting him to clasp it. Instead he lifted it to his lips, kissing the palm very gently, then the soft skin of her wrist.

A ripple of pleasure moved up her arm, and her eyes widened.

"John!"

"There are many way to please a lady," he told her, his eyes dancing. "Did your louse of a husband never teach you that? Ways which do not necessarily need all the body parts to be in prime working order."

She gazed at him in amazement. "Jerod was more—more concerned with his contentment than with mine, I think."

"I can well believe it," John said. "Then we have delightful hours of exploration ahead of us, my love. And this Sunday, it will be our banns the vicar can read."

He kissed her palm again, and she laughed aloud, thinking of the wonders of the life they could enjoy together.

Six weeks later Maddie was much more disheartened, and she knew little more than she did at the beginning, except to wonder just how Adrian's mad cousin could locate him amid an island nation apparently teeming with tall, dark-haired men. She had traced a dozen such to dead ends, sure that each was her husband, and each had been a crushing disappointment.

She was tired and often wept into her pillow at night. Maddie was at least glad that Bess had insisted on coming with her. The good-hearted maid was her only link to home, and she could assure her mistress that her emotional responses to not just big setbacks but small things like a stale biscuit or a too cool cup of tea were sometimes only a result of her approaching motherhood. Otherwise, Maddie would have been sure she was losing her mind.

But she was very very tired and quite despondent, and she didn't know what to do next. She had written home of her lack of success. She had written to her sisters, with no response, and she couldn't understand how the twins, at least, still had not returned home to their London addresses. And she was so lonely she wanted to go to bed and not get up.

She feared she would never see her husband again. What if Adrian died alone, somewhere, and she didn't even know? She thought of Felicity, determined to at least make sure her former husband's new wife knew the fate of her nefarious spouse and did not suffer the awful suspense of waiting and waiting and never being sure what had become of him.

That made the too-ready tears well up again, and she dashed them away, muttering words she had not known till they started this trip.

Bess had gone down to fetch tea and biscuits; Maddie had taken to wanting a bedtime snack. She paced up and down the small inn room or peered out the dusty windowpane into the still noisy street below. The sun had just set, and they had had dinner in a private parlor. At least Adrian's money made traveling easier. For the poverty-stricken Miss Applegate it would have been impossible. But if she had not been seeking her husband, she would not have been on this quest, she thought.

She picked up a sheet of the local newspaper and glanced over it once more. This time her gaze stopped on an advertisement she had ignored earlier.

Bess, when she returned with her tray, was surprised to see that her mistress's mood had suffered a radical change.

"Bess, we are going out!" Maddie exclaimed. She had already put on her bonnet and pelisse.

"But, Miss Madeline, I mean, Lady Weller," Bess added belatedly, "I've got yer tea, and it's nice and hot. Anyhow, it's late."

"It doesn't matter. I have a hunch, and I want to check it out."

She took a quick sip of the tea, almost scalding herself, and giving Bess only time to put on her cape and bonnet, they were soon off to the hotel that listed the approaching opening of "The Duke's Daughter and Other Follies."

Here she had a lively exchange with the clerk on duty at the desk, but after an exchange of coins, she had the information she wanted. She and Bess headed for an upper floor.

At last she was able to knock on a door from which a noisy conversation seemed to ensue.

A chambermaid with a tray in her arms opened the door. "Who shall I say is calling, miss?" she asked.

Maddie stood up straighter. She must really be tired. "Lady Weller," she said crisply, thinking that there were times when she did enjoy having Adrian's title to flaunt.

The conversation in the room paused, and she distinctly heard a light voice she knew well say, "Who on earth—" and another shush her.

The chambermaid curtsied, not easy with the tray still in her hands, and said, "Yes, my lady, please to go in. I'll be back with fresh tea, ma'am," she added over her shoulder to the people within.

The door opened wider, and Maddie went through. She was gratified to see the shock and pleasure that broke out on the two identical faces of the women in front of her.

"Madeline!" they shrieked in unison. "Whatever are you doing here?"

And of course she burst into tears as her twin sisters grabbed her from either side and enveloped her with enthused embraces.

Seventeen

*T*here were endless questions, of course.

"How on earth did you become 'Lady Weller'?" Ophelia demanded. "When we left England, you didn't even have a suitor!"

"And what are you doing in York wandering about with only Bess?" the other twin, Cordelia, added. "Is Papa all right?" She sounded anxious.

Maddie sighed. "Have you had none of my letters?"

Cordelia's husband, a dark-haired, gray-eyed man with a slightly cynical expression, lifted his brows. "It's your hen-witted housekeeper's fault again, Ophelia, you know it is."

"Oh, dear, you're likely right, Ransom." Ophelia said. "She's probably still sending our mail on to the hotel in Dover, even though we left there a fortnight or more ago. I'm sorry, Madeline. We've not caught up to our mail in months. Do tell us what is going on, and *when* did you get married?"

"When did you fall in love? And where is your husband?" Cordelia added.

"I wish I knew," Maddie said, trying not to cry again.

"You've misplaced him?" Ophelia's eyes grew big.

Cordelia poked her in the side. "Stop imagining plots. This is not one of your plays, this is real!"

"Of course it is, and my own dear sister, too. I'm totally distraught for you," Ophelia exclaimed, giving her twin a hurt look. "Why, I miss my darling Giles so much—"

Maddie looked around for the other husband; there was a slight imbalance of the sexes. "Where is Giles?"

"Oh, he was asked to take the place, temporarily, though it is still a great honor, of the Bishop of Berwick upon Tweed, who is eighty and ill, although they had better not ask him to stay—the weather there is dreadful, not to mention being so far out of the way—"

"And what are you doing here, and why didn't you come to see your family on the way?" Maddie interrupted, as Ophelia's stories tended to go on forever.

"We were going to later, but the new London theater is not yet completed, and the actors are on tour. They wanted me to be on hand while they opened the new play, in case they needed changes made in the script—there are always changes needed, you know."

Maddie didn't, but she nodded, anyhow.

"And Giles didn't want her coming alone, so Ransom and I came to keep her company. How on earth did you find us?" Cordelia, the more practical twin, asked.

"I saw the advertisement for the play opening this week, and I recognized Ophelia's pen name, so I came at once. I've been writing to you both for weeks and getting no answer—you missed my wedding!" Maddie told them.

"Oh, I am so sorry," Cordelia said, and Ophelia looked woebegone. "That's dreadful."

"Oh, it's more than that." And Maddie told them about

the mad cousin who had interrupted their first try at a wedding ceremony, and Ophelia's eyes grew so wide they looked like saucers.

"Even I would not think to write such a scene—my heavens, Madeline!"

"You should try living through it," she told them.

"Weller went off and left you?" Ransom interjected, frowning. "Perhaps we do need to find him and tell him a thing or two about—"

"You must not judge him," Maddie said quickly. "He thought it the safest thing to do. His cousin threatens me, as well."

Then she had to explain about the duel, and the other cousin's death, and now how they had discovered the flyers, and the whole tangled scheme.

"Good gracious, it does sound like one of Ophelia's plays," Cordelia said, her voice faint. "You must be at your wits' end, Madeline, you poor darling."

This time, she did lose her self-control, and suddenly she was weeping again. "And I miss him so," she wailed. "And I—I—" She looked at Ransom and tried to pull herself together.

"Ah," Cordelia said. "My dearest, why don't you take a walk? I'm sure you are in need of fresh air."

"I'm sure I am," her husband agreed, his tone pleasant. "I'll be gone at least an hour. It is a pleasure to see you again, sister Madeline."

Maddie tried to give him a smile, but wasn't sure she succeeded.

When he had left the room, all three sisters piled onto the sofa, with a twin on either side of her.

"Oh, I have missed you both so." Maddie told them. "First, I must tell you how sorry I am about those dreadful letters I sent you after you ran away to London."

Ophelia looked embarrassed. "They were quite well deserved, considering our—especially my—behavior, and you apologized to us already, dear Madeline, so please—"

"Yes, but I don't like to remember them, so I must just say that I am really, really sorry!"

"Only if you don't mention them again," Cordelia said, her tone firm. "I'm sure you have been lonely. With Juliana and her husband always traveling, and only Lauryn near at hand—"

"But she isn't!" Maddie told them. "Lauryn stayed with the squire. Which would be well and good, but the squire has gone to London, and Lauryn feels she has to remain with him. She is so heavy with guilt at not having given him an heir before her husband died—"

"He is still dragging her around? Oh, that is too bad of him," Ophelia retorted.

"So you have been alone with only Papa? Not that Papa is not good company, but still—oh, Madeline." Cordelia gripped one of Maddie's hands, and Ophelia had the other, and for a moment, they were silent, but Maddie felt surrounded by love. She sighed in contentment.

In a few minutes the chambermaid returned with a full tray of tea and bread and butter and cakes, and Maddie could wipe her face and feel more composed as she drank tea and ate.

Bess, who had quietly sat back and allowed her mistress to catch up with her sisters, looked well pleased to see the girls reunited. She had also been given hugs by the twins, whom she had helped raise after their mother had died. She was also supplied with tea and edibles, and she sat down again and listened to all the gossip.

"You will find him," Cordelia was telling her older sister now. "I'm sure you will, Madeline."

"But it is well nigh impossible," she wailed. "There are so many men, and he does a good job of disappearing, I must tell you. I do not see how his cousin ever picks up his trail, and if it were not for the flyers, as we now know, I don't see how he ever would. And we are wasting precious time, that is the worst of it—and I don't know how much time we have to waste!"

The wrenching pain of the last statement cut her to her heart. Maddie drew a deep breath, touching her belly, now beginning to swell slightly, though the loose cut of the current fashions did not easily reveal it.

Cordelia looked startled, and Maddie realized there was one thing she had not told them.

"Madeline, you don't mean—"

She nodded, smiling.

"Oh, so are we!"

"What?" Maddie was the one surprised now. "Both of you?"

Ophelia grinned. "You didn't expect me to allow Cordelia to get ahead of me, did you?"

Maddie laughed. No, when did one twin not keep up with the other?

"Oh, what fun all the cousins will have together!" Cordelia predicted. "Do you think we can manage to all have boys? Or all have girls?"

"It will be wonderful," Ophelia said, "whatever we have."

Maddie smiled, but she still had to push back a twist of anxiety. Wonderful to have a child, but she wanted a husband, too! Where was Adrian, and how would she ever find him?

Then she looked at the sheets of newsprint lying around the hotel room, and suddenly an idea came to her.

Adrian was in Aberdeen when he saw the newspaper. He had drifted through village after village, not particularly caring where he went. If he could not be with Madeline, one location was as good—or as banal—as another.

He kept an eye on the newspapers even though he knew the time for the infant to be born was months away—he thought about the baby often late at night. Wondered if the child would be a girl with Madeline's sweet expression and her lovely green gold eyes, or a boy whom he could teach to shoot and ride. Either way, he wanted to hold the babe, to lift it up, and to make it laugh and see it light up with pleasure because it knew its father.

He wanted to be there, dammit. He wanted his wife. He wanted to touch the sweet curve of her breast and kiss her soft lips. He wanted to talk to her, hear her voice, lie next to her in bed, and hear the slight sigh of her breathing just as she dropped off to sleep.

He wanted her. He missed her. Life, such as it was, was not worth living without her. Yet he had to keep living; he owed it to her. Damned conundrum—he spent his existence wrestling with enigmas.

Running away had never seemed such a hardship before. Now he hated every step he took. He wanted to turn and confront his damned lunatic relative. Except he didn't know where Francis was, so he wasn't sure how to do that, either. And if he simply turned and went back to Yorkshire, he might draw the mad marksman back to endanger Madeline, and he refused to risk that. Now he would jeopardize not one precious life but two!

If his cousin had even a hint that Adrian had an heir growing inside Madeline's lovely body, he would drop his quest for Adrian and turn all his powers toward murdering his wife. And that did not bear thinking of. So Adrian had to keep running, had to keep drawing the madman away, as far away as he could.

There had been one attempt in Northumberland, and

Adrian had shot back, had tried to track down the shooter, but his cousin had again slipped away. So the cat and mouse game had continued. Now here he was even further north in Aberdeen, dining on kippers and eggs as tough as the far from loquacious Scotsmen who shared the small inn with him.

Adrian took a bite of the fish and lifted the paper to read the small print. What he read made him drop his fork, and then stand and push back his plate.

The maid who'd brought him his breakfast stared at him in surprise. "Be ye ill, me lord? Ye're as pale as a banshee wailing o' the moor."

"Tally up my charges," he told her, ignoring the question. "I'm leaving at once."

Maddie was in the draper's shop at the end of Main Street when she heard the commotion. She had sent Bess to collect some new potatoes, so she was alone for the moment. Not sure if the noise could be anything to do with her or simply some farmer's escaped pig, she went to the door of the shop to peek out.

At first she could not see what was making the ado. She heard dogs barking and someone shouting, probably nothing important, she told herself, and was about to turn and go back in, when someone grabbed her arm.

She tried to jerk free, and as the door swung shut, she saw who held her.

It was the cold, pale face of Adrian's cousin.

She was the one who felt cold, now.

"Oh, well played, Lady Weller," the man said, in his high, fluting voice, "but perhaps I saw your bait before your wandering husband did."

"I don't know what you mean," she said. She stood up straighter, determined not to show fear in front of this sadistic madman.

"Of course you do. 'Lady Weller gravely injured.' A wonderful line to bring a missing husband hurrying home. Did you not think I might read it, too?"

Actually, she hadn't, and now Maddie cursed herself for not seeing the gaping hole in her plan.

It hadn't occurred to her that Adrian's cousin could be so devious as to figure out—and so quickly—how her scheme had been laid.

Damn him to perdition and back. All she needed now was for some villager to come up and ask her about how her "interesting condition" was proceeding, she thought bitterly. Not that she had told a soul, but somehow the maids had nosed it out, and then the whole village had seemed to find it out, too.

She tried again to pull away from his grip, but the man had hands like vises. He kept her arm inside his, and they were walking along the path beside Main Street, looking more or less normal to observers, perhaps.

Maddie considered shouting for help, but few of the villagers would be armed, and she was sure that Francis was. Adrian had said he was deadly accurate, too.

"Are you still as good a shot as you were?" she asked, keeping her tone even. As he jerked her along, she might as well try to distract him.

He giggled, a weird sound to come from a man. "But of course, my dear. I try out my skill regularly, using your husband for target practice. How do you know I didn't leave his bloody, broken body lying dead on the heath just days ago?"

Her heart seemed to turn to ice, and her foot slipped off a stone, almost making her ankle twist. She caught herself just in time.

Adrian dead?

No, she didn't believe it. If so, why was Francis here? Making sure Adrian had no heir, she answered herself, still feeling chilled. No, he just wanted to taunt her, Maddie told herself. She would not believe that Adrian was dead— she would not!

Although if she were about to be murdered, it would shortly make no difference.

She had to think about herself for a moment, and the baby she carried, Adrian's baby. How could she get away, without harming innocent lives around them?

Maddie tried to think. Only a few houses and shops remained, and then the street would fall away, then the man could pull her into the open space and take her where he wished, to shoot and dispose of her body without witnesses. She had to do something quickly.

Just as she braced herself to try once more to pull out of his grip, she heard a voice call her name, and she thought her heart would stop.

"Adrian!"

It was he, standing at the end of the street, just in the center, holding a pistol pointed at her captor. He was a beautiful sight; she wished she had the liberty to enjoy it.

"Step aside, Francis," her husband said, his voice clear and steady, "and release your hold on my wife."

"You'd like that, would you?" his cousin responded, jerking Maddie even closer to his body, so that she smelled the cloying scent that he used in much too heavy abandon. "No, no, you must shoot around her, an amusing little problem, yes?"

People at the side of the street shouted and exclaimed. A rush of villagers grabbed their children and pushed to get inside doors and out of the way of flying bullets. But even then, Maddie saw from the corner of her eye a variety of faces at the windows peeking cautiously to see what would transpire.

A strange quiet fell over the street, with only a lone dog still barking at these intruders, and the animal retreated behind a box that had spilled its load of potatoes.

Maddie winced as the madman held her in front of him so that she shielded his body. He lifted his own gun to better position Adrian in his sights.

What would Adrian do—withdraw again?

Although her husband looked pale, he stood his ground, his expression resolute, and his pistol was steady.

She had to get out of the way. Francis's grip on her arm still felt like an iron vice. But surely firing with one hand must be awkward, she thought, and holding her with one hand gave him little leverage. She would not be a party to murdering her own husband.

She sat down.

Dropping her full weight into the dust of the street, it was impossible for the madman to hold her. She simply allowed herself to fall, and when her body met the street, she kept on going, throwing her head down and covering it with her arms, holding her breath as gunfire exploded above her.

Two shots—the heavy thud of another body falling. She was afraid to look up, afraid to see who was still standing, or were both men dead?

Oh please, God, she prayed, please, not Adrian!

Then she heard rushing footsteps, and someone was lifting her.

"Madeline, are you hurt? Speak to me!" She knew that voice, the anxious tone.

With a cry of joy, Maddie lifted her head and threw her arms about her husband's neck, weeping tears of joy on his shoulder.

"With all the dust in your face and hair, you are going to end up a quagmire, if you keep crying like that," Adrian observed, his tone a bit gruff, "and you are breaking my heart in two, as well, so perhaps you could manage to stop?"

She lifted her face and smiled at him.

"Are you hurt?" he asked again.

"We are fine," she told him. "But Adrian, there is blood on your coat!"

"Just a crease across the ribs," he assured her. "We must get you home."

"Oh, yes," she agreed. "My sisters are here, or the twins at least. You can meet them finally."

"I look forward to it," he agreed. "But not as much as I do being alone with my wife again, and this time, with no one to shoot out our windows!"

She looked down at the body sprawled across the dusty street, and she shuddered. "Oh, Adrian, what a long and terrible road we have traveled!"

Nodding, he kissed the top of her head.

Someone had come up behind them, and Adrian turned. It was a stout little man, looking flustered but determined to be of help. "Are ye all right, me lord? Me lady? Such a terrible man, what was he about, trying to harm me lady like that?"

"He was an evil man, mad as a hatter," Adrian agreed. "Lady Weller is unhurt, but she is obviously shaken. I am going to take her home. If you could see to the disposal of the—um—body, I will pay whatever the charges are, later."

"Of course, of course," the man said. "Pity the squire's not at 'ome; 'e's our magistrate, but we'll see about what needs to be done."

"Thank you," Adrian said.

Madeline had just had a strange sort of flashback. The stout little man was the village baker, the same one who had come upon them in the gazebo, the first time Adrian and she had met under such improper and unpropitious circumstances. He had been rather less helpful then. She remembered his shocked and disapproving face.

"Adrian," she whispered into his ear as her husband carried her easily off the street. "Do you realize who—"

"Yes." He grinned at her as they shared the private joke. "An old friend of ours. And now it's 'my lord' this and 'my lady' that, despite the fact that we are littering the village with corpses. Did I not promise you I would restore your reputation?"

She made a face at him, but when he paused to kiss her, forgot to be indignant. "So you did," she said. "Oh, Adrian, I have missed you so!"

"Since you have filled my empty life with such love, I think I have had the best of the bargain," he told her, his voice husky. "And now you have saved my life, so you must allow me to devote the rest of it to you, and our child—or, I hope—our children!"

That reminded her of the bullet fragment buried deep in his chest, and the wave of happiness that had warmed her suddenly checked. "Oh, but Adrian. What about the bullet? You must tell me the truth. How long did the doctor say you might expect?"

He lifted her to the horse that he had left tied to a small tree, then untied the reins. "Perhaps six, nine months."

Such a little time? She gazed at him in horror. Would he not even see their child born? "But, Adrian, when did he make this forecast?"

His look was hard to read. "Close to two years ago."

"What?" She almost fell off the horse. "Adrian! Have you not considered that the doctor may not know what he's speaking of?"

"Most of them don't, my darling," he told her calmly. "I have stopped reflecting on it. But I did think, in fairness, I should tell you what he had opined before you married me."

"So you don't think it is an accurate prediction?" She could not quite put her fear away.

"Let us say," he told her, meeting her gaze this time with serious eyes, "we all live with fear, with the specter of our life and our love being cut short, my dearest. But I hope not, because this time, I have so much that I wish to live for."

Holding to the saddle, she leaned over, and he put one foot into the stirrup so he could rise up to give her a quick kiss.

"I expect to enjoy a lifetime with you, Madeline, my love," he told her.

And this time, when he smiled, she could smile back with a light heart.

Author's Note

The story of Ophelia and Cordelia Applegate's shocking
adventures may be found in *A Lady of Scandal*. Available
from Berkley Sensation.

Turn the page for a preview of
Nicole Byrd's
next historical romance

Enticing the Earl

Coming soon
from Berkley Sensation!

"*They do say he's desperate handsome*," the first housemaid said as she scrubbed the door panel. "And a wild man in bed!"

"Tell me some'un I ain't 'eard," the second maid jeered. "The earl's famous for 'is way wid the ladies. And I 'ear 'e's dumped the 'igh priced ladybird 'e's been supportin' in such style. She'll 'ave to find some'un else to pay for 'er 'igh perch carriages and diamond studded boots. Wish I 'ad a chance to take over her post, and she could 'ave this 'ere mop!"

Grinning at this fantasy involving the Quality's love lives, she sloshed her mop about on the staircase landing, splattering drops of dirty water. Thick with muscle, her arms wielded the handle with ease.

"Ha!" The first servant snorted. "You and me and half of London, besides. He's probably built her a castle and—and—God knows! Who wouldn't want to be mollycoddled with jewels and pretty clothes, and made love to night an' day?"

"It'd jolly me just to spend a few 'ours alone wid a man like that!" The other maid groaned in mock ecstasy, and both servants dissolved into fits of giggles.

Who indeed?

Seated on the stairs a flight above them, Lauryn Applegate Harris wrapped her arms about her knees, feet drawn up beneath her, and wondered if she would ever meet such a man. It didn't seem likely.

She had been in London for six months, and this—eavesdropping on the hotel maids as they worked—was as close as she had come to any social life. Not that Lauryn had clothes suitable for entering Society, anyhow. She was still wearing the rusty black gowns she had dyed for her unexpected widowhood, and now she lacked the money to replace them. Just this morning she had found a hole in her last pair of good stockings. Being poor was enough to make a saint curse.

And she was no saint—just a young widow who was acutely weary of always making do with too little and forever covering up her own sadness as she tried to help her father-in-law, the squire, cope with his. He had taken the loss of his only son so hard that she'd feared more than once for his sanity. And the only comfort that might have assuaged his misery was beyond her power to offer. If she had only given him, and her late husband, an heir . . .

Then Squire Harris would have had something to console him and take his mind off the terrible deprivation they both felt. And she would have had some part of her husband to hold on to, and a child to love.

She pushed away the guilt which rode as constant companion with her lingering grief. She had to look forward, not back, as her sisters reminded her in their letters.

"If you will not come home, if you are determined to stay and aid the squire, please try not to dwell on the past," her older sister Madeline had written. "You know we love you, Lauryn. I write this for your own good."

Everyone had advice. Easy for Madeline to say, Lauryn thought, as her sister cuddled her own firstborn with a husband beside her to offer his strength and support. But Lauryn knew the counsel was sincere. Early on, she had made herself ill with grief, and at some point, she'd realized she could bear no more tears and sleepless nights. None of it would bring Robert back. Now, if she could just have a little laughter again, once in a while an outing and a pretty dress—Was she terribly selfish to think such thoughts?

She'd had few enough such entertainments to enjoy even before Robert's death. Sighing, she glanced at the sewing basket beside her and the abandoned the stocking she'd been trying to darn.

Wedding her childhood sweetheart when both were quite young, Lauryn had expected to live an agreeable life with her husband, bearing many children with long, happy years to enjoy them together. But the babies had not come, and as the years passed, Robert had seemed to accept their childless marriage.

Their first flush of postwedding passion had drifted into occasional love making and pleasant companionship, and her husband had amused himself instead with hunting and shooting and the details of running their small estate. Perhaps more aware of time's relentless passage, Robert's father, the squire, had appeared more concerned about the lack of an heir—the next male in the Harris family line was a distant cousin whom the squire detested—and Lauryn herself had felt the guilty burden of her barren state.

Then Robert had been struck down by a sudden illness. Now, at the age of nine and twenty, Lauryn found herself a widow, doomed to a life of sitting on the sidelines, wearing her widow's weeds and her matron's cap, and watching other young ladies dance—if, indeed, she ever had the chance to attend a ball again, which didn't seem probable.

And now—

A new brightly colored dress, nothing black or gray or even violet . . . a handsome man with eyes only for her . . . a man who made her blood quicken once again, a man who made her feel alive, not in the grave with her poor, struck down too soon, young husband . . .

Oh, was she a terrible person to allow such wistful reflections to dwell in the farthest reaches of her mind?

Despite herself, Lauryn's reflections turned to the scandalous Earl of Sutton. What did he look like, this much talked about lord? What would it be like to be the lady he sought out? For a moment, her pulse quickened, then the fantasy faded. Turning back to her basket, she picked up the wooden darning egg which she thrust into the heel of her stocking. She'd better darn that hole, unless she wished for cold feet, as she and licentious earls were most unlike to meet!

Hours later when her father-in-law returned at long last, his face appeared gray with fatigue. He had looked weary before, but this was worse. His eyes had seemed lifeless ever since Robert had died, but now—now, the light inside them had retreated even farther.

Lauryn opened the door to their rooms for him. Observing his slumped shoulders, she swallowed hard. "Are you all right, sir?"

"I've lost it all, Lauryn. All. I'm an old fool."

Her first feeling was one of relief. Perhaps now he would return to Yorkshire and give up this reckless behavior, drinking too much, gambling with men with deeper pockets. The squire had never spent so much time in the city before. Normally, he was content in his own shire, on his own acres, but after losing Robert, it seemed as if he could not stand the sight of his own land, not without the son who should have inherited it.

Without an heir . . . Guilt moved once more inside her, and she tried to push it back.

"Do you have enough left to pay the hotel's charges? We can return to Yorkshire—"

"You're not attending, child. There's nothing to go back to." He rubbed his hand across his face.

"What?" She felt the first stirring of panic.

The squire's voice shook a little, and she could smell the drink thick on his breath. That had likely not helped his skill at cards, but she would not remark on it. It did little good to offer censure after the fact.

"I don't know how I shall pay the hotel, or how we shall eat. The pot had gotten so large, and I was in so deep—it was all I had left to cover my losses. I thought with just one more good hand, I might redeem it all—"

He named a figure that made her blanch and reach for the support of the back of a chair to keep her legs from folding.

"And then I lost again. Now the land is gone, the estate in Yorkshire, and the worst of it is, I don't think the earl even wants it. He was making jokes about moth-eaten sheep to the rest of the table when I took my leave. I've already written him out a deed—best to get the thing over with, don't you know—but he'll like as not toss it away or throw it into tonight's card game."

The squire dropped down onto the side of the bed as if his legs would not hold him. He buried his face in his hands.

She patted his shoulder, but her stomach roiled, and she thought she might be ill. The squire's land—the land that had been in his family for generations, the land that should have been Robert's some day—gone in a game of cards? The squire wouldn't survive this!

"Who is it—To whom did you lose it?" she asked, when she could make her voice work. Could she call on some of her brothers-in-law to come together and loan the squire enough to get his land back? Would his pride endure such a lowering blow? She doubted she could get his permission to even ask.

"The Earl of Sutton," he told her, his tone grim. "It might as well be the devil himself . . . He has the devil's luck at cards, I can tell you."

Lauryn was glad her father-in-law was lost in his own misery and not watching her face as he lay back on the bed. She had gone quite rigid.

Sutton? The notorious rake the hotel maids loved to gossip about? He was the one who now possessed the squire's deed and other vowels? Good heavens!

Was the earl a cruel man? Had the gossip about him ignored that side of him—Was this an aspect she had not realized as she painted him in her daydreams? Or were such men just ignorant of all real life outside of the patter of cards and the skill or the luck that determined who came out on top?

And if the squire had been lost in the deepening circle of his despair, would not someone, if not the earl, have been bound to win . . . Should she blame the earl for being the winner or was it just fate?

Yet why should she let the earl off the hook? She didn't even know the man! It was the Squire who was suffering, who would suffer—Was there anything she could do to help?

That land had been in the Harris family for scores of years. Even though not formally entailed, it was meant to stay in their family. She had not dreamed of anything else, and she knew the squire hadn't, either, so what momentary madness had led him to offer it up as collateral . . . Could Lauryn do anything? She had always been the one to offer help, the middle child who looked out for her younger sisters, who assisted around the house when her mother had died too young, who had made her father smile by being mature beyond her years—it was second nature.

And to be truthful, if it brought her into contact with a handsome, dissolute lord who might bring some excitement into her quiet, bleak existence—she felt a small thrill deep inside, and she was aware that idea didn't exactly displease her, either.

Feeling guilty at once, she pushed the feeling back. She had to think first of the Squire. She went back to check on him and found him dropping off to sleep.

Lauren pulled a blanket up over her father-in-law as he shut his eyes and fell into a troubled slumber, then she went into the next small room and paced up and down as she tried to think.

Despite the lateness of the hour, she was suddenly wide awake. She went to the window and opened the pane, leaning out to look and listen. The street was still busy with carriages returning from evening engagements, elegant carriages, some with family crests on their doors.

Lauryn thought of the affluent, perhaps titled personages inside, with their fancy clothes and rich and privileged lives. That was the existence the Earl of Sutton must lead. What would he want with the squire's small Yorkshire estate, and how could she convince him to release it? If she told him how devastated the squire was and why—no, no, it would be unfair to strip away all her father-in-law's dignity. Plus, if he should find out, he would never forgive her.

Men were stubborn, as well, about gambling winnings—it could become an affair of honor if she were not careful. And then both men's hands would be tied as to what they could do.

Sighing, Lauryn rubbed her temples, which all at once threatened to ache. She must have something of worth to give the earl in return, in order to get the squire's estate back, but that was near impossible. She looked down at her empty hands. She had nothing of value to give. She had no jewelry, except a few trinkets that Robert had given her, and they had sentimental value, little else. She had had no real dowry, her own family was not wealthy.

For some time her thoughts flew from one impractical scheme to another. And then the obvious answer came to her.

She had only herself . . .

Lauryn blinked. What about—no, no, that was unthinkable . . .

Was it?

She jumped up and went to the one small looking glass on the wall and strained to see her reflection in the faint light now coming from the window as the sun fought to rise over London's horizon, its weak rays pushing valiantly through the haze of coal dust from countless chimneys.

In her girlhood she had been called pretty by swains in her shire. She made out a familiar pale heart-shaped face, with large green eyes, delicate features, and long hair of a golden hue with reddish highlights, just now pulled back behind her head. No longer the girl she had been, but not totally repellant, surely. Was it enough to satisfy an earl known for his discerning taste in women? If she went to him and pledged to serve as a courtesan, would he engage her?

How did such a woman work?

Her heart dropped. She had no clothes! How could one look alluring in faded black mourning gowns?

Still, perhaps she could ask for a wardrobe as one of her terms of engagement, Lauryn told herself. That would solve the problem quickly.

Was that typical of courtesans? She wished she knew more of such women. But really, how could she be expected to? Ladies were never informed about that side of life. Lauryn bit her lip. The earl must not know her background, or he might not retain her—even the notorious Earl of Sutton might have some scruples to overcome.

She would just have to hope for the best. She balled her hands into fists, wondering if she had the nerve to carry through with such an outrageous, highly improper scheme.

If anyone found out, she would be ruined for life. Still, it wasn't as if she expected to ever have the chance to marry again. She had no money to attract another husband, and her first husband's property, even if they should get it back, would stay with his family line. It would be different if she had borne him children, but—

What would her father, her sisters, say?

Perhaps they would not have to know.

Even if the earl agreed to such an arrangement, he would surely tire of her quickly. She had a dim idea that men like that did, and didn't the maids' gossip bear that out? Then she could return to her real life. And courtesans did not go into company with ladies of quality. Lauryn knew that much!

She would use an assumed name, she would stay away from anyone who knew her, and no one in London did know her, as she had not been out in company, not having the clothes or the money to do so.

And she was not an innocent young thing, virginal and untouched. She was a married woman, or at least, a widow now, but the main thing was she had experience in the marriage bed. She would not be shocked, Lauryn told herself, and she could—she hoped—keep him interested for a few weeks, at least, enough to make their bargain valid.

She paced up and down again for several hours, trying to think of possible loopholes, likely weaknesses in her scheme. Was there any better way to save the squire's home? She could think of none.

Finally, she looked into the looking glass again and saw the look of determination on her face. She tucked a few straying locks into place before she picked up her simple bonnet with the black ribbon.

If she were going to do such a thing, she had to do it now, before she lost her nerve, Lauryn told herself. She checked on the squire, who still slept, his breathing heavy with the aftermath of too much drink.

She hesitated for a moment at the door to the hall. Was she really going to go through with this insane idea? It was madness.

But a thrill of excitement moved inside her at the thought of living with a handsome lord, of being indiscreet, of kissing and romancing an experienced lover—surely she deserved a few weeks of being wicked after spending most of her life obediently toeing propriety's line.

After Robert had died, she had ached for him, and their bed had seemed so painfully lonely. She had been so agonizingly aware of how much her body had craved a man's touch . . .

Could she not try life as a bad girl just briefly, just for once? Surely a man who had sought out so many women must know how to please a lady . . . or any woman at all . . .

And it would be for some greater good if she could retrieve the squire's land. She couldn't bring back Robert, she couldn't supply an heir, but she could give his father back his home.

Taking a deep breath, Lauryn headed down the stairs.

                            ≈

Sutton was halfway through a stack of letters, most of it business and all of it, sadly, demanding his personal attention, when his butler coughed from the doorway.

It was the "your attention is needed, truly needed, my lord, or I would not interrupt you" cough, so he reluctantly raised his head.

"There is a young lady to see you, my lord. She says the matter is urgent."

"At this time of day?" Sutton knew his tone was skeptical, but most young ladies of the Ton were still abed at nine in the morning, or at the most out riding in Hyde Park, where they could be seen by other fashionable ladies or admired by young sprigs of fashion.

He had been up late himself, playing cards at a smoky gaming hell in a disreputable part of town, but he never indulged himself by sleeping late when he had business to be seen to, and besides he hoped to leave London by tomorrow.

His brother Carter was at the Lincolnshire estate, and if left to himself, was sure to get into trouble.

And what the hell did she want of him?

"Did you make my excuses?" The butler was usually good about shielding him from those kindly souls collecting for good works or from matchmaking mamas foolishly endeavoring to introduce him to giddy daughters. "I am in no mood for charity seekers."

"I did, my lord, but she is quite—ah—persistent," Parker said, his usually bland expression covering some emotion Sutton could not quite read.

The earl was aware of a flicker of curiosity.

"Very well, show her in, but warn her I have time for only a short interview." He put the paper, a ship's bill of lading, back on his desk.

At first glance, the female who entered his study did not seem particularly prepossessing. Of medium height, dressed in shapeless, drab black garments, her figure was obscured, and beneath a bonnet that had seen better days even before it had developed a fatal droop, her face was hard to make out.

Standing, he motioned to a chair in front of his desk. When she sat down and loosened the hat, removing it so that he got his first good look at her, his interest quickened. She had the face of a classical beauty, pale skin and delicate features, and hair of a pale reddish gold. She met his gaze with her chin up and a defiant intelligence burning in her eyes, and that stirred his curiosity even more.

"How may I help you, Miss—?"

"Smith, Mrs. Smith," she said quickly. "I-I have come to you seeking employment, my lord."

"Indeed." He paused, not sure how to go on. She might be poverty-stricken. Indeed, she looked it in a genteel kind of way, as a country parson's daughter might, but she was, in her speech and her deportment, obviously a lady, so how on earth she could expect to serve in his household, he could not think. She could not mistakenly think he was married with children and be looking for a post as a governess? It was about the only situation in which indigent ladies could earn a respectable income. He opened his mouth to disabuse her of the notion, when she spoke again.

"I realize—I realize this is unexpected, but—but I have need of a position, and I-I have reason to think that you have a vacant—that is, that is I have heard gossip—I mean, I have heard comment—"

She stopped again, her face flushing as she seemed to search for words. She was not looking for a post as governess, he decided.

Fascinated, Sutton gave up trying to guess. This was too entertaining, even though he knew it was too bad of him to be amused by her discomfort.

"I wish to obtain a post as—as a courtesan," she blurted.

Sutton knew that his eyes must have bulged. "What?"

"Yes," she said, looking relieved that the word was out. "That's it. I realize I have no recommendations—"

The earl had to hold his breath to keep from whooping—he wanted to laugh so badly he had to ball his fists and stiffen his whole body. "I see. That is a problem," he managed to say.

She stared at him anxiously. "But I do have experience, my lord, and I assure you that you would not regret taking me on."

With a surge of heightened awareness flooding his whole body, he had a sudden image of tipping her over the desk and "taking her on," then and there. He drew a deep breath.

Perhaps she also realized how the term could be construed. Blushing, she turned her gaze toward the marble fireplace.

"Indeed," he said, his tone neutral.

Oh, God, he thought, wondering that he had been so bored this morning that he had longed to walk out on the desk full of business and social correspondence. Now he wanted to roar with laughter and—and more. He wanted to tilt up that heart-shaped face and try out those "experienced" lips and see just how much of a hoax this all was!

What in hell was she playing at?

"And what kind of wages are you expecting, may I ask?" he inquired, his tone very polite.

"Oh, the—the usual," she said, her voice airy. She waved one hand. "A-a new wardrobe, of course."

He nodded. "Of course." He would burn that black gown she currently wore with absolute pleasure, he thought. It made her look like a pudding insufficiently cooked. But her slim hands and the well-shaped ankles he had had just a glimpse of when she had sat down suggested that her figure deserved much better.

She glanced at him, as if to gauge his response. "You may—you may shower me with jewels, if you like," she suggested.

Managing with some effort to keep a straight face, Sutton swallowed another shout of laughter. "I will consider it," he said instead.

Had she been reading the worst of the scandal sheets? This must have to do with his recent "retirement" of his poorly chosen and short-lived—ah—courtesan, as this surprising guest chose to call it; harpy would have served for his last companion. Greedy, scheming, selfish, and untrustworthy were a few other terms that came to mind.

"But the main thing," she went on, and this time he saw the effort it cost her to keep her voice level and her expression calm, "the main thing is that I should like a small estate."

"Really?" He narrowed his brows, watching her. "That would make it quite a costly proposition, Miss—Mrs. Smith."

"It does not have to be close to London," she added quickly. "So it does not have to be quite so costly, my lord. In fact, it can be a good deal farther away, perhaps in the North Country, somewhere like Yorkshire . . ."

So that was it, the earl thought grimly. Had Squire Harris sent this innocent to get back what he'd lost? If the man had done this in cold blood—What was she, young wife, daughter?

His face must have shown his disgust, because the young lady in front of him looked alarmed. Sutton tried to smooth out his expression.

"Yorkshire, you say?"

Still watching him anxiously, she nodded.

"It seems to me I might have recently won a small estate such as that in a card game. I will turn out the contents of my pockets and peruse my winnings. Then I will give some thought to your proposition. But now it is your turn."

"My turn?" She stared at him as if he had turned into a bear from the circus.

"I must see a sample of the wares if I am to consider buying," he told her, his tone pleasant and noncommital. "That is a reasonable request, as you know."

Her eyes widened, and she looked as if she might slide off the chair. But she pulled herself together quickly.

"Oh—oh, of course, my lord," she stuttered. "What do you wish me to do?"

"Take off your gown," he ordered.